# SALVAGE

## A Ghost Story

## Duncan Ralston

Shadow Work Publishing

This story is a work of fiction. Names, characters, places and incidents are either the product of the author's imagination or are used fictitiously. Any resemblance to actual persons, living or dead, is entirely coincidental.

No part of this eBook may be reproduced or transmitted in any form or by any means, electronic or mechanical, including photocopying, recording or by any information storage and retrieval system, without written permission from the author.

**SHADOW WORK PUBLISHING**

# Praise for SALVAGE

"Much more than a ghost story. A lot of people that read this book will end up connecting with it in many more ways than they thought and would probably admit to."

— Confessions of a Reviewer

"A spectacular ghost story."

— DLS Reviews

"*Salvage* is a fantastic debut novel that demonstrates Duncan Ralston's innate ability as an author to truly connect with his audience."

— Two Book Lovers Reviews

"*Salvage* is a highly original, very well thought out book that's different from just about anything else I've read. Readers who discover *Salvage* will discover some true buried horror treasure here."

— Silver Screen Videos

# ALSO BY DUNCAN RALSTON

*Gristle & Bone* (collection)

*Salvage* (novella)

*Wildfire* (novella)

*Woom* (novella)

*The Method* (novel)

*Video Nasties* (collection)

*Ebenezer* (novella)

*Ghostland* (novel)

*In Every Dark Corner* (collection)

*Afterlife: Ghostland 2.0* (novel)

*Ghostland: Infinite* (novel)

*Gross Out* (novel)

*Ghostland: Ghost Hunter Edition* (omnibus)

*Try Not to Die: At Ghostland* w/ Mark Tullius (gameboook)

*Puzzle House* (novel)

*Pedo Island Bloodbath* (novel)

*Helloween* (novel - Fall 2024)

# Contents

*For Mom and Dad,*
*whose house built me.*

*After death, no reviving;*
*After the grave, no meeting again.*

— THESSALONIAN INSCRIPTION ON A TOMB

## SUFFER THE CHILDREN

WHEN OWEN SADDLER was thirteen years old and his sister Lori was five, the two of them went down to the cool, clear waters of China Cove to play, on a rare summer day when the whole family was together. Owen loved his sister, but he'd taken her along with him only begrudgingly. What he didn't like, more than anything, was being told what to do, and as it was his stepfather who'd stuck him with looking after Lori, he liked the task even less.

Already he felt a strong loathing toward the man pretending to be his father, a man Owen's mother had told him to call "Dad," but whom she herself called "Gerald," and never "Gerry." Owen couldn't remember his real father, but he was certain the man couldn't have been more different from Gerald. His real father had been a *strong* man, a *determined* man. He knew this because his mother had often said so, and Owen had a vague sense—not enough to be called a memory—of its truth. Gerald was neither of these, but he was tall, was often quick to anger, and he usually drank so much on these infrequent little trips that Owen's mother would have to drive them home. Yet for all the man's faults, he had given Owen a younger sister to pal around with (or ignore, depending on his mood), so Owen supposed he owed the man at least a little credit.

Lori plodded along in her candy-striped tank top and Adidas swim shorts, scooping up bottle caps, pop tabs, and candy wrappers with her shovel, crinkling her nose in disgust, and flicking them away in a scattering of sand. Owen followed along a short distance behind her. Farther down the beach, some older boys were throwing a football, chasing each other, and laughing once they'd piled on top of one another, fighting over the ball. Owen made sure not to be caught too close to Lori, for fear the boys might lump him in the same category as her and call him a baby.

"Let's go back this way, okay?" he said, taking her hand and directing her away from the boys.

"I wanna go swimming," Lori said, pouting. She knew all about his dislike of water, of lakes in particular—he didn't like to call it "fear," but truthfully that was what it was—and he supposed she knew he wouldn't take her much closer, let alone join her. The sun beat down on the beach in China Cove, where the islands of Georgian Bay and the endless blue of Lake Huron came together. Owen wore a *Teenage Mutant Ninja Turtles* T-shirt to cover his scrawny chest (the smart one, Donatello, was his favourite), long board shorts, and his shoes and socks. He had grown too hot not to cool off his legs, but just the idea of stepping into the shallow surf troubled him. There was no reason for it, as far as he knew. Gerald had called it a "phobia." His mother had held her tongue when he'd said it, something Owen had thought unlike her.

"Mom said no swimming," he lied.

Lori's scowl was deepened by the shadow of her sun hat. "That's not true!"

"It is. Go ask her if you don't believe me."

Lori turned away from the water, toward the trees, where Gerald and their mother sat in the shade, her reading, him blowing the foam off a can of beer from the cooler. It was too far to shout, so Lori squinted up at her brother as if to assess his honesty. He struggled to keep a straight face. "Fine," she said finally, sulking until he let go of her hand.

Owen recalled snippets of a hushed conversation in the car on their way up to the lake, while Lori sang along to the music from her colorful "My First Sony" Walkman. Their mother hadn't wanted to come here, that much he'd been able to hear. But Gerald, who was usually neither strong nor determined, had put his foot down—literally, stepping on the accelerator—and had refused to reply to Margaret Saddler's passive-aggressive comments about Gerald's impending drunkenness until she'd finally given up her protests, saying "Fine," in the same sulky tone their daughter did now.

Lori trudged to within a few paces of the water and peered back, apparently waiting for Owen to follow. He did, but only after realizing, too late, what she'd had in mind. Once she'd figured out he was too far away to catch up to her, she turned and ran: the sort of deke-out the boys playing football might have applauded.

"Cripes," he muttered, and chased after her.

Lori's little legs carried her into the surf before Owen had made it halfway to the water's edge. She was already up to her waist when he stopped dead where the waves left shapes in the sand as they retreated, disintegrating bit by bit a small mound of wet earth that had once been a sandcastle. Suddenly Owen no longer felt the sun's baking heat; instead, a cold, shuddering fear gripped him from head to toe.

There were creatures in the water with sharp teeth and spiny fins. There were bloodsucking leeches and turtles with vicious alligator snouts. There were slippery, slimy things that squirmed in the muck at the bottom of the lake, hideous blind invertebrates that had never seen daylight.

A wind whipped his hair. He turned and watched as it swished through the trees, tilting pines and rustling the branches of enormous maples. A steel-gray cloud suddenly blocked the sun. Owen frowned uneasily, and turned back toward the water to see Lori's sun hat blowing from her head. She cried out, half-laughing, and chased it farther out into the lake.

Out where it should have been too deep to stand, a man Owen hadn't noticed before was standing up to his ankles in the lake. Dressed in a white buttoned shirt and loose-fitting black pants, from whose right pocket Owen caught a glimmer of gold, the man locked eyes with him, and Owen found himself unable to look away. The wind caught the man's dark hair, and a malicious grin spread below his moustache. The man stretched out a hand toward Owen.

*"Lori!"*

Owen hadn't meant to scream, had only meant to call her out of the water. But the boys farther down the beach looked over at the sound of his cracking voice and snickered. Owen wheeled around to see Gerald and his mother rising from the picnic blanket. *Oh God, they're coming over*, he thought, feeling the familiar warmth return, rising up his neck to his cheeks as embarrassment seized him.

"What's the big idea?" Lori grumbled, having retrieved her hat and waded back to where Owen now stood. She looked back out over the water, following his troubled gaze toward the man standing in the lake.

"That man," Owen said. The dark grin on the man's vaguely familiar face widened. "I think he's dangerous."

Lori shaded her eyes with a hand and squinted out at the lake. Owen was certain she was looking right at the man, but Lori turned back to her brother with a look of curiosity in her blue eyes. "What man?"

"Right there! You don't see him?" Owen jabbed a finger at the man, whose grin widened even further as he began to stride toward them, his brown leather shoes splashing on the surface of the lake, dampening the cuffs of his pants. "He's *right there!*"

"Who's right there?" Gerald said, approaching the children with a smirk. Owen turned to face him. Gerald stopped just in front of Owen, and planted the hand not holding a can of Old Vienna beer on his hip, in a posture of obstinateness with which Owen was all too familiar.

"Nobody," Owen said to him, still feeling the presence of the man behind them, wanting to turn and look, as he would have when retreating from a darkened basement. Watching for the monster. Sensing its approach. Finally, he couldn't stop himself from turning back to look. But there was no one. The surface of the water was clear, flat, empty. The man was gone.

Owen turned to Gerald, not comprehending. His mother approached then, and stood behind her husband wearing a disapproving scowl under her mass of brown curls. Owen felt tears begin to well up as a wild urge to defend himself overcame him, despite his reluctance to admit what he'd just seen. The man had been *there*. He'd *seen* him. A man walking on water. It wasn't possible... was it?

*Seeing things*, he thought.

Lori peered up at him sympathetically.

"There was a man," Owen said, his voice starting to quaver, his lower lip quivering: the telltale onset of weeping. "He was... he was standing on the water. He was *right there!*"

His mother and Gerald made a show of peering out at the bay where Owen pointed, but it was obvious they didn't believe him. Owen wouldn't have believed himself if he hadn't seen it with his own eyes.

"I don't see anyone," Gerald said.

"That's because he's *gone* now. He must have... he must have gone underwater."

"Owen, don't be silly," his mother said.

"I *saw* him, Mom."

"It was your imagination," she said, scowling off toward the water herself.

"You don't know what's in my head."

"Don't sass your mother," Gerald said.

"Shut up, *Gerald*!"

"Owen!" his mother scolded.

Gerald crushed the beer can, his face expressionless. Gerald with his pale legs and potbelly, with his lame jokes and stupid crumpled Panama hat. "All right," he said calmly. "This has gone on long enough." He let the crushed can fall from his fingers into the wet sand, then made toward Owen. Lori saw it coming and stepped out of their way.

"Gerald...?" Concern like broken glass in his mother's voice.

Owen backed away from Gerald's reach, glancing cautiously at the water behind him. "What are you doing? Get away from me!"

"No more phobias," Gerald said, snatching out at Owen, who quickly sidestepped out of his reach. The fear Owen had seen in his mother's eyes caused tears that had been standing in his own to brim and fall. "You're going in that *lake*!" Gerald growled. His long fingers nabbed Owen's right arm, squeezing so hard the flesh around them went stark white. Owen swung with his weak left fist, pounding feebly at Gerald's ribs while the much larger man dragged him toward the water.

"Let me go! Let me *GO*!"

Tears streamed down his face. Lori followed their progress with wide, fearful eyes. The older boys stopped playing to watch the spectacle.

*Baby. Crybaby. Little loser. I deserve this.*

Owen stopped fighting and let Gerald drag him in, shoes

and all, up to his knees. He wept silently as the cold water filled his shoes.

"There's nothing to be afraid of," Gerald yelled, his face red, raised veins zigzagging his temples, the tendons in his neck stretched taut. "See?" He dragged Owen farther in, up to the cuffs of his shorts. Owen came along like one of Lori's stuffed animals, held by the arm, his muscles lax. Gerald shook him until his teeth clacked. But the cold had numbed Owen; he felt far away. "*See?*"

"GERALD!"

The scream snapped Owen from his stupor. Gerald's grip loosened, but not enough for Owen to pull away. Gerald's hat fell off his balding head and he snatched it up, squaring it back on his head with a sheepish look.

Margaret Saddler had ventured into the water up to her ankles. The wind fluttered her curls and the hem of her sundress. In the shadow provided by a cloud, she was beauty and fury. "You let my son go this instant!"

Gerald held firm. They stood several feet apart, the water lapping at Margaret's ankles and at Gerald's knees, staring each other down. Behind her, Lori's fear was palpable.

He let go.

Owen splashed down onto his hands and knees. He stood up quickly, shaking off like a wet dog, and scurried to shore, blowing right past his mother. She watched him go. All of her rage had apparently vanished; she appeared deflated, weary.

They caught up to Owen at the parking lot, where he'd been mindlessly chucking gravel at the surrounding trees, enjoying the hollow, wooden *thock*. Gerald lugged the cooler, unnaturally quiet, sulking, while Margaret carried the knapsack and held Lori's hand. As Gerald and their mother loaded everything into the car, Lori sauntered up to Owen, who attempted to ignore her until she tugged on his shirt.

Owen hefted the small stone in his hand. "What d'you want, squirt?"

Lori reached out and took his hand, her small fingers squeezing his. "I believe you," she whispered. Owen looked down at her, certain she was messing with him. But the sincerity of her smile had his tears threatening to return.

He ruffled her hair, breaking the spell. Lori grunted and

shook her head free of his grasp. "You're a good kid, you know that?" he said.

"So are you," she said.

"Nah." She was always saying stuff like that, making him feel good when all he'd wanted was to feel rotten, to feel like the jerk kid he was.

"Course, you are," she assured him. "You're the best older brother I ever had."

Owen smiled at this, mystified, as his little sister—so much older than him in many ways—scampered off to the car and got in the back seat.

After some time, he followed her.

# PART ONE

---

## SON

# CHAPTER 1

## IN HIS IMAGE

I

WHEN OWEN WAS forty, the people of St. John's Norway Cemetery put his sister Lori in the ground. Had she lived, she would have turned thirty-two in a month.

The non-denominational minister, who had been provided by the funeral home, read the standard verses: the one about the deceased being not dead but merely sleeping, followed by a bit of Psalm 23, John 3:16's "only begotten Son," and then another about ashes and dust—nothing particularly inspired or personal. Owen saw his mother's jaw clench as she ground her teeth. Distaste for religious platitudes was one thing they still had in common, aside from their love of Lori, who was dead and soon to be buried.

Even Lori's headstone was just like the others beside and behind it. Speckled granite with too much polish, more like a jewel than a grave marker. The artificial grass was too green, sterile. Owen had expected to see dirt, a small sign of the grim business being done, but aside from a few specks along the too-smooth edges of the hole, there was none. What had been taken out—and subsequently covered by more green plastic shag—had been expertly removed, leaving a perfectly rectangular chasm in which Lori, Owen's little sister, would lay until time wore her bones to the minister's dust and ash.

Owen was glad for the few mourners who cried, because he couldn't seem to manage tears himself. Even when he thought back to the last time he'd seen his sister alive, and the bad way they'd left things, he felt cold, detached. The others, the people who smiled for her life instead of weeping over her death, he wanted to grab by their shoulders, shaking away their smiles, the way he'd shake away bad art on an Etch A Sketch. He wanted to shout in their faces, *She's dead! Stop smiling! Lori's dead, you maniacs, and she's never coming back!*

He couldn't, though. Not because doing so would violate social norms he cared little about at the moment, but because he lacked the courage. Stewing in impotent rage, Owen shoved his hands deep into his pockets and watched the casket sink into the ground, sinking the way Lori had sunk in that lake up north —whose name he couldn't recall—before she'd finally begun to float again, not from the force of her own will, but from the gases of her decomposition.

*Death is lighter than water*, he thought.

"For today we grieve the loss of a good soul," said the minister. "But rest assured, life will go on, and happiness will surely find us once more."

*Surely*, Owen thought grimly. In his right pocket was a handful of dirt, smooth and without stones. Between his fingers, it felt something like ashes.

———

2

"YOU LOOK JUST LIKE HIM, you know."

Owen had faked civility through countless condolences, had worn a painful smile for every "Sorry for your loss," "She was such a spectacular human being," and "God has a plan for everyone." But when the old man had said *You look just like him*, Owen took a step back to evaluate the phrase and the man who'd spoken it, falling out of line from where he stood between his mother and Gerald Kinsman, who'd already been Owen's stepfather for a handful of years by the time Lori had been born.

*Just like* who? Owen wondered.

The old man held Owen's hand firmly, his frail arm fully extended once Owen had stepped back. He was dressed in a cheap gray suit with moth-eaten cuffs, his white beard stained yellow-brown by what appeared to be cigarette tar. The handshake was palsied, his gray eyes quivering in their sockets as the old man struggled to maintain a nearly savage eye contact.

Owen turned to Gerald on his right: Gerald, with his ginger comb over, was tall to the point of being gangly, a full foot taller than Owen. Even their facial features were nothing alike. Gerald's nose was wide and flat, and as red as his hair from years of drinking. His chin was bulbous, and his potbelly was a round thing below his nearly concave chest. "He's not my fath—" Owen started to say, but the old man released his hand and moved on, briefly shaking hands with Owen's mother, who seemed to be obliged to fight back a snarl.

*You look just like him.*

Owen shook the hand of another mourner, a woman he didn't know who offered another bland cliché. He looked down the aisle of shuffling men and women, all in black attire, but the old man was gone, lost among the crowd gathered to mourn the loss of Lori Jean Saddler, dead much too young at the age of thirty-two.

Owen's uncle Ralph played "Greensleeves" on the pub's upright piano, the instrument nicked and scratched from years of shattered glasses and dart playing. The dartboard hung very near Uncle Ralph's head while he played, mesmerizing his audience, most of whom had postponed their drinking for the song's duration after realizing the man was no novice piano player.

If there was ever a time to cry, it was then, and for a moment Owen thought he might be able to squeeze out a tear or two. But the song ended before he could conjure up the necessary emotion, and everyone who'd gathered around the piano was clapping and cheering. The moment had come and gone. His eyes remained dry.

Lori's death a little over a week earlier had shaken him, yet he hadn't wept then, either. The words "Your sister's had an accident" had struck him like a bulldozer. He'd felt her death as an aching emptiness in his chest—a feeling that should have brought tears in a functioning human being, popping the cork that held back the waterworks. On an intellectual level, he knew he was sad. Lori had meant the world to him—had *saved* him, really. He'd been shy before her arrival in the world, withdrawn. But, in many ways, having her in his life had helped him bloom. Without her courage to inspire him, he might never have come out of his shell to acquire the few friends he'd made (and subsequently lost) over the years. Without her encouragement to dampen his doubts and fears—of rejection, of failure, of never being quite good enough for anything or anyone—he might never have graduated high school or gone on to university to become an architect or built homes and hospital additions and green roofs on skyscrapers hundreds of feet in the air. Even the wind farm, his current project located a few dozen kilometers north of the city, owed itself to Lori's prodding.

Without having had Lori in his life, Owen might have been lost. Now, with her gone, he truly *was* lost. He felt untethered to reality, with only his mother left to keep him grounded. And still, the tears wouldn't come.

"Don't you just wanna knock the smiles off all these fucking people's faces?"

Trevor, one of Lori's childhood friends, stood beside Owen at the table of *hors d'oeuvres*. Uncle Ralph was playing an upbeat tune Owen didn't recognize. Mourners wore smiles and chatted again, raising glasses in toasts and moving their heads to the music. Owen chewed the mouthful of cracker and Hungarian salami—which he'd just shoved into his face before Trevor had interrupted—and swallowed it dry.

"It's nice they're smiling," Owen lied. "Isn't that what wakes are for? To celebrate life?"

"Sure, but *look* at them." His whisper was conspiratorial, a devil on Owen's shoulder. Trevor wore a neatly tailored black suit jacket atop a kilt, the black of his jacket sharply offset by splashes of blood red in his pocket square and thick knee-high socks, over which he wore sandals. His caramel-brown pate, shaved to the skin, glistened under the bar lights. "You'd think this was a *wedding*," he remarked.

"The way that minister was going on," Owen said, "she might've married Lori to Jesus."

Trevor snickered and clapped him on the back. "You're sick, man."

Owen mused at how accurate Trevor's comment was, despite being a backhanded compliment.

"It's really too bad about Lori, man," Trevor said. "She was a good kid. I'm really gonna miss her."

Owen nodded and stuffed another cheese-laden cracker into his mouth.

Trevor watched him chew for a moment. He seemed to recognize the mouthful had been meant to halt the conversation, and returned Owen's nod. "You take it easy, Ownsy," he said. He eyed Owen queerly and moved past.

Owen swallowed. "Yeah," he said, still half-chewing and glad for the easy out. "You, too." He watched while Trevor ambled over to another crowd of friends. Trevor glanced back at him with another strange look, and then raised his glass for a toast. The others responded by raising theirs.

Owen stood alone by the food table—reliving those junior school dance parties all over again—and began to wonder how much longer his mother intended to be here. He'd already had drinks with some of Lori's friends, and he knew they were likely to celebrate into the wee hours, then move on in search of an after-party. He decided that, if he and his mother were obligated to stay until the last of the mourners decided to call it a night, then he would excuse himself early.

A young white guy dressed in a Middle Eastern *kurta* approached the table, picked up a napkin and plate, and began loading the plate with enough food for a group of three. "Excuse me," he said, reaching the place where Owen had planted himself. "Oh, hey. You're Lori's brother, aren't you? Don't tell me..."

"Owen."

"Of course." The kid smiled pleasantly. His whitened teeth gleamed against his deep tan. "I'm Hanson," he said, holding up his free hand in a motionless wave.

"We met at Lori's twentieth. You're the diver, right?"

"Did we?" Hanson said absently. "Yes, diving is one of my passions." He gestured toward one of the snacks on the table. "Are these vegan, do you think?" He answered his own question with a shake of his head. "Best not to risk it."

"You taught Lori how to dive," Owen said.

"That sounds like it might be an accusation," Hanson replied, though it didn't seem to bother him enough to spoil his appetite.

"It's not—" Owen hadn't meant to accuse the kid of criminal negligence, but he supposed *somebody* had to be to blame for Lori's drowning, and her diving instructor seemed to him the likeliest culprit. Still, he didn't want to get into a fight at his sister's funeral. "I don't mean it's your—"

"Have you ever dived before, Owen?"

"Not unless I was pushed."

Hanson chuckled. "Well, Owen, it's an unfortunate fact that things like this happen. It's a tragedy, of course, but it's something you have to consider when you go under. Something as simple as a kink in the hose could—sorry to be blunt—kill you. You can die of *panic* if the water's deep enough. Think about *that* for a second. We call it blue orb syndrome. You become disoriented; you can't decide what's up or down, the bottom or the surface. You *hyperventilate*. You may see things that aren't necessarily there."

"I guess," was all Owen could think to say.

"Respectfully, Owen, you're not qualified to guess."

*Oh, but I do know*, Owen thought. *I know too much.*

According to the officer involved in the case, they had found Lori's body in the low, muddy reeds where fishermen trolled for smallmouth bass. Owen had pressed for details when he and his mother had gone to the police station, but his mother had strangely not wanted to hear them, and in fact had insisted he take her home without receiving any answers—but death was no longer a mystery. Police dramas and murder books, especially the ones by Martin Savage that his mother liked to read, had filled in the details like some macabre checklist, so that Owen and his mother knew all the signs a forensics team would have looked for: blood in the lungs, burst blood vessels in the eyes, bloating, a bluish tinge to the flesh, dirt and algae under the fingernails, metabolic acidosis, acute renal failure. He had called later to talk to the officer in charge, but they had ended up playing phone tag. He knew from a handful of television programs that proving homicide in a drowning case could be extremely difficult. Still, some dark part of him suspected foul play must have been involved.

"You're right," Owen said, distracted—not by thoughts of Lori's death, but by his mother, who seemed to have gotten into an argument with the old, jittery-eyed man who'd accused him of looking like his stepfather. "How would I know about drowning?" he said, watching his mother show the old man to the door with a fierce thrust of her hand.

Hanson squinted at him. "It's all right to grieve," he said, laying a hand on Owen's shoulder. Owen looked down at it and said nothing, while across the large, dim room, the old man leaned in close to Margaret Saddler to voice his parting words. She slapped the old man hard across the face. Owen had never seen his mother slap someone before, despite the countless times she'd lost her temper, and wondered what he must have said to deserve it. The old man gave a disheartened nod, turned his reddened cheek away from her, and slinked away.

"Just know that Lori isn't just *here*," Hanson was saying, and when he laid a palm flat on Owen's chest, Owen snapped his gaze back to the kid. "She's also *here*," the kid said, and swept a robed arm to encompass the totality of the pub, indicating Lori's eternal oneness with Everything.

Owen looked around himself, not quite getting it. His sister's philosophical friend scowled, and took that moment to slip away.

3

A FEW HOURS LATER, Owen sat on the steps outside the pub, clearing his head. A light rain was falling, a cool mist on his skin, the sun sinking behind the big Anglican church down the street, when Gerald stepped outside for a smoke.

"Hiya, Owen," Gerald said. He wore his characteristic hangdog expression. Not that he necessarily felt guilty for anything—though he had much to feel guilty about, in Owen's opinion. It was just how his eyes were shaped, drooped at the corners, his mouth downturned from the weight of his jowls.

"Gerald," Owen said, avoiding eye contact, looking instead at the passing traffic.

"You know," Gerald said, hovering behind him, "Lori and I were reconnecting before—well, before she went up to that *place*."

*Reconnecting*, Owen scoffed. *More like meeting for the first time.* Gerald Kinsman had only been around full-time for the first five years of her life, and had been blind drunk through most of those.

"She told me."

"Any idea what she was doing up there?"

"Where?" Owen said, his tone laced with anger.

"*Chapel Lake*. Did Lori... did she *tell* you anything, Owen? She never said anything to me about going up there, never even called, like she promised—"

"Why would she tell you *anything*, Gerald? You were barely in her life. She didn't even *know* you."

The man's stubbly Adam's apple bobbed as he choked back an emotional response: whether exasperation or grief, it was difficult to tell. "Someday you'll understand how hard it is, walking into a family that's not yours," he said, his tone eerily calm. "Being the outsider. Trying to step into the shoes of a father who was never there to a kid who never wanted one."

"Like you ever tried," Owen said. He wanted to hit the old man as hard as he could, this man who'd once claimed to want to be his father, pretender to the throne in the Saddler house. He wanted to dig his hand into his pocket and fling Lori's ashes —not really ashes at all, he reminded himself, only unnaturally smooth sand—right in Gerald's face. Instead, he said the worst thing he could say to a recovering alcoholic: "All you did was *drink*."

"That's a goddamn lie!" Gerald shouted back. He shot a look into the bar, where gatherers still drank, oblivious to the argument outside.

"I *saw* it, Gerald. But you were good at it, I'll give you that. It's just too bad you couldn't make a career out of *that*."

"I haven't had a sip of booze for over a year," Gerald said, breathing deep through his nose to calm himself. "I'm *trying*, Owen. Can't you see that?" His eyes expressed concern. "Why do you have to be so closed-off all the time? What made you so damned unforgiving, huh? Even your mother's forgiven me. Why the hell can't *you*?"

Margaret Saddler emerged from inside, just then, wiping her hands on her tweed pants. "Well, the hand dryer didn't work, so I'll have to sit with wet pants."

Gerald put on a smile. Owen's mother smiled back politely.

Neither of them acted as if Owen was there at all. "They'll dry soon enough," he said.

"Speaking of dry," she said, "it's a genuine pleasure to see you're off the sauce again."

Gerald blushed. "Every day is a struggle, but we persevere."

"Yes, we do."

They shared a strained smile, the awkwardness so palpable Owen forgot about his anger and just marveled.

"Well, it was good to see you again, Margaret," Gerald said, "even if it wasn't under the best of circumstances."

"You, as well," Margaret said with a deferent nod. "Well?" she said, turning to Owen. "Shall we go?"

Owen rose from his place on the stairs.

"Take care of your mother, Owen," Gerald said at his back. "And yourself."

Owen ushered his mother down the steps without a word.

"Don't be rude," she scolded him.

So Owen said, "You, too."

———

4

"WHO WAS that man you were arguing with earlier?" Owen asked as they drove home. He was staying with his mother for a few days at the house in the suburbs where he'd grown up, he and his mother having moved there when he was five.

"Man?" she said, flummoxed.

"The man with the beard. You two were in a pretty heated debate, from the look of it." She couldn't have forgotten already, but he supposed she had been distracted. They'd both been distracted. "You slapped him in the face?"

"Oh," she said, and clucked her tongue. "Pish posh."

She went straight into the house once they were parked, plopping herself down in front of the TV. The two of them sat for a bit watching reruns of old sitcoms, or rather, his mother watching and Owen staring vacantly, his mind on more important matters. *How did it feel gasping for breath in those last moments?* he wondered. *Did she lose consciousness right away? Was it like drifting off to sleep? Blacking out drunk? Or was it agony, her lungs filling with water, feeling every single molecule of oxygen dissolve, the crackling inhalations, her heartbeat slowing, her liver bloating and extremities trembling, growing cold and numb, knowing with each breath the next could be her last?*

The credits from *Growing Pains* flashed in the darkened room. His mother had put the commercials on mute, and hadn't turned the volume up. For some reason Owen had never understood, she disliked TV theme songs. Even the song from *Cheers*, probably the most universally-loved, she'd kept on mute. This was another secret he and Lori had shared, learning the songs from videos they'd taped and chanting them together while their mother was at work.

He got up from the couch and kissed his mother perfunctorily on the forehead, her wrinkles lightly dusted with a pale, floral-scented makeup, then he left her in front of the TV. Eying the pea green carpeting on the stairs on the way up to his old room, he recalled that he and Lori were supposed to have torn it up together, a fun project for the two of them, the summer after his first year at university—yet another reminder of his failures as a son and brother.

"Do you remember...?"

Owen turned at the sound of her voice with his head just below the second floor landing, looking down at Margaret Saddler through the stair rails. She hadn't spoken a word to him all day that hadn't been dragged out of her, and the sudden sound of her voice, broken, unsteady, startled him.

"Do I remember what, Mom?"

She didn't look back. He noticed with sadness that her white hair had thinned in the back, another sign of death creeping ever closer. Soon she'd be gone, too, and aside from his work colleagues, he would come completely untethered, like a boat without a sail, with nothing and no one left to keep him around any longer.

"When you were little," she said, her words flat, without emotion, "the two of us used to argue all the time."

"I don't remember that, no."

"We did." She never turned from the television. "You'd scream bloody murder over any old thing and go charging up those stairs to your room. You'd slam the door and you wouldn't even come out for supper."

It sounded vaguely familiar. He remembered he'd been so mad about some nonsense once that he'd refused to let her take him out for his own birthday dinner, and he hadn't backed down no matter how much she'd pleaded. He'd really been an angry little shit back then, screaming, crying in public for attention. Swearing at his teachers, his mother. Punching kids for no particular reason. The thought of it made him ashamed. He was glad his mother hadn't turned around to look at him right then or he might have broken down in tears.

"Then Lori came along, and that all changed. I saw it in your eyes the first time she grabbed your finger in her chubby little hand." Finally she dared a look over her shoulder, her eyes filled with tears. "All of that *fury* you had stored up in you like a fire... it all just went away. In an instant, you became that perfect little boy I'd always known you could be."

Owen offered a sorrowful smile. His nose tickled and his eyes felt prickly. He fought the feeling back, swallowed it bitterly. "She did that with everyone, didn't she? Brought out the best in them."

"Yes," she smiled. "She did." When she nodded, the tears she'd been struggling against finally spilled down her cheeks onto her shoulders. These were the first tears she'd allowed herself all day, unless she'd wept in the bathroom while Owen had been sitting on the stairs. In many ways, he and his mother were the same. *The dam broke*, Owen thought, and the coldness of the thought stopped his own tears before they could come. *Here comes the flood*.

Margaret swiped at them with the back of a hand, a thin smile on her painted lips, and sniffled.

"G'night, Mom," he said.

"Mmm," was her reply. The television had caught her attention again, and the volume came back on canned laughter. Owen stood looking at his mother a moment longer, this brave woman who'd raised two children on her own and had never asked for a thing in return. He studied her pale, shiny scalp through her thinning hair. Then he continued up the steps to the second floor.

Lori's old bedroom was on the way to his own, the door closed. If it had been opened, he would have been obliged to go in, to look over her trophies and photographs; the notes from lovers she'd still kept in contact with, who'd likely held no hard feelings; the letters from orphaned children in Rwanda and countless other places she'd traveled to share her time and friendship. It would only make him feel bad about his own selfish life. But the door was closed, so he moved past to his own bedroom at the end of the hall.

Aside from clean sheets and the lack of dirty clothes piled in every empty space on the floor, the old room was just as he'd left it. His mother hadn't even taken any of his clothes to Goodwill. He looked over the posters on the walls: Iron Maiden, Van Halen, Stevie Wonder—it was hard for him to believe he'd ever been into Creed, but there was the evidence above his old scratched-up rolltop desk. He seemed to recall something about the band had spoken to him back then, but he couldn't for the life of him imagine listening to them now.

He slipped off his shoes and sat on the edge of the creaky single bed. The bedspread had a fabric softener odor he recalled fondly from childhood, some sugary-sweet flower like an old lady's perfume. Lying back against the spongy pillow, he thought about the box his mother had left on his sister's bed: inside was everything Lori had brought with her when she died, what the detective had called her "personal effects." His mother hadn't had the courage to go through it, and neither had Owen, though he could guess at some of its contents. The silver pendant in the shape of a unicorn he'd given her would be among them, with its recent addition of the small silver crucifix he'd thought at first was meant to be ironic: the unicorn and the cross. The macramé wallet she'd made in crafts class as a kid would be there with very little money inside—just a tattered birth certificate, a bank card, a social insurance card, maybe a few concert ticket stubs and receipts, and the picture of them at Wild Water Splash Park one summer when they were all young, even their mother, the great big colorful tubes of one ride or another in soft focus behind them.

He yawned. *Such a long day. Rest my eyes for a bit, maybe. Then do some reading...*

Owen peered out at the cold dark water, a landscape of lush green, a decrepit dock, knots missing in old gray boards leaving round holes where the water showed through if you looked down and covered your eyes. He stood at the edge of the water, holding his sister's hand. Somewhere, a loon called out, followed by the low rumble of thunder in the distance. Beyond the trees, streaks of slate gray reached down from the clouds, a curtain of rain darkening the horizon.

Brother and sister jumped into the lake. The water was icy. She cried out and the two of them laughed. They treaded water. Swimming still felt somewhat unnatural to Owen, but after Lori had taught him how, he'd gradually come to enjoy it. He swam in a semicircle to face the opposite shore, languidly kicking his feet while a large turtle slipped off a rock into the water. When he turned back, Lori was gone. Where she'd been, the water rippled out in widening circles.

He called out her name. He turned, thinking she must have gotten behind him, that she was playing. "Lori!" Another rough circle. He thought about the last time he'd seen her, looking up the stairs at him from the front door of their mother's house. He remembered calling out to her as he did now: *"LORI!"*

Something grasped his leg, pulling him down. Not Lori. He sensed something dark in its scrabbling fingers... something sinister, yet familiar. It dragged him down; it had always dragged him down. He gagged, choking up water, thrashing his limbs, struggling against the thing below him in the deep. Drowning, just like Lori had.

He woke himself with a shout, and inhaled deeply. His first instinct was to cough. No water came up; no water surrounded him. It had all been a dream. But the sensation of drowning was still there, too strong to be ignored... and the thought that Lori was somewhere nearby made him glance hopefully toward the open door, as if the events leading up to her funeral had been a dream.

The night-light in a hall socket cast a dim yellow glow, throwing the shadow of the banister against the far wall. The hall itself was empty.

Owen sighed and rolled over, still fully dressed, and peered out the window at the darkened sky, the halo surrounding a streetlamp. The alarm clock he'd used in high school, SNOOZE worn off the button from pressing it so often, showed the time at just past two. He'd been sleeping maybe three hours. Mid-July, and the little room was stifling. He'd sweated through the sheet, which he supposed would explain the sensation of drowning. The sweat-dampened sheet had knotted itself around his ankles, explaining the creature that had pulled him under.

Lori had still drowned. Nothing would change the stark and irrefutable fact of her death. She'd gone night diving alone at a lake up north, and her oxygen had run out. Some deeper part of him had always expected Lori to leave and never come back. Each trip she took, a voice would speak up in his mind: *This could be the last time you see her.* He'd imagine Lori falling under the spell of some Svengali or religious guru, her mind so open to new experiences and ways of seeing the world, she'd let anything in. He would see her parachute sailing out into the blue, detached from its pack, and Lori hurtling, freefalling toward the earth. He would picture her mangled body in the high branches of a tree or some farmer's field, a cow grazing nearby, oblivious. He'd see her flung from her airboat in the Everglades, splashing into the swampy reeds to be gobbled up by gators. He'd watch her two-prop plane take a sputtering nosedive into lush green mountains; see her take a wrong step during a jungle trek into a waist-deep pool teeming with piranhas; the small, wooden planks on the sheer face of a cliff snapping beneath her feet; approaching an isolated South American tribe with her hands held out in peace only to be gunned down by a naked tribesman's Kalashnikov. Each time she left, he'd suffer these vivid premonitions and hug her with a ferocity that would make her laugh. "I'll only be gone a month!" she would assure him—or a week, or a day—as she readjusted the hefty knapsack on her strong shoulders. Lori must have thought she was invincible, her life as elastic as a bungee cable. But Owen had witnessed her death a hundred times. Her world was limitless, while his was well-ordered, routine.

She had never told them her purpose for going up there, nor what she'd felt had been so significant or interesting about that particular lake, this Chapel Lake. She'd just left. He supposed she might have gone up there to some religious retreat, considering the name. Religion had never been a part of their household, yet Lori had embraced it, always going against the grain. He'd guessed it had something to do with her burgeoning relationship with her father—a concept Owen couldn't understand, his own father having left his life at the same age Lori's had left them—and his recent involvement with the cult of sobriety.

The last time the Saddler children had been home together, Lori had shown up to dinner with a crucifix nestled against the unicorn pendant he'd bought her when they were kids. She'd claimed to have had a religious awakening while trekking through some war-torn country, and their mother had replied that it was all well and good, but she politely and firmly asked that her daughter remove it at the dinner table.

*Never seen Mom so mad*, he thought.

In the bathroom, the faucet dripped.

Curious, Owen pushed himself out of bed. *How long has that been running?* he wondered. *Since I shaved for the funeral?* He skirted past Lori's room, past his mother's, to the bathroom. The floor was dry. That was a relief, at least. He watched the sink for a drip, and quickly realized the sound was coming from the shower behind him.

He peered down into the darkened hall, to the lighted stairwell where the muted sound of canned laughter floated up, to his own doorway and the foot of his bed. The slit of darkness under Lori's door unnerved him. Anyone could be in there, lurking about. *Anyone.*

Another heavy drop, not the hollow *plink* of water on enameled steel but the large *plunk!* of water into a tub already full of it. The plug must have fallen in and lodged itself in the drain. But the shower curtain was drawn. He'd left it open this morning, and he'd been the last to shower, he was sure of that much. Maybe his mother had drawn it closed before they'd left for the funeral. It seemed like something she might do.

A shadow moved behind the clear frosted vinyl of the shower curtain. He saw only its dark, gauzy reflection, and he froze, his heart beginning to hammer.

Owen forced himself to approach the tub, more cautious than he'd meant to, the hesitation in his approach redoubling his fear, imagination running amok. He'd seen *something*, the shadow of the door in the hall light, or his own shadow caught in the corner of his eye, and he'd mistaken it for the figure of a man or a woman standing in the shower. *Or a girl*, his mind whispered, before he could prevent the thought from surfacing. The dark, ethereal shape moved again behind the shower curtain. Whatever it was, it hadn't just been his imagination. The head of the figure moved slowly back and forth, as if assessing him, and the water continued to drip. *Drip.*

*Drip.*

He tore the curtain aside—

His heart leapt as he saw it, the empty shower, the tub devoid of water, not knowing quite what to think of that, nor the fact that he no longer heard the drip that had drawn him to the bathroom in the first place. The plug lay where he'd left it, where it had been before his morning shower, beside his mother's shampoo and body wash. One of Lori's tar soaps was still tangled with her blonde hair from her last visit; no mistaking it for anyone's but Lori's, as Owen and his mother both had dark brown hair. He remembered thinking just that morning how unlike his mother it was not to wash the hair down the drain, or to have thrown away the soap, for that matter, and buy Lori a new bar the next time she visited. With lavender shampoo running down into his eyes, he'd considered it was as if she had somehow *known* Lori would never be home again, that she'd kept the soap and hair on purpose. She *couldn't* have known— of course she couldn't have. But that was what he'd thought.

He continued to the toilet, used it, and flushed before washing his hands, eyeing himself in the mirror in the semi-dark. Unshaven, hair a mess, brown eyes sallow, as if he hadn't slept in days—he certainly hadn't slept well since they'd heard about Lori. He ran a finger over the old scar on his eyebrow from an injury he didn't recall, the vertical scar that made kids in later grades call him Vanilla Ice. It stood out stark white against his dark eyebrow, a constant reminder of the lost memories from his early years.

As he stepped back from his reflection, his gaze fell on Lori, standing in the shower behind him. Nerves freezing, he held himself perfectly still, afraid if he moved she would vanish, heart pounding as he studied her in the mirror. She wore a plain white robe he'd never seen before, dampened up to her knees, blonde hair wet and hanging in her face. She opened her mouth to speak, voicing words he could neither hear nor discern by the shapes her lips made.

*"Lori..."* he said, and before he could ask her what she'd meant to tell him, her form shivered, became translucent, then

broke apart into tiny droplets, like water, and splashed down heavily into the tub.

Owen whipped around from the mirror, falling to his knees at the edge of the bath, reaching it as the last of the water—the last of *Lori*—gurgled down the drain.

"God, Lori..." he sobbed. "Lori... Lori..."

A door creaked open down the hall. He looked up as his mother stepped out of her room, bleary-eyed and blinking. "Owen? What's going on?"

Owen cleared his throat, pushing himself up from the bathroom rug. "Nothing," he said. "I just... I lost a contact, that's all."

Dressed in a nightgown a similar shade to Lori's white robe, she gave him a skeptical look. "Since when do you wear glasses?"

"A while ago, Mom. Go back to bed, okay? You had a long day."

She scowled. "I don't need you telling me what to do, Owen. I haven't before, and I certainly don't now."

He nodded. "Okay, Mom. G'night."

She half turned. "You really should put on the light, if you're looking for something." Her peace made, she went back to her room, closing the door behind her.

"Seeing things that aren't necessarily there," he muttered to himself as he headed down the darkened hall, remembering what Lori's dive instructor had said about that syndrome with the peculiar name. "And I'm not even underwater..."

He blew out a breath through his teeth, trying to relax himself. Still, he couldn't shake the idea that Lori had been trying to tell him something. That she'd come back for a reason. These troubles followed him into sleep.

# CHAPTER 2

## BAPTISM

I

OWEN FELT CONFLICTED leaving his mother alone when he returned to his downtown condo late Sunday night. She was a strong woman, he reasoned. She'd survived years before him, before Lori, and she'd survive even now that one of her brood was gone for good.

He knew he was just making excuses for abandoning her, but he needed to get back to work sooner or later—sooner seemed the best option for his own health, if not for his sanity, considering what he'd seen, or *thought* he'd seen, in her bathroom. The wind farm project wasn't going to finish itself, and although Teri Avery, his business partner, could handle herself in the boardroom and the work site, it wasn't fair to leave her to handle the protesters, too. So he determined to throw himself into his work. It was the best way to get through the grieving process, he decided, to move beyond all the morbid imagery and imaginings, to stop his mind from wandering to thoughts of death and drowning and lakes up north where the water was dark and cold and deep enough to drown in.

All well and good, as his mother might have said, except that it didn't work. By Tuesday, he found himself stopping in front of a dive shop on his way out of town, and on Thursday, he actually dared to go in. An hour later, after a quick call placed to Avery to let her know he'd be a little late, he came out with a shopping cart full of stuff, some of which he didn't even know what to call, let alone what they were for: wet suit, fins and booties, a regulator, something called a "safety sausage," another thing the sun-ravaged clerk had called a "pony" (which looked like a smaller version of the large scuba tank), and an underwater camera. It all came with a free T-shirt branded with the store logo on the lapel and DIVERS DO IT DEEPER stenciled on the back. The clerk had a good chuckle over this, and Owen laughed along amiably even though he hadn't found it funny. It would make a decent rag, at the very least.

Driving to the job site with the equipment heaped on the passenger seat, he felt incredibly pleased with himself, as if he'd taken a big step toward recovery, and hadn't just plunged head-first into the initial stages of obsession.

Protesters were there in large numbers when he finally made it to the site. So many angry faces, their rage directed at his car as he passed, shaking their signs like swords at their enemy. Since they'd broken ground on the site three weeks back, the marshy area leading up to the site had been packed with the usual suspects: the environmental activist groups (Save the Wetlands was in charge this time, since the wind farm project was otherwise a benefit to "Mother Earth"); a First Nations group, some wearing traditional garb and waving the flags of their tribes; the youth groups, their faces and bodies painted with slogans, their chants aggravatingly catchy ("One, two, three, four," they sang, "we know what we're fighting for!" *Do tell*, Owen thought with gentle mirth); the NIMBY people, who weren't protesting the project, but its location, and their polar opposite, local citizens who would benefit from the jobs created, there to protest the protesters. Hence, the final component necessary for any good protest, the Provincial Police, a half dozen officers standing sentry in strategic positions between the factions.

With so many reasons for protest, their signs were an odd jumble. A silver-haired man shook a NO MORE WIND TURBINES sign at Owen's windshield. Flanking the car was a group with matching professional SAVE THE GRAY TREE FROG! signs. Many of them likely didn't know exactly what to make of Owen driving through in a hybrid. Standing side-by-side among the environmentalists were others who likely did: they held hand-painted signs demanding Owen and his partners STOP GREEN FASCISM and LEAVE JACKSON'S FIELD ALONE! The few enviro kiddies caught up in this group appeared lost, but continued their chant, calling out like the gray tree frog to prospective mates.

Owen caught a lone man's eye as he drove through the throng, long, shaggy dark hair hanging over the man's spooky blue eyes. He wore torn blue jeans and a stained white T-shirt, holding a JOHN 3:16 sign up lazily at his side, unmoving.

"What the hell...?" Owen muttered, twisting to look back as the crowd swelled in, packing tight around his small car. He shot a glance in the rearview, but the strange man and his out-of-place sign were long gone.

Police held the protesters back from the site itself, where Suburbans and Volvos and Avery's BMW were parked alongside dozers and trailers. Owen swung his feet out the driver door and tugged on his steel-toes before trudging out to meet Avery in the middle of what locals called Jackson's Field.

She stood with five guys in hard hats and steel-toes going over the technical drawings, swinging a long arm out to indicate to the men where the future towers would stand. In a group of men, Avery held her own; it didn't hurt that she towered over most of them, but even if she hadn't, her knowledge and experience had carried her far. There was never a time when Owen wasn't glad to have her as a partner. He doubted Avery could say the same of him.

The group broke up their huddle and went about their various duties. Avery spotted Owen as he approached, and shook her head. "Lot more protesters today," she said. "I thought the freaks only came out at night?"

"Did you see the guy with the John 3:16 sign? What's that about?"

She glanced over his shoulder. "Must've thought he'd found himself a backwoods wrestling match," Avery said, and Owen chuckled. "You look like you're in a brighter mood today. Good to see it."

"Feeling much better, actually. Thanks."

Avery eyeballed him a few more seconds before squinting off at the marshy field. "You ever see one of these green tree frogs they're chanting about?" It didn't seem to Owen it was what she'd *wanted* to say. He assumed she wanted to press him about how he was doing, and couldn't bring herself to. They didn't have that kind of relationship. He'd never had that kind of relationship with anyone but Lori. Even the few women he'd dated had accused him of being closed-off—*Wasn't that what Gerald called me?*—a state of being that had eventually, inevitably, ended the relationships. Only Lori had known his true self. Even so, he'd shut her out near the end, too. He'd told himself they were growing apart, as siblings often do, but the truth was he'd been pushing her away.

"They're *gray* tree frogs, I think," he said. He remembered catching one when he was little, younger than he could ever recall being, and it had peed in his hand. Whether it had done it out of self-defense or fear, he'd never known. Either way, he'd had no special feelings for the animal. "The fact that there's maybe one single tree in this whole goddamn field doesn't make me believe we'll being doing any harm to their habitat, though."

Avery chuckled. "No, I wouldn't think so."

"When's the Premier supposed to be showing up?" The Ontario Premier had been scheduled to break ground today, a fact Avery had reminded Owen of when he'd called to say he'd be a bit late. Owen hadn't forgotten; the idea of the smiling dignitary stomping on a brand-new shovel while the press snapped photos and shot footage filled him with mild dread.

Breaking ground reminded him of the clean little four-by-ten burial plot in St. John's Norway where Lori's body quietly decomposed, and he was afraid his mask of composure might slip in front of the cameras. How would that look for the little company they'd built, he and Avery, with one of its lead architects looking like his sister had just died, on the front page of every paper?

Avery glanced at her watch. "Little after twelve," she said. "It's almost eleven now."

"Good, good," Owen said. There was a skirmish in the crowd, but the police quickly broke it up. A man and a woman shouting at each other. The woman belonged to the workers' side, the man was a NIMBY. The cop held them back from each other, then made them shake hands and mutter apologies. *A uniquely Canadian brawl*, Owen thought. It wasn't very funny, but he felt it deserved a grin.

The bustle cleared, opening the way for the man with the spooky eyes and his JOHN 3:16 placard, which he'd raised to shoulder-height. He stood immobile, his gaze fixed on Owen.

Owen felt his heart quicken as anger flooded his veins. *He's provoking me*, he thought, remembering the chapter and verse from Lori's funeral. *Don't let it get to you.*

"What's the matter?" Avery said.

"Nothing."

But the man turned the sign, his expression unchanging, the board still resting on his shoulder. The backside was painted in red, curdled like streaks of blood:

## LORI'S WITH US NOW, OWEN

Without a thought, without even blinking, Owen rushed out into the muddy parking lot, ignoring Avery's cries for him to stop. Just beyond the cars, he fell to his knees in muck, getting a reaction from the crowd, laughter and shock. He pushed himself up, muddying his hands, and stormed toward the man with the sign.

"Who are you?" he demanded. "How do you know who I am?" The man said nothing, only pushed his icy blue stare further into Owen's skull, a mesmerist's trick. Childish rage spilled over, and Owen shoved the man in the center of his chest, leaving a muddy palm print against the man's dingy white T-shirt.

"Owen!" Avery sounded both terrified and angry. She grabbed him by the shoulder and drew him away from the man. "Are you *nuts*? What the hell are you doing?" She whispered this, harshly, and threw a smile over Owen's shoulder at the man with the sign. "I'm terribly sorry, sir. He's had a bad week."

"Bad *week*?" Owen shouted, incredulous. "Avery, this fucking guy—"

But as he struggled to remove her hand he took in the sign's message: STOP GREEN FASCISM. No John 3:16, and zero mention of his or Lori's names. Owen's muscles slackened at the realization: *the hallucinations were still happening*. Twice now; three times, counting the lucid dream. Avery was still pulling him away from the man with the sign, and he fell into her arms. She gave him a one-armed hug, patting him cursorily on the back.

"Is everything okay here, ma'am?" A young cop had sashayed over, looking apprehensive to dive into the fray.

"Don't ma'am me, Sonny Jim," she snapped, a classic Avery-ism. "And yes, we're fine. It's a misunderstanding, that's all."

The troubled officer turned to the spooky-eyed man for confirmation.

"I'm really sorry," Owen said, and he meant it. "I thought you were... someone else."

"No harm no foul," the man said.

"I'll pay for the dry-cleaning, if you—"

"I got six more shirts like this at home, fella. Like I said, water under the bridge."

These last words slugged Owen in the chest, but he wouldn't allow the feeling to express itself on his face. Avery, meanwhile, stared the cop down until he reluctantly moved away. Then she turned back to Owen and said, "Go home, Owen." She spoke directly into his ear. "Take some time off. You need it."

"I *don't*," he said, his voice nearing a whine. "I need to work."

"Work doesn't need *you*. *I* don't need you. The lion's share is done, you know that. It's all PR bullshit now, nitpicky little detail-work you're no good at anyway. You're a big-picture guy. Take a week off." It was a demand, not a request, and though she couldn't exactly give him orders, she could easily make things difficult for him at the office. "Shit, take *two*. Let yourself *grieve*."

But Owen was looking past her at the rise of green before the land gave way to swamp, where his sister stood, her damp hair and white gown caught in the same wind that rocked him.

"I don't want to grieve," he said, watching Lori mouth her voiceless plea, wondering why she couldn't just *leave him alone*.

"Nobody does, Owen," she said. He saw sympathy in Avery's eyes, revealing an emotional side she'd kept hidden from him in the eleven years they'd been partners. "If people did, they'd call it something else."

When he looked again, his sister was gone.

———

2

THE FUNERAL BILL arrived that day. He'd known his mother couldn't afford it on her fixed income, so he'd asked that they send it to him. He hadn't been expecting it so soon, though, with the wound still fresh, and after his breakdown earlier in the day, it hit him hard. It was a business, he supposed, like any other, and businesses needed to be paid. But they could have waited a few weeks, at least, in his opinion. Out of compassion.

"Something wrong?"

Owen turned at the vaguely familiar voice. The girl from the condo next door stood behind him, the key to her mailbox held between slender fingers, nails painted black, chipped and bitten. Her face was as white as the wall behind her. She might have blended in entirely, like a ghost, if not for her dark clothes.

He'd seen the young woman around the building before, in the elevators, in the underground lot. Seen her entering the condo next to his, and said nothing, had only given her a brief smile. After the first missed opportunity, it felt awkward to speak up on subsequent meetings in the hall. He knew her last name was Huang, because they'd gotten their mail mixed up once, her coupon for some hair product left in his mailbox, his receipt for some charitable donation in hers.

"Nothing's wrong," he said, shrugging up his shoulders a little too high. He realized he must have been standing in the mail room for some time, staring at the bill in his hand, a handful of flyers in the other.

"Oh. You just seem depressed is all," she said.

His breath caught. He felt as if he were drowning, water in his lungs choking out his breath—*Is that what this is? Depression?*

Funny how it was so obvious, that a woman he'd only just met had read it on his face, in a single phrase, a single gesture, but he'd never once considered it himself. *Did Avery notice before today?* Owen wondered. *Have clients?* In that moment of self-reflection, he realized his head had been drooped, his chin almost touching his chest, his mouth downturned on one side like a man with Bell's palsy, but in a way that seemed to feel natural. He straightened immediately, forcing his mouth into a tight smile. Christ, how long had it been like that? Hours? Days? *Weeks?*

She eyed the envelope in his hand with the funeral home's

letterhead, and the corners of her own lips turned down. "Oh," she said, suddenly flustered. "I'm so sorry, I didn't mean—"

"No, it's—I'm—"

"I didn't mean to pry," she said. "I just... You know we live right beside each other and I don't think we've ever said a word. Our bathroom walls touch—that's kind of intimate, I think, maybe I'm just weird—and I don't even know your name. That's a bit odd, isn't it?"

"I guess it is a little strange," Owen admitted, as much for the fact that neighbors of three years didn't know each other's first names as for her belief that their toilet tanks being separated by a foot-thick wall of concrete was a form of intimacy. He shifted the mail to his left hand, shook hers with his right. Her hand was fragile, anemically cold. "I'm Owen."

"Sophie. I'm sorry for your loss." She frowned. "Wow, that really does sound meaningless from a stranger, doesn't it? 'Sorry for your loss.' As if I know anything about you." She glanced at his chest, causing Owen to wonder if she was trying to get a look at his heart. "Your pain," she added, and he supposed she must have been.

He nodded, forcing a smile. "It's fine. Thank you."

She smiled wanly back, small features set in a pale face surrounded by single-shade brown hair chopped into bangs. He hadn't really noticed her before, hadn't clued in to the fact that a not-unattractive woman lived next door to him.

*When's the last time you thought about anyone sexually?* he asked himself, and he knew he must have been depressed for a very long time when he realized he couldn't answer the question.

The silence drew out. Finally Sophie nodded, brushed her bangs aside. She opened her mailbox, grabbed the mail from inside, and locked it again. "Well," she said, "it was nice to meet you, Owen."

"Yeah, you too..." He'd lost her name already.

"Sophie," she reminded him with a patient smile. "If you need anything, to talk or whatever, my door's always open. I mean, of course, it's *locked*. In this neighborhood, are you kidding me? Just... you know, *knock*." With a shrug, she added, "I know what it's like to lose someone."

"Okay," he said, deciding at worst she'd lost a childhood pet, a tabby with fur the same single-shade brown as her hair, dead of feline diabetes. The last thing he needed was some stranger who knew nothing of real loss trying to yank him out of this— and he called it what it was—*depression*. Hope only exists to make the disappointments deeper. Hadn't his mother told him that often enough? He forced another smile. "Thanks again."

She stood there waiting for more. When he offered nothing, she nodded again and headed for the elevators.

Owen dumped the flyers in the recycling, considered tossing the bill from the funeral home in with it, and then took it with him. Sophie would be waiting for the elevator still; they were always slow. He hung back behind the corner of the wall, listening for the ding. Once the doors slid shut with Sophie nestled inside, he stepped back out into the empty foyer.

———

3

OWEN SAT on the leather sofa in his simple suite, off-white and black and deep, rich brown like Sophie Huang's hair. He was thinking about the man with the John 3:16 sign, which had turned out to be something entirely different, and wondering why his mind had made such a bizarre connection. *LORI'S WITH US NOW, OWEN.*

"Us," he muttered. "Is that what she was trying to tell me?" But of course, *she* wasn't trying to tell him anything; it was his own subconscious speaking to him through her, through the protest sign. The television, on mute, showed the reenactment of a murder in hazy colors. The killer looped a strand of wire around the throat of this week's female victim, and *pulled*...

Clearly, he still had doubts about her death. When he'd finally gotten through to the officer in charge, the officer had seemed certain Lori's drowning had been accidental. There was little Owen could do but speculate.

According to the police, Lori had rented a cottage on Chapel Lake with the purpose of going diving, but the whole thing had seemed entirely unlike her. Lori was more of a Cayman Islands diver, parti-colored fish and pink coral reefs and underwater caverns, with long sandy beaches to dry out and tan on. Owen couldn't imagine what she possibly would have been hoping to find, diving in cottage country where, aside from shape and size, all the lakes were virtually identical.

*I have to know. Everything. All of it. Why she went and how it happened. I have to know.*

Owen opened his laptop and looked up the lake. Peterborough Township's website said Chapel Lake was man-made, created in October of 1979 as a reservoir for a hydroelectric dam. He clicked the link to the town's website, and it came up a dead end: WEB PAGE NOT AVAILABLE. Even the cached site was blank. He scrolled through the other links. None of them were for Chapel Lake, either the town or the lake itself. According to one site he was able to find, the original town had been named Peace Falls, after the white settlers' name for the nearby Mushkoweban Falls. The present town of Chapel Lake lay on land meant for expansion of its neighboring village, Dunsmuir —a familiar name, Owen thought. They'd incorporated Dunsmuir into the new town of Chapel Lake before the dam was built and the old town submerged.

His search finally hit pay dirt in images: photo after photo of underwater wreckage filled the screen, green-gray neighborhoods of ruined buildings, swarming with freshwater fish. In one photo, an old wooden boat rotted on the caved-in roof of a shack, its hull encrusted with zebra-striped barnacles. Another showed a rusted swing set, chains hanging loose and furry with green and brown algae, the seats themselves missing, like some makeshift torture device.

Several photos showed why it had been named Chapel Lake: a church steeple standing like an obelisk in the middle of the water—an eerie sight, despite the sun-shiny setting. He might have thought it was a Photoshop job if photos hadn't been taken at so many different angles and times of day. In some, there were boats and water-skiers and Jet Skis shooting by in the background. In others, the water was low enough to see the church's bell tower. Several more were shot from underwater, some at a wide angle, distorting the church's features, shot low to capture bright ripples where the cross broke through the surface.

Owen closed the laptop, satisfied with what he'd found. But his curiosity lingered. He could see how Lori might have been interested enough to check out the lake for herself, as an experienced diver. She'd done wreck salvage before. She'd even worked as an underwater welder for a few months to make money for her next trip, much to the displeasure of Owen and their mother, who feared her death on a daily basis. This was salvage on a larger scale, though he supposed if the town had been sunk in 1979, there would be very little left of worth under Chapel Lake. Since she'd likely seen the same photos he'd just looked at and found the same scant information, she'd likely have come to the same conclusion herself.

*There's gotta be more to it than that*, he reasoned. *Lori's a smart girl. She wouldn't have wasted her time up there, unless she knew something I don't.*

Without access to what she'd been thinking in the last weeks and days of her life, without a computer or a diary to work with, he supposed he'd never know. Lori hadn't kept an apartment the past few years, drifting from sublet to sublet, often sleeping on a friend's couch in between expeditions, or, as a last resort, Mom's house. Her computer, if she'd even owned one, and her diary, if she'd kept one, would likely be in the box at the house, gathering dust on her old bed.

He considered calling his mother and asking her to look, but when he'd brought up the idea of going through it himself, she'd been mortified, yet another nonstarter conversation in the Saddler house.

*What then?*

His thoughts traveled down to the parking garage and his hybrid (a car he'd bought after Lori's constant badgering that his previous one was damaging the environment), to where his brand-new diving equipment lay in the cool semi-darkness.

*Should I try it?*

On the way back from the job site, he'd considered recreating Lori's dive: to put on the wetsuit and mask, to let out enough oxygen from the tank so when he finally dunked himself underwater there would only be enough good air for a few minutes' breathing at most.

It would take too long, though, and by the time he got everything ready, he'd be likely to lose his nerve. Still, the idea was enticing, so much so that he stood up without further thought and crossed to the bathroom, where he began filling the cast-iron tub. As he undressed, his mind returned to the previous Saturday, to the imagined *drip-drip-drip* of the faucet in his mother's house. *It was calling to me even then*, he thought, and when he asked himself exactly *what* had been calling to him, he spoke the answer aloud: "The water."

All he needed was a little taste of what it had been like. More than anything, he needed to know. He might not figure out what had happened to her, but he couldn't shake the feeling that, before he made his way to Chapel Lake, this was the logical first step in his journey. To be close to her again. To feel how she'd felt. To know how it had ended. The moment he felt himself starting to choke, wanting to suck in air, breathing water instead...

"I'll call off the experiment," he told himself, standing naked before the tub full of water, and he flicked out the bathroom light, plunging himself into semi-darkness. Lori had drowned night diving. In the small amount of light from a lamp in the living room, he eased himself into water as cool as the lake in his dream. There might not have been moonlight when Lori went under, but there would have at least been minimal light from the cottage she'd rented on Chapel Lake. His imagination filled in the details for him: the cabin had oil lamps, providing her with a nice orange glow. The Himalayan salt lamp by the sofa would be a suitable equivalent.

He lay back, resting the base of his skull against the edge of the tub. When he did have baths—a rarity—he'd use an inflatable pillow. This time, he wanted nothing to come between him and the fantasy. The tub was large enough for him to stretch out comfortably, but a foot might sink too low and thump against the bottom, an elbow might thud against the side and spoil the illusion.

*This has to be perfect*, he thought.

In water up to his neck, the nightmare came rushing back. The thrashing, the splashing, the choking for breath. He pushed the thoughts away, hoping to calm his nerves. Now was no time to chicken out, not when he was so close to knowing how it had felt. Like the handful of dirt he'd reached out and snatched from her graveside when all eyes had been on the minister, the need to feel how Lori had when she'd drowned was inexplicable, a morbid compulsion he couldn't deny. A part of him knew no good would come of it, but that part was small, and easily ignored.

He took a measured breath, let it out slowly. He took another, thinking, *This is how she died.*

Then he slipped all the way under.

The water magnified every sound to near-supernatural proportions. He heard the radio in Sophie's condo, blasting some talk show, though the voices were muffled. Somewhere, someone zipped along on an exercise machine, a stair climber or an elliptical. The clatter of dishes from above or below, he couldn't tell; a toilet flushing; the rattle of a small animal chewing on its cage.

Soon all of these sounds drifted away. He heard his heart, thrumming steadily in his ears, and nothing more.

Ten seconds passed this way, thirty... until the urge to release his breath pressed heavily on his lungs. Finally, he opened his eyes.

A man stood over him.

More than a mere shadow this time, more than the dark shape he'd seen behind the shower curtain at his mother's house before Lori had shown herself to him the first time. He could make out the man's face, distorted yet familiar, through the ripples on the surface: a gaunt, wild-eyed face with dark, receding hair beginning to gray at the temples, and a dark mustache over an even darker smile. He wore a white loose-fitting work shirt and black slacks. A thin chain of burnished gold or brass hung from his wide, deep pants pocket to a belt loop. Owen took in all of this in the mere moments before his heart began to race and he instinctively drew back, plunging deeper under the water.

*It's him,* he thought. *The one I saw that day, walking on water. Lori's ghost.*

More rippling forms appeared behind the man, peering down at Owen's nakedness: eight stone-faced men and women in all, and a young blonde girl, all of them dressed in white garments. *Flock* was the word that sprung to mind, and he found himself thinking: *He tends to his flock like a shepherd.*

Behind them all, Lori stood shivering, fear evident in her eyes, while the man in the white shirt—*Shepherd*, he thought—rolled up his sleeves. Terrified and confused, Owen sprang up from the bottom of the tub. Breath exploded from his lungs, bubbling up toward the surface.

The Shepherd's hand plunged into the water, pushing down with enormous strength against Owen's sternum. He felt an ache from the man's strong hand like a bruise on his heart, a pain much like the loss of his sister, and he kicked out, soaking his attacker's shirt through to the undershirt beneath it, splashing the others, who stood huddled around the tub, watching without flinching, without mercy—even the child, the young blonde girl, didn't blink.

Only Lori turned away, apparently unable to watch.

Owen grasped the ghost's forearm. Horrifying images filled his head the moment his hand touched the man's bare skin—of fat, overfed beetles scrabbling out of skulls with scraps of withered gray flesh and a single eyeball floating in a red froth, its ocular nerve thrashing behind it like a fin, and of naked white bones strewn across a plain of sediment—and he jerked his hand away, strange black tendrils forming between the Shepherd's flesh and his palm and stretching out like saliva before being whisked away in the churning water. He gulped for air, desperately, his mouth filled with liquid. He tasted his own sweat, the dirt he'd unintentionally washed from his body, choking as it filled his nose, his throat, worse than the dream, worse than the nightmare. Strangely, the man's brown eyes held no malice; what Owen saw was something like bliss, a profound joy mirrored now in the faces of his flock, all except Lori—who, from her similar gown, was most certainly "one of them," just like the message he'd thought he'd seen during the protest.

*Joined them. Joined this cult. Joined her ghost. The man who walked on water.*

Suddenly his vision shifted, and a very clear image that was either a hallucination or a vision overcame him. This same hand held Lori down, forcing her under the dark water. She kicked and screamed under its weight, unable to rise to the surface. The image vanished suddenly, returning him to the tub, where pinpricks of light danced before this vision. The room beyond began to gray, the witnesses to his death only visible in the whites of their eyes. He was losing consciousness.

Owen screamed, hoping for his neighbors to hear, hoping

for the Shepherd and his flock to forgive whatever sin he'd committed against them. But the water stifled his cries.

The tub had grown impossibly deep. The Shepherd's arm seemed to stretch down to such an incredible depth that, even if the man let him go now, Owen wouldn't have the strength to swim to the surface. Far above the Shepherd's head, at an even greater distance, the ceiling split open like a wound, and the darkening sky began to show itself, rain pattering down on the surface of the water.

The lake was cool and dark and inviting, the sky overcast, the rain that had been threatening in the west all morning just beginning to drizzle down around them. Lori slipped under the water, disappearing in a wake of concentric ripples.

Owen gulped in another mouthful of water and followed her down.

# CHAPTER 3

## LOST AND FOUND

I

OWEN SHIVERED, GASPING for breath.

He was breathing again, his lungs taking in air instead of water, and the sensation made him realize he must have been dreaming. The water, the trees, the sky, all of it peeled back like a stage backdrop. Lori disappeared. He floated in a cold and shapeless void, an emptiness so thorough he couldn't feel his own body.

*Am I dead...?*

The thought seemed to arise from nowhere. His body was gone, his thoughts mere electrical impulses in the ether.

A moment later, his surroundings came into view as if illuminated by a flashbulb. Sensation returned to his limbs, his chest, neck, and head. He'd been floating in a senseless abyss, but now he felt he was lying down. His hair was damp, heavy on his head, wrapped in something from his knees to his chest, fuzzy and warm, and yet he still shivered. A scent hung in the air: floral, powdery. A perfume? But whose? Not Lori's; not his mother's. Familiar, though. Something he'd smelled very recently. A window was open behind him, issuing a cool breeze. Directly across from him, the television was tuned to a rerun of *Columbo,* where Columbo was on vacation, wearing a Hawaiian shirt.

*Am I still dreaming?*

"My mother..." A woman's voice, swimming toward him in the gauzy half-light.

His eyes flickered toward the voice, as familiar as the scent. He saw the photo on the table of the three Saddlers at the water park before fully realizing where he was: *My condo, my living room.* It seemed he remembered very little, not least of which how he'd ended up here, on the sofa, shivering and wet and wrapped like the dead.

He turned his head, a difficult task. Just breathing was difficult. It seemed as though an invisible weight was on his chest, pressing him down—

The events from the bathroom returned, and he sat up abruptly, pushing against the sudden crushing pain in his chest. He'd been wrapped up snug in a pale blue terry cloth towel. The Shepherd's hand wasn't there—had never *been* there. Yet he still felt it, like a weight. Like something pushing him down.

She sat on the chair opposite: Sophie Huang from next door. The world was still somewhat blurry. He blinked until he could see her properly. She'd said something, hadn't she? He was barely able to croak, "W-what?"

"I lost my mother," she said, and brought her eyes up, looking at him intensely. "A year ago. She'd smoked for as long as I can remember. Probably even smoked through her pregnancy, for all I know. Maybe that's why I'm so fucked up."

Sophie put the tips of her fingers to her naked lips in a gesture of surprise. "Sorry," she said, with a self-conscious downward glance. "TMI. Anyway, she hadn't been sleeping well for months. Stayed up all night watching those late-night infomercials, hoping they'd put her to sleep. Of course they didn't, she just ended up with an apartment full of unopened junk. Then one night, she fell asleep in her chair with a lit cigarette. The medical examiner said she probably died in her sleep of asphyxiation before she could feel herself burning to death. Cold comfort. I'd always said that ratty old chair was a fire hazard." She uttered a morbid chuckle.

Owen wondered how Sophie could manage to talk about it so calmly. It must still have been painful, with her mother only in her grave a year. He let the silence draw out, unsure how to respond. Finally, he managed to say, "Sorry for your loss."

Her sudden laughter startled him. After a moment, he realized what she'd found funny: she'd said the same thing to him when they'd met in the mail room. He grinned. It would have been too painful to laugh, even if he'd found it funny himself.

"There was water all over the floor when I came in," she said, when her laughter died. "I thought maybe the dishwasher was leaking; mine does that sometimes. Then I saw the bathroom door open..." She gave him a look so intense he wanted to shrink away from her. "I thought you were dead. You were so pale, you weren't breathing or anything. Just floating there. It's funny, you looked so peaceful."

They sat in silence a moment.

"I tried to kill myself once," she said, matter-of-factly.

"I wasn't trying to kill myself."

"Of course you weren't. I never said you were." Judging by her tone, though, she didn't believe him. But pressing the issue would have made it seem more like he was lying, so he let it go. She'd just saved his life; by how much, he wasn't sure. Now was hardly the time to quibble.

"It was just after my mother died," she said, and for a second he had no idea what she'd meant. His thoughts were disjointed; he couldn't seem to focus. An aftereffect of having nearly drowned, he supposed, and determined to try harder.

"Couple of weeks, I think." She was looking off at the big windows that faced the Harbourfront as she spoke, at the lights of all the other condos, a poor substitute for the stars that couldn't be seen with so much light. "I stood in front of the subway tracks for—God, it must have been over an hour, willing myself to jump every time a train pulled into the station."

She considered it a moment, scowling off in silence, at her own foolishness or the thought of how close she'd come to death, Owen wasn't sure. "But I couldn't do it. You know, it's funny, I used to worry every time I stood close to the tracks and someone passed behind me, I'd keep them in my peripheral vision to make sure they couldn't push me, and if they tried, I'd see them and be ready. I'd steel myself for the push, make sure I had my footing and wouldn't fall out onto the tracks if it came. But that day, I *prayed* for someone to see me there and just... give me a little nudge. Just a little shove and all of my stupid little troubles would be over." She chuckled softly, perhaps at the dark simplicity of it. "But nobody did. Eventually, the station attendant or someone came over and asked me if I was all right. I told him I was lost, so he gave me directions." She shook her head, a very slight movement. "I really was lost, but not in a way directions could've helped." Looking up, Sophie held his gaze. "I was lost from *myself.*"

Owen nodded. He let the silence draw out again, because it seemed a moment of silence was required. Then he said, "Well thanks for not letting me throw in the towel," indicating with a nod the towel she must have wrapped around his naked waist. She laughed again, a big, hearty laugh that apparently surprised her so much she tried to stifle it with her hand. It wouldn't hold back her snickering, so she snorted and made noises in her throat behind a balled-up fist.

Owen grinned, pleased to be able to lighten the mood, while proving—he hoped—that he wasn't in a suicidal mood. But he didn't laugh with her. When her giggle fit was through, he said, "Sorry."

"It's okay," she said, and chuckled again. "After what happened in there," she nodded toward the bathroom, "I guess I must have needed a good laugh."

"Thanks again," he said. "Honestly."

"Just thank your lucky stars I know CPR."

"Sorry if I wasn't the best kisser," he said. "I'm much better when I'm conscious, I swear."

She laughed again, not quite as heartily, and her cheeks flushed a little. She'd pulled him naked from the tub and resuscitated him before drying him with the towel, and mentioning it clearly embarrassed her.

"Why did you come here?" he asked her. "I mean, I'm glad you did, obviously. It just seems a little—"

"*Deus ex machina?*" she said, and grinned.

"Exactly."

"I found this mixed in with my mail." She picked up what looked like a postcard and held it out to him. Owen took it from her. "It's weird, I was going to give it to you the next time I saw you in the mail room, but my mother told me to get moving, and when mother talks, I listen."

Owen nodded before her words had a chance to sink in. "Wait... *your mother* told you?"

"Uh-huh," she said, then tilted her head. "I take it you don't believe in ghosts."

Owen scowled. "No. I don't. But thank your mother for me next time you see her." He realized how rude it sounded, and backtracked. "I'm sorry, I just—"

Sophie shrugged, expressionless. "You're a skeptic. I get it. It's tough not to be cynical these days. Anyway, you have to admit it was fortunate I came when I did."

"It was. Again, I'm sorry. I didn't mean to be dismissive."

Sophie brushed it off and launched into a monologue, but Owen only half-listened. The photo on the postcard had caught his attention: a lake nestled among some trees, sparkling with diamond glints of sunshine. At the center of the photo was the rotted crown of a white church steeple, its cross rising from the water. Printed across the top were the words, GREETINGS FROM CHAPEL LAKE!

*Speaking of ghosts*, he thought.

"You know, you shouldn't keep your door unlocked," Sophie was saying. "It's not the best neighborhood."

Owen turned the card around and was staring at the words on the back. The postmark was dated June 20, just over three weeks earlier. He recognized his sister's neat handwriting:

> *Come as soon as you can, Owns.*
> *He's here. Zip.*

To an outsider, it must have seemed like gibberish, but to Owen—who knew what his sister had meant by "zip," and who also now had a strong suspicion who *he* was, though the terrifying incident in the bath must surely have been a hallucination brought on by hypoxia—they filled him with a sudden and overwhelming certainty. Lori hadn't gone into Chapel Lake by choice the night she died, he understood that now. Somehow this man, whoever he was, had *drawn* her to the water. Though he might never know for certain, Owen felt the truth of it like a chill in his bones. And though it might have been too late to save Lori, he could still do something about the people he believed had been her killers. The flock. And the man who'd walked on water.

"Is she the one who passed?" Sophie asked.

"Thank you, Sophie," he said, ignoring her question. "Really. For everything." The postcard rattled between his quivering fingers. "But I have to look into this, and I should probably get dressed, so..."

"Oh, no, that's fine. I'm sorry if I overstepped."

"No, not at all," he said.

Sophie gave him a tight-lipped smile, then nodded and crossed to the door. She stopped by the kitchen counter, then turned, her eyebrows raised in concern to where they'd disappeared behind her bangs. "Are you sure you'll be okay?"

"Mm-hmm," he answered much too quickly. With an immense amount of physical concentration, he lowered Lori's postcard to the coffee table as if it were easy. He could tell Sophie didn't believe him, so he forced a smile. "I'm good," he said, a little more aggressively than he'd meant.

"Okay," she said. "You know where I live if you need to talk."

---

2

OWEN DRESSED QUICKLY in the clothes he'd left in the bathroom cubby, and looked up Chapel Lake again, this time for a map. The town and lake went by the same name, both nestled in a patch of forest along with hundreds of other small lakes —called the Kawartha Lakes or, simply, the Kawarthas—crisscrossed by provincial highways, communities, and country roads in Peterborough County, a little over two hours' drive northeast of Toronto. The map became a steel gray, forest green blur of blocky pixels, the closer he zoomed in on Chapel Lake.

Looking over the postcard again, the wording seemed needlessly enigmatic. He wondered why she hadn't written more, why she hadn't mentioned the *he* by name—why she hadn't sent a whole letter, for that matter. Or an email. Or *called*. If she'd written *I am here* or *He is here*, like the game they'd made up as kids: the time he'd written *I am in a painful place* on their little index cards, meaning the cactus pot, and after nearly twenty minutes of searching he'd inexplicably found Lori kneeling in their mother's closet. But she'd used the contraction this time—*He's here*—as if the phrase had no connection to her game at all.

It had happened so long ago, when they were still so young, he could barely remember the incident at all. Just some photos, a Bible, and Lori sitting among a dozen shoes, their pairs seemingly missing.

*Zip* he knew. Zip meant *zip it*, as in *Zip it, Owns. Don't tell Mom.* The fact Lori didn't want their mother to know what she'd been doing up there meant Margaret Saddler wouldn't have approved. But the list of things their mother frowned upon was virtually endless.

"I need to go up there, ask around. See if she went there looking for her ghost, or..."

*...or if he'd followed her up there*, he finished in his mind, not wanting to speak the words aloud.

The thought occurred that the last time he'd needed to know about Lori's death he'd nearly killed himself, *would have*, if not for an incredibly fortuitous series of events: for the postal employee to accidently put Lori's postcard—of all things—in Sophie's mailbox, and for Sophie to choose the perfect moment to return it.

*Sophie's mother chose the moment*, he thought. *Sophie was just acting out her mother's wishes. Following in the footsteps of a ghost. Or so she claims...*

Rationally, he knew the harm of this venture: that by going up to Chapel Lake he would be fully committing to what had begun with Lori's drowning and should have ended tonight in the tub. That, because he'd hallucinated some backwoods Bible-thumper holding him underwater while his unsympathetic flock stood by and watched, he'd already driven halfway down the back roads to Crazy Town. That this little guilt trip of his was irrational, harmful. *Dangerous.* The second step on a gravely obsessive quest that had already nearly taken his life. Continuing any further down the path would lead toward an inevitable downward spiral.

*But if Lori's ghost really is a real person... If she'd gone up there to Chapel Lake and* found *him...*

Owen printed out the directions, laying them on the kitchen counter by the dish where he kept his keys, pocket change, and dead batteries. After the highway, the country roads to Chapel Lake would undoubtedly punish his car. He'd put in a call to Avery, explain the situation and what he'd planned. She might argue, but eventually she'd admit that having him gone for a week was far better than the guilt trip he'd give her by forcing him to stay.

First things first: he needed a few hours of sleep. He was exhausted, despite the brief lapse of consciousness. He fell into bed, was asleep within minutes, and he slept like the dead.

By some miracle, there were no dreams.

3

THE MAP HADN'T LIED. After the highway, there were only fields and trees and rolling green hills. Some roads were paved, others macadam. Driving them was like sitting on one of those vibrating chairs in the mall.

The drive itself was peaceful. The farther he got from home, the more he focused on the act of driving itself, the better he began to feel. A few times, he thought of Lori, he pictured her in the roadside shops rifling through moccasins and dream-catchers and cheap sunglasses, wondering if she had stopped and gotten out at the Peterborough Lift Locks or Burleigh Falls (he hadn't himself, had only marveled at them as he drove by). He imagined her, but didn't see her: there were no more hallucinations of Lori in her damp white gown, mouthing words he couldn't hear. He quickly pushed away thoughts of Lori's tormented spirit and the man who'd walked on water, forcing himself to enjoy the road, the scenery, the smells. The smells of sweet hay, sour dung, chip truck potatoes, spicy conifers, chalky gravel—the perfume of the countryside—blew in through the open windows, filling him with pure good feelings, and vague, fragmented memories of a childhood half-forgotten. His mood seemed to brighten, the fog of depression seeming to lift, though he knew it couldn't last.

Passing through a small town very near his destination, he noticed the gas was low. In his hurry to beat traffic, he'd forgotten to gas up. On the outskirts of Chapel Lake, a service station parking lot shimmered in the late-morning sun. He pulled the car up to the pumps. The sign said FULL SERVE, something Owen thought had disappeared with the advent of debit cards. A bell dinged when his tires rolled over the rubber cable on the blacktop.

"We don't got none a them battery charger doohickeys, if that's what yer waitin on."

The voice startled him. The attendant had approached from behind, dressed in coveralls and scuffed steel-toed shoes, his bushy brown eyebrows raised in mild curiosity. His scruffy hair of the same color rustled like feathers below a trucker's cap with the ESSO logo, although this station appeared to be no-name. There was a garage in back, from where the gas jockey must have come, and a grease-slathered kid who stood eyeballing them from the open doorway, ratchet in hand.

"Oh, it takes gas," Owen said.

The attendant peered down at the gas cap and nodded thoughtfully. "Headin' up the Chapel, are ya?"

"Huh?"

"I said, 'you headin' up Chapel Lake?'" The guy was mid-fifties, maybe younger, his face *leathered and weathered*, as Margaret Saddler had once said while swooning over Clint Eastwood. He wiped his grimy fingers with a dirty rag, which only served to smear oil further into the creases in his skin.

"Oh," Owen said. "Yup. I guess you don't see a lot of city folk out here."

The man raised a bushy eyebrow. "That s'posed to be cute?"

"No." It was. "How did you know I'm headed out there?"

"Saw that Scoobie 'quipment in yer backseat. Figgered you're either headin' up the Chapel, or just come f'm it and got yersef turned around sommers up the road there. Either way, we're glad to have yer b'ness."

The man's country patter made Owen grin. The name stenciled on the lapel of his overalls read, BEAU, and unless he'd been a beautiful baby, Owen thought, it had been one hell of a practical joke to play on a kid.

"Want me to filler up then?"

"That'd be great, Beau."

The attendant looked down at his own lapel, then back at Owen with mild irritation. "It's *Bew*."

Owen suppressed the urge to laugh, and Beau/Bew went about pumping the tank full. The numbers rattled up, the cost per gallon seemingly incongruous with the age of the pump itself, which appeared to be an antique. He looked in the rearview, expecting to see Beau's kid—or whoever's kid he was —still standing there with the ratchet in his hand like some movie maniac. But the kid was hard at work on a lawnmower engine, with a slightly bent, unlit cigarette poised between his lips, and Owen felt a twinge of guilt thinking the kid was potentially a homicidal hillbilly.

Beau whacked the squeegee against the inside of the holder, ridding it of the excess water.

"Don't worry about the windows," Owen said, and the bushy brown caterpillar resting over the old man's left eye rose. "They're only gonna get dirty again once I hit that road to the lake."

Beau shrugged and tossed the squeegee back in the holder with a splash of gray water. He lifted his hat to scratch absently at his sunburned scalp. "Yee-ep," he said, as if they'd been talking all along. "Gonna be a scorcher."

Owen considered whether or not a reply was required, but the pump dinged, sparing him the effort. Beau put his cap back on, pushing it right down to his small ears. He jerked the nozzle out and set it back in its cradle. Then he unfolded a pair of bifocals from his hip pocket—the medical tape wrapped around its bridge looked like the cocoon his caterpillar eyebrows might have formed—shook them open, and used them like opera glasses to squint at the gauge.

"That'd be forty-eight forty-five," he said, dropping the glasses back into his pocket. "Now, will that be cash or Master Charge?"

<hr>

## 4

OWEN HAD GLEANED a strange fact about Chapel Lake in his research: the village itself had no actual chapel, aside from the one submerged under the lake. The nearest church was fifteen kilometers northeast in a town called—in what was likely an unintentionally ironic biblical reference—Locust. He'd read this on the blog of a salvage diver who seemed to think it was not just peculiar but disturbing, and had speculated that the townspeople still held cabalistic gatherings in the old chapel under the lake. An odd leap of logic, in Owen's opinion, but the idea had conjured up a haunting image of a gloomy under-water church filled with men, women, and children in diving gear, listening to a similarly equipped preacher via transceiver.

The first thing he'd noticed driving into the village of Chapel Lake was its lack of signage. Most other villages would have some kind of flowery town sign with a cutesy or folksy sort of motto, often carved out of wood. Lacking that, a simple green metal road sign with the town's name in tall white letters, the kind that shined when high beams hit it at night. Chapel Lake had neither. What it had instead was a big wooden water tower with CHAPEL LAKE painted on the side the color of dried blood. Much of the paint had flaked off, and as he drove past, Owen realized you couldn't spell Chapel Lake without an H, an E, and two Ls.

The town wasn't exactly thriving, either. Many small towns had become havens for retirees, meaning big business from Baby Boomers, well-to-do folk trying to escape the city, the rat race, the teenagers and immigrants. Chapel Lake, it seemed, was not one of those towns.

Maybe a dozen years ago it had been a decent-sized tourist trap (the run-down B&Bs were evidence of that), but not today. Windows of a bakery advertising "Authentic Canadian pastries" were lined with newspaper, the door adorned with WE ARE CLOSED FOR BUSINESS FOREVER printed on dot-matrix computer paper. In a small park, no one posed for photos in front of the oversized cedar canoe. The post office's sad red and white maple leaf hung from the rusted pole like a wet rag. The hardware store—NOW HIRING, according to a sign in the window—was closed, and the outdoor market sparsely popu-lated: a few meager displays of peaches-and-cream corncobs and strawberry baskets, the remnants of a half-assed Mennonite fur-niture venture, and something called Miss Betty's Jams 'N Pre-serves. All of this Owen saw as he drove through town, while curious citizens shaded their eyes and squinted back at Owen in his fancy little car.

"You people can roll out the welcome wagon anytime, now," he muttered, waiting at the flashing red light in the center of town. An elderly lady turned to look down at him from the sidewalk with a thunderous expression, though she couldn't possibly have heard him with the windows rolled up and the air conditioning on. He suspected she might cast the same glower of disapproval on anyone she didn't recognize, particularly upon such an obvious out-of-towner. The lights changed and she shuffled her walker across the street. Owen turned left.

Potholes were more common than usable road beyond Chapel Lake's business district. The realtor renting out the cottage had an office on the north end of town. Between there and what passed for the "downtown core" were turn-of-the-century homes gone to seed, a fenced-off auto yard, a small antiques "shoppe," and a closed-down Dairy Queen.

Wickman Realty was a small square one-story building, the kind of off-white stucco eyesore with a flat roof that could just as easily be a dentist's office or a chiropractor's, except for the storefront windows. The lawn was neatly manicured, one of the few in the area. The windows held neat photo displays of houses and cottages for sale, lease, or rent. Owen scanned them for the cottage Lori had stayed in, but since he didn't know what to look for, and had just hoped something would leap out at him, he gave up, disappointed.

A young couple with a baby sat at Skip Wickman's desk when Owen stepped in, the bell above the door tinkling. The couple peered back over their shoulders.

"I'll be with you in a moment," Skip said.

It was cool inside, like a fridge, compared to the street. More photos of houses, trailers, cottages and empty lots were posted on a photo board. A rack by the door displayed brochures for towns, townships, and lakes in the region. Children playing in the water. Couples holding hands at sunset. Horse carriages, speedboats, canoes, fishermen, the Mushkoweban Falls Hydro-electric Dam (*Power for Our Future!*), the Peterborough Lift Lock, a bridge called the James A. Gifford Causeway across Chemong Lake, pinecones, snowmobiles and skiers, village fairs and festivals, cotton candy and livestock, trees and trees and even more trees.

Finally, Skip shook hands with the husband and wife, who looked to be in their early twenties and had probably just signed the lease on their first mobile home. He led them out of the office, holding the door for them. As they thanked him again,

Owen noticed the woman had teared up a little. Their baby boy began to cry the moment they stepped back out into the heat.

Skip Wickman turned from the closing door, its bell tinkling. "God loves His children, but they sure do test His patience with all that crying," he said, more to himself than to Owen, his realtor's smile still affixed, turning it like high beams toward Owen. He was in his early fifties, hair salt-and-pepper at the temples, beige suit and slacks creased just so, his tie nearly the same shade of brown as his skin. "Now, how can I—?"

Skip's mouth remained open but no words came out. He stood there, still holding the door handle, looking Owen up and down.

"You okay?" Owen asked.

Skip closed his mouth. "I'm sorry. You must be Mr. Saddler." His eyes narrowed. "You know, it's uncanny how much you look like her." The man swallowed hard. He seemed to consider how to proceed, having perhaps said too much. "I was so sorry to hear about your sister. Lovely girl." After a pause, he stuck out a hand. Owen shook it. Skip's handshake was firm, his palm as cool and dry as his office.

"She was," Owen agreed, not expecting how much it would hurt to speak of her in the past tense. "On the phone, you said the cottage—"

"*House*," Skip corrected. "Belonged to one of the Hordyke boys. Their family founded Peace Falls. Jim Hordyke built the house by hand in the mid-'50s. There's a plaque put up by the Historical Society, a sort of honorary commemoration, I'm sure, it being the only house from Peace Falls still standing, after the flood, where it had been built. But nobody cares much for historical footnotes like that anymore. When he'd built the house—old Jimmy Junior, who was actually the *fourth* in a long line of Jimmys—it lay on the top of the hill overlooking the town of Peace Falls, about as far away from the water as you could get."

Skip opened a palm toward his desk, the only one in the office. "Can I offer you a drink? I've got terrible coffee and lukewarm water." He grinned. "Not to oversell either."

Owen chuckled. "I'm fine, thanks." He sat in one of the gray tweed chairs: threadbare, a bit wobbly, but comfortable enough. He'd avoided the other, where the young father had been sitting, having noticed a suspicious dark stain on the seat. Skip sat opposite, in a weathered but still serviceable leather chair.

"He was a fisherman," Skip continued, "which explains the 'fisherman' part of its name, Fisherman's Wharf, but not the 'wharf.' I believe some of the locals started it as a bit of a joke. Now, of course, Jimmy's probably laughing from his grave at all those old fools who'd made their jokes at his expense. Now that they've flooded the valley for their hydroelectric dam," he said with obvious scorn, "the house rests neatly on the shore of Chapel Lake. So in a way, I suppose you could make the argument that Jimmy Junior was somewhat of a prophet."

Skip reached into his desk, brought out a pack of gum, and gobbled up a stick. He held the pack out to Owen, who shook his head. The man shrugged and tucked it back in the drawer. "Bank took it away not long after the dam went up. Whether Jimmy Hordyke was a prophet or not, the bank still had to make one. A profit, I mean." He smiled lightly at the pun. "When he'd built it, in the 1950s, I suspect property taxes weren't much of an issue. The '80s changed that quickly enough. Even more people are foreclosing around here these days than they were back then, I'm sorry to say."

Skip lowered his head and paid them a moment's respect. "I suppose one could also say old Jim Junior was a pioneer in that respect, as well. Not that it's anything one would want to be a pioneer *of*." He chewed his gum thoughtfully a moment. In the silence, Owen heard a chainsaw in the distance.

"Now that you know the history of Fisherman's Wharf," Skip said finally, "I wonder if I might ask you something. I'm not usually one to pry, but it does concern me a fair bit, and I feel I would be remiss not to ask. If I offend you in the process, let me apologize sincerely in advance."

Owen supposed he should have seen it coming. Out-of-towners likely didn't die under mysterious circumstances very often in a town this small, as they might, say, from the more-typical drinking and boating incident. He knew there would be more questions once people around town realized his connection with Lori, most of whom probably thought of her as "the dead girl." Best to answer now and get it out of the way. With any luck Skip Wickman was a bit of a gossip, and word would be all over town by tomorrow.

"You want to know why I've come all the way out here to stay at the house where my sister was staying when she died," he said.

"If it's not too much to ask."

"Mr. Wickman—"

"Skip. Please."

"Skip, I promise you I'm not here to cause trouble. I just need to follow in my sister's footsteps for a while. Give myself a sense of closure, for what it's worth."

The chair squeaked as Skip leaned back and clasped his hands behind his head, making himself comfortable, now that the serious business was through. "Well, I suppose that's understandable." He nodded toward Owen's car out the big storefront windows. "I see you've brought your equipment. Have you done much diving?"

*Aside from almost drowning in my own bathtub, you mean?* "Not really, no," he said.

"I'm a bit of an enthusiast myself," Skip said, with an emphasis on the last syllable: enthusi-*ast*.

"Oh?"

"Indeed."

"I may do a bit," Owen admitted.

"Your sister said much the same." Skip sat forward with another squeak of the chair, and clasped his hands above the desk, leaning closer to Owen. "I suspect—and I'm not alone in thinking this, Owen—your sister may have had more on her mind than just diving."

Owen wasn't sure how to respond. He'd suspected it himself; this was as close to proof as he'd come. *He's here*, she'd written. She'd been out here *looking* for someone: for *him*, whoever the hell *he* happened to be. Likely the man who walked on water. Lori's ghost.

"She told me she was looking for some underwater town?" Owen said, forcing himself not to ask the many questions he had. "Thought it would make a decent photo-essay."

Skip grinned, then leaned back in his chair. "She was hugging that camera of hers like a babe in arms when I first saw her. Didn't look like much of a thing to me. A '70s job, not one of those fancy digital things kids have these days. She asked to take my picture. Who am I to say no? With this face? *C'mon.*" He chuckled in false modesty.

"Yeah, she always had that thing slung around her neck, even at Christmas dinner," Owen mused, grinning at the thought of Lori carrying her ugly camera around, taking pictures of dinner, of Owen and their mother, of anything that caught her eye. Always snapping photographs. Even, apparently, of strangers like Skip Wickman. Owen thought it was a sly way of snooping, snapping photos of the town and its inhabitants. "I bet she probably took pictures of just about everyone in town, huh?"

Skip laughed. "Just about." He checked his watch. "Darn. Owen, I could talk all day, but I've got a showing in fifteen minutes. If I sign over the key, would you be all right heading out there without me?"

Owen assured Skip he'd manage, glad to have the conversation done and to be allowed to go to the house on his own. He wouldn't have to fake geniality any longer, though it was an easier task with a decent conversationalist like Skip.

"Now, where is that key...?" Skip rummaged through his desk drawers, patted his jacket pockets, pushed aside legal documents on the desk, and even checked inside the I LOVE MY YORKIE mug he used as a pen holder. "Where is that damn thing?" he said, reaching into his pants pockets, patting his chest.

Owen began to feel uncomfortable, watching Skip's search grow more frantic, unable to do anything to further its process. "Can I help?" he asked, as Skip rifled through his drawers again.

The realtor looked up with a scowl. "No, no. I'm sure I just overlooked it."

Owen couldn't watch anymore. It was uncomfortable, seeing such a put-together man unravel over a key. He peered down at his own feet, tapping impatiently on the gray carpeting, and found what Skip was looking for.

Owen bent to pick up the clunky, rusted old brass thing, and held it up for Skip to see. "Is this it?" He didn't need to ask; either this was the key, or it opened the doors to Hogwarts.

"Oh, *thank God,*" Skip said, plopping himself down in his chair with a hefty sigh. "That's the key, all right. Where did you find it?"

"Right there by my feet."

Skip frowned. "How did it—?" Then he shook his head. "Well, at least it's found. That key opens most of the doors in the house, but I think you've already figured that out."

"It's a skeleton key," Owen said.

"A skeleton key," Skip repeated. "I realize it doesn't instill much confidence for security, but believe me, Owen, nobody would want to break into that house." He caught himself. "Not that it's not a nice rental. I just mean if anyone had wanted to, they would have a long time ago. Being as isolated as it is, out there by the lake, no neighbors, it would be quite easy to break a window and loot the entire place without causing a stir." He grinned. "There I go overselling again."

"I'll be sure to keep a night-light on," Owen said.

The realtor chuckled. "You be sure and do that." He stood with the look of a man who couldn't wait to be gone. "Now, if you'll excuse me." Owen stood to take the hand Skip offered. "Any problems with the house, Owen—*anything at all*—I'm just a phone call away."

"Why would there be problems?" Owen half-joked, covering how spooked he'd suddenly become, a tingle running up his spine as if he were the dandy hero of some gothic horror story. An isolated house with a history, opened by a skeleton key. A ghost town under the lake where his sister had drowned. No neighbors, and no one to hear him scream. It was such a cliché that Owen nearly laughed. He stopped himself before it had a chance to escape, making a sound like a stifled sneeze. Skip Wickman probably considered him a bit nuts already, knowing he'd driven all the way out here to shadow his dead sister. No use adding fuel to the suspicion.

The realtor offered an obligatory "Bless you." He turned the door sign to CLOSED and ushered Owen into the street. They shook hands, and Skip repeated his invitation to call no matter how small the problem (although, this time Owen doubted the sincerity of it), then rushed off to his shiny new Cadillac.

The moment Owen closed himself in his car, he burst out laughing.

# CHAPTER 4

## TAKE ME TO THE WATER

I

FISHERMAN'S WHARF WAS only a few kilometers from town. The final lap of his journey was a winding single lane dirt road. About five minutes after turning onto it, he reached a fork in the road. To the right, according to a green road sign, was the PEACE FALLS TRAILER PARK. To the left, a smaller, hand-painted wooden sign said, HORDYKE'S WHARF .5 KM. He turned left.

The house stood a hundred or so feet from the road, obscured by trees and protected by an open gate. Owen got out. He saw the Historical Society plaque behind an overgrown bush: big, brass, and painted blue, with the words HORDYKE HOUSE (rather than the name given to it by the locals) embossed beneath the Ontario coat of arms. Below that was a description of the house, but Skip Wickman had already told him most of what had been inscribed. What Skip hadn't said, Owen had already gleaned from the photos—*A milled-log house of the American style, hand-crafted on the hill above Peace Falls by James Hordyke Jr., and his son, in 1953.* Contrary to what the sign indicated, milled-log houses were not handcrafted, but hewn in a mill, and assembled onsite like a jigsaw puzzle. Local historians should have been aware of this, but it was a minor mistake, given the laudable sentiment.

Gravel crackled beneath the tires as he drove up to Fisherman's Wharf.

James Hordyke Jr. had built a two-story log house with a

stone chimney in the middle, its only interesting feature. Otherwise, the house was virtually unremarkable in every respect, except its disrepair. The logs had grayed almost to the color of the limestone. Owen got out for a closer look, noting casement windows that were likely original, insulated by untrimmed mounds of multiple caulking attempts, brown shutters that had been nailed open like insect wings tacked to a display board, and chipped paint that showed its molting colors: white, green, and orange, the color of pumpkin innards. The chimney looked as though it might have a few more years left before it toppled in a cluster of stones and mortar to the tawny carpet of pine needles surrounding the house. The front door, with its skeleton keyhole, was noticeably lopsided.

The skeleton key felt heavy in his pocket. He took it out and approached the crooked door.

Owen couldn't see the lake from the front door—or back door, depending on your method of approach, by car or by boat —but he heard it lapping against something, along with a squeaking sound, an old dock, perhaps, with rusted hinges that lay somewhere beyond all the trees and brambles, dense spruce and broad white pines heavy with cones. Wind swished through their needles like the long sweep of a broom. Somewhere a red squirrel chittered its maniacal, high-pitched laugh. Much nearer, a cicada confirmed the heat.

"This place really is in the middle of nowhere," Owen said to himself. "God's country." He glanced over his shoulder at the outhouse, with its carved cross, and chuckled. "If I can't relax here, I might need to check myself into a motel with padded walls."

Owen slid the key into the lock with a scrape and clack, and twisted it. The door burst outward as if someone had kicked it from the inside, and he sidestepped out of its path, an inch from having his nose broken. It banged against the side of the house so hard it almost came back a full ninety-degrees. It swung toward the wall again, then slowed to a stop and hung loose and unbalanced, creaking gently.

"Foundation's slanted," he told himself as his heartbeat slowed. "That's the problem."

He wrinkled his nose at the dank smell that wafted out. There were ugly, musty old rugs curled up at the corners, covering obvious indents and bumps in the hardwood floor. Above, a ceiling fan rattled. Even having the windows open had done nothing for the mustiness. The house was open concept, though he doubted that Jim Hordyke, a fisherman by trade, had known he was repeating a design attributed to Frank Lloyd Wright.

Through the kitchen windows, the lake shimmered in the afternoon sun. The sight unnerved him, an image plucked straight out of his dreams and dropped in front of his eyes. He hadn't been here before, as far as he knew. Even if he had and couldn't remember it, his mother surely would have mentioned it. *Oh by the way, that lake your sister drowned in, we went there when the two of you were little, sorry I forgot to mention it. Probably doesn't mean anything, though. Don't bother looking into it.*

Owen crossed the house to the red-brown door. He hesitated only a moment, scanning the deck. A chipmunk had been nibbling peanut shells and scampered off when Owen stepped up to the window. An old orange charcoal barbeque, open and full of pine needles, stood beside a paint-flecked Muskoka chair. Owen unlatched and opened the door, and stepped outside.

Beyond the deck railing, a cobbled path led down to the water. At the shore, a small tin boat, painted purple with green stripes, banged against an ugly unpainted dock, gray as old bones. A canoe lay pulled up on the shore under a tarp. Owen headed down the stone path. The day had heated up. He wanted nothing more than to take his shoes off, roll up his pants, and stand in the water. Cool off a bit. Maybe even take a dip, if he felt brave.

He followed the path to a set of stone stairs leading directly into the lake. At the water's edge he peeled off his shoes and socks, tugged his pant legs up, and dipped the big toe of his right foot in. The water was cold, refreshing. Slicked with algae, the steps ended at the sandy lake bottom, which he could barely see. He steeled himself with a sharp inhale.

"Just like peeling off a Band-Aid," he said, and plunged both feet in. He went down two steps quickly, up to his knees. The frigid water sent a shock straight through to his bones, and he howled in a mixture of delight and holy terror. In the distance, a loon responded with its distinctive cry. For a moment he felt like he might black out, then his bones grew accustomed to the chill, and he wiggled his toes, pallid under water the color of weak tea.

Fat little minnows fearlessly circled his bare legs. Owen breathed deeply the smell of the lake, the trees, and fresh, clean air. Other than the faint smell of gasoline and engine oil from the boat, there appeared to be no sign of human intrusion. No Jet Skis zipped back and forth monotonously in front of the dock, causing wave after wave to pummel the shore. No fishermen trolled past, surreptitiously eyeballing the property. This cabin, in its uninhabited corner of the bay, sheltered from view from the rest of the lake, felt entirely unspoiled by civilization.

On either side of the stairs, white foam with curls of yellow-brown algae washed up, breaking on a rock wall that extended in either direction to prevent erosion of the shore. The dock lay to his right, its hinges creaking as it swayed, the purple and green tin monster thunking against the side. A spider the size of his palm crawled out from one of the stones to his left, dark brown legs with gray stripes, and skittered beneath another.

This was paradise. An Eden among the trees.

It felt fine. *He* felt fine.

He'd barely finished the thought when a piece of trash rose from the depths, caught in a collision between two small waves, and floated toward him. The blue sheet of paper, folded and crumpled but not yet disintegrated, plastered itself on his leg, like slime against his skin. He tore it off in disgust, made to throw it right back into the water, but its message caught his eye, bold black letters streaked across the top:

WILL YOU BE EMBRACED
BY THE ARMS OF THE FATHER?

*A religious pamphlet*, he thought. *Should've just tossed it back.*

His gaze skimmed the surface of the lake for others. A couple of gulls were squawking and fighting over a dead fish on the opposite shore, but that was all. The tract must have floated up from somewhere on the main lake.

The warning bubbled up from his subconscious: *She's with us now, Owen.*

This tract belonged to the Shepherd and his flock.

Owen read the first paragraph aloud. "'In those days before the flood they were eating and drinking right up to the day Noah went into the Ark, and they did not understand until the flood came and destroyed them all.' Well, that's pleasant," he remarked. The quote was attributed to Matthew 24:38-39. The one below it was from Job: *The dead are in deep anguish, those beneath the waters and all that live in them. The realm of the deadis naked before God; Abaddonlies uncovered.*

"What the hell is *Abaddon*?" Cold shivered up his spine from the water at his feet. *Those beneath the waters*, he thought. *The realm of the dead. Christ!*

"Will I be embraced by the arms of the Father?" Owen said smugly, squishing the pamphlet into a wet blue ball and lobbing it back where it came from. "If He's as much a deadbeat as *my* dad, not bloody likely."

A chorus of voices carried on the slight breeze startled him. He stepped down into the wet sand, going in above his knees, to peer around the thick boughs of a sturdy white pine. Needles swished and swayed between him and a stout man who stood hip-deep in the lake, his flowing white robe blossoming like some heavenly flower in the water around him. An unkempt sunset-orange and gray beard sprouted from his nostrils and ears, and fluttered in the breeze as he sang:

> *My soul is sick, my heart is sore*
> *Now I'm coming home*
> *My strength renew, my home restore,*
> *Lord, I'm coming home.*

Owen saw the others then, standing together in the water closer to shore, their own pristine white robes caught in the sunlight between the dancing branches as they sang along with their minister. A mother held a baby girl dressed in a christening gown, a miniature version of the robes her parents, relatives, and friends wore. She huddled close to her husband; both wore beatific smiles. The golden curl high on the baby's crown gave her the look of a cherub.

A high wind whipped through the trees, momentarily obscuring the backwoods baptism. When the branches settled, the minister was not the same man Owen had seen a moment ago:

he had dropped fifty pounds, his bushy beard had been trimmed to a neat black mustache, and instead of robes, the man wore a white work shirt, rolled up at the sleeves. Water lapped round his loose black slacks. The crooked smile, stern dark eyes set in deep sockets, flesh the color of a dead fish belly: Owen recognized the man immediately, and fear twisted his guts.

*He's here!* Owen thought. *Lori's ghost...*

Stumbling backward in fright, his right heel struck a rock, and he fell butt-first into the chilly water. He was able to throw a hand back just in time, stopping himself just shy of going under, his teeth clacking together as he sat down hard in the muck. But he was soaked to the shoulders, and chilled to his bones.

"Having trouble over there, son?" the preacher said. The low pine bough swayed in the wind, giving Owen a clear view of the ceremony for the first time. On one side of the baby and parents stood a youngish man with tattoos on his arms and a stern-faced woman with German plaits in her hair. On the other side, a stout, apple-cheeked woman stood next to an older man, possibly the grandfather.

The voice belonged to the plump, jovial-looking country minister with the downy orange-gray beard—not the Shepherd. Nor were these others the ghostly apparitions of the Shepherd's flock. They smiled at Owen with compassionate but confused looks. The minister, himself casting a sympathetic look through the boughs at Owen, awaited a reply.

*Not him*, Owen thought. *Seeing things again*—still.

"I, uh..." Stammering, he pushed himself to his feet. "I just thought you were someone else," he finished weakly, the sound of his clothes dripping into the lake reminding him of the water in his mother's tub. Even though he was soaked and chilled right through to the marrow, he was relieved to find these people weren't who he'd first thought they were.

The minister gave him a quizzical, playful grin. "Pray tell, just who did you *think* I was, young man?"

"I don't know," Owen said. "Just... someone else."

The grin fell from the minister's face. "Well, the Devil has many faces, does he not, my brothers and sisters?" His congregation agreed with nods and mutters of *Amen*. The young mother squeezed her child to her bosom, and the father protected them both in his strong arms. The mother looked somehow familiar, with an older-style haircut and no makeup. The father appeared ashamed.

"Tell me, son," the bearded minister said, "have you borne witness to the Mystery?"

Owen shrugged. "Not that I know of."

The man was struck dumb for a moment, his big ruddy jaw slapping shut. Then he laughed wholeheartedly, a high-pitched cackle of a laugh that seemed to fit the man perfectly. His people laughed with him as he rolled his eyes toward them in wonderment. Once they'd quieted down, he asked, "Have you been *baptized*, son?"

"I don't think so." Owen thought about his mother's feelings toward religion, which he and Lori had eventually discovered were a facade. "Maybe?"

Again the minister chuckled. "You don't seem very sure of yourself, friend. But the Lord," the pastor smiled, "well, the Lord is sure of *you*."

Owen looked out at the open lake—he could see the main bay from here—where frothy white peaks had begun to form, growing larger as they slinked their way toward shore. He wondered what harm it could do, playing along. At least he'd have something amusing to tell Avery. She was always going on about her born-again brother and sister-in-law, both of whom had found Jesus after years of drug abuse. She'd go apeshit thinking they had brainwashed her partner, too.

*Maybe they're the same people Lori came up here to see?* Owen thought. *Maybe this guy with the beard is one of the Shepherd's favorite sons, preaching His word while the Shepherd's in his compound, being tended to by a harem of innocent young girls.*

He shrugged the thought away, not wanting to think of Lori in such circumstances. She was too strong to be lured into something so lurid... though he supposed many of these people had once been strong, too.

"Come, brother!" The minister ushered Owen toward them with a hand. "You're welcome to join us, if the spirit moves you. Come and be cleansed!"

His people nodded, waving Owen over. The baby girl cried out for attention. Her mother laid a kiss on her forehead, then took her little cherubic hand and used it to wave him toward them.

Owen shrugged, knowing he'd be fine among them if he was prepared against any attempt to convert him. "Okay," he said, already beginning to wade over.

"*Welcome*, son!" the minister said. "Welcome, welcome! I am Brother Woodrow, son, and these good people and I belong to the, uh... Blessed Trinity Mission."

"Thanks," Owen said, stepping into the fold. "Hey there," he said with a timid wave, as the congregation patted him on the shoulders, delighted voices greeting him, and then began singing *Oh come to me, co-o-ome, let the little children come.* When he reached Brother Woodrow, Owen realized he had begun to smile.

"What, may I ask, is *your* name, son?"

"Owen," he said, taking in all the smiling, singing faces, the clapping hands and swaying bodies. "Owen Saddler."

"*Saddler*," the minister repeated dubiously. A ripple of discontent flowed through his parishioners before they fell suddenly quiet, unmoving, watching Owen with seeming distrust. Amid their silence, Owen noticed the baby—the only one still making a noise, her little features pinched together as she wailed —had a small blue cross embroidered on the dress near her heart, the kind with clubs at the ends of each arm, like the ones on playing cards. *A budded cross*, Owen thought, unsure how he knew it.

"Now, hush, now," the minister said, holding out his hands in supplication. "The boy comes to us for *salvation*. Who are we to turn him away? We are *all* God's children, are we not?"

Tentative nods met this. Owen didn't like the vibe he was getting, and suddenly—*desperately*—he wanted nothing more than to creep away, to dive under the minister's legs and *swim* if he had to.

"Well, okay, then," said Brother Woodrow. "We've come down here to the lake to bestow upon this child the Sacrament of Immersion, or baptism, if you prefer, though we do *not*." He smiled over his congregation again, settling his eyes and his smile upon the child in his mother's arms. "But we are always looking for Seekers like us, aren't we, brothers and sisters?"

The congregation agreed.

"Seekers?" Owen wondered aloud.

"Of the Mystery," the minister explained, as if it were obvious. "Of our Father's Eternal Love."

"Right," Owen said, and hoped his sarcasm hadn't been noticeable. "You know, I think one of your tracts washed up over there. Blue thing. Stuff about the days before the flood and whatnot." He remembered the word that had troubled him. "And something called Abaddon?"

Brother Woodrow sneered. "*Abaddon!*" he scoffed. "I assure you, Owen, we don't issue anything so vile as *tracts*, and if you are referring to our, uh... *religious readings*, you are similarly mistaken. We carry nothing but the clothes on our backs and the word of the Lord to the Immersion, isn't that right, brothers and sisters? Excepting, of course, for my very own personal copy of the Good Book." At this, he patted the rectangular lump in the deep breast pocket of his robe.

"Oh," Owen said. He hadn't meant to offend them, but he seemed to have stumbled into something. "Sorry."

"No apology necessary," the minister said, replacing the sneer with his big, bushy smile. "Now, if you'll just step a touch closer to me and turn to face our brethren and sistren, we can begin."

Owen trudged out to Brother Woodrow, and turned to face the others. He crossed his arms over his chest as he'd seen people do in the movies and TV when they "went down to the water," crouching before Brother Woodrow, who laid his right hand gently on Owen's chest. The left hand, Woodrow raised toward the heavens.

"In the name of the Father, the Son, and the Holy Ghost—"

The congregants said, "*Amen.*"

A sudden chill came over Owen. Another holy-rolling ghost had tried to baptize him just last night—baptize him or *murder* him—while his flock had looked on, just like these people watched now. Brother Woodrow's hand pressed on Owen's chest like the Shepherd's had, and Owen suddenly feared *this* was a hallucination, not the men and women he'd seen before. *Abaddon lies uncovered.* If these people were products of his weary mind, he was in more danger here than he'd been in the tub. Last night he'd merely been in three feet of water. Here he had an *entire lake* to drown in, the same lake that had taken his sister.

And it was very likely these were the same people who'd sold Lori salvation. They'd filled her full of old time religion, and drowned her for her sins.

Owen slipped out from under the holy man's hand, rising quickly from the water. "I'm sorry," he said, so cold he was shaking. "It's the water. I can't—" He considered how not to further offend them. "I don't like going under," he said, and after last night, it wasn't exactly a lie.

"But *immersion* is necessary for *salvation*," the minister blustered, a look of caution on his ruddy face. "We must be cleansed of our sins and the sins of our fathers before we are permitted passage into His Heavenly Kingdom!"

"I know," Owen said. "I know. But I just don't think it's right for me. At this time."

The people looked to their minister. Brother Woodrow remained silent, favoring Owen with a grim smile. "Very well," the minister said flatly. "You know where to find us, should you change your mind." Then he added, somewhat ominously, "Or should it be changed for you."

Owen remembered the name. "Blessed Trinity Mission." *She's with us now, Owen.*

Brother Woodrow nodded reflectively. "Go in peace, brother. We have a young, uh... *soul* here to save."

The mother smiled and gently bounced her weeping child, the crowd parting like the Red Sea. Owen trudged through the frigid water, feeling the stares of Woodrow's ministry as he stepped through them, backing away from their circle. He stopped before the heavy pine bough and looked back. Gently shushing the baby in his arms, Brother Woodrow nodded brusquely to Owen, bidding him a silent farewell before he began his magical incantation over the innocent child.

*Get 'em while they're young, padre,* Owen thought, his fear lessening. He pushed the bough aside and stepped out in front of the Hordyke property. The branch swung back behind him, hiding the Blessed Trinity—*Father, Son, Holy Ghost,* Owen thought reflexively—from view.

The parishioners raised their voices in song again: *I'm on my way, praise God, I'm on my way...* The sweetly sung words followed him to the house, where he peeled off his dripping clothes down to his boxers, reflecting on the strange event he'd just been part of, and tossed his shirt and pants over the porch railing. Inside, he went upstairs, peeled off his underwear into the sink, and toweled off in the bathroom.

By the time he was dry and in fresh clothes, he was starving. The clock showed just past two, but it had to be later than that. His digital watch said 3:20. The kitchen clock must have run out of batteries. He told himself to find some later, get it started again, but right now, feeding himself was imperative. His stomach growled as if he hadn't eaten in days. He took a can of chicken noodle soup down from the pantry and opened it with a rusted can opener. *Soup for the soul*, he mused. It smelled okay, not spoiled. The stove lit on the first click with a whiff of sulfur.

*Isn't sulfur the same as brimstone?*

Owen peeked out the window as he placed the pot on the burner and stirred. By now, the Blessed Trinity Missionaries were likely all dried off and holy-rolling it back to their respective homes, comforted in the belief that they'd spared a young soul from eternal damnation, though likely irked that they hadn't been able to convert the stranger next door.

Tomorrow, he'd go back down to the water, but not to pray. The diving gear was calling to him; despite what he'd told Brother Woodrow, he was eager to go under, out in the main lake. But already he was exhausted. Tonight, all he could hope for was some mindless cable TV, or a decent book to read among the ones lining the wall.

Anything but the Bible.

# CHAPTER 5

## THE BOOK OF REVELATIONS

1

OWEN DREAMED OF his sister.

She wore the flowing white nightgown, its hem soaked by the dark waters of Chapel Lake. Owen watched her from where he sat in a wooden rowboat. Between them, a black silhouette split the surface of the water: the cross of the church beneath the lake. Shallow waves rippled around it, catching glints of moonlight. Standing before the steeple was the man who walked on water, the Shepherd, holding out his arms to them in welcome.

Lori reached out toward Owen, mouthing her soundless plea. Without an oar, his desperate efforts to reach her were no match for the current steadily drawing him away. Worse, the boat was taking on water from a hole in the bottom, which was rising alarmingly fast. Owen searched for something to bail the water, and found nothing but a rusty old can with no bottom.

The boat was going down. He jumped out into the water, splashing against the current toward his sister, the steeple between them, the cross looming above him, eclipsing the sun. He clutched at its slimy wooden shingles. Waves struck his face. He spat, blinked water from his eyes, and began climbing to the cross, hugging it—

Lori was gone, and so was her ghost.

As the realization struck him, a bony hand burst from the water and clutched his ankle, its gray, chicken-skin flesh, cold

71

and slimy; and as more hands broke the surface to drag Owen down to their watery grave, the words from the religious tract came back to him: *The dead are in deep anguish, those beneath the waters and all that live in them...*

He awoke to his own voice, shouting: "*Abaddon!*"

Rattled, he tried to get his bearings as his heartbeat began to slow. Dark. Cool. The bed stood lengthwise between an open doorway and a small, dim window, not the large, bright windows of his condo, and had a wardrobe at the foot of it (filled with unfashionable women's attire from an earlier era, he recalled). For a moment, he thought he must be at his mother's, but the smell of old wood and musty bed coverings, along with a slight fishy odor, brought everything back. He'd trudged upstairs to the single bed at Fisherman's Wharf after a short evening of mindless TV with fuzzy reception, and had fallen asleep almost immediately.

*I saw Lori!* he marveled, sitting up in the dark. He wanted to go back to sleep right away, to return to what he'd been dreaming before the things below the water had grabbed him, to see her again. She might have been dead in the real world, but in his dreams she was still very much alive. *Trying to tell me something—but what?*

He got up, stepping in a wet spot on the carpet, further evidence of cracks in the roof, and trudged down the hall to the small bathroom to urinate. When he stepped out again, the flush gurgling down the pipes, a light came on downstairs.

Fear gave way to reason. "Probably on a timer," he told himself. In the dim light, he glanced at the clock in the bedroom. Just past two in the morning.

*Who the hell would set the lights to come on so late?*

He answered himself right away: *Someone without a proper alarm clock, that's who. Someone who wanted to get up in the dead of the night to go diving. Someone like Lori.*

The light downstairs dimmed, then brightened again.

"Lori did this," he said. Downstairs, the light dimmed and brightened once more.

*It's your imagination. A trick of light, like the shadow in the shower. The light's not dimming—or maybe it is, but not because of... It's faulty wiring. Happens all the time. Don't mistake poor craftsmanship with paranormal activity.*

"There's no such thing as ghosts," he said aloud, though he didn't sound convinced, even to himself.

The light dimmed and brightened.

"Screw it," he said, and peered over the railing to the living room. The light by the chair at the bookshelf was on, barely enough to brighten the darkest corners of the room. Under the table, behind the sofa, anyone could be hiding.

"Hello?" he called out. Another flicker of the reading lamp seemed to answer him.

The darkened windows made him uneasy as he crossed to the lamp. *You can look in*, he thought, *but you can't see out*. He reached for the light switch. The bulb dimmed with a buzz. Brightened again.

*That happened. Not my imagination. Gotta screw it in tighter.*

Taking a tissue from the box on the end table to protect his fingers from the hot bulb, he reached up under the lampshade—

*POW!*

The bulb shattered, sharp little bits striking his fingers, plunging the house into darkness. Owen jerked his hand free, cursing under his breath. It hadn't cut him, but it had scared the living bejesus out of him, and now he couldn't see a thing.

*What are the odds of that happening, huh, Mr. Home Inspector? You didn't even touch the bulb and it* bursts *like that?*

"I don't know," he said, the wavering in his voice fueling his terror in the dark. He stood perfectly still, waiting for his heart to slow. Floorboards creaked and groaned, probably the house settling. Something tinkled to his right, at the bookshelf—not broken glass, but a small metallic sound. At least he could see through the windows now, black branches swaying in the cool night breeze. Cold comfort.

*Can't stand here forever.*

Finally his eyes adjusted to the dark enough to move. The main light switches were near the front door, so he headed there, careful of his footing, aware there was a low table around here some—*there it is*. He felt his way around it, bending to touch the tabletop. *Past the table, you're home-free all the way to the door.*

He bumped into something tall and fuzzy, and nearly stumbled back in fright of a shadow the size and shape of a man. He threw up his hands to defend himself from the intruder, and then squinted into the gloom.

*Just the coat rack, idiot.*

Chuckling nervously, he reached past it, slipped his fingers along the rough log wall until they grasped the light switch. He flicked on the overhead lights.

In his bare feet, he remained mindful of the glass, turned off the lamp and unplugged it, worried it might short circuit and shut out all the power in the house. He crossed to the kitchen, got the broom and dustpan, and swept up as many shards of the light bulb as he could find. He dumped them in the trash before returning to the lamp.

"Piece of crap," he said, looking down at the pale yellow-brown lampshade, decorated with dark brown beavers using logs as toothpicks. "Probably been here since they built the place."

Again, the delicate metallic tinkling came from the bookshelf. Curious, he moved toward it. Dozens of books lined the shelves, mostly mysteries—though likely not the same Mystery that Brother Woodrow spoke of—with titles by Agatha Christie, James M. Cain, Dashiell Hammett, and Sir Arthur Conan Doyle, who'd allegedly believed in ghosts. There were a few others of various genres, plays by Ibsen and George Bernard Shaw, the collected works of Dickens and Shakespeare, a few novels which had spawned movies and movie franchises. Owen selected a book at random, *The Dice Man* by Luke Reinhart, and was about to retrieve it when the small metallic chiming drew his attention again.

Tucked in among the books was a pendant on a thin chain. He recognized it right away: *Lori's necklace.* The unicorn hung loose against the clasp, but when he pulled the rest of it free, the crucifix was nowhere to be found. The chain had broken, snapped at three-quarters its length, and was still clasped. The crucifix must have fallen off, lost somewhere in the house. He pulled down a book, with a shiny black cover, that held the chain in place, newer than the rest of the dusty volumes and almost twice as tall as the paperbacks. Then he pushed the others aside to feel around to the back of the dusty shelf for the trinket, but he came up empty-handed.

*Maybe she kept it with her*, he thought. *Ward off evil.*

*It didn't work though, did it? Why did you put this here? Was it for me to find? Did you make it rattle so I'd find it?*

"Are you here with me?" he asked the eerily quiet house, and peered around himself, suddenly certain he'd find Lori standing in the second floor hall, dressed in the damp white gown from his dream. But the house was empty. In the kitchen, the fridge ticked away in place of the stopped clock, while an animal chewed on the underside of the house.

Owen slipped the necklace and pendant into his pocket, then happened to glance down at the table where he'd left the book he'd pulled down to hunt for Lori's crucifix.

It was a notebook. His breath caught in his throat when he recognized the handwriting on the first page. His knees buckled.

"*Lori,*" he said, dropping down into the recliner. Too excited now to go back to bed, despite his exhaustion, Owen began to read:

*June 8, 2014*

*First things first, I feel I should apologize for how I left things with you and Mom. I was under a lot of stress, and if you read on, you'll understand why—*

His heartbeat quickened. *She wrote this for me.* She'd put it where he might find it, and he'd found the treasure without their usual game of clues. *I am on a dusty shelf*, he mused, and read on.

*—I have so many things to tell you, and hopefully this won't have all been for nothing. It's my first day in the house, but it took a fair bit of recon to get me here. Fisherman's Wharf, they call it. The realtor, with the incredibly silly name of Skip Wickman, told me why they called it that, but I'm sure he's told you, so I won't repeat it here. Needless to say, there's a lot of local colour, and that's just the tip of the proverbial iceberg, I'm sure. I'm looking forward to talking with some of the people who were here before the flood, see what they think of it all. I've got a feeling I should be cautious, though; there's likely still some sour grapes about the whole deal. I mean, wouldn't you be pissed if the government took your home or your farm because it hap-*

*pened to be in a deep enough valley along a river some consul-
tant said would make a suitable source for a hydroelectric dam?*

*I know talk like this might bug you, Owns, considering you
might've had to expropriate land for a few of your own projects.
I'm thinking about the wind farm, in particular. I know there's
been quite a bit of protest against it, but you have to remember,
in cases like that, the end justifies the means. And I guess I
should remember that here. They may have lost their land, but
because of it, hundreds of thousands of people don't have to rely
on fossil fuels to power their smart fridges and cell phones. That's
pretty amazing, dontcha think?!*

Owen ran a hand through his hair. Having never really
looked at the wind farm issue from the community's perspective, he'd assumed they were the typical old biddies and angry
landowners who would just as likely protest a big box store or
subdivision or any other form of urban encroachment in their
quiet rural area. But Lori had made him consider it now, as
she'd made him consider many other perspectives, and he felt he
understood a little better. He'd have to remember to be less dismissive of them back at the job site.

He read the rest of the entry:

*I wish I could call you, but I need to know for sure I'm right be-
fore I do. I came here for you, Owen, and after what we'd talked
about the last time I saw you, I know I'm right to have come.
But I don't want to upset the life you've made for yourself, considering how important this is, and what it might mean to you.
About you.*

*It's too soon to tell you, I know it is, so I guess I'll just have to
suck it up. The past few times we've all gotten together as a family, watching you made me think of a sandcastle built too close to
shore. I look at you and worry you'll break apart into itsy-bitsy
pieces under that first lap of untested water. I know that what
I'm doing out here will help you. It's pretty obvious the issue has
been following you, for as long as I've been your sister, at least...
but it's too soon. I don't know enough yet. So I'll save it until I
know for sure.*

The urge to skip ahead was difficult to ignore, to find out

what Lori had thought was so terribly important to him—*about* him. To decide if it was a secret worth killing her over. He had too many questions. Why had she hidden her notebook, when she could have left it out for him? And what had she meant comparing him to a sandcastle? Was she saying he was *fragile*? That he couldn't handle whatever big, important secret she'd uncovered, without buckling under the weight of it?

"She knew," he said to himself, a lump forming in his throat. "The whole time she knew I was—" He swallowed. "I *am* depressed. That's why she came up here, isn't it? To help me. To save *me* from drowning. But what did she find...?"

His curiosity too much to bear, he flipped through to June 12, where he found what he'd been looking for:

> *I guess I should tell you a little about why I'm here.*
>
> *I've always had a feeling Mom wasn't telling the full truth about your father. All that stuff about how he was a "great mind" who "wandered away." What was that supposed to mean, anyway? That he abandoned you both? That he wandered into the arms of some other woman? It never really worked for me, and I bet it never worked for you, either.*

Owen paused, his mouth incredibly dry, his nerves jangling. The mention of his father had shocked him.

*That's who she'd come here to find? My father? Why couldn't she just leave it alone?*

He was relieved, though, in a way. It meant she hadn't joined a cult after all, and her death could easily have been an accident. But the mystery only deepened: why would she have come all the way up here, to Chapel Lake, to find his father? He supposed there was only one way to find out, so he dove back into her journal.

> *What always bugged me most about Mom was the way she'd shun any sort of religion or spiritual talk. There's atheism, and then there's <u>anti</u>-theism, know what I mean? Atheists don't believe in God, but they don't care if <u>you</u> do, so long as you're not forcing it on others. <u>Anti</u>-theists seem to have <u>declared war</u> on God. I feel like this type of thinking might be triggered by an event a person feels is an injustice to them, like a personal slight*

*from God. Something minor, maybe, but maybe something big, an illness, a death, and it festers inside them like a cancer. The anger and bitterness toward religious groups, looking down on the religious. Pitying them. I'm sure we both agree Mom was one of those. Remember that whole thing about the Lord's Prayer? Of course you do. You're probably still traumatized by it, ha ha.*

*That day we were playing our little game, and you said "I'm in a shameful place," or whatever it was. And my first thought was Mom's closet, because of the time I heard her crying after one of your big stupid arguments about nothing, and when I opened the door I found her kneeling there under the dusty yellow bulb surrounded by shoes. I still remember the musty, mothball smell of that closet like it happened yesterday. When I asked what she was doing, she tucked something awkwardly into a shoebox and wiped away her tears. She had to think for a second before telling me she couldn't find her Sunday shoes.*

*Well, I guess I didn't think much of it at the time, only wondered why she'd be crying over shoes, and go on to scold me for crying over a skinned knee. But that day I hid in the closet, I remembered Mom crying for her lost shoes, and I found the shoebox with her Bible and all that other stuff in it... Well, you remember. That was when we started the whole "zip" thing, wasn't it? You said, if Mom hid it away in a box, she must have been ashamed of it. You never considered she might have kept it there as a keepsake, but I guess it was easier for you to think of Mom in a bad light back then. You had a lot of anger in you, and I think now I understand why.*

*Anyway, I sort of forgot about all of this until Thanksgiving last year. I snuck upstairs to her closet after dinner, and found a few pictures of the two of you before you moved to the city, and you were SMILING in them, Owns! Crazy, huh? (Such a sweetie, btw. Never imagined you'd had blond hair!)*

*I found her birth certificate in the same box. I don't suppose I have to tell you it said Peace Falls, but just in case you need Closed Captioning for the Subtlety Impaired, Mom was born here. I think the "zip" is implied, but please, Owns. ZIP. 'Kay?*

That was the end of June 12th's entry. He skipped ahead, desperate to know more. Lori had always been the insightful one in the family. Already she'd filled in gaps in their mother's life and his own that he'd never even considered before: *Mom was* born *here*, he thought. *Incredible!* It explained a fair bit, he supposed, but posed more questions than it answered. He flipped pages until he came across one written in heavy, scrawling pen, dated June 15th.

*I've found him! Finally!*

*Spoke to an elderly man today who knows quite a bit about the old church since he was a parishioner before what he called "The Rift." Most other people refer to it as "The Schism," if they refer to it at all, and when they do, it's usually with pretty obvious contempt. Once, an old woman from the retirement home said, "the bother with that two-faced Bible-thumper," and after she'd said it spit on her own rug. I had to bite my lip so I wouldn't laugh.*

Owen paused a moment, wondering if the "two-faced Bible-thumper" was the man he'd seen the day before: Brother Woodrow and his Blessed Trinity Mission. The holy man would have been young at the time, if he'd been the minister of "the old church"—which was likely Chapel Lake's namesake, the church under the water, since there was no other church in town.

*That's where Mom comes in. I always knew she wasn't quite telling the full truth about where you were from, and now I've found the proof. This man Pete Jebson was there, and he knew Mom personally—except he calls her Maggie, which we both know Mom <u>hates</u>.*

*And guess what? You were born here too, Owen! In Peace Falls! I've always said the past is a bright and shining beacon, lighting the way home, and now it's brought us to yours! That house where you spent the first five years of your life is under that lake still, this man Mr. Jebson told me. He doesn't dive himself (afraid of the water, supposedly—a grown man afraid of the water! Can you imagine?), but he pretty much assured me yours is one of the houses still intact. Problem is, even though he's showed me the door to the gold mine, he won't give up the key: he's withholding important elements (like which house WAS IT? blerg!) and I suspect it's because he hasn't had the attention of a pretty young girl in a long time. He's flirtatious, but in an awkward way, instead of creepy. I kind of feel sorry for him.*

*What he says about Mom is that she was married (see? you aren't a bastard, after all! haha) to someone in the church. He was there when you were <u>baptized</u>. (Okay. Weird, I know.) He said you were "your Momma's blue-eyed boy," and "the apple of her eye," which doesn't really sound like Mom at all, does it? He also called you "Israel's favourite son," though I can't find the name Israel among the church people, so I assume it's a Biblical or Torahic reference. Or likening Peace Falls to Israel?*

"Joseph," Owen told her, as if she were in the room. He wasn't sure how he knew it, though he supposed now he understood how he knew many of the Biblical references that sprang to mind here and there, without ever having studied them. *Someone* had taught him as a child; he'd been a part of this church, with his mother and, apparently, his father. "*Jacob's* favorite son was Joseph," he said, surprising himself by remembering more. "He gave Joseph the coat of many colors, except that's a mistranslation. What Jacob actually gave him was a *long-sleeved* robe. Only, in the Book of Genesis, God renames Jacob 'Israel,' so you could say, he's *Israel's* favorite son."

*Whatever he means, you were obviously thought to be a Very Special Boy—a favouritism no one ever seems to bestow upon the daughters, by the way. (Don't worry, Owns, I won't grandstand. I'm just saying.)*

*Anyway, I'm getting a little off-track, when the whole point of this story is to tell you <u>I've found your father</u>! One: I know now he was someone from the church <u>before</u> and <u>after</u> the Schism. Two: he was married to Mom, which means there would have to be a marriage certificate on file somewhere. And three: I've got a photo of the church members my dad gave to me as a reference. He said he'd found it in a box of Mom's stuff (probably the same box she'd kept her Bible and the other Peace Falls stuff in), and she'd let slip once that one of the men in it was your father.*

*Apparently they had a big argument about whether or not she should tell you (Gerald was on your side, Owen, though you probably won't believe it), and she put her foot down against it. He took the photo when she wasn't looking to give to you anyway.*

> *The last time he and I met he said you wouldn't talk to him, not that I needed to be reminded, so he asked me to give it to you. I had a better idea: instead of just a picture, why not give you <u>your father himself</u>? I've taped the photo to the back cover so you can have a look and see if you can figure it out. So far, no one seems to stick out for me...*
>
> *One of those men is YOUR FATHER, Owns! He's <u>here</u>!*

Owen stopped reading, the words from her postcard—*He's here*—echoing in his mind, blood thumping in his ears as he flipped as slowly as his anxious fingers would allow to the back. Part of him didn't want to see. So many times he'd caught sight of an older man on the subway or in the street with a vague resemblance to himself and thought, *Is that him? Is he my dad?* He'd consider talking to the man, but always that angry child in the deeper regions of his mind had held him back, the voice that said, *Fuck him. He's a deadbeat. He* abandoned *me. He "wandered away." Don't even give that piece of shit the satisfaction of recognizing him. Don't let him think you give one single goddamn squirt of piss about him.*

On the back page was a strip of tape, torn at one end and speckled with dust—but nothing else. Lori had removed the photograph.

His hopes sank. He hadn't expected to learn much from the photo, since Lori hadn't been able to recognize his father by sight, but Lori had never actually *seen* his father, and Owen had. He'd spent the first five years of his life in the man's shadow, or so he assumed, and for anyone with a somewhat decent memory the recognition should be instant. His memory had never been particularly good, though, and the few things he recalled from early childhood could have been the memories of a dream.

He wanted to see his mother as she'd looked when she was young. He wanted to see himself as a blond-haired boy.

*Baptized!* he thought. *How can I remember pointless little scraps from Sunday school sessions I don't even remember attending, but I don't remember my own baptism? Why can't I remember a single thing about the man who sired me?*

*Trauma,* his mind countered. *Isn't there something about childhood trauma causing depression and memory loss? Maybe something happened to me when I was five. Something bad.*

He thought of the worst thing he knew that had happened

in Peace Falls, then backtracked, counting with his fingers to the date. "Born in '74," he said aloud, "so in '75 I was one. That means I turned two in 1976, three in '77, four in '78. That's it then, isn't it? It's gotta be it."

In October of 1979, the approximate date of the flood, Owen Saddler would have just turned five years old.

# Interlude

## The Dark Places

WHEN OWEN WAS fifteen years old and his sister Lori was seven, the two of them sat in the living room on a typical winter day when no one else was home. Outside, the world was white and getting whiter, as more snow fell in large flakes past the big front windows.

"*Frère* Owen, *frère* Owen, *dormez-vous? Dormez-vous?*" Lori sang, sitting upside down on the loveseat, her head hanging over the edge, face turning red, blonde hair touching the floor. "*Sonnez les matines, sonnez les matines, ding dang dong, ding dang dong.*" Having sung the whole thing without breathing, she inhaled deeply, and puffed the breath out again. "I'm *bored.*"

"No shit, Sherlock." Owen glanced up from playing *6 Golden Coins* on his Game Boy, his nimble thumbs making Mario leap and smash. "If you weren't such a little squirt, I could be doing something else instead of babysitting your ass."

"I'm not a baby." She turned right-side-up, the color rushing out of her face. "And quit calling me squirt. You're barely even taller than me."

Owen mimicked her. She stuck out her tongue and sat cross-legged on the chair. After a long moment of watching the snow fall, she said, "Let's do something."

"I *am* doing something," Owen said with a grin, not looking up from his game. "I'm ignoring *you.*"

Lori leapt off the chair and approached him. She flicked his shoulder.

"Get lost, shrimp!" He shooed her with a swish of his hand.

"I thought you were ignoring me."

"Who said that?" Owen said. "Must be a ghost."

Lori scowled. She flopped down beside him on the sofa. After a while watching over his shoulder while he played, she sighed. "Why can't we have a Christmas tree like everyone else?"

"You know why."

"No I don't."

"Sure you do. You 'member how nuts Mom got when Gerald tried to get us to pray that one time before dinner?"

"Boy, do I." Lori rolled her eyes. "What does that have to do with gettin' presents?"

"Christmas is religious, dumbwit."

"Oh yeah." She slumped her shoulders. "I guess that means Mom's not gonna let Dad take me to the Christmas concert?"

Owen raised an eyebrow in her direction. "At the church? Are you crazy?"

She slumped further. The telephone rang in the kitchen. Owen paused his game and got up from the couch. He'd been waiting on a call from his sort-of friends about a party that night, and thought it might be one of them. He hurried to grab it, catching it on the third ring. "Hello?"

The caller was a telemarketer, looking for his mother. "I'm waiting on a phone call," Owen said curtly, then slammed the receiver down.

Back in the living room, he saw that Lori had left. "Good," he said. He loved his sister, but he hated having to stay home with her while their mother worked. Not that he had much else to do. Aside from a handful of burnouts and losers, there were very few people he'd call friends. He sat back down on the sofa before realizing his Game Boy was gone. "That little asshole," he muttered, pushing back up. "Squirt!" He went to the stairs, and shouted up, "Hey, squirt! Get your ass back here with my Nintendo, or I'm gonna kick it!"

Silence greeted him.

"Lori...?"

He returned to the kitchen. A scrap of notepad paper lay beside the phone. On it, Lori had written *I am in a dark place*.

Lori's game. They hadn't played it in... must have been two or three years.

"A dark place," Owen said, thinking. He tucked the page in his pocket and went looking, vaguely aware she had tricked him into playing with her, and realizing he didn't mind so much. At least it would take his mind off of the phone call he suspected he'd never receive.

He opened the basement door and slid his hand along the cold stone for the switch. Flicking it, a bare bulb came on downstairs, illuminating the small space: the clean concrete floor; a shelf filled with old paint cans and cleaning supplies; the door leading to the furnace. It smelled damp, and certainly it held many dark places for Lori to hide. But there was no way she would have gone down there without the light.

He flicked it off again and back-stepped into the kitchen, not wanting to turn away from the darkened basement until the door was safely shut.

*Where else? The shed?* No, she would have had to get past him to go out back, unless she'd gone out the front, and he would have heard the heavy front door shut if she'd gone out that way.

*Where then? One of the closets?*

A stifled giggle signalled her location. Owen followed the sound back to the living room.

"I heard you, you little twerp..." A dark place. There were no dark places in the living room, except... "Aha!" he said, leaping onto the sofa and peeking over the edge. Lori sat crouched in the space behind it, holding the Game Boy. She burst out laughing as he snatched it from her.

"Nice one, wiener," Lori said.

"That's dim, not dark."

Lori stood. "Picky picky."

Owen sat back down and took the game out of pause. Lori hoisted herself over the back of the couch and sat beside him. "Aw, c'*mon*. Let's play some more, huh?"

He put down the game with a melodramatic groan, loathe to admit he'd had a good time in the short while they'd been playing. "All right, but no more cheating."

"Whatever," she said, rolling her eyes.

For the next twenty minutes, they hid objects from around the house and wrote each other clues. Lori hid a pen in the cookie jar (*I am in a sweet place*), which he found quickly, and Owen hid one of her My Little Ponies in the laundry hamper (*I am in a dirty place*). It took her many trips around the house to find it, and after she'd dug it out of his dirty socks and under-wear, pinched between two fingers, she slugged him in the shoulder. Because of this, he'd assumed *I am in a wet place* meant she'd put something in the toilet, but when he'd lifted the lids to the bowl, she'd snickered at him behind her hand.

"I am in a painful place," she read aloud, the two of them now standing in the kitchen. She looked up at him, at a loss.

He shrugged, having saved the best for last. "No hints."

She gave him a shrewd look. "It better not be in a mousetrap."

Owen laughed, wishing he'd thought of it. She took off hunting, peeking under the dining room table and behind the blinds. She came back and reached for the basement door han-dle. "It's not in the basement," he told her. He avoided the base-ment when he could, and wouldn't go down there by himself for a stupid game. Lori shrugged and moved on. As she mounted the stairs to the second floor, the telephone rang again. He snatched it off the hook.

"Hello!" Owen said excitedly, but the tone of Darius's greeting told him what he'd already suspected. Darius, a friend since the fourth grade, had somehow propelled to cool status when the two of them transitioned to high school, and he'd since maintained their friendship with obvious begrudging. He had promised to ask Wendy Packer, whose parents were away for the weekend and had planned a big party with no supervi-sion, if Owen could come as his guest.

"Yeah, so uh, Wendy didn't invite you, so it's probably a good idea if you don't tag along," Darius said.

*Tag along.* Owen had grown tired of hearing those words. In fact, he was pretty sure Darius hadn't even asked Wendy at all. "That's cool," he lied, holding back tears. "I didn't really want to go anyway."

Darius begged off, worried he'd be late for the party, and Owen hung up, swallowing a bitter lump of sadness. It was just like his so-called friends to leave him behind. Everyone left him, eventually.

"*Fuck* them," Owen muttered to himself, the forbidden word feeling good on his tongue as he threw the pen and notepad at the wall. He slumped back to the living room and took the Game Boy out of pause, before remembering what he'd been doing when the disappointing phone call had interrupted him.

He crossed to the table by the window, where their mother kept potted flowers in the sun, most of them still blooming even in the winter. The pendant and chain were just where he'd left them, draped over the cactus. Owen plucked it off carefully and tucked it in his pocket, then went hunting for Lori.

Not in her closet, not in his; she wasn't under her bed, and she couldn't have hidden under his, because it had drawers. Owen crept into their mother's bedroom, wary of the forbidden territory, and lifted the duvet cover to peer under the large bed. Nothing. Before he got to his feet, he spotted a slat of light on the floor, and followed it to its source: the closet.

"Gotcha," he said under his breath, and approached the closet door.

He tore the door open, startling Lori into dropping the thing she'd been holding. The black book fell on its back, the words HOLY BIBLE in burnished gold glimmering under the bare bulb. Lori looked up from where she sat cross-legged on the floor amid their mother's many pairs of shoes, caught. She breathed a sigh when she saw it was just Owen.

"Mom'll kill you if she finds out you've been in here," Owen warned, looking down at the mess she'd made: an opened shoebox stuffed with papers and old photographs. He knelt down beside her. "What is all this stuff?"

"Just a whole bunch of old pictures and junk. Here's one of Mom." Lori plucked one from the box and held it up for Owen to see. Their mother, much younger, stood in front of an old white house in a winter jacket on a crisp-looking day, squinting from the sun in her eyes. "She was pretty," Lori remarked. Owen shrugged, not wanting to think of his mother in such a way, more concerned with the Bible, anyhow. Considering the time his mother had yanked him out of class, scolding the teacher for subjecting him to "religious oppression," it was surprising to see a Bible in her closet.

"You ever wonder how come Mom doesn't have any pictures of you when you were little? I mean *really* little?"

"No," he lied. Of course he had wondered. He rifled through the photos in the box, hoping to find some, but they were all of strangers, except the ones that also had their mother, and in many of these she was actually smiling.

"Who are all those people?"

"Mom's old friends, I guess," he said, tucking them back in the box. "How come you came in here, anyway?"

"Your clue said *I'm in a painful place*. This is where Mom comes to cry."

Owen picked up the Bible. He turned it over in his hand. The cover was worn, and the pages were wrinkled along the edges, as if something had been spilled on it, or it had been left near water.

*Comes to cry?* he thought. *Mom never cries.*

*She never smiles either*, he reminded himself, *except in all those old pictures.*

"You better make sure you put all this stuff back in the right place," he said absently, leafing through the book. *In the beginning, God created the heavens and the earth. Nowtheeearth was formless and empty, darkness was overthesurface ofthedeep, andtheSpirit of God was hovering overthewaters. And God said, "Letthere be light," andthere was light.*

Owen read the words again: *Let there be light*. He thumbed through the pages like a flip-book. It stuck on a thicker page, and he opened the book, revealing an old, sepia-toned photo.

His breath caught. Lori looked up from putting the photos back in the shoebox with a questioning look. She looked at the photograph in his trembling hand. The closet suddenly felt very small, as if the walls were closing in on him, and his vision grew swimmy as the world around the photograph grew dim, narrowing like an iris wipe in an old movie.

"Who's that man?" she asked.

Lori's words snapped him from his trance. He tucked the photo back into the Bible, stacked the book on the photos, and the lid on the box. "Nothing. It's nobody."

"That's him, isn't it?"

"Him, who?" He stood. "You're not making any sense, squirt."

"*The ghost*," she said, invoking the name she'd given the man Owen had seen the day they'd gone to the beach at China Cove, when Lori had made a run for the water and the man—the *ghost* —had been standing up to his shins where it had been far too deep to stand. And now, to see the same man in an old photo his mother kept as a place-marker in the Bible they never knew she had...

*Was he a ghost?*

The squeak and rumble of tires coming up the snowy drive startled them. They turned to each other with mortified looks, saying, "Mom's home" in unison, both of them scrabbling out of the closet. Owen flicked off the light, thinking: *Let there be dark*. He closed the door behind them and they scurried downstairs, back to where this had all begun, on the sofa and the loveseat, trying to slow their panting as their mother stepped in through the front door.

All throughout dinner that night, Owen wondered about the man in the picture. Who was he? Why did their mother have a picture of him? What had he been doing in the lake that day, standing above the water?

*Forget it*, he told himself. And why not? He'd already forgotten the man before, hadn't he? Until just then in the closet?

But he couldn't seem to put the man out of his mind, even later that night. He'd been playing his Game Boy on his bed, distracted by thoughts of the man in the lake, when Lori knocked on the door.

"What do you want?"

Lori sidled by the doorjamb. "I've been thinking..."

"I thought I heard the little hamster wheel squeaking."

She scowled. "Ha ha." She plodded into the room and sat down on the edge of the bed. "I think we should look at that stuff in Mom's closet again tomorrow. While she's at work."

"No way, José. If she finds out we've been in there, we're in big trouble."

"She *won't* find out." She mimed zipping her lips. "Zip it, remember?"

"I remember."

Lori sat silently, kicking her feet on the mattress, while he pretended to be interested in his game. Finally she said what he suspected had been on her mind: "We need to figure out who the ghost is. I was thinking if we make a photocopy of the picture, maybe we could do a library search—"

*"Would you forget about the stupid man?"* he yelled.

Both of them looked at the open door. Downstairs, their

mother had the TV on, and was washing dishes during the commercial breaks. She obviously hadn't heard him.

Owen seized on an idea, something to get her mind off the ghost. "You never did find what I hid," he said.

Lori scowled, seemingly not knowing what he meant. Then she clued in. "Where was it?"

"In the cactus pot," Owen said.

"A painful place," she said, nodding.

He brought the shiny thing out of his pocket and dangled it in front of her eyes.

"Wowee!" Lori cried. "Is that for me?"

"No, it's for your imaginary friend."

She took it from him, at first holding it by the delicate chain, then grasping the unicorn pendant between the thumb and forefinger of her left hand and twisting it in the light. Owen saw the rainbow prisms it threw on the wall and ceiling.

"This is the best!" she said, unsnapping it and looping it around her neck. "Can you do the clasp?"

Owen made a show of grudgingly sliding over to where she sat. She lifted her hair, and with a little finagling, he snapped it closed. She got up off the bed and rushed over to the mirror, marveling at the shiny unicorn resting above the neckline of her busy sweater. Prisms flickered over the walls from the pendant itself, and from its reflection. "It's so *pretty*. What's it for?"

"For Christmas, dumb-wit. Zip it, though. If Mom asks, tell her it's a late birthday present."

Lori nodded, dazzled by the gift. She turned to him with a serious look. "I promise I won't talk about the man anymore, if that's what you want. But can I just ask you one more thing first?"

Owen shook his head, but he said, "Fine."

"What if the man's not a ghost?" She approached the bed, holding the pendant in a closed fist. "What if he's an *angel*?"

But Owen, who'd never in his memory had a thought that wasn't poisoned with pessimism, wondered, *What if he's the Devil?*

# Part Two

---

## Father

# CHAPTER 6

## SEEK AND YE SHALL FIND

I

OWEN STOOD ON the swaying dock, looking out at the bay. The wetsuit felt snug on his hips and bulged at the waist, giving him a gut.

"Beautiful day, isn't it?"

He started at the voice, and turned to see a man with a white streak of sunscreen on his nose, his bald pate already sunburnt. The man sat cross-legged in the back of a cedar canoe, a paddle on his knees. Below a pair of safari shorts, he'd hiked the white socks he wore over his sandals up to his knobby knees. His fishing vest sparkled with dangling lures.

"Sure is," Owen agreed. "Nice canoe."

The man shrugged humbly. "Thank you kindly. Built it myself. I'm Dink Deakins."

"Dink...?"

"Deakins. You must be Owen Saddler. I've heard a lot about you."

"Word travels fast."

"Actually, I spoke with your sister. Damn shame what happened to her, Owen. Can I call you Owen?"

Owen shrugged. "It's my name."

Dink dipped the paddle lazily. The canoe drifted toward the dock on the weak current, and Dink Deakins grabbed at it to steady the canoe.

"You spoke to her?"

Dink squinted up at him, the sun in his eyes. "Oh, you bet."

"Do you mind telling me what you talked about?"

"Do I mind? I didn't paddle all this way to sell you life insurance!"

Owen nodded. The man looked at him a moment longer before continuing. "Hmm, let's see... Oh. We talked about your mother, though I have to say, I never really knew her. Didn't run in the same circles." He flashed an apologetic smile. "What else, what else? Oh, right. The church. She asked a fair bit about the church, about the Schism, mostly. Wanted to know about the preacher who ran it, but like I told her, I didn't know a lot about the man. Was never big on religion, personally. The only kind of assurance I need pays a steady sum to my beneficiaries, am I right?"

Owen faked a smile and nodded. The man's patter had a false quality to it, the feel of something rehearsed. He couldn't be sure if the man was outright lying, but he suspected he wasn't being entirely truthful. "So she didn't ask you anything about me, is that right?"

"About you? Ha! Well, someone's got an ego, huh? I'm kidding, of course. You know, I don't remember her asking anything about you. Come to think of it, she didn't mention she had a brother at all."

"Well, I appreciate you coming by, but if you don't mind, I was about to—"

"Do some diving," Dink said. "I've got to confess, Owen. I did have an ulterior motive for paddling by."

*Here it comes*, Owen thought.

"Are you covered? Do you have a plan?"

"A plan?"

"Life insurance!" Dink exclaimed, as if Owen were being obtuse. "The wife told me it'd probably be a little gauche to ask you, after what happened to your sister, but I couldn't help but wonder what would happen to your poor mother if, God forbid..." He gulped dramatically. "You know..."

Owen stepped on the canoe's gunwale. "You might want to consider listening to your wife next time," he said, and pushed Dink away from the dock.

"Roger that," Dink said, dipping the paddle to steady himself. "Ten-four, good buddy, I hear you loud and clear. But if you change your mind..."

"I'll be sure and call you," Owen said. "...An asshole," he added under his breath, waving cheerily.

"You be careful out there on the lake," Dink said, throwing a hand in the air as he paddled away.

"What a prick."

A loud rumble shook the ground, rattling the windows. "What now?" Owen wondered. He stepped off the dock and padded back to the house. When he reached the driveway, a garbage truck had pulled up in front of the house. The buzz of flies and the fetid stink of rotting food struck him immediately. He'd assumed it was the garbage truck, until he noticed that the trash cans had been tipped, their contents torn and strewn across a carpet of pine needles. Flies zigzagged from one piece of trash to another. The pudgy trash man jumped down from the driver's seat to get a better look.

"Cwapcakes!" the trash man said, looking down at the mess with gloved hands on his hips, shaking his head. His pudgy, hairy belly stuck out from a stained black T-shirt. Sandy brown hair fell shaggily from a trucker hat declaring HAP CRAPPENS—which appeared to be a statement, not the name of his business, since the truck itself had HOWIE HAUL-IT stenciled on the side. The trash man's eyes goggled at the sight of Owen from behind transition sunglasses, currently midway between light and dark. He laughed uproariously. "Nice muffin top, buddy!" he said with the same lisp Owen had noticed earlier, pointing to the bulge in his wetsuit.

"Thanks."

"Cwazy mess you left here for me," the trash man, likely the Howie of Howie Haul-It, said. Along with a wispy beard, Howie had some of the facial features characteristic of Down syndrome: puffy, slightly downturned eyes, pudgy cheeks and a small chin.

"That's not mine."

The trash man's eyes clouded with suspicion. "Oh, I guess it musta been the ghosts then, huh? Ghosts that eat—" He kicked a can with the toe of his boot, and examined it. "—SpaghettiOs and waw vegan oatmeal?"

"I meant, the raccoons must have done it," Owen said. "And really, it's not my trash. I just got here last night. I don't know who—" He left the thought unspoken. Of course he knew whose garbage it was: the rental's last occupant, Lori.

The trash man blinked. "S'matter? Cat gotcha tongue?"

"I don't know whose trash that is," Owen finished. "How often do you pick up the garbage around here?"

"Oh, so, this is *my* fault?"

"No. I'm not suggesting... I'm just wondering if trash collection—"

"Wefuse," Howie interjected, hands on hips again.

"What?"

"It's wefuse. *Wefuse* collection."

"Fine. I'm wondering if *refuse* collection is once a week, or two."

"Biweekly. Biweekly wefuse collection."

"Is that once every two weeks, or twice a week?"

"*Twice a week?*" the refuse man said, uproariously. "Who do you think pays the taxes around here? Donald Twump?"

Owen laughed. "It's Howie, right?"

"That's what it says on the twuck."

"Okay, Howie, I'm sorry about the mess, even though it belongs to someone else—"

"Ghosts," Howie said without a trace of superstition.

"*Whosever's* it is, I'll help you get it into the truck, if you need me to, all right?"

Howie's face clouded. "I can take care of it myself. You think this is bad, you should wide along with me some day."

"I bet," Owen said, already itching to go. He felt rude just leaving, but he was losing the day. "So you're good with this?"

Howie grimaced at the trash. "I'm not gonna *like* it, but I got it covered."

"Well, okay. Good luck. And thanks. I'll be down in the water if you change your mind." He hoped it wouldn't come to that, but better to fake civility than skip off like an asshole.

"Going diving, huh?" Howie said.

"Yup."

"I wouldn't get in that water if you paid me." Howie shook his head, his eyes pinched shut. "Not on my *life*."

"Oh, yeah? Why's that?"

"Township dump's over on the other side of the lake," Howie said, pointing a gloved finger toward the bay. "Mighta been a pwetty good location when it was still a valley, but not anymore. My dad says the lake went all the way up to the dump 'cause the power company never did a pwoper survey before they flooded, and he should know, 'cause he's on the town council." Howie let this hang, as if it were important. Owen offered an impressed nod, which seemed to please him. "So what do you think happens when it wains?"

"When it rains?"

"What'd I just say? Yeesh!" Howie waggled his eyebrows, the gesture reminding Owen of a marionette. "All that garbage juice seeps wight into the gwound water, and I bet you know where that gwound water ends up, don't ya?" He jabbed his grimy gloved finger toward the bay again. "Wight back in the lake!"

"That is gross."

"You're damn tooting!" Howie said. "That's why you'll never catch me in Chapel Lake. Not even a stinkin' *toe*."

"I don't blame you."

"Yeah. I'd wather swim in a heap of dirty diapers. And heck, I'm in up to my elbows in wefuse every single day, so put that in your snorkel and smoke it, buddy." Howie laughed at this, a squeaky giggle that shook his whole body.

Owen grinned back. "I will."

"Well, all wight then," Howie said, satisfied he'd made his point. He grabbed the closest garbage can and tipped it beside the spill, grunting as he got down on his haunches to scoop raw garbage into it with his gloved hands, his hairy ass crack clearly visible where his T-shirt hitched up above his jeans.

"You sure you don't need a hand?"

Howie didn't even look up from his work. "Who's paying who here, huh? *Yeesh!*"

"If I find any treasure out there," Owen said, "I'll give you a share."

"If I find any tweasure *in here*, don't expect *me* to share!" Howie said, rolling his eyes. "Tweasure... Good luck with *that*, buddy." Howie chuckled again, shoving handfuls of wet garbage into the can. "Only thing you'll find in that lake is loon shit, and I should know."

"I thought you didn't go in the water?"

"I *don't*. But my dad pays top dollar for salvage. Let's just say he hasn't had to open his wallet a whole bunch the last few years. He says the lake's all used up. Nothin' out there but loon shit."

With a whole town under the lake, Owen found it difficult to believe it had been entirely picked clean. But Howie had a point. If no one had brought his father any salvage, chances were pretty good there was nothing to find, unless the divers were keeping it all to themselves.

"Does your dad dive at all?"

Howie shook his head and looked up at Owen shrewdly. "Are you cwazy? My dad's afwaid to swim!"

2

OWEN STEADIED himself as the dock rocked from the waves of a speedboat out in the main bay, hinges clattering and boards creaking, the old tin boat battering against it and tearing at its hooks.

Birds called out *yooooo-hoo* to each other from the brush along the shoreline. Owen recognized the song but not the birds, until they voiced their distinct *chicka-dee-dee-dee-dee*, reminding him vaguely of those lost early years spent with his mother and father in a home that was now beneath the lake.

The clattering stopped, and the dock became stable. He'd lugged all his diving equipment down there, meaning to dive right in... but the thought of getting in the water after everything he'd been through the past week, after the dream last night, after what had happened to Lori... now that he stood there ready to go, he hesitated.

"Stop being a wimp," he told himself, looking down at the impenetrable surface, still as tinted glass. "You heard Howie. Nothing out there but loon shit."

*No ghosts, anyway.*

He kneeled at the end of the dock and prepared the equipment: spitting in his mask and rinsing it out, inflating the buoyancy jacket thingy (he couldn't remember what the store owner had called it), testing each of the deflation valves before strapping it over his chest, snapping on the weight belt, and making sure the release snaps weren't covered by the jacket, lugging on his tank and pony and checking the pressure with the gauge.

Lori had taught him to swim when they were children, which in turn had helped him overcome his fear of the water. When they were older, she'd managed to convince him to take a scuba course with her at the local community center. The teacher had called him a "natural," but without anything to see underwater, having taken place in a swimming pool, the lessons had been a tad boring. Lori had continued with diving, taking further lessons with her smug friend, Hanson. Owen had let the skill wither, though he hoped it would be like climbing back on a bike.

When he'd finished checking the equipment, he sat at the edge of the dock with his fins in the water and took a big gulp of fresh air, then bit down on the regulator, breathing in the slight chemical taste of oxygen. Once he was used to the technique and breathing normally again, he slipped into the water.

He floated in place for a bit, kicking gently as he bobbed in the waves from a boat out in the main bay. Then he released some air from the buoyancy compensator, and slowly sank to the bottom, raising a greenish cloud of silt. A bone-white crayfish skittered backwards away from his fins and hid under a rock.

His breathing came too quick. He knew it was bad, but as he sank to the bottom, he couldn't stop himself. *Blue orbs*, he thought. *That's what'll get you when you're under.* He couldn't decide whether to inflate the jacket or drop the weights, or do neither.

*You're losing it, Owns. Keep it together.*

Thinking in Lori's voice helped him focus. His breathing steadied. He stopped panicking, and kicked out languidly.

In control again, he twirled around to face the dock. Lumpy pink Styrofoam bobbed under the dock boards, coated with years of algae and dirt, keeping the dock afloat. The lake bottom was sun-bright, and though he hadn't been able to see it from the surface, it was incredibly clear now, aside from the area under the dock's shadow, cold and dark as a cave.

He stood on a mucky patch of rocks and marveled at what he was seeing. Before him lay a world not many people experienced: the world of the fish, the turtle, the freshwater crustacean. A realm of murky gloom, of muted greens and browns; not colorfully exotic, like tropical diving. Under the lake, the marvels were mainly human, the lost detritus of civilization: old boots and discarded tires; paint-flecked propane tanks and moldering doll heads; faded pop cans and rusted boat motors. He didn't expect to find the treasure from his dream down here, but somewhere out there were the remains of Peace Falls, and the chapel that had given this man-made lake its name. The church itself appeared to be intact, from the photos he'd seen.

Somewhere his lost childhood awaited him, and he meant to rediscover it. He took his first literal step toward that goal now, raising a cloud of silt with a fin and beginning to walk sluggishly forward, the weight of the water fighting back against him as he stepped under the shadow of the dock.

It was colder here, as he'd suspected, but the warmth of the water inside his wetsuit kept him from experiencing the sting of it. Things down here hadn't seen the light of day for God knew how long; no sun-bleached rocks stood out like beacons from the gloom. Another crayfish propelled itself backward over his left fin, hiding under a sleet-gray stone. A fat brown-green bass, or trout—he had no idea how to make the distinction; it could have been a pike for all he knew, though he had an idea pikes were much larger—twisted itself in his direction and floated there, a slick, whiskered gatekeeper scrutinizing this interloper in its turbid domain.

*Hey, George. How's the water?* Owen thought. Then he grinned, accidentally sucking a bit of watery sediment in through the exposed sides of his mouth, and he swallowed it with a grimace. He considered that, even if the fish had con-scious thought, it likely wouldn't know what *water* was. For a moment, he'd believed he was able to behave as if he were still on land without consequence, and he'd tasted a mouthful of Howie's loon shit for his ignorance.

George swished off lazily toward warmer climates, leaving Owen to his business under the dock. If anything had been dropped in the water accidentally, it was more likely to have happened while standing on the dock than anywhere else. Loose change, keys, virtually anything someone might keep in their pocket (*aside from a pocketful of dirt*, he supposed, snarkily reminding himself of the shameful thing he'd done at

Lori's funeral)—he'd find it down here. So he kicked outward with his fin, raising a cloud of silt. He felt like an archeologist, brushing aside centuries of dust to get at his quarry, though anything he'd find under here could only be as old as the lake itself, and Chapel Lake was younger than Owen.

When the cloud settled, he'd exposed a pile of small stones, and a Royal Crown Cola can so old it had pull tabs yet was entirely undamaged, its reds and whites still as crisp as if it had just come off the line because of its limited contact with the sun. He thought he might be able to make a few bucks from it on the internet, but decided it wasn't worth the effort.

He took another few steps, crouching now as he approached the shore, and kicked out again. The cloud this time rose thick enough so he couldn't see beyond it, with less space to disperse it between the ground and the underside of the dock. A flat, skinny fish with muted rainbow colors twiddled out of the cloud and veered around Owen. When the sediment cleared, a fat, shiny quarter glinted in a crack of light from between the dock boards.

He bent to fish it out of the muck, and brought it close to see. It wasn't a quarter at all, but a Jamaican ten-dollar coin. Probably only worth a quarter, anyhow—or *less*—but what it represented was worth more than anything he'd found so far: Lori had been to Jamaica *within the last six months*. A trip with girlfriends, one of the few they'd been able to coax her into that hadn't been about saving someone less fortunate than herself. A *vacation*, in other words, with no agenda other than to have some fun in the sun.

She'd called from the airport hotel when she got back home, told him she'd had a great time with the girls, but couldn't help feeling guilty about all the poor people kept outside the gates of the resort. She'd gone into town on her own, despite warnings from resort staff, and spent a night in some Kingston ghetto with backpackers and locals, getting some "local flavor," as she'd called it—which Owen guessed had meant getting high and dancing to some street band, maybe getting frisky with one of the locals if she'd felt particularly adventurous.

This coin was a souvenir of that trip, he was sure of it. He imagined it falling out of her macramé coin purse as she opened it, looking for her lighter to fire up a joint while she tanned on the dock. The coin must have clattered across the dock and rolled down between the cracks before she could snatch it back. It had sunk into the muck below, waiting for low tide to reveal it, or to be buried forever.

*Lori held this*, he thought excitedly. *Maybe even dropped it down here deliberately for me to find. Another link in the chain...*

He found other coins, though no more Jamaican currency. The lakebed was littered with quarters, dimes, nickels, loonies, toonies and pennies. He plucked each of them up and tucked them into his fanny pack. *Might as well collect 'em all*, he thought. *Probably won't waste much time down here again, when there's a whole town of ruins out in the lake.*

A long, sleek fish, green and spotted, with a beak full of sharp, tiny teeth, drifted toward him. His knee-jerk reaction was to wriggle out of its way. It looked just big and mean enough to take a decent chunk out of his arm. But he breathed in, then out, thinking it through. Nothing in the water meant him any harm, save for some mindlessly dangerous bacteria. The animals down here were more afraid of him than he was of them, if they felt fear at all. He summoned up his courage, then reached out and grazed the fish's back with gloved fingers as it floated by. It didn't react at all to his touch, only swam by until it vanished in a pool of dark.

Surfacing, Owen spat out the regulator and took a breath of real air. He was so relieved his first experience had gone well that he decided to get right out on the lake.

<hr>

3

THE WATER WAS CHOPPY, wind whipping up froth across the lake and bending trees on the mainland. Waves curled over the side of the boat, splashing him, the bow of the ugly purple and green monster rising up spastically as it ascended before slamming down heavily on the other side. If he hadn't already been wearing his wetsuit, he would have been drenched in seconds. By the time he reached the church, the inside of the boat was covered with several inches of scummy water.

Only a few die-hard water skiers and Jet Skiers were out today, bouncing crazily over the pounding waves. A sailboat on big yellow pontoons leaned nearly vertical as it slashed across the lake, sails pregnant with wind. One hardy kayaker fought against the current. It was hard not to feel bad for the guy, every one or two paddles forward he was pushed back two boat-lengths on the next wave. Owen didn't see a single canoe, and figured that was probably for the best.

The second he hit the chop on the main bay, the urge to turn the boat around and go back was strong. The weather was a bad omen. He could already see plenty of silt and foam and reeds churned up underwater as he slowed the boat down to navigate the waves, worried he might tip it. But he fought the urge to give up, telling himself that, down near the bottom where the town lay, it was likely just as still and silent as the grave, and so he continued on against the current.

Out near the church steeple, intermittently visible above the waves, a large dock in the shape of an E had been anchored, most likely for divers to moor their boats. Several boats flopped and banged against big bumpers fixed to the dock. Since the boats were empty, he assumed the divers must be diving under the turmoil, all except a single woman trying to get into her flippers, her attempts rocked by the heavy waves.

Owen's first try at parking was thwarted by a simple beginner's mistake: forgetting that the handle of the motor needed to be pushed in the direction *opposite* the way he wanted to go. Consequently, he swung out wide, missing the dock by ten feet or more. The woman on the dock seemed to shake her head, though it could easily have been directed at her misbehaving flippers, or an unintentional motion caused by the waves. He brought the boat around again in a wide arc, then slipped it into the space between an expensive inboard bow rider and a tin boat like his, painted yellow and black like a giant wasp flecked with rust. The bow slammed into the dock, screeching as the waves dragged it along the side. He cut the motor and reached out to snag one of the bumpers before the boat could whip away from the dock again. Then he latched it quickly to the cleats and got out, feeling impressed with the job he'd done.

"Nice work," the woman said. She'd finally managed to get her flippers on and was sitting at the edge of the dock, riding the waves like a woman on a bucking bronco.

"First time," Owen said.

"No shit." She wore a wetsuit, skin-tight, with a full cap and face mask. She could have been anyone. Her voice had a distinct rasp to it he would have recalled if he'd heard it before, which added to her edgy tone. "There's nothing down there," she assured him. *"No hay tesoro."* Off his questioning look, she explained testily, "No treasure. If you're looking for salvage, you're gonna be leaving disappointed."

He eyed her with suspicion. "What makes you think I'm looking for treasure?"

Her expression softened momentarily; then she reapplied her scowl with renewed vigor. "Why else would you be here? You drive up from the city with your brand new certifications and fancy gear to pick the old girl clean."

"I don't have a certificate," he said. It seemed like the only way to distinguish himself from the rest of them without confessing his true motive, from the people in the speedboat and the big fancy fishing boat on the other side of the dock whom she'd already judged as harshly.

She gaped at him behind her mask for a moment, then burst into laughter. "Oh, that's *perfect*!" she said, still laughing. He thought he caught her mutter, "Golden boy doesn't even know how to swim," but he couldn't be sure, since it seemed unlikely for her to call him 'golden boy' when they'd only just met.

"I know how to swim," he shot back.

*"We'll see,"* she said, and bit down on her regulator. Without another word, she slipped into the chop.

"Yeah, we *will* see." The comeback felt pathetic as he'd said it, but the woman hadn't heard it anyhow, having already dropped beneath the waves.

Owen hurried to prep his equipment, hoping to meet her down there and prove to her he knew what he was doing—though, frankly, he was nervous about the weather, and the lack of visibility it likely would have stirred up underwater. He spat in the mask and rinsed it clean. It squeaked as he worked it over the dive cap. He bit the regulator, flipped his legs over the edge of the dock, fins splashing in and out of the water as the dock rose and fell. It wouldn't be an easy dive, as it had been back at Hordyke House. He regretted not having had the time to learn from an instructor, even if it had come down to Lori's friend, whatever his name was—the white suburban kid who'd dressed like a yogi at her wake.

*So stupid*, he scolded himself. *They'll use my death as a lesson to wannabe divers.*

He muttered, "Fuck it," and pushed off feet-first, finding himself underneath the waves before he could change his mind.

The water was milky green as he descended, flecks and clumps of dirt and algae swirling in the maelstrom. A long, fuzzy weed glommed onto his mask, partially obscuring his vision. He tore it off, then circled, looking skyward for the dock —but it was gone. Already he'd lost his point of reference. He thought of blue orbs. His breathing grew frantic.

He saw a hazy black shape in the gloom now, the only thing down there not moving violently, and he swam for it, its permanence among the churning chaos, its *everlastingness*, calming him. His breathing evened. He swam with the current now, though below the surface its drag wasn't so forceful. The closer he got to the church, the more it drew him toward it, like someone tugging him on an invisible rope. He saw it clearly, could make out individual boards and roof tiles. Above him, rising waves revealed the cross—it vanished again as they receded. He swam for it, the surf pulling him up, and a moment later he was standing on the steeple's tiles, grasping at the large, rusted metal cross like a life preserver. His head rose above the surface, the waves pushing and pulling at his chest, threatening to tear him apart.

He thought: *This is it. This is the end. I'm gonna die hugging this cross.*

With that in mind, he heaved himself back underwater, hugging the roof, scaling it in reverse. Gradually, the current's hold began to slacken. The cross appeared and vanished above his head, appeared and vanished. His right flipper slipped under the fascia. He felt a momentary vertigo as he lost his footing, then he thrust himself downward with all his strength.

Facing an open window, he found the bell that had once called people to church, a bell he could almost hear inside his own head, encrusted now with decades of rust and zebra-striped barnacles. Strands of algae reached out toward him with the current like long, slimy fingers, detracted, and reached again, but the big, heavy bell remained still. It would never ring again.

As he descended below the window, the current finally lost its hold on him. He swam freely, the way becoming clearer, the murk dispersing. The church was clearly visible now; other buildings came into view a good distance away, the street below pitted and cratered. Here was a bicycle, overtaken by the same zebra-striped creatures that had claimed the church bell. A toilet rested on its side, flat plants like elongated blades of grass in its bowl and tank swaying languidly in the sluggish current. Elsewhere, teams of small fish zipped in and out of the windows of an old junker car, like a scene from an aquarium, an entire ecosystem of plants, barnacles, and bacterium living in its trunk and hood.

A flash of light startled him. Near the truck, a diver snapped photos with a big underwater camera of a lamppost bent so sharply its mantle touched the road. Two other divers swam hand-in-hand a few feet above the street, moving away from where he stood near the church, on what had once been a sidewalk, now cracked and raised like a collection of tectonic plates as it lead up to the grand double doors of the church.

What he saw before him was like a badly distorted memory, a sort of dreamy mishmash in which objects and places were no longer where they belonged. He'd stood here before, he knew that the moment he looked up at the old dilapidated church, its windows boarded, its doors chained, the cladding loose and rotting or missing entirely, leaving deep black gaps beyond which anything could be lurking. Even though the church he saw was entirely different from the church in his mind's eye, he knew its shape as he would the silhouette of a long-lost relative, or an old friend.

The memory came back with perfect clarity of him and his mother standing here, his hand in hers, his mother much taller than him. She'd hesitated at the steps, deciding, he supposed, whether or not to enter. Why, he had no idea. She could have forgotten something at home—her Sunday shoes, maybe?—or realized she'd gotten a run in her stocking and had to go back to change them. She could have been dithering on whether to enter the church for the first time, to offer up herself and her son into the fold... or uncertain whether they should go in one last time, after the "Schism" had turned its parishioners into pariahs.

Whatever the reason, adult Owen couldn't go in, either. The church stood in opposition to entry, large and ugly and intimidating. It had somehow withstood a force of nature—man-made, but a flood nonetheless—that had turned most of these structures to rubble, though it was no longer a place of sanctuary. Within its walls lived creatures that had never worshipped, had never seen the sun. Any history would have been obliterated with the deluge, leaving only death and decay and a silence almost as long as Owen was old. His breath became hurried at the thought of violating that quiet, that deathly stillness. A burst of bubbles rose from his regulator and ascended to the surface, where the water churned the sky and the church's cross rose and sank as if on the sharp end of a Crusader's lance.

*Now or never, Owns.* Lori's name for him rang in his head like the toll of the old bell, sending a shiver up his spine. *This is what she brought you here for. Can't give up now, when you're so close to knowing the truth.*

*But how the Hell do I get in with all the windows barricaded? The door's got chains on it, for God's sake!* Somebody *wants to keep us out—probably for our own safety.*

*In and out quick, then. If the thing decides to fall down after all these years, what are the odds it'll fall on me?*

But this was *his* domain: the Shepherd's. This had been his church, Owen was sure of it, and he and his mother had been a part of his congregation, his *flock.* He was as certain of that as he was that the image of him and his mother standing below the church had been a memory and not his imagination.

He stood on the steps below the final walkway now, just four rough blocks of concrete leading to the wooden stairs and the doors beyond. He realized suddenly that, all the time he'd been arguing with himself, he'd been unknowingly moving closer, tugged by the slow current. He'd come close enough to see knotholes in the cladding, the sharp remains of stained glass behind old grayed planks nailed to the sash, and just as his gaze fell on one of the windows—the farthest right on the second floor—the boards on it began to shudder, as if merely looking at them made them tremble.

Fear seized his muscles, freezing him where he stood, his imagination conjuring up a beast large enough to disturb those planks, to split them outward and separate them from the rusted nails until the rotted boards splintered into sharp bits and fluttered lazily to the lake bed.

The creature emerged from the ancient dark of the church, black and formless, worming out through the hole it had made, and as it descended it unfurled. Owen saw its limbs, four of them, a perfectly normal number, and the limbs splayed out and propelled it forward, and in the instant it turned its very human shape toward him, he recognized—the woman from the dock. She'd opened up a means of entry to the church. She'd shown him the way.

*The past is a bright, shining beacon*, he thought, *lighting the way home.*

The woman fluttered down to where Owen stood. Immediately, his muscles loosened, his heart rate slowed. His breath evened, steadying. Her dark eyes, dark enough to drown in, studied him for a moment. She raised her left arm and pointed at the diver's watch strapped to it, and then she jerked her head back in the direction of the opened window. When she looked at him again, she raised her eyebrows with a quick shrug: *Do you have enough air to take a look?*

Owen checked his gauge. Plenty of air left. He nodded, pointed to her, then at the black hole in the face of the church —an empty eye socket in an old, bare skull: *You first.*

She pointed to him, and then rotated a bunched fist by her right eye. *Crybaby.*

Owen pried the fingers of his heavy glove down to flip her the bird. A smile showed in her eyes. She turned to swim away, heading up toward the gap. Owen followed in the cloudy wake she'd kicked up from the bottom.

She was waiting for him at the window, hands on either side of the jagged opening. When he caught up, she twisted her body to slip into the hole and immediately propelled herself into the darkness. Owen put his head through, peering in after her and seeing nothing but black.

*Can't follow her in there. What if it's a trap? What if she's with him? With the Shepherd? She could be leading me right into his* house. *God's not home right now—but his Messenger could be in here waiting for me. He'll hold me down, and maybe this time he won't let me up.*

With his hands still on the sill, a flicker of light from behind the church caught his eye.

A modest two-story home stood nearly hidden on the small rise behind the church, reminding him of the house behind the Bates Motel, where Mother had sat in her chair in the window. He guessed it must have been the priest or minister's house, and like the chapel, it seemed to have suffered very little damage from the flood. There were two windows on either side of the front door, two on the second floor, and an octagonal, slatted opening for an attic crawl space. Its concrete steps had eroded and were covered over in algae. The windows were all gaping black mouths—except the second floor window on the right, from which a light had begun flickering across the glass of his mask, as if someone were signaling to him with a mirror. Dread seized his muscles as he wondered whether objects could reflect sunlight at such intensity, so deep underwater.

*Of course they can*, he thought, shaking off his doubts. *If they couldn't, you wouldn't be seeing it.*

He realized it was not particularly sound logic, coming from someone whose world now included hallucinations of a psychotic preacher and flock drowning him in his own bathtub. But it persuaded him enough to approach.

Another flicker came as he swam toward the house, blindingly bright, as if someone had captured the sun and was shining it directly at his eyes through the window. *Nobody's there*, he reminded himself, though he supposed it could have been another diver, hunting for treasure.

*Something's in there, though. Something shiny. Maybe something valuable.*

Behind the church stood a small cemetery, several of its headstones upturned, eerily tranquil. He saw no divers. No fish, either; not even a small crustacean visible within the gloom. It was as if life refused to dwell in the long, heavy shadow of the church.

Thoughts of death stirred a sudden fear for his own life, and Owen checked his oxygen gauge. Half-full. He rapped it with his knuckles. The needle moved, and then settled around 200; still roughly half. He must have been down a good half hour already. Another ten minutes wouldn't hurt.

Assuaging any further doubts, the light in the house flashed again. He was reminded of his encounter with the reading lamp last night, its brightening and dimming. He hoped this time there wouldn't be a bang.

Swimming to the window, he flicked on the LED. Its green light washed over a small bedroom, but didn't seem to catch on anything particularly shiny. Everything inside seemed to be covered in a thick layer of lake scum. Nothing moved inside. Even the shadows seemed static as the beam illuminated the room.

He pulled himself in and stepped down onto a single bed, a sodden mattress resting haphazardly on rusted springs and clumped with more of those striped mussels, like a particularly bad case of bedbugs. Up close, they looked like some kind of tacky jewelry. Some wise entrepreneur would do well selling the invasive organisms as earrings and pendants.

It was a child's bed, in a child's bedroom. Across the room a rocking horse had suffered a fate similar to that of the mattress. Bits and pieces of flocked wallpaper still stuck here and there on bare gray boards, though it could just as likely have been mold. At the foot of the bed, much like in his room at Fisherman's Wharf, a trunk lay opened on the dirty rug. Owen rooted through the few remaining toys inside, finding them impossible to tell apart, many of them stuck together in stony clumps.

A dark shape moved at the other side of the room. Owen froze in place, heart racing, keeping his eye on the spot where he'd seen the movement. He waited, saw the shape sink as he sank, and realized he was seeing his own reflection in a mirror on a vanity. A teddy bear leaned against it, covered with the same barnacles and algae as everything else. He allowed himself to sigh, bubbles rising to the blackened ceiling.

Had the mirror brought him in here? He'd seen the light— *so to speak*, he thought with an inward grin—from outside, seen it flashing him in the face three, four times. Could it have been reflecting off this ugly old mirror, its face scaled with algae?

He exhaled irritably, and sat on the crusty mattress, exhausted, disappointed. Sitting in some kid's bedroom with his head cradled in his hands, particles of God knew what settling on his head and shoulders, wondering what the hell he was doing out here at Chapel Lake at all, let alone fifty feet below its surface. Lori had died out here, but who was he serving by following her? Following in her footsteps was a somewhat morbid way to memorialize a family member, an obsessive's attempt to preserve her memory. His mother would have been mortified if she'd known what he was doing, where he sat right now.

Had Lori really called out to him from beyond the grave? Had her letter been meant to draw him here, or steer him away? Coming here was an idea he'd jumped on with the immediacy of a fixation, like an addict on a possible score.

*Will you be embraced by the arms of the Father?*

Owen chuckled contemptuously.

*Jesus, don't get caught up on Papa Saddler again. You know as well as Mom, that deadbeat skipped town and left you with nothing. Less than nothing. Even entertaining the idea he's out here is expending more energy than the man's worth.*

He knew that. Margaret Saddler knew it, too. All Lori had ever known was hearsay.

Suddenly the flicker came again, from directly behind him, a widening circle of light trailing past his shadow as it swung across the wall and back. Two circles, actually; a larger one surrounded the smaller. Owen turned, expecting to find nothing. But there, hanging from one of the coat hooks on the door, was a shiny yellow chain.

Forgetting he was underwater for a moment, he leapt from the bed, certain he'd found his salvage. The weight of the water caused a dreamlike slowness, worsened by his flippers, which hadn't been made for walking forward. After what seemed like an eternity, he reached it and held the chain in his hand. No unicorn was attached to this one; no crucifix, either. It was a pocket watch. Grime scaled its face, but he was certain this had been the cause of the flashes. He wiped away the dirt. Its little gold hand had frozen at two, the big one stopped a few minutes past. There was an inscription on the back, but it was too green and faded to read even in the dim light of his LED.

He tucked the watch in his fanny pack, zipped it securely— a fastidiously languid motion, zipping a zipper under the water —and checked his gauge.

Bubbles rose from his lips as his eyes widened in horror—*In the red, oh God, it's in the red!* He didn't know how much air that actually left him, but he wouldn't wait to find out the hard way. He swam for the window, but just as he reached for freedom something jerked him backward. He struggled forward, kicking madly, but couldn't budge.

He was caught. Something held him in place.

Dark eyes met his in the mirror, a cold, pale green face glaring grimly over his shoulder, holding him fast to the wall.

*Followed me! Waited for me!*

The same rolled-up sleeves on the same white work shirt, sodden and grimy now. The same loose black pants. His watch and chain were tucked away in Owen's fanny pack. The Shepherd seemed to take no pleasure in drowning him—it was clear from the look in his eyes. It was simply his lot in life, his God-given duty. Those unsmiling lips began to open, and a viscous fluid flowed from them, jet-black tendrils spilling over Owen's shoulder and slipping around his bare throat.

It struck him then, as his oxygen level dipped further into the red, that this man—this *thing*—must have done the same to Lori. He'd drowned her in the name of his corrupt God, and would offer Owen the same fate as long as Owen remained frozen, mesmerized by the dead man's reflection in the mirror.

The knife was on his belt, in its sheath. Not very long, but sharp. Inky filth from the Shepherd's mouth obscured Owen's movements in the mirror. He'd have it out and plunged into the dead man's heart—if it still *had* one—before the Shepherd knew what was coming for him.

The button unsnapped. The Shepherd's eyes remained transfixed on his, the expression on his gaunt face as unchanged as a post-mortem photograph, while thick ribbons of black vomit gushed up from his innards. Owen saw his own elbow rise ever so slightly as he pulled the knife free.

The Shepherd's mouth closed suddenly, the wet, hollow clack of his rotted teeth resounding in Owen's ears, his face pinching into a scowl.

*Now or never, Owns...*

He swung the knife over his shoulder, its blade glinting in the same light that had caught in the face of the pocket watch. It plunged to the hilt in the Shepherd's chest, the blade sinking into flesh that was like thick gelatin, the dead man's eyes widening as he realized his fate. The wooden *THOCK* as the blade hit the wall echoed in the small, submerged room, an explosion of bubbles bursting over Owen's shoulder. His eyes widened as the black hose slithered out like a snake, spewing oxygen. In his haste to get free of the Shepherd's grip, he'd cut his own oxygen line.

But he *was* free. That was something, at least. He shot off toward the window in a flash, without even a look back to see if the Shepherd had gotten free and was following him, just swam, holding his breath, heading for the light.

As he passed through the window, he was grabbed by the shoulders and jerked roughly to the side of the house, and his mouthpiece was torn from his lips. With cold finality, Owen turned to look his killer in the eye, one dead man to another, readying himself for Death's cold embrace.

She wedged the regulator into his mouth.

He felt his lungs fill with precious air—not with death, but life. She took the air away, this woman he didn't know, his *savior*, and gave him a brief, apologetic smile, before yanking him up, up toward the sky, toward air, toward *life*.

They broke the surface between the steeple and a large orange buoy, and he gasped for air that had never tasted so sweet. She dragged him to the dock, grunting as she swam until he was able to use his own arms. She helped him up onto the dock, the two of them groaning from the effort. He doubled over suddenly, every single inch of him seizing in excruciating pain, and puked up everything still in his guts from that morning.

"You all right?" she said, dusty blonde hair matted to her head. Her face was tanned, and the heavy lids gave her eyes a look of perpetual sadness.

Owen coughed up bile. It splattered on the surface of the lake where the rest of his vomit lay in a disgusting froth, the water calmed now, looking like glass. He was too dazed and queasy to appreciate it. "I think so."

She was scowling at him when he plopped down on his ass. "What the hell were you doing in that house?"

"Nothing, I..."

She prompted him to go on with her dark, sad eyes.

"I just thought I saw something."

"Saw what?" she asked, more suspicious than curious.

"I don't know. Nothing, I guess." He spat into the water again. "I guess I must have caught my hose on something."

She looked at the hose, severed clean and hanging from the tank. "I guess *so*," she said, seemingly unconvinced. She started peeling off her flippers. "You think you'll be okay to drive? I could give you a tow if—"

"I'm okay," he said.

"You sure?"

He nodded, catching a deep breath. "Yeah. And thanks. If you hadn't helped me..."

"You would have drowned?"

He thought of Sophie Huang, her embarrassment when he'd mentioned her heroics. "Yeah," he said, smiling genuinely for the first time in as long as he could remember. "My name's Owen, by the way."

"I know what your name is. Everyone in town knows who you are." Her right fin sucked against her bare foot as she pulled it free. "Owen Saddler, brother of the dead girl."

He flinched. The smile fell from his face as swiftly as if he'd been slapped. "That's a harsh way to put it."

"It's true, isn't it? You spend your whole life tiptoeing around death, it won't make it any easier when you lose someone else you care about."

"True, I suppose," he said—not wanting to concede, but she had just saved his life. "What's your name? Just so I know who saved my ass."

"It doesn't matter," she said, wringing out her hair onto the dock. "You won't see me again."

"You seem pretty sure of that."

"I am. 'Cause even you can't be stupid enough to come back out here and try this again."

"Even me?"

"Yeah." She held his gaze. "The guy whose sister drowned maybe ten feet from where he's sitting? Even you."

The blow struck hard. He didn't know how to respond without expressing his anger. The cold, unidentified bitch stood and crossed the dock to her boat, the tin Bumble Bee. He was glad he hadn't told her about the Shepherd, nor the watch he'd found, despite her assurance he'd find nothing down there. She stepped in, the boat wobbling, and sat down in front of the motor.

"Nice talking to you," Owen called to her as she started the motor and pushed the boat away from the dock. He watched her drive away, cutting west across the lake until she disappeared from sight.

He stood up on weary legs, wiped his lips again, and peered over the edge into the water. Somewhere down there, the house with the child's room lay silent. His deadly hallucinations had followed him all the way to Chapel Lake. He'd caught on something in the wall and had imagined the Shepherd holding him down. Easy enough to make himself believe it, considering he'd only seen the dead man in an old, worn mirror covered in sludge.

"Left my knife down there, too," he said. "Probably still stuck in the wall."

*Even I wouldn't be stupid enough to go back down there and get it*, he thought. *Would I...?*

# Chapter 7

## Salvage

I

OWEN SAT ON the back deck of the house with a root beer in his hand and Lori's journal on his lap, enjoying the gorgeous afternoon, looking down at the lake every so often to remind himself how lucky he was just to be alive.

Chickadees twittered in the trees above, and while he was reading, the chipmunk had climbed onto the deck near him to nibble at a pile of peanuts Lori must have left, mostly little bits of shells now. The sun was hot, but he'd moved the chair to a place in the shade. As he read, the tree's shadow moved across the deck, and Owen moved with it.

She had tried to go out on the lake one morning, only to find that the boat motor had been "tampered with," according to the marina mechanic; and the power seemed to flicker and sometimes go out entirely at the least convenient times, like when she was showering or standing in front of the mirror brushing her teeth in the sink. Her investigations had come to a standstill, too; nobody in town wanted to talk to her, and Dink Deakins and Peter Jebson had both stopped returning her calls, shunning her when she'd gone to visit their houses.

In her June 20th entry, the same day she'd sent the postcard —*GREETINGS FROM CHAPEL LAKE!*—Lori was describing the seemingly indestructible and impenetrable church, when she finally revealed her true motivation:

*I said before I sometimes think you're like a kid's sandcastle built too close to shore, and you sure didn't get it from Mom. She's as solid as a rock, except for that one time I caught her crying over her lost shoes. I think you've been quick to become depressed for as long as I've known you, but it didn't hit me until a few years back, when you were in that funk after you and Allison split, that it might be clinical.*

*I asked Mom about it, if there was any history of mental illness in the family. Grandma and Granddad always seemed pretty well-adjusted, aside from being WASPs, but you never know, and Uncle Ralph has his problem with pills. Mom looked at me like she'd seen a ghost. "What are you implying?" she said, and tried desperately to change the subject. You know how she is: Mom kept mum.*

*But I wasn't going to drop it just like that, and when I asked about your dad, she got upset. Said her spiel about him being a "great mind who'd wandered away." But her mouth slammed shut like a castle drawbridge all of the sudden, and that's when it finally clicked what she'd meant all that time about wandering away.*

*It wasn't <u>your father</u> who'd wandered away, Owns, it was <u>his great mind</u>. All that time she'd been dropping hints to the Terrible Truth and neither of us knew it.*

*Your father didn't leave you and Mom. <u>He went crazy</u>.*

Owen read those final three words for a second, then a third time, then let the journal settle in his lap. A horn sounded out in the bay, loud and long, like a ferry horn calling its passengers, like a church bell calling to the flock.

If his father had been crazy—whatever that meant—it could have been hereditary. Clinical depression was one thing, but seeing dead preachers intent on choking the life from him could mean schizophrenia, and if left untreated, it could be very bad for both himself and, possibly, others.

He closed Lori's journal with finality and tucked it under his arm. The sun had begun to sink behind the trees, still far from setting, but cooling the air considerably. At the edge of the deck the chipmunk nibbled greedily at scraps of shell. High above them both, a gull cried in the clear, pale blue sky.

His mother would be no help. Like Lori wrote, Mom would keep mum. But somewhere in town, *someone* had to know who his father was, and what had happened to him. Owen determined to find that someone tonight.

If not the man himself.

———

2

His car had been idling at the intersection of the cottage road and the paved county road, when the Howie Haul-It truck stopped in front of him and Howie laid on the horn.

Owen snapped out of his daze, wondering how long he'd been sitting at this lonely intersection staring out at a stretch of empty farmland, worrying about his predicament.

Howie leaned over the passenger seat and peered out the window. "Find any tweasure?" he said, waggling his eyebrows in heavy sarcasm.

"I did, actually," Owen said, startling the trash man. With brash eagerness, he took the pocket watch from the change tray and dangled it for Howie to see. Its double-circle reflection swung in an arc across Howie's truck, momentarily blinding the man. Howie threw up a hand to protect his eyes.

"What the jeepers! Wight in my peepers!"

"Sorry," Owen said, palming the watch like a yo-yo.

Howie blinked hard, and with his eyebrows waggling, it was almost comical. "You found that down there?"

"Yessir."

Howie rolled his head on his shoulders in a gesture that seemed to indicate that, all this time, he'd been missing out. "You gotta be *kidding* me!"

"I kid you not."

"Well, cwipes on a cwacker. Nice find, Indiana. I guess it ain't loon shit, but it still pwoves my theowy."

"What theory is that?"

"You can find just as much in the twash as you do in the lake." He began to rummage. "Check out *this* puppy," he said, and held up a small metallic object. It glinted in the sun, but was too small to make out.

"What is it?"

"A cross," Howie said, though it sounded more like *cwoss*. "I found it in your wefuse."

Owen started. "Can I see it?"

Howie pocketed it greedily. "Tell ya what: why don't you follow me to the Pony? You can meet my dad, and maybe he'll give you a few bucks for that watch, if it isn't a piece a junk."

Owen didn't want to get rid of the watch, didn't think Howie's father would be interested in it even if he did, with its large crack and dead hands. He'd wound it and changed the time, but the thing still refused to work. He was interested to meet the man, though, and if anyone knew what had been taken out of that lake, a man who paid top-dollar for salvage likely would. "Do they have food?" he asked, suddenly realizing he was starving.

The question mystified Howie. "Sheah!" he said. "Only the best damn hot wings in town!"

"Then let's go."

"Coolio. Follow me."

Howie threw the truck into gear and took off with a grunt of his hemi. Owen zipped behind him in the hybrid, hoping like hell he could keep up.

<hr>

3

THEY MET AGAIN in the parking lot, a mess of weeds and crumbled paving blocks. Two rat-shit pickups were already parked, one with a Union Jack covering its back windows. Howie got away from him on one of the residential streets, but once Owen found King Street it wasn't difficult to find the Red Pony, as it appeared to be the only bar in town. At four in the afternoon, it had already gathered a decent crowd on the front patio. A neon sign advertised Labatt Ice on tap; a handwritten sign announced Karaoke Thursdays.

"You caught up," Howie said, pulling off his gloves and tossing them into the open passenger window.

"Yeah, sorry. Didn't want to speed in a school zone."

"Kids are in class," Howie said dismissively.

"So, let's see what you got."

Howie grinned wide and dug into his big grimy pockets. He

held the shiny trinket out between them. A single word cried out in Owen's mind—*Lori!*—and he grabbed at it. Howie closed and retracted his hand, looking wounded. "*Hey*, now. Haven't you ever heard of finders keepers?"

"That belongs to my sister," Owen said, certain it was the crucifix from her necklace. It had been at the house—and in the trash, of all places.

*What was it doing in the garbage?* he wondered.

*Maybe seeing her ghost again turned her off religion for good*, he answered, aware that a man so worried about late-onset schizophrenia should be careful how he talked to himself.

Howie gave Owen a suspicious glare from behind his tinted glasses. "Are you pulling my leg?"

Owen heaved a sigh. "My sister Lori stayed at Fisherman's Wharf for a while. She must have swept it into the trash before she—what?" Reacting to Howie's vacant stare, he corrected himself, "*Refuse*, sorry."

"That girl was *your sister*? The one that..." He nodded in a vague direction. "In the lake?"

Owen nodded.

Howie looked hangdog down at his dirty boots. "Sorry for what I said about ghosts in the house. I didn't know she was your sister."

"It's all right," he said, remembering the woman who'd saved his life this morning. As far as callous comments went, hers would be hard to top.

"Here," Howie said, holding out the necklace. "Take it."

"You sure? What about finders keepers?"

"You want me to change my mind, or what? Finders keepers is a buncha bullcwap, anyhow."

Owen took the crucifix, surprised—and glad—Howie had managed to find the missing piece of her necklace. *She could've easily snapped the chain with her camera strap around her neck, but why would she throw it out? That's what I need to figure out.*

*Another mystery*, he thought miserably. *Wouldn't Brother Woodrow be glad.*

"Thanks for finding it," he said to Howie, tucking it into the watch slot in his right pocket. He brought out the Jamaican coin he'd found for Howie to see. "I found this under the dock, if you want it."

Howie glanced at it. He rolled his eyes. "Oh, big whoop. I've got hundreds of quarters in a jar at home."

"Look closer," Owen said with a sly grin.

Howie did. He blinked comically at it, then raised his glasses from his nose to get a good close look. "Holy jeez! Lemme look at that thing."

"How 'bout I give it to you instead?"

Howie looked up from the coin, uncertain whether Owen was "pulling his leg" or not. "*Give* it to me?"

"Yup."

Howie gave him another suspicious look. "Are you *sure*?" When Owen nodded, Howie said, "Well, okay then!" He took the coin and brought it very close to his face. Then his lips peeled back in a big goofy grin. "Let's go show my dad!" he said cheerily.

Just as Howie had said, a sign by the door of the Red Pony proclaimed: TRY THE BEST DAMN HOT WINGS IN TOWN! The tavern had been named after the miniature dive tank, Howie said on their way to the front door, not the miniature horse, and it wasn't just a literal dive bar, it was also a place where likeminded men and women got together to get blitzed to the gills and shoot the shit about their favorite pastime.

Stained glass lampshades threw multicolored light on what was basically a long room with a bar and tables along either side, and with the typical product signage along the walls: the Bud, the Keith's, the Johnnie Walker Red. The air had a smoky quality to it, despite no one smoking. A jukebox stood near the doors, illuminated with bright colors, with an ancient cigarette machine beside it, empty and dark.

The bartender, a plump woman with a perpetual smile, her dark eyebrows drawn or tattooed on her brow beneath a mound of dyed-blonde hair and dark roots, was chatting up a couple of scruffy-looking trucker types at the far end of the bar when Owen stepped in behind Howie. The guy sitting beside them looked out of place, a man with mussed gray hair and a wildly colored cravat under a tweed jacket, his suede elbows resting on the bar in front of an amber liquid on ice, probably scotch. He looked to Owen like a scotch man.

"Heya, Howie!" the bartender called out. Her belly, under a tight-fitting black T-shirt, had folded over her money belt, and she had to shift it out of the way to get change for one of the guys in a trucker hat and plaid jacket.

"What's shakin', Tina?"

"Just my ass," Tina said, and jiggled a little. This made Howie and the trucker fellas laugh raucously. Professor Scotch only glowered over his drink. The guy looked pretty plastered. "Who's your friend?" Tina asked.

"This is Owen. Fancies himself a tweasure hunter."

The woman sized Owen up, seemed to see something worth a second look around the back of him. "Don't they all?" she said suggestively. "Well, what can I get ya, Indiana?"

Howie said, "That's what *I* called him," as he slipped by behind Owen.

Owen shrugged. "What's on tap?"

Tina nodded at the row of taps directly in front of Owen. Feeling a bit stupid, Owen called out a random beer. He'd never been much of a drinker, let alone a connoisseur; had always felt that the choice of poison didn't so much matter as the company. The occupants of the Red Pony had a sort of small town repartee he took to immediately, like a small town *Cheers*, where everybody knew everyone's name. And though the diver from this morning had said everyone already knew his, these people didn't seem to have gotten the memo.

Howie plopped down beside the professor. "Heya, Pops," Howie said, laying a hand on the old man's shoulder. The professor's head rose waveringly. His eyes twinkled when he saw his son sitting next to him.

"Howie!" he said, pasting on a crooked smile and kissing Howie on the forehead. Howie pretended to wipe it off as the old man seemed to grow confused, his bushy gray eyebrows knitting together. "What time is it?"

One of the truckers, the one wearing blue plaid, as opposed to his friend who wore the standard red, smiled and said, "Happy hour. Drink up, Lansall!" Howie's Dad looked surprised. "You're early," he said.

"Got a fwiend here I want you to meet," Howie said by way of explaining.

Owen guessed that was his cue to come over. He'd gotten his beer and paid for it, and sipped it through the foam as he approached father and son.

"Owen, this is my dad."

The old man swallowed an apparently bitter sip of scotch before offering a hand that trembled in Owen's grip. "Pleasure to make your acquaintance," he said with a British burr. Whether it was authentic or a put-on, Owen couldn't tell, but it explained Howie's use of the word *refuse* for trash. "Howard James Lansall, the Second," the old man said, which would make *Howie* Howard Lansall, the Third—a pretty highfalutin name for a refuse collector, in Owen's opinion.

"Good to meet ya," Owen said, suppressing a grin. "Owen Saddler."

Howie's father perked up at this. "*Saddler*, hmm?" He gave Owen a brief inquisitive look, and then seemed undecided whether to glower or smile. His face settled somewhere between an awkward grin and sympathy, but the expression looked as phony as his accent, as if he were trying to mask an altogether different emotion.

*Pretty awful poker face*, Owen thought. Whatever Howie's father did for a living, the man had all the characteristics of a career alcoholic: palsy, halitosis, bloodshot eyes, ruddy complexion. "Howie said you pay top dollar for salvage," Owen told the man.

Now the smile looked genuine. Howard draped an arm over his son's shoulders, startling Howie as he gulped the Caesar he'd ordered. "The boy makes quite an advertisement."

"And you never considered diving yourself?" Owen said, remembering as he asked that Howie had mentioned his father was afraid of the water.

Howard gave him a distrustful glance. "One doesn't buy a dog only to bark himself, does one? Anyhow, it's all about the breathing, isn't it, and alas, I'm quite apneic." He let Howie go, leaning in toward Owen with a faux-conspiratorial air. "There are those on the town council who would have you believe it's because I'm full of hot air, but I assure you, Mr. Saddler, the sentiment is quite mutual."

"Tell him about the watch," Howie said, pushing aside the celery to get a mouthful of the blood-red concoction.

"Watch?" The old man's bushy eyebrows rose to the middle of his forehead.

"Yeah, I uh... I found this pocket watch," Owen said, feeling slightly embarrassed to have been put on the spot, the elder Lansall studying him with bleary-eyed intensity. "I don't know if it's anything. I mean, it's probably not worth much with the face cracked."

Owen's humility seemed to amuse the elder Lansall, but it only seemed to annoy Howie. "Just *show* him alweady."

Shrugging, Owen took the watch from his pocket and laid it face up on the bar. It looked even worse under the bar lighting, the glass not only cracked but scratched, the brass nicked, the hands bent, the three and five unstuck and rattling loose under the crystal.

Howard's father squinted at it, furrowing his brow. "May I hold it?" he asked.

"Be my guest."

Howard plucked it up gingerly, turned it over in his trembling fingers. "The cover is missing," he said.

"Oh?"

"Indeed. See here?"

He held it up for Owen to inspect. Owen caught what he was meant to see immediately. "Broken hinges."

"Sharp eye, son," Howard said.

Owen caught the jealous glance Howie gave his father before gnawing off the end of his celery stalk. "Thanks," he said humbly, not wanting to get between father and son.

The bartender came back from the kitchen and slid a heaping plate of wings and fries in front of Owen, and fish and chips before Howie. The sugary, acidic smell made Owen's stomach rumble. Howie shook malt vinegar onto his food while Owen devoured a drumette. Crispy, juicy, and tender, not too sugary, salty, or tangy. Best damn wings Owen had ever tasted, though he hadn't had much occasion to eat them, since he didn't frequent pubs.

"This is what's known as a hunter-case pocket watch," Howard told him. "Without the lid, it's an open-faced or Lépine pocket watch. He's the Frenchman who invented the slimmer design. In his time, he was renowned as one of the finest craftsmen in the world."

"Wow."

"Yes," Howard agreed. "Unfortunately, this is a worthless hunk of scrap. Even if it weren't in such disrepair, it wouldn't be worth much. If I had to guess, I'd say it's a 1920's design. Nicely made, but American or Canadian, likely, not Swiss or French, or even German."

"That's bad?"

"In the case of stem-wind lever-set watches, I'm afraid so. This was a mandatory design for rail workers. The lever is here, next to where the five would be, if it hadn't come loose. Pull the lever," he demonstrated with the long, neat nails of his palsied fingers, "and twist the stem," which he did, setting the crooked hands to noon. Or midnight. "*Et voila*."

"Oh," Owen said, pleasantly surprised. "I thought it was broken. I was just twisting the top thingy. The stem."

"It *is* broken, dear boy. Quite broken. These hands shan't move again on their own, I'm afraid." He seemed genuinely distressed by this; the compassion of a collector. "A watchmaker could repair it for you, if the inner workings aren't too rusted, but bearing in mind all its other defects, I'd say it's worth neither the expense nor the trouble." He turned it over and pooched out his lower lip. "This engraving might tell you more about its owner—or *legend*, you might call it—but it's too worn to be legible, I'm afraid. One might be able to remove some of the sediment using methylated spirits or acetone. Recover some of its original luster." He smiled, almost wistfully. "One must be prudent with acetone, however, as it is *quite* an aggressive solvent." He gave Owen a serious look. "Under *no* circumstances should one use ammonium hydroxide. Brass is a *porous* metal. At the very least, you will have made it more susceptible to tarnishing. At worst, you will have given the metal an undesirable pink coloration."

Owen finished chewing and then swallowed before saying, "That's not good." The old man had gone off on a bit of a rant, and some of the bar regulars were listening intently. Howie, on the other hand, was absorbed by his fish and chips, having likely heard all of this countless times before. It was a lot for Owen to take in, but the gist of it was clear: he'd found a treasure that had no value in a monetary sense. Someone in town may have been missing it, and might be glad to have it returned to them. But the memory of the watch, as it had been, might be tarnished by what it had become in its current condition.

"What if it was in good condition?" Owen said. "How much would it be worth, do you think?"

Howard grinned. "You've got a touch of the fever, I believe. Got that lusssster in your eye," he said, drawing out the sibilance.

"Maybe a little," Owen admitted, wiping his saucy fingers on a napkin.

"A gold hunter's watch in good condition, as you say, could garner anywhere between fifteen-hundred and sixty-five-hundred dollars at auction, depending on its origins. For this, maybe a few hundred dollars."

"Oh." Owen's shoulders slumped.

"*However*, the true worth of a find like this is its rarity," Howard said, running a thumb over the etched lettering. "I've always told Howie there's nowt left in Chapel Lake but loon shit, *je m'excuse mon Français terrible*. But here you've proven me wrong. Countless divers have combed those depths for weeks and months and come up sour of countenance, lamenting their ill fortune. You've earned their jealousy, at the very least."

"Cool," Owen said.

"'Cool'!" Howard repeated, chortling at his audience, who joined in halfheartedly. "*That*, my boy, is what we in the salvage business refer to as an understatement." Howard winked at him, and Owen chuckled dutifully. "May I ask where you found it?" he said.

Owen opened his mouth to tell him, and then thought better of it. Howard apparently noticed the hesitation, and raised a bushy brow. "It was in an old junker car," Owen said. "In the glove compartment."

Howard hummed in consideration.

"I guess you wouldn't want to take it off my hands."

"It's true, as Howie might have told you, the treasures I'm looking for are of a more personal nature. Alas, this is of no value to me. It belongs to you, son. It's an *achievement*. Treasure it as such."

Owen grinned, amused by the old man's hyperbole. Howard Sr. jingled the ice in his otherwise empty glass to get the bartender's attention.

"What are you drinking?" Owen asked.

"Chivas Regal," the old man said, and waved a dismissive

hand when Owen rose up from his stool for his wallet. "Don't trouble yourself."

"I insist."

The old man smiled. "Well, if we must drink to buried treasure, let's the both of us have something from a slightly higher shelf, hmm? Say, Macallan 18?"

He raised an eyebrow at Tina, who'd just sidled over. She gave Owen a look: *Are you sure?*

"Macallan 18," Owen nodded. "For the three of us."

Howie seemed to light up at this, but Howard nixed his son's participation with a wave of his hand. "Oh, Howard doesn't drink scotch. Says it tastes like turpentine—isn't that right, Howie, my boy?"

"Wight-o, Pops," Howie mocked, grimly eyeing his plate as he smeared the last chip in the dredges of ketchup and plopped it into his mouth.

"Two Macallan 18s, dear."

"And another Ceaser for Howie," Owen added, hoping to shore up the father-son rift.

The bartender shrugged and went to the shelf. Howie wiped his mouth and dropped the napkin on his spotless plate, having swiped the last of the ketchup with his thumb and eaten it plain. He pushed the plate forward with deliberate loudness, and stood to belch softly with a fist held at his sternum. "Twy the fish next time, Owen. It was *dee*-lish." Howie grinned over his unintended bon mot. "That fish was delish," he repeated, chuckling as he made his way around the bar.

Owen hadn't made a dent in his wings yet, having been more interested in Howard's lesson than his food. "So what *are* you interested in, Howard? Can I call you Howard?"

"I insist that you do." Howard's eyes lit up as Tina brought over the scotches. He took his immediately and savored its bouquet, nostrils flaring. "You can practically *taste* the peat," he said, which Owen had to guess was meant as praise. He couldn't imagine Howard being able to smell much of anything, with the tangle of gray hairs in his nostrils. The old man downed the scotch in one gulp. Owen raised his to his nose and took in a whiff of moldering butterscotch. He considered plugging his nose, thought it might offend the old man, and drank it in two volcanic gulps. The heat kicked him in the chest, much hotter than the hot wings, and he slammed down the glass with a fiery gasp.

Howard laughed and patted him on the back. "Not much of a drinker, are you?"

"No," Owen croaked on a fiery breath.

"You'll have to do better than that if you want to play with the big boys, as they say. You've got salvage fever in your blood now. I expect to see you anon with a fanciful yarn or two."

Owen grinned. The heat had mellowed to a pleasant warmth in his belly. "Howie must be fun at home," he said.

"A queer fish, that boy," Howard remarked, peering blearily across the bar at his son, who stood in front of the jukebox bobbing his head to unheard music. "But I love him to death."

"He is pretty amusing," Owen agreed.

"Amusing *how*?" Howard said, scowling at Owen with his owlish eyebrows as if he'd been offended.

Hoping the old man didn't think he was making fun of Howie, Owen quickly added, "He's got a great sense of humor."

Howard Sr. seemed mystified now, rather than upset. "*Does* he?"

"Sure," Owen said, amazed the old man hadn't noticed. "He could do stand-up."

Howard seemed to think this over. His brow furrowed deeply. "It's not bloody cricket what happened to Howie and his mother, but he seems to be making a good fist with the cards he's been dealt, and his sister Nan does well by him. His refuse operation does quite well, too, and I'm glad of that." He exhaled deeply, shoulders sagging as if he were a deflating balloon. "Still, it's difficult, on occasion, not to feel as though one has suffered the trials of Job."

"Job?"

"From the Bible," Howard said, mild exasperation in his tone.

"I know Job," Owen told him. In fact, he knew much more about Job than he'd previously thought, the memories of his Bible teachings dredged up by his proximity to the lake. "I guess I'm not sure what you mean."

Howard smiled patronizingly and patted Owen's hand. "You will, dear boy. In good time, you'll know exactly what I mean."

The implications of this sort of talk bothered Owen, and he decided to change the subject before the conversation grew any-more melancholy. "You mentioned personal treasure before. Did you used to live down there in Peace Falls?"

"For quite some time, yes. I was a barrister once. Money for old rope, being a financial barrister in the Square Mile. After I left for Canada—had an uncle in Dunsmuir, you know—I did a good heap of pro bono work to even out the score with the master of the house." He grunted a melancholic laugh; now that Howie was off by himself, his father appeared to have slipped headfirst into Sad Drunk mode, and Owen wasn't prepared to enable him much longer. He'd suffered Gerald's drunken rants because his young age had prevented him from speaking up, or being heard. "And still, He plagues me with sores," the old man finished—or if he wasn't finished, Owen was done with him.

"Right," he said, raising his hand for the bill. Tina caught his eye and winked.

"No, I mean literally," Howard said, his head swaying drunkenly. "I've got hemorrhoids the size of walnuts, I tell you."

Tina came by with the bill, and Owen—who had polished off his chicken wings and celery, but had left the carrot sticks, as they weren't his favorite—paid her in cash. Then he tipped her with some of the change he'd found under the dock, which he'd rinsed in the bathroom sink at Fisherman's Wharf.

"Well, Howard, it was really nice to meet you," he said, having to shout over music that had begun to blast over the speakers from the juke. A strident trumpet solo, a jazzy beat brushed on a snare.

Howie stepped over to the bar, picked up the fresh Caesar Owen had bought him, and took a defiant bite out of the celery garnish. As he did, Sinatra began to sing, his voice unmistak-able, telling his fans to forget their problems and just get happy. Somebody at the tables groaned.

The old man seemed oblivious to the music, though he'd had to raise his voice to be heard over it. "A genuine pleasure to meet you again, Owen," he said, raising a drunk-limp hand to-ward Owen. They'd never met before, Owen made to say, but the music was too loud, too eerily familiar. Instead, he took the man's hand and shook it gently. "And do let me know how your treasure hunting goes. I'm anxious to see what you find."

Meanwhile, Sinatra kept on telling the bar to get happy in time for Judgment Day—not exactly something to be happy about, in Owen's opinion. It reminded him of his encounter with the Blessed Trinity Mission and their attempt to "save" him, and suddenly an image came back to him with such force it could only be a memory: a man's large, rough hands laying him in frigid, turgid water, teaching him to swim. Did he have a life jacket on? He couldn't tell. He didn't even know how old he'd been. All he knew for certain was he'd been frightened, and this man, who must have been his father, had been uncannily determined for young Owen to submit to his will.

Red Trucker turned to Blue Trucker and said, "Christ, not *again*."

Something beyond Owen's comprehension was happening here—the atmosphere was electric. Howie had stormed off to put this song on the jukebox, something he'd apparently done at least once before to warrant exasperation from the regulars. And for some reason, Owen had connected this song with a repressed memory of his father. Meanwhile, Howard's right eye had begun to twitch irritably.

"Would you excuse me a moment, dear boy?" Without waiting for a reply, the old man scooched loudly off his stool and staggered around the bar.

"There goes trouble," the trucker in red remarked.

"Shucky darn," said his friend.

Howard stopped at the foot of the jukebox, while trumpets swelled and jazzy drums kept the beat. Howie sipped his drink with a mischievous grin, watching his father bend to yank the plug.

The music ended abruptly as the Chairman of the Board sang about washing away sins—but the old man's pained yelp filled the silence as he grasped blindly at his back with both hands.

Howie sprang up from his seat and ran to his father with the speed of an EMT, laying a gentle hand on the old man's back. Owen got up to see if he could lend a hand, though not as swiftly, his core muscles still sore from vomiting at the lake. Others stood up from their seats and gaped, but didn't come to the old man's aid.

"I'm sorry, Daddy," Howie cooed, throwing his father's arm

over his shoulder and ushering him to a seat at the closest table. "I'm sorry. I'm stupid. I'm so stupid."

"No, no," Howard groaned, eyes narrowed in agony. "It's my fault. I occasionally forget how decrepit I am. Tina!" he called over Howie's shoulder. "Would you be a lamb and call the paramedics?" The bartender picked up the telephone. "There's a girl," the old man said with a pained smile, as his son shushed him, smoothing the straggly hair on his crown.

———

4

IT TOOK AN EXCEPTIONALLY long time for the paramedics to arrive, but the volunteer firefighters came first, and an OPP officer who introduced himself as Constable Selkie, a name he recognized. Once things had settled down, and the senior Howard's vitals had been taken, Owen stood with Selkie out front of the Pony. Howie threw Owen a cheerful wave from a seat in the back of the ambulance as the EMTs closed the doors and carted them off to the hospital in Peterborough.

"So," the police officer said, once Tina and the regulars had shuffled back inside. "You're the brother, are you?"

Owen turned to him, ready for it. Selkie was young, with sharp, handsome features, his cheeks as smooth as a baby's, dark hair slicked back on his pale scalp. He'd been rocking back and forth on his immaculately shined boots as he watched the paramedics help the elder Howard into the ambulance, which seemed to be a nervous habit.

"Name's Mike," Constable Selkie said. "Howie Lansall and his pop are my in-laws."

"Really?" He had seemed especially familiar with the two, and Owen had just chalked it up to small town friendliness. Now it made sense. He shook the man's hand.

"You bet," Selkie said. It was a firm grip, but Owen hadn't expected anything less.

"They're good people," Owen said. "Real friendly."

"Yup, just the best." He rocked on his boots. "Lot of friendly people in the Chapel," he said, and for a second, Owen thought he meant the chapel in the lake. A drop of cold sweat struck his ribs as he thought of that cold, murky tomb, and the house on the hill underwater, where he'd almost died. "Lotta friendly people in the Chapel," the cop repeated, then gave Owen a serious look over the rim of his sunglasses. "Quite a few people eager to get *un*friendly to out-of-towners asking the wrong kind of questions, if you know what I mean."

Owen nodded. "Mr. Wickman already gave me the spiel."

"Well, that's fine. I'm sure he did. Now I warned your sister the same as I'm warning you, to keep you two out of trouble, and I don't mean any disrespect to you or your family, but she didn't exactly heed my advice."

"Meaning... what?"

"I'm just saying, be careful, is all."

"You don't think what happened to her was an accident?"

Constable Selkie went pale. He held up a hand, palm-out. "Now, wait a second, I am *not* saying anything like that. You're putting words in my mouth, sir."

"Then, what are you saying?"

"Look, your sister had suspicions somebody was putting the screws to her, and I was the officer who got the call."

*Putting the screws?* Owen thought. *Do people actually say that outside of dime-store murder books?*

The cop gave him another suspicious look over his sunglasses, then settled them back on the bridge of his nose. "Look, I just want to make sure you're careful about who you ask... certain things."

"About the church."

"You got it. For your edification, we received two calls stating you were seen snooping around the church today, and that was well before noon. I'm sure the news spread pretty quick, especially after what happened with your sister. My condolences, by the way. She seemed like a real nice girl."

"She was," Owen said. Funny how much easier it was to think of her in the past tense now that he was so much closer to her. "Somebody really called the police about me?"

"You gotta understand, Chapel Lake breeds a special kind of what I politely like to call 'people watchers,'" the cop said. "Some of these older folks, they spend their whole day smoking ciggies and peeping out the blinds through binoculars. Some of them have *telescopes*—and that's not to look at the stars, Mr.

Saddler, no sir. It's to see what other people are *up to*. They may call it Neighborhood Watch—say they're performing a civic duty—but it's *spying*, to speak plainly, and honestly, it disgusts me. *Busybodies*." He sneered. "Nothing better to do than meddle in other people's business and waste the force's time and resources."

"It's a shame," Owen said, only because it seemed Selkie expected commiseration.

"You're damn right it is."

A cicada chirped in the silence that followed. Constable Selkie looked down the hill in the direction of the lake, the last of the day's sun glinting off his shades. Desperate to fill the silence, Owen said: "You wouldn't happen to know a blonde woman, a local, about my age, would you?"

Selkie turned to him, glasses darkening. "You're gonna have to narrow it down."

"She's a diver."

"Oh," Selkie said. "You must mean Jo Dunsmuir. Yeah, I hear her and your sister got pretty friendly before..." He trailed off, muttering an apology.

"My sister?" Owen repeated. The name Dunsmuir had a familiar ring to it, but what concerned him more was her relationship with his sister.

"Yup. From what I hear, Crazy Jo was the only one around here who'd give her the time of day by then. Her, and my father-in-law."

"'Crazy Jo'?"

"That's what some folks call her. I guess I shouldn't be telling tales out of class, but she's the main reason people started to distrust your sister."

"You say Howard talked to my sister?"

"Yeah-huh. Lookin' into old church business, from what I understand," Constable Selkie said with a nod. "Howard was their lawyer, at least that's what Nance tells me. She's my wife, his daughter. Anyway, it's probably not important. But listen, next time you feel like you need to dive in the good spot, you might think about parking that boat elsewhere. Everyone knows it's the Hordyke boat. Don't park at the marina, either. People will see you getting in the water there and figure out what you're doing. Pull it up in a nice covered space, lots of trees, a little ways from Peace Falls. Plenty of inlets to do that."

"I will," Owen agreed, thinking it was smart to be more careful about who knew where he was and when. Especially if Selkie was right about Lori.

"Good. Now people are going to see that I'm talking to you right now—"

"Right now?" Owen searched the street and saw no one but a man in a brown suit standing outside an accountant's office, smoking an e-cigarette. But there were several stores, and more than one of them had drawn their window blinds against the sun.

"Most likely," Constable Selkie said, squinting behind his shades. "One of Chapel Lake's finest tattlers lives right over there—see that bungalow with the unfashionable lawn jockey on the porch?" He pointed to the residential street just south of the post office, where several bungalows stood. Owen picked out the one he meant. A Canadian flag fluttered in a light breeze from the porch, only a few feet above the offending object. "That's old Thelma Birch. Complains to anyone who'll listen about starlings swooping in and stealing nests from other birds —you know, those little black birds that look like miniature crows? Well, you can be damned sure she's talking about the African-American family who moved in next door to her, because she's eyeballing their house the whole time she's saying it. I don't know why people listen. I guess because she talks so damn loud you can't help it." He shook his head in exasperation. "So do me a favor and give a good nod, like you understand what you've done is wrong and you won't do it again, Mr. Officer."

Owen made a big, sulky nod he hoped didn't look too phony, feeling like his mother had just made him apologize to a childhood bully. He shot a glance down the street and thought he saw the blinds move in this Thelma Birch's decrepit house with its single large, dirty window.

"That'll do," the cop told him. "Now, anything you need, you be sure and look for me." He thumbed his nametag toward the sunlight. "That's Constable Selkie. Mike, if you like. You're friends with Howie, you're pretty much part of the family. That kid don't take to just anyone."

"I'm honored. Thanks for the help, Mike."

"Least I could do. I kinda feel a little like I owe you, not being able to do anything for your sister, and all."

"Well, I appreciate it. I'm sure you did all you could."

"Thanks. You know, I was born here, Owen, not like most of my fellow officers, and that gives me an obligation to these people other officers might not understand. I don't treat everyone like a suspect without provocation, and I take what happens here to heart." He left a pause, in which Owen wondered if he was meant to express his gratitude again. "Well, okay," Selkie said with finality. "You take care now."

"You too, Constable. Thanks again."

Selkie gave him one last look over his sunglasses, as if he thought it might be the last time he'd see Owen alive, then strode to his cruiser, peered around himself in a very cop-like way, as if looking for danger, before climbing in to the driver's seat.

Owen thrust his right hand reflexively into his pocket to finger Lori's necklace. It was only then that he realized Howard hadn't given him back the watch.

# CHAPTER 8

## THE MYSTERY

I

NOBODY IN THE bar had seen the pocket watch in all the commotion, though it was difficult to tell if the regulars were saying so because one of them had taken it for themselves, and the others were too loyal to turn him in—or *her*, Tina being just as likely a culprit.

"Maybe the old man palmed it in the hubbub," the trucker in blue suggested, and shrugged as if it didn't make much of a difference to him either way. "Shucky darn," his friend said, and the two of them guffawed.

Owen dropped the subject. They were right. It was just as likely Howard had accidentally taken it as it was that someone else had stolen it. He thanked them and left, giving Howie's truck a quick once-over as he walked by. The cab was filthy, which didn't surprise Owen much, considering the man's job. There were cassette cases scattered on the passenger seat—'80s stuff: Dire Straits and Wham! and Michael Jackson's *Thriller*.

Back at Hordyke House, Owen loafed around for the rest of the day, too tired to dive again or even take the boat out on the lake. He brought a Muskoka chair from the back porch down to the dock and sat looking out at the lake, enjoying the sunshine.

The day was spectacular: the lake sparkled in the sun; the cicadas and birds chirped their content. Out on the water, kids went by on water skis and bobbed on Jet Skis across the bay. He'd found an old pair of binoculars in the house, and brought them up to his eyes every once in a while to get a better look, feeling a little like one of the busybodies Selkie had sneered about earlier, but his interest was just curiosity, not gossip.

A gray stork-like creature flew very close to the dock. Owen snatched up the binoculars, getting a good look at its hindquarters before it swooped out of view. A hummingbird buzzed over the dock, paused near Owen's chair, then zipped off, searching for a sugar fix. Two teenaged girls in a canoe paddled past on their way along the shore, their brightly colored bikinis a sharp contrast to their deep summer tans. The girl in front threw Owen a cautious wave, perhaps charmed by his unwavering smile, and he returned it. They giggled, dipping their paddles, and vanished behind the trees.

While he sat there enjoying everything the day gave him, he mulled over what he'd learned since his arrival in town. Lori's journal had provided him with a goal—to find his possibly insane father—but, so far, not much had pointed to anyone in particular.

He supposed he had to at least consider the idea that the senior Howard was his father, particularly in light of the chummy way the old man had called him "son." He decided to visit Howard in the hospital tomorrow, and while he was there, he'd ask him about his business with Lori, and if she'd mentioned anything about her troubles with other locals, and at the house.

But first, he would dive. Out there, an entire town waited to be plundered, if not for treasure, then for its secrets, a place where people had lived and worked and played. Some of those houses, workplaces, and schoolyards, were still intact, their remains a testament to those who had lived there. Someone—a Hordyke, Owen recalled, an ancestor of the fisherman who'd built the Wharf—had discovered a nice little plot of land in Southern Ontario, though it might have been called Upper Canada then, and had founded the town of Peace Falls there, had built a community there, had lived and grown old there. Had been *buried* there.

Now the entire town was buried, submerged under fifty, maybe a hundred feet of water. Down there with the fishes, an entire town festered, rotted, grew scales. *A ghost town*. Peace Falls was a ghost town in the classical sense, and at least a few of the residents of Chapel Lake were still haunted by what the dam had done to their community—to their *lives*.

Eminent domain, or "expropriation," was a strange and frustrating law that, when broken down, meant no individual ever truly owned a property. Families would be forced into "selling" to the government; they had no choice, really. Take the offer, or live with the low-ball offer later. He'd seen old photos on the internet of a parade of houses rolling up a hill on trailers to the cheers of bystanders. Owen wondered if graves had been moved with them. He'd seen the cemetery down there behind the chapel, and its graves would have been disinterred, by law. But he was willing to bet there were dozens of dog and cat skeletons slowly decaying under the earth in what had once been backyards, but was now the bottom of a lake. Maybe even a few stray human corpses had been left in that cemetery, if they'd stacked graves.

As he thought this, a lumpy brown thing rose from the water a few feet off the end of the dock. Owen brought the binoculars up, racked the focus, and saw the turtle's grumpy face—a snapper, by the look, with its hooked beak. The ugly thing blinked, not looking anywhere in particular, just bobbing on the light waves while Owen peered at it. Then it dipped back out of sight, leaving small ripples in its wake.

The barometer hanging by the backdoor called for dry weather. He rapped it with his knuckles, sure he must have seen the gesture in his youth, and the needle moved from *Dry* toward *Very Dry*. The undulating whine of cicadas in the early evening assured him tomorrow would be hot: a perfect day to spend in the cool water.

2

OWEN WOKE from a claustrophobic dream that drifted away upon awakening, and sat bolt upright for a few moments, looking at the clock.

"Two again," he said, his voice in the dim light making him edgy. *At least the lights didn't come on this time. Forgot to check for the timer last night, though. Bulb broke and then Lori's diary —you forgot to check the switch.*

He wasn't about to get out of bed and check now, and he didn't need to use the washroom. Nothing left to do but lie back down and get some rest. He'd need it for his big dive tomorrow.

*Maybe I'll see* her *again*, he thought, not Lori but the woman from the lake, and the prospect made him anxious. He wasn't sure whether it was a good anxious or bad, both repelled and drawn to her. She was attractive, there was no doubting that. But she was also rude. She'd saved his life, but she'd turned him away before and after.

Picturing her pouting scowl, her curves as she'd twisted to squeeze the water from her hair, Owen began to feel as if he were no longer alone in the room. Somebody stood over him, a dim shadow only gradually coming into sight as his eyes adjusted to the dark.

He sucked in a quick breath, but didn't dare move.

Even before he could see the man's face clearly, he knew him: it was Shepherd, the man who'd tried to drown him twice. He stood sopping wet before Owen, dripping filth from his white dress shirt and loose-fitting black pants on the carpet: *pat-pat-pat-pat*. His gaunt face was white as soap, his eyes as black as the mud at the bottom of the lake. Looking at this face was like peering into a mirror between the living world and the land of the dead.

*Jesus Christ—I really am losing my mind.*

The dead man's tendons creaked as he opened his mouth. A gurgling arose from the Shepherd's throat, and a viscous black fluid like gritty oil spilled from his lips, pattering on the carpet. Instead of words, a fat, dark beetle crawled out onto the Shepherd's desiccated tongue, spread its chitinous wings, and fell heavily onto the bedspread. Owen drew back and flicked at the bed in revulsion but the beetle merely crawled away, its hairy claws clinging to the fabric, oblivious to his efforts, and plunked heavily to the floor.

Distracted, Owen didn't see the Shepherd shamble out of the room, just the wet footprints the dead man had left on the carpet and the bare floorboards in the hall. Nerves still tight with anger, certain he was still dreaming, Owen leaped out of bed, mindful of the scurrying beetle, and rushed after him. The Shepherd's wet prints on the rug squelched under the soles of his feet, cold and slimy, as he stepped out into the hall and gazed out over the railing. The moon cast its dim glow over the bookshelf, the furniture. The room stank of sweet rot and muck—

*Have I dreamed* smells *before? I can't remember if I have or not...*

Headlights swept through the curtains, brightening the house as he descended the stairs. Caught in the jaundiced light of a truck or car out on the cottage road, he saw the dead man, as solid as his surroundings, and when the headlights passed, returning the house to its post-midnight gloom, the Shepherd seemed somehow more real than the rest of it, like a man standing in the midst of a hologram.

Then he was gone, leaving only wet footprints behind.

Owen scurried and stumbled down the stairs. The back door stood wide open, the Shepherd's silhouette slipping out into the distant night. Owen ran to the door, but by the time he got there, the dead man had disappeared. He pressed on into the darkness, following in the Shepherd's footsteps, which glistened under the moon. It wasn't until he reached the stairs leading to that lake that Owen finally caught sight of the dead man again, hobbling down the stone walkway toward the water. Fear clutched at Owen's throat with sudden urgency. Dream or not, the Shepherd was luring him toward the lake, was leading him toward a violent, thrashing death.

*Will I wake before it happens?* he wondered, but another idea occurred to him, much more sickening: *It this what happened to Lori?*

Owen stood under the cloudless sky, bright pinpricks of stars peeking through night-black fronds of pines and cedars. At the end of the path, where water lapped against the cement steps, the Shepherd turned his lamplight-white face up to his follower.

*Come on in, Owen,* those dead eyes seemed to say. *Join the congregation.*

"No." Owen shook his head fiercely—not a dream. Everything he'd seen, everything he'd felt and smelled, was real, or *real enough.* He'd die down there if he went any further. "I won't do it," he said, trying to convince himself. "I'm not going down there. I don't care who you are, you can't make me. You *can't."*

The dead man swept out a damp arm, still dripping, toward the black water. Owen had a vague idea the man was *always* wet, that he would remain so for eternity. The dead man held his hand palm up, not pointing, not ordering Owen toward his death, only indicating the lake itself, as if to show him something of grave importance.

*It's a trick,* he thought, but still, he followed.

A moment later he stood at the preacher's side, skin crawling, following the dead man's gaze to the moonlit lake. Pale figures rose from the water then, breaking the surface in the glittery path of the moon. Owen saw them clearly: men, women, and the blonde-haired cherub, dressed in clothes belonging to the 1970s or early-'80s, all wide collars and muted colors. They were the same people he'd seen the day before in the lake, *the exact same,* and only then did he connect them with the people who'd watched him drown in his tub. The young mother, whose face had wrinkled in the water to the texture and color of a prune, held her baby's sagging corpse in her arms like a rotted pumpkin, and the hollow-eyed father kept his gristly arm around them both.

Owen thought, *The realm of the dead. Abaddon uncovered.*

The congregation of the dead opened their mouths together. At first, Owen thought they meant to speak to him, as Lori had in his dream. Instead, their decayed windpipes began to chant in a toneless croak:

> *My soul is sick, my heart is sore*
> *Now I'm coming home*
> *My strength renew, my home restore,*
> *Lord, I'm coming home.*

The dead stopped singing abruptly, the wet, oozing messes that remained of their eyes and mouths widening as if in dread, their left hands rising to point in unison toward the shore. Toward *him.*

The hair on the back of Owen's neck bristled in nerve-twisting dread as he turned to the man at his side—but the Shepherd no longer stood with him. It was Brother Woodrow.

"The Devil wears many faces," the man of God said, smiling darkly. He was as dead as the others, his red beard straggly and sparse, his eyes sunken in yellow-brown pits, his smile lipless. He drew the brass watch from the Bible pocket of his filthy, tattered robe, and flicked open the lid to give its smooth, undamaged face a brief look. In that moment, Owen saw the time was 2:06.

"It's time, son," Brother Woodrow croaked. "Do you see the Mystery?" His wild, bulging eyes twinkled under the dark heavens as he looked over his flock, and he drew an arm over Owen's shoulders, pulling him in to a friendly, chilling embrace. The dead man's flesh writhed against Owen, as if his robe had been stuffed full of snakes.

Owen snapped awake, twisted up in the sweat-dampened covers. It took a few tries to tear and shake himself free, long enough to think he'd awakened to yet another nightmare, to wonder if the dreams would go on happening over and over, wondering if he'd ever wake for real. Then he was free, gasping as if he'd been underwater and had just come up for air. He kicked the sheet away and sat up in bed. The morning sun had already warmed the room.

He sat in bed thinking about the frighteningly lucid dream for several minutes before deciding it was silly to waste a day made for getting out in the lake. He climbed out of bed on the window side. The sun shone through gauzy brown curtains, and when he peered out between them, the lake looked like a polished jewel. Already people were out and about, kids climbing the rocks across the bay, and a man and boy fishing from a small tin boat in the shallows.

He threw on a pair of shorts and a T-shirt, trying to forget about his dream as he dressed. Heading for the door, he squelched down in a wet spot on the carpet, and a shiver stole over him. He froze where he stood, the soles of his feet damp, just as they'd been in his dream.

"Nope," he assured himself. "Probably a leaky roof. Washed-out shingles and exposed nails, remember?" He lifted his foot carefully from the cold wet stain and looked down. It had left a print. "That's *my* footprint, not—" With a hard swallow, he tried to make himself believe it. "—not *his*. It's rising damp.

Wood rot in the floorboards. This place is a money pit, not a haunted house."

Feeling as though something in the room might be watching him, he added more forcefully, "*There's no such thing as ghosts.*"

Then he tromped over the vague footprints leading out into the hall, obliterating them from sight, but not from mind.

<hr>

### 3

HE ATE A HURRIED BREAKFAST, cereal and toast with jam, then headed for the back door. As he passed, he saw the red light on the answering machine blinking. Someone must have turned off the ringer. Either that or he'd slept through the call.

"Message one," the robotic voice announced.

"Hi, Owen, it's, uh... It's Constable Selkie. I don't know how to tell you this; I'm not even sure why I'm calling you... I just... Nance has locked herself in the bathroom, and Howard's in an MRI... I've got no one else to talk to."

Selkie's voice quavered, as if he was crying. In the background was a bustling of people, chattering, scurrying.

"*Christ*, man... He was just a *kid*. Call me when you get this, okay? Just... Please."

The phone was cradled improperly. Owen pressed STOP.

"Didn't leave a number," he said to the machine. He dialed 911. "The number you have dialed is not in service," the automated voice told him. "Please hang up, and try—"

He hung up. Dialed 0, hoping to speak to a person.

"Hello. Information."

"Hi, I need the number for the police. I tried 911 but it said it's not in service."

"Right. We don't have 911 up here. You'll have to dial the full number."

"Okay, if you could just do that for me, that'd be great. It's kind of an emergency— Actually, do you have the number for a Michael Selkie? Maybe I should call him directly."

"If this is an emergency call, I can connect you with the police—"

"No, it's not an emergency. I mean, I'm not sure what it is, exactly."

"Sir, do you want me to dial the police, or don't you?"

"Dial Michael Selkie," he said, frustrated. "*Constable* Michael Selkie. Please."

"One moment," the operator said, annoyed.

The phone rang. Selkie picked it up on the first ring.

"Constable Selkie," he said, his voice ragged.

"Mike, it's Owen. Owen Saddler."

"Owen! Oh, thank God, you called back."

"I just got your message," he said, dragging a kitchen chair over to sit by the phone. "Is everything okay? You sounded—"

"Owen..." Selkie sighed heavily. "Howie's dead."

"How—?" He wasn't sure if he'd meant to ask if he'd heard Selkie correctly, that Howie was dead, or if he'd meant how had it happened. Selkie took it for the latter.

"Drowned," he said, incredulous. "He fucking *drowned*, Owen."

"That's not possible. He told me he wouldn't be caught—" He'd almost said the d-word, and he knew, he *knew*, that it was somehow the fault of Brother Woodrow, that Woodrow and the Shepherd were somehow, invariably, one and the same. "He said he'd never set foot in that lake."

"I know," Selkie said. "I know."

"Well how did it happen, did they say...?"

"Dump owner found him at eight a.m. Figure he musta gone out there to dump some trash, maybe got a little closer to the lake than he'd thought. The garbage goes right down to the water over there—"

"He told me."

"His truck rolled right over him, pushed him right into the lake. It looked like there was a washout, a small flash flood—I dunno how that's even *possible*. His head's pretty... Oh, *Jesus*, Owen, it's just a mess. It's a *mess*—" His words cut off in a choked sob.

"I'm so sorry, Mike." *I just saw him yesterday*, Owen thought, as if it made a difference, as if having seen him made his death less real. *He waved to us from the ambulance.*

"How'm I gonna tell my wife?" Selkie was saying. "My little girl, Owen—Jesus! I just don't *get* it."

But Owen knew. He'd stood with Howie's murderer. He'd seen the Mystery. "'The dead are in deep anguish,'" he said, "'those beneath the waters and all that live in them.'"

"What?" Selkie said, angry, confused, and Owen realized that he must have said it aloud.

"It's from Job," he said, unable to cover. "The Bible."

"What does it *mean*, though?"

Owen weighed his options: he could dive down to the church under the lake, hoping to find answers among the dead, or try to wrestle information out of a grieving father, to find out what the old man knew about Brother Woodrow and his Blessed Trinity Mission.

Suddenly, the thought of getting in that lake didn't seem quite so inviting. Suddenly, it was the *absolute last* thing he wanted to do.

"Owen...?"

"I need to talk to Howard," he said.

4

THE OLD MAN sat at the window in a small room with a single bed, wrapped in a rough wool blanket as gray as his mood. His hair was unkempt, bristles of stubble as white as snow on his chin and cheeks. A pleasant Filipino nurse in blue scrubs with a Mickey Mouse print had shown Owen the way and left him at the door. He knocked on the outside wall.

"I won't roll up my damned sleeves for *one more* bloody test!" Howard grumbled, squinting out at the sun. "I don't care on whose authority you've been sent. I'm in mourning, God damn you."

"It's me, Howard. Owen."

The old man turned. His foggy gaze settled on Owen and showed no recognition. Then the old man's face brightened. "Owen, my boy!" His smile turned down at the edges. "I suppose you've heard the dreadful news. All over town already, I'd imagine. They do like to natter, flapping their gums without saying much of worth."

"I'm so sorry about Howie," Owen said, sitting down on the radiator beside him.

Howard gave Owen a hopeful look, and ushered him near with a jittery hand. Owen leaned in, the old man's hot, sour breath filling his nostrils. "You didn't happen to bring any—?" He made a gesture as if swigging from a glass. *Drinky-poo*, he meant.

"Sorry, it didn't even occur to me." Of course it *had* occurred to him, having lived with an alcoholic, but now was probably the worst time to support Howard's habit.

"Probably for the best," Howard Sr. agreed. "I'd just get shit-faced and have to go through the DTs all over again. Did you know they don't even have a smoking lounge anymore?"

"That's awful," Owen said, thinking the opposite.

"Sodding prison camp, is what it is. Thank bloody hell that Gestapo nurse of mine's on a day off. At least I can have a wank with a modicum of privacy."

Owen laughed.

"You laugh, but it's true. You get a stiffy at my age, it's a point of pride to beat that wormy bastard with all you've got." Howard giggled along with him, until his cheeks went beet red and his eyes began to water. He broke into tears somewhere amid the laughter, looking off at an unfinished puzzle Owen just now noticed lay on the mattress, an enlarged photo of Chapel Lake on a partly cloudy day. He hadn't seen it from the doorway, obscured as it was by the heavy blue-green curtain.

Howard put a hand on Owen's knee. "He hated the lake, Owen. *Hated* it. I don't understand why he'd have been any-where close enough to—" He choked on the word. "—to *drown*."

Owen put a hand on the old man's. Howard's hand quivered against Owen's knee, then slipped free and fell to his side, over the edge of his wheelchair.

"Michael said it happened near the dump. A flash flood, or some such thing."

Owen knew better, but Howard didn't need to know the truth: that his son was just another casualty of that terrible church beneath the lake.

"A flash flood, can you imagine? It doesn't seem likely to me." Squinting again, the old man brought a shaky hand up to shield his eyes. "Will you close the blinds?" He gestured toward the cord tied in a knot halfway up the window, just out of his reach. Owen yanked it and the blinds dropped. Slats of light and dark fell over the room. "Merciless thing, the sun."

Owen didn't know how to respond, and so he said nothing.

"My son never hurt anyone," Howard said. "He was a wonderful boy, a good boy. Never caused any trouble. Oh, certainly, he was a handful in his early years, but his mother took care of all that. I was always—" The old man pulled a resentful face. "—always *working*. When he was born, there were those who pitied us, Charlotte and me." He wrung his hands together, obsessively, the sound of his dry palms distracting. "There were actually people who thought we'd have been better off if he'd died in his crib, if we'd drowned him in the tub. Because of his disorder. His Down's syndrome. I heard them, you see. They were always nattering."

"That's awful."

"Yes," Howard said. A slow, repetitive nod shook loose a tear. It streaked down the deep valleys of his face and came to rest at the corner of his lips, where he licked it away absent-mindedly. "I couldn't fault them for it. When the doctor informed us of Howie's condition—the cheeky prick actually had the nerve to call it *mongolism*, if you can believe that, as if we still lived in the nineteenth century!—and when I saw my boy for the first time... God help me, *I considered it myself*. A child can be a burden to his parents under the best of circumstances, and when I looked into his little eyes, I saw only trouble ahead for us, Charlotte and me."

Owen nodded, but of course he couldn't understand, only sympathize, with baby Howie as much as with his parents.

"He wept so much in those first weeks at the house. Some nights I lay awake believing I was cursed. I *cried out to God*, Owen, to take the poor boy while he slept. To make it quick..." His lower lip quivered at the thought. "...and painless. But a quick and painless death is death nonetheless. One final gasp expelled into the ether, and then... Poof. *Rien*. Nothing. And I wished this on *my own son*, you understand. My own *flesh and blood*."

In a sudden rage, Howard struck the mattress, scattering the pieces of the puzzle across the mattress. He calmed himself with a thin, jittery exhale through his teeth, squinting out through the slatted blinds.

Owen grasped the old man's hand, and squeezed it until Howard looked up at him. "This didn't happen to Howie because you prayed for him to die," Owen said. "If people died because someone prayed for it, this world would be a lot less crowded."

Howard smiled through his tears. "Yes, I suppose you're right." He studied Owen amusedly. "That's a rather cruel brand of optimism, wouldn't you say?"

"I learned it from my mother," Owen said with a brief smile. "Try to forgive yourself, Howard. I'm sure Howie would have."

"Mmn." His dry tongue peeked out to moisten his cracked lips. "But has Crouch...?" A strange segue, in Owen's opinion—*Who or what is Crouch?* Howard's gaze drifted from Owen's left eye to the other, searching for something. "Close the door," he said then, nodding toward it.

Owen stood and crossed the room. He peered out into the hall, which bustled with activity, then pulled the door shut with the serpent's hiss of its hydraulic hinge. He locked it, in case a nurse wanted to take more of the old man's blood, and returned to his seat at the radiator.

"What I say here, you don't repeat," Howard said, sotto voce, despite the privacy. "Do you understand?"

"Of course."

The old man nodded. He opened his mouth to speak, and then appeared to reconsider his words. Finally, he began: "The schism in that church began quite suddenly, I recall. One Sunday, it was business as usual, *God is love* and all that, and the next, it was agitated talk of *interlopers* and *Satan's pimps.*"

"Imps?"

"*Pimps.* I'll explain in a moment." The old man swished a hand out toward the tray table, where his breakfast lay untouched, congealed scrambled eggs and dry bacon. "Would you be a lamb and fetch me that juice?"

Owen stood and brought it over.

"There's a lad." He tore off the top with jittery fingers. "With any luck it'll trick my liver into believing it's a screwdriver," he explained, and raised the container in a mock toast. "Chin chin." He drank the contents greedily, with a slurping, bubbly sound that reminded Owen, for one sick moment, of the bubbles from his severed oxygen tube as he drowned in the house at the bottom of the lake. He shivered, despite the warmth of the radiator.

The old man sucked out the last drops, smacked his lips, and shrugged, neither satisfied nor dissatisfied, before setting it down on the window ledge. "Where was I?"

"Satan's pimps."

"Right, right. It is my contention, Owen, that the church's sudden change of direction was caused by a certain revelation, so to speak, at town council that very Wednesday. There'd been a guest speaker, you see, a government official from out of town, and he'd carried with him word of a certain impending development in the community—"

"The hydroelectric dam."

Howard winked. "Now you're playing catch-up. As you can imagine, word got around quickly. He was a wolf in sheep's clothing, as the minister himself might have said in one of his homilies. The phrase spreading around town was *Satan's pimp*. Having met with the man myself, I must admit, I rather liked the term. He'd come offering money, you see. What he'd called *fair compensation*. But it was understood the development would move forward with or without our consent. As an architect, I'm sure you're familiar with the concept of expropriation."

Had he told anyone about his job? Owen didn't recall, but he supposed it was just another example of small town curiosity. "More than I'd like to be," he said.

"As was Crouch."

That name again. "Who's this Crouch?"

"Our local pastor, in those days of milk and honey," Howard said.

"Not Woodrow?"

Howard eyed him queerly. "*Woodrow?* Where the Devil did you hear that name?"

"I met him, my first day here."

"You met—?" The old man flustered. "No, no, son, the pastor was *Crouch*. Everett Crouch." He gave Owen a sidelong glance, and then squinted out through the blinds as red lights flashed through them. Owen peered out. Down below, an ambulance had pulled up, and EMTs scrambled to open the back doors for an elderly woman wrapped on the gurney, who peered confusedly at all the commotion. He let the blinds fall back with a metallic swish.

"After the town hall meeting," Howard continued, "Crouch's sermons perverted into angry, paranoid rants of Noah and the Great Flood, about Babylon and Sodom and Gomorrah. All the wonderful examples we find in the Bible of God's everlasting wrath." He pronounced it like a last name: *Roth*. "Crouch even had new windows put in—this great, God-awful stained glass depiction of Moses parting the Red Sea."

"Mike said you used to be their lawyer."

"It's true. I separated from the church after the Schism, but Madge, your mother, stayed with him." He shook his head, Owen supposed, at her foolishness. "I suppose we always believed Crouch would have a change of heart. But he never did. When the flood came, your mother and I, along with many others, fled the church. We abandoned him. I suppose in Crouch's mind, we betrayed him."

"What happened down there in that church, Howard?"

"Crouch and his flock chose to stand against the flood. Crouch had them believing some madness about how God would spare His faithful. They stood against the deluge to protect their church. Little did those poor people know, they would have lost it with or without the flood." Howard nodded as if Owen had challenged him. "Flat broke, so they were. Everett Crouch had run that church into the ground well before the water overtook it."

"How does a church go broke?"

"Lack of membership. It was stripped of its tax-free status after the Schism. There were accusations of cult-like behavior, and with the events in Guyana still fresh in our collective subconscious, the government took the allegations quite seriously. You know, the Chinese call suicide *abandoning the body*," he said, still wringing his hands obsessively.

"Suicide? You think—?"

"Oh, quite certainly. It was never proven, but it's what I believe. It's why I pay for salvage. I suppose a rather morbid part of me expects to one day have evidence that Crouch and the rest of them died in that flood, to hold it in my hands. His final words to me were, 'Earth, do not cover my blood. May my cry never be laid to rest.'" Howard let the words hang before remarking, "It's from the Book of Job. I had to look it up." At last he turned to the puzzle he'd shattered, regarding it the way he would a mess made by a child. "I really wish I hadn't done that."

"You can put it back together."

"Howie wanted me to help him with it. I told him it was a child's game." His eyes never left the unassembled pieces. "I wasn't much of a father to him, I'm afraid. I hope he knew that I loved him, at the very least."

"I'm sure he did," Owen said, remembering the twinkle in the old man's eyes when he'd seen his son at the Pony, and the reverential way Howie had spoken to Owen of his father.

"Crouch and his Blessed Trinity killed themselves," Howard said with dismal finality. "Your mother and I tried to save them from him, and we failed. I suspect it's that failure we've all been hiding, the ones who escaped, as much as the dead themselves."

"But you have no proof."

"Belief is stronger than proof, Owen. The Reverend Crouch knew that more than anyone."

"But why would they kill themselves? Just because they were going to lose their church?"

Howard eyed Owen with cold cynicism. "Why does anyone do anything, son? For their *beliefs*. Out of *conviction*. Because God told them to," he added with a vicious sneer. "Or the Devil."

*The Devil has many faces*, Owen thought, remembering the words of Brother Woodrow, and again he shivered. "Why didn't you tell the police?"

The old man let out a resigned sigh, as if he'd told the story a hundred times before. "I spoke with Detective Selkie," he said. "He'd held similar theories, but without evidence, we'd have been holding up the town to unneeded media scrutiny, like Waco, Texas, after the siege. Like Jonestown. Houses had been *moved*, Owen. *Lives* disrupted."

"How many others? No one else believed you?"

"A chosen few," the old man admitted. "Oh, there are whispers. Never doubt that. The darkest secrets are always perceptible to others. The guilty wear them like badges, whether they choose to believe so or not. And Crouch has never forgiven us," Howard said grimly. "He took my boy into that lake with him out of vengeance. They wanted to be martyrs, you see. They wanted their deaths to remind us we were *all* victims of the flood. Of that *bloody* dam. 'Earth, do not cover my blood...'"

A long moment passed in relative silence, but for the muted sounds of the hospital beyond the door.

"Howard, did you know my father?"

"Naturally."

Owen eyed him with suspicion. "You're not...?"

The old man burst out in a good, hearty laugh. "Your father? Good God, no! I loved your mother dearly, Owen, but ours was a strictly platonic relationship. She'd made certain of that."

"But you do know something you're not telling me."

Howard squinted, appearing to be in thought. "Get my satchel, will you?" he said after a moment. "It's over there in the closet." Owen stood and opened the closet door. Howard had put his clothes on hooks and his shoes on the closet floor. A brown leather bag lay beside them. He brought it to Howard at the window.

The old man unzipped it and rummaged. His trembling fingers came up holding a photograph with rounded corners and muted colors, creased and smoothed out flat again. He handed the photo to Owen, who recognized several of the faces right away: his mother, youthful and smiling vibrantly, her dark hair in a stylish bob, and Howard on the other side of the group from her, much younger, handsome, his hair dark but still wild. There was the blond boy Lori had told him about, the boy he'd once been, sitting at Margaret Saddler's feet with a blonde girl about his age. There was Skip Wickman, young and smiling. The others were the same men and women he'd seen the other day in the lake, in his dream, in the tub—he was certain of it. They were the Blessed Trinity Mission... and their Reverend stood at the center of them, smiling wide, the sleeves of his white work shirt rolled up to the elbows, not Brother Woodrow, but the Shepherd, a man named Everett Crouch.

The photo nearly fell from his fingers.

He pointed, his hand shaking as badly as the old man's. "That's him? That's Crouch?"

"The very same," Howard said. "You remember him?"

The words stuck in his throat. After a moment, he managed

to choke them out, "I do." He turned the photo over. The words *BLESSED TRINITY MISSION, July 1979* were scrawled on the back.

"My father's one of these people?"

Howard nodded.

"You won't tell me which one."

"Your mother would kill me."

Owen nodded. He'd already gotten much more out of the old man than he'd expected, and he didn't want to put up a fight. "Can I keep this?"

"It's yours," Howard said. Owen recalled he'd said the same thing, in the same way, about the watch.

"Thanks." Owen tucked it into his pocket. "Hey, you didn't happen to take that pocket watch with you yesterday, did you? I can't find it anywhere."

"The watch? I gave it back to you, didn't I?"

Owen shook his head. "I guess I must have forgotten it on the bar in all the commotion."

"I suppose you must have," Howard agreed. "Sorry to hear it."

"Oh well. It was a piece of junk, anyway."

"Yes, but it was *your* piece of junk. One man's trash..."

"Yeah," Owen said, standing up. "I'll come and check in on you tomorrow, if you're still around."

"Thank you kindly, my dear boy. And thank you for listening to an old man's ramblings. I don't know what came over me."

"Confession is good for the soul," Owen said, and patted him on the shoulder. Howard put a hand on his and shook it vigorously. He let it fall to his side while Owen crossed to the door. He had it unlocked and open when Howard spoke again. "When you speak to your mother, tell her I said, 'I still do.'"

"You still do what?"

Howard smiled wistfully. "She'll know what it means." Then he turned to face the window, his back to Owen, narrowing his eyes at the cloud-darkened sky.

# CHAPTER 9

## THE GOOD SHEPHERD/SHAME THE DEVIL

I

OWEN BUMPED INTO Constable Selkie on his way out. They were both distracted, Owen with thoughts of dead preachers, and Selkie with the death of his brother-in-law, his puffy red eyes watching his feet.

"Hey, watch it, pal," Selkie said, realizing too late who he'd bumped into. He grabbed Owen's arm affably then, his glower softening. "Shit, I'm sorry, Owen. I didn't know it was you."

"That's okay," Owen said. "I guess I should have been watching where I was going."

"Just come from the old man, huh?"

"Yeah. We had a good talk."

"Oh, yeah?"

"About Howie," Owen said, hoping the policeman wouldn't see through his half-lie. "I really wish it didn't have to happen."

"You and me both." He patted Owen on the shoulder. "Hey, listen, you doing anything right now? I could use someone to talk to. Or *at*, I guess."

Twenty minutes later they had crossed town in separate vehicles and were sitting in a small, bright, under-populated diner close to where the Trent River opened up to Little Lake. Where Chapel Lake had a church steeple at its center, Little Lake had a large fountain, its white spray caught in a strong wind while Jet Skis zipped back and forth through the rainbow it created.

A grumbly server brought their bills with the coffee, slapping them down on the wobbly table overlooking the lake. A tuft of thick black hair rose from the back of his white T-shirt, his apron stained with grease and blood.

"You know, most places, it's kind of expected cops get their coffee free," Selkie said with a seemingly smug grin.

"Don't I pay your salary? I gotta give you free coffee, too?"

The server wandered back to the grill, where he cracked some eggs and turned sausages for the only other paying customer, an old man sitting at the counter reading the paper.

"The guy's a grumpy old bastard, but I'd take his coffee over Timmie's, any day."

Owen raised his mug in a half-hearted cheer, and blew on it while Selkie poured sugar into his own. "You know, there's a lot of folks in town who think that lake is cursed." As if predicting a reaction from Owen, he held up a hand. "Not me, of course. I love the lake. Used to get drunk on Camp Island just about every weekend with a bunch of crazy kids from school. Even got my first hand job from a trailer park girl in a rented canoe on Heron Bay." He laughed at the memory. "This old dude trawled through on a fishing boat and just about lost it when he saw this girl, I don't even remember her name, with her bikini top yanked down pushing up her tits, jerking on my dick like she was pulling a stubborn boat motor."

The both of them chuckled at that, though Owen did so mainly to be genial.

"So no, I've never thought it was cursed. But some of the older kids had stories. Weird stories. Shit you wouldn't believe —*couldn't* believe, if you wanted to keep your sanity, you know what I'm saying?"

*Oh, I know*, he thought, and said, "I think so."

Selkie chuckled scornfully, like Owen had no idea. "My dad," he said, "he always thought the Blessed Trinity people were murdered in that lake. He was a cop, too. Got a cop's mind. Always on the lookout for trouble."

"Murdered?"

"My dad was watching the flood, like everyone else, but he got this funny idea in his head, like he wanted to sit in that old wooden boat of his while the valley filled up. Like a rubber duck when some kid's running a bath."

Owen flashed to the tub, Crouch standing over him,

pushing him under while the Blessed Trinity watched. He shuddered unintentionally.

"Anyway, funny idea, right? He was floating for a while, just enjoying himself while the current took him from door to door, all the houses and buildings people had been too poor or too cheap to move up the hill. You know, bouncing back and forth like a pinball, pushing himself off with a paddle so he wouldn't beach himself on someone's porch. Ma thought he was nuts, and I guess he probably was a bit nuts by then. He got shot on duty, the bullet lodged near his spine, not paralyzing him, thank God, but bad enough he had to go on Disability. He woulda got fired for drinking on the job eventually, if he hadn't, most likely, and after that, he just loafed around most of the day watching *Barney Miller* and reruns of *Dragnet*. You remember that one? With the song? *Duhhh duh-duh duh*," he sang unmusically. "So the old man's probably drunk as a goddamn skunk, probably giggling his ass off down there, when he sees two or three guys come out back of the church and head up the hill. He thought nothing of it, thought maybe it was the Trinity people coming back to get something they'd forgotten in the church before it was underwater for good. But a little while later, he thought he heard a gunshot."

"A gunshot?"

"Just one, real faint, so as it could have been the wind, or his imagination, or one of the little kiddies up there on the hill, for all he knew. It didn't occur to him until later, when Crouch and the others were found missing—that's a weird expression, huh? '*Found* missing.' Like 'living dead.' It's a, what do you call it?"

"An oxymoron. Your father didn't report it?"

"He did, but no one believed him. He was drinking a lot by then. They told him it was probably just a tree branch cracking under the water. Anyway, it didn't hit him until the rumors started going around, you know how those busybodies are, and the paper that week with this big headline, 'Whatever Happened to the Blessed Trinity Cult?' Then he started thinking it could have been the scream of someone drowning, down there in the church. Can you imagine? I mean, I'm not saying I believe it, but if it's true—how could God let something like that happen?"

Owen thought to say *The Lord works in mysterious ways,*

but after what had happened in the lake this morning, he thought better of it. "Your father, is he still around?"

"No sir."

"Dead?"

Selkie laughed. "*My* dad? Dead *broke*, maybe. Last I heard he was living with some bar skank out near the casino, spending every red cent of his disability on video blackjack."

"So what do other people think about it?"

"They think the Mission just skipped town, and I agree with them. They were fighting a losing battle: against the government, against the bank—hell, against just about everybody in town. If they ran off, all the better, right?"

"The police didn't look into your father's allegations?"

"They led dozens of dives to that church. Eventually they sealed it up when it got too dangerous. Some kid died down there during a dive trip with his folks. Hundred pound Crucified Jesus fell right on top of him. Crushed the poor kid's head in. After that, nobody was allowed to go inside the church, and I guess the police gave up looking. I was just a kid myself when it happened, for the record."

"Of course. What about the others? The rest of the church—they didn't believe your dad, either? Skip Wickman—"

Selkie nodded. "And my father-in-law, who you've met."

"Can you do me a favor?"

"Sure, why not?"

Owen took Howard's photo from his pocket and put it face-up on the table. "Can you name these people for me?"

Selkie slid the photo beside his coffee, took a sip, and flipped it over. "July, 1979. Isn't that when disco died?" Owen shook his head, not getting it. "Never mind. Looks like this was taped to something. A photo album, maybe." He indicated a piece of torn tape stuck to the top, peeled and black at the edges as if someone had tried to remove it. He flipped it back face-up and pointed. "That one there, that's Howard." He pointed again. "And there's your mom, but you probably already guessed that."

Owen silently agreed.

"I guess that'd make this kid you. The other kid, the girl, that's Crazy Jo, the one your sister was talking with. I heard you and her had a little run-in yesterday, by the way. She's a scary one, huh?"

*The diver*, Owen thought. *No wonder she's on my case about the church.* "She's interesting, I'll give her that."

Selkie pooched out his lower lip, considering Owen's response. "This guy," he said, pointing to the slim black man with a short afro and muttonchops, "is Wickman, of course. I guess that'd make these two the Dunsmuirs, Jo's folks." He bent to give it a closer look. "These three, I dunno," he said, pointing out the elderly man Owen remembered from the lake, and two young women, one looking chubby in a sundress, the other dour-faced in black pants, like Crouch, and a chambray work shirt. "The Poindexter is Dink Deakins," he said, pointing to a lanky guy with Buddy Holly glasses and brown hair pomaded to the side. "He was good friends with my father-in-law, back before the flood. They've drifted apart, since. And this kid here," he'd pressed his finger down on a teenaged boy with bad acne, "I think that's Beau Parish. He runs the gas bar on the county road." He slid the photo back to Owen. "You know, your sister was asking questions just like this. What is it the two of you are looking for?"

"One of these men might be my father."

Selkie laughed again. "Well, if it's one of those guys, my bet's on Senior. Dink Deakins probably never got laid before he met his wife. And it's probably not Skip, not unless you're hiding a big black dick in those pants."

Owen thought to point out the offensiveness of Selkie's joke, but doing so would have been counterproductive. "It's not Howard. He said my mom and him were just friends."

"Oh, yeah?" Selkie shrugged. "Well, hell, I guess it could be anybody then."

"Yeah," Owen said, disappointed again. Then he thought of something, something that had bothered him since he'd woken up in the middle of that first night at Fisherman's Wharf. "Hey, did your dad happen to say when he heard those screams?"

"Yeah, he did. He remembered because he checked his watch right before. It'd been about two or three hours since the flood started, and his boat was only floating about ten feet from the ground. He was wondering how long he'd have to sit there before the damn lake filled up entirely."

"And the scream...?"

"Woulda been right after that. He paddled home when he ran outta booze. He never followed through with a damn thing in his life, except a bottle. Got home around..." He thought back. "Three, maybe? I remember, because he sat his fat ass right down in front of the TV to watch *Dragnet*, and *Dragnet* started at three. Three?" he asked himself, then nodded. "Yeah, three. Eyewitness testimony," he said, and shook his head derisively.

"So what would that make it? A little after two when he heard the scream?"

"Jeez, now you're starting to sound like the cop." He grinned. "Yeah, I guess it musta been around two. Does it make a difference?"

A little after 2PM. When the watch he'd found had cracked, when the clock in the house had stopped, and when the reading lamp had flickered, waking him from his dream of Lori.

"Not really," he said. "Just curious."

---

2

BACK AT FISHERMAN'S WHARF, Owen stood on the cement steps at the foot of the lake. He hadn't bothered to put on the wetsuit, which still lay on the porch railing, and hadn't brought the tank and equipment down from the kitchen. As badly as he wanted to find the "Blessed Trinity Cult," as the Chapel Lake paper had called them when the remaining members had disappeared, he knew he couldn't bring himself to go back in the water. He'd narrowly escaped death twice, but the third time was always the charmer. He couldn't go down there alone.

He'd tried to look up Jo or J. Dunsmuir in the phone book, but neither name was listed. Jo and his sister had been working together, according to Selkie—he needed to know what Crazy Jo had told Lori, and how much the two of them together had known. He could also use a competent diving partner, someone who knew the lake better than he did. A dark part of him worried that Jo—who he supposed must be the same blonde girl he vaguely recalled from dreams—would suffer the same fate as Lori, as Howie; the same fate Jo had spared him the other day, racing him away from the homicidal Revered Everett Crouch.

Crouch wanted him dead, him and all the rest of the Blessed Trinity exiles and their kin—they'd taken Howard's son, Margaret's daughter. *The Lord is merciful and forgiving*, or so it was written, but Crouch was unforgiving, merciless; he'd obviously forgotten that famous Biblical verse, *Vengeance is mine, saith the Lord*. The Blessed Trinity had sacrificed themselves for their church, so far as Howard and Constable Selkie's father believed. Those who had abandoned them in their time of suffering would soon be reunited with the congregation they'd left for dead.

Owen slipped his shoes back on and headed up to the house. Lori's journal awaited, along with a cold bottle of root beer. He brought them both out to the deck and read, finding more revelations almost immediately: Lori wrote of a faceless man dressed in black from head to toe who'd stood over her bed. Owen shuddered reading this, thinking of his own dream the night before, and the wet spot Crouch had left on the bedroom floor that Owen had dismissed as rising damp.

*It was rising damp, all right*, he thought—*only this damp rose all the way from the grave.*

He laughed bitterly.

On June 24th, Lori had come to the same conclusion Owen himself had only a short while ago:

*He's there in that church, Owns. The preacher's there, I know it! But I can't prove it if I don't find his remains... This is a bad place. There are ghosts in Chapel Lake, and I don't mean skeletons in the closet. I'm starting to think all of the things that happened to me in this house—the power flickering, the shadows and creaks in the night, the clocks all stopped at 2:06 no matter how many times I set them and change the batteries—can't just be explained away anymore. Either I'm going absolutely crazy, or this place really is haunted.*

*The trouble is, I don't believe in ghosts! Ghosts can't exist in the same world as God. Either God exists and our souls are saved or damned, or our spirits carry on in this world, haunted by our own transgressions, haunting the living in the dead of night. Purgatory is a made-up place. It's not even mentioned in the Bible—I guess you'd probably know, since you were part of that church. Did Everett Crouch teach you these things? Did Crouch ever explain to you about the difference between the spirits of the Bible and what we call "ghosts"?*

*It doesn't matter. I don't know what to believe anymore. Last night I dreamed he came back, only this time he led me down to the water—*

*The same dream*, Owen thought. *How could we have the same dream?*

*Because it wasn't a dream*, he answered himself. *Crouch came for us, he lured us down to that lake. He's had his hook in me ever since that night in the tub, and he's been reeling me in.*

Owen swigged his root beer, his mouth suddenly as dry as the town of Peace Falls before the flood.

Crouch had lured Lori here, too, somehow—Owen was sure of it. He'd cast his sister into the water and used her as bait, to draw the big game out from hiding.

*Why does he want me so bad? Wasn't taking Lori enough? Wasn't* Howie?

No. It would never be enough, he was sure of that now. Crouch's poisoned soul wouldn't rest until the last of them were dragged down to their watery graves. Not until the last members of the Blessed Trinity had been returned to the fold.

*The Good Shepherd lays down his life for the Sheep...*

He didn't want to read anymore, but he couldn't close the book in the middle of Lori's story.

*—and they rose out of the lake, bloated and black, the corpses of the Blessed Trinity Cult. It was <u>horrible</u>, Owns, but the worst part was when I woke up there was a puddle beside the bed where he'd stood in my dream.*

*How is that possible if he's not real?*

Owen wondered if she had also been asked about "the Mystery," as Brother Woodrow had asked him. He supposed he'd never know unless he kept reading, so he dove right back in as the sun began to sink behind the trees on the opposite shore, and the happy cries of suntanned children in the trailer park died away.

After the visit from Crouch, her dives began to focus on the church, but she could never manage to get inside. She'd gone so far as to drag a street sign to the window to use as a battering ram, but the force required to smash even the rotted wood boarding up the lower windows was dulled and deadened underwater. She'd left unrewarded.

Lori *had* been able to enter the house behind the church, and had done some snooping. As Owen had thought, it seemed to be the home of the church's minister, this Everett Crouch, and aside from the fact that there'd been two moldering double beds pushed together in the master bedroom, and a single bed in the room next to it—evidence of this man of the cloth having had a child—she'd found little of interest.

"Why didn't she find the watch?" he wondered aloud, scaring away the chipmunk who'd come to feast on the dust of his previous meals.

*Because it* belongs *to me*, he thought, *just like Howard said. Whether it really is mine or not, I was* meant *to find it. Crouch used it to draw me into that room, just like he used Lori to draw me to the lake. He wanted me there all to himself, to fill me full of his filth, whatever the hell that black stuff was that came out of him. His poison. His perverted religion. His* disease.

The sun was a glorious fire on the horizon, but it was too dark to read out here anymore. He brought the book and the empty root beer bottle inside.

Craving red meat, the bloodier the better, Owen fried himself some hamburgers and left them so juicy that they soaked through the buns and made his fingers greasy. When he'd finished, he let out a loud, satisfied burp—*That one's for you*, he said to the darkened living room, hoping Crouch and his holy ghosts were listening—and licked his fingers clean. He threw the dirty plate in the sink. The faucet was leaky, dripping into the chipped enamel pan, but he didn't care. He let it drip; no matter if it reminded him of the tub at his mother's house, no matter that it reminded him of Crouch. He felt defiant.

If the Shepherd wanted him, he'd have to come get him. There was no way he was getting in that lake again, not unless he was dragged.

A splashing sound drew him back to the sink, where the drips still plunked hollowly. He peered out the window above, expecting to see Crouch's pallid face framed by the darkness beyond the glass. Nothing stirred in the darkened woods. The black pillars of trees, the dock, pale and skeletal under the moon, and the dapples of silver light out on the water were all he saw.

Another splashing sound. This time it drew his attention toward the lake, where a dark shape slipped across the surface of the water, ripples radiating from the dock, dispersing the glitter path of the moon.

"What *now*?" he said.

The thing turned back, moonlight revealing a pale ovular form rising above the water with something long, sleek, and dark trailing behind it—*Hair*, he thought. *It's a woman.*

His immediate thought was that this was one of the women from the Blessed Trinity. Whoever she was, she threw her arms up onto the dock and pulled herself up, and he saw that, aside from her damp hair and the dark place where her legs came together, the rest of her glimmered wet and pale in the silver moon, naked as Eve.

*The realm of the dead is naked before God...*

Owen stepped out into the cool night air. Frogs chirped and moaned in the shallow water, mosquitoes droned. A lonely loon cried somewhere out on the lake. A bat fluttered by, black against black.

The woman stood as Owen approached—not as cautiously as he might have if she hadn't been nude—and she turned her shoulders to squeeze out her hair on the dock. He recognized the gesture immediately: Crazy Jo Dunsmuir. The blonde girl from the photo of the Blessed Trinity. The childhood friend he barely remembered.

"She really is nuts," he said, and hurried down to the lake.

Jo dove in again before he could warn her, her smooth white form plunging headfirst into the wet dark of the Blessed Trinity's grave. For a long moment, as he bounded onto the dock, he was sure she wouldn't resurface—that Crouch and his undead minions would have pulled her down there with them for good. That he'd be forced to dive in after her, to save her life as she'd saved his.

He hurried down to the dock, suddenly more worried about her life than his own. Then she broke the surface, blowing water from her lips, and shook her hair. Her eyes, dark jewels in the moonlight, found him instantly. A smile came to her red lips, and she swam for him.

She treaded water at his feet, looking up at him in amusement. "You act like you've never seen someone skinny-dip before," she said.

He held out a hand. "You really should get out of the water."

"You really should get in here with me. The water's *fine*."

Owen shook his head. "I'm not getting in that lake. Not after what happened this morning."

"Oh, poor baby."

"A man *died* today," Owen said. "Don't you have any respect?"

She gave him a pitying look. "People die all the time, in or out of the water. It's a fact of life. You can't let that make you afraid to live."

"Cruel optimism," he said, recalling what Howard had said about him.

"What?"

"It doesn't matter."

"Exactly. It doesn't matter." She smiled again, coyly. "All that matters is there's a reasonably attractive naked woman at your feet, and you're too worried about dying to take advantage."

"Advantage...?"

"We're not kids anymore, Owen, running around with our clothes off. When adults get naked, it's either to get clean..." She reached up and stroked his bare leg. "...or *dirty*."

He felt himself stiffening in his shorts. "I can't," he said—nearly gulped.

"Fine then. Why don't you fuck off crying back home to your mother?"

"What the hell is *wrong* with you?"

Crazy Jo scowled and blew water from her lips again. "You want me to write you out a list?" She swam backward, kicking away from the dock, splashing his legs. Once she was in shallow water, she stood, revealing herself. "Last chance, golden boy," she warned him, sliding a hand over her wet, erect nipples and down between her legs. "Come get a piece before it gets cold."

His shorts jutted out at an angry angle, his prick throbbing painfully against the fabric. He couldn't conceal his desire for her any longer. His hard-on sprung free as he stripped off his shorts. Owen couldn't remember the last time he'd kissed a woman, let alone slept with one. He supposed it would have been Allison, and that doomed relationship had ended over a year ago.

"I'm coming," he said.

He caught her smirk. "Not yet, I hope," she said.

Owen dove in over his head.

She met him halfway, her hands finding him in the dark below, tugging at him. Their lips met for a second time—though now with a powerful, aggressive hunger. Their tongues danced. He reached between her legs, finding her warm and slick in the cool water. The frenzied movement of their right hands stirred the surface. With his left, he cupped her head, fingers slipping into her wet hair, pulling her close. Her left hand reached below her right and cupped him as well.

Owen's eyes fluttered open. Over Jo's shoulder he saw a fat black snake slope into the water from the shore and slither across the surface. He thought of the Tree in the Garden as the water snake slipped by, oblivious, out into the dark. Jo bit the shallow above his clavicle, moaning against his skin, and he grunted in pleasure, forgetting the snake, forgetting Eden.

Jo pulled him into a close embrace, her breasts and hardened nipples pressing against him, and jerked him roughly inside of her. He thrust, and she mimicked his movement, a little off-rhythm at first, then finding it, relearning all the old steps. Their trembling bodies bucked together, splashing, thrashing, both of them finally groaning in orgasm, crying out to God. She gasped and buried her face in his neck, and they stood silently, catching their breath, his cock throbbing inside her until it slipped out on its own, cooling and trickling sperm into the lake.

"That was a long time coming," he said, not meaning to make a bad pun. Jo laughed anyway. It took a moment for him to realize she wasn't laughing, but *crying*.

"What's wrong?"

She looked up at him, eyes filled with tears. "I promised myself I wouldn't do it," she said. "I wouldn't fuck you. It's exactly what he would have wanted, isn't it? The two of us, his golden children, repopulating the earth after the Great Flood."

"What? That's cra—" He stopped himself from saying it, from calling her *crazy*. She'd likely heard it enough over the years. He could only imagine the survivor guilt she must have suffered, growing up the child of mass suicide. Owen hadn't even known the sorrow that darkened his past and had still grown up angry, lonely, cynical, and clinically depressed.

"All of his sermons about how you'd spare us from the flood didn't amount to shit," she said. "You left, and the flood washed it all away."

"What do you mean 'spare' you? What's the flood got to do with me?"

Jo shook her head. "I envy you, you know that? You don't remember anything. I can't *stop* remembering."

"I was *five*," he said. "You want me to feel bad for you, believe me, I do. But if you're expecting me to feel guilty, you can forget it. What did you want me to do? Beg my mother to turn the car around?"

"Yes!" she cried. "*I* would have."

"Hell, Jo, for all I know, I *might* have! I don't even remember this town, I barely remember *you*. I don't even know my own *father*, for God's sake!"

She muttered something, her eyes downcast.

"What did you say?"

"I said, 'Yes, you do.'"

"How the hell would you know what I know or don't know?"

Jo shook her head, chuckling at his stupidity. "You know who he is, Owen," she said. "Why do you think he wanted you here so badly—bad enough to murder a girl who had absolutely nothing to do with us, with that church? A girl who wasn't even *born* when they were already dead!"

Owen swallowed hard. He should have known—Crouch had made it so simple for him. Even he should have been able to see the Mystery. "What are you saying?" he said, refusing to believe it. "You're saying he—Crouch is...?"

"Everett Crouch is your father," she said.

## YE OF LITTLE FAITH

LORI HAD BEEN home for two days when Owen stepped through the front door, unlocking it with his mother's spare key. "The prodigal son returneth!" she exclaimed, grabbing him up in a hug.

"It's almost like you were expecting me," he said, fumbling with his baggage as she squeezed the life out of him. Loose dreads of her blonde hair pricked his chin. "Where's Mom?"

"In the kitchen with my dad." She took Owen's bag from him. "Take off your coat, stay a while."

"Gerald's here?" Owen hung his coat on the rack while he kicked off his boots. Early October, and it was already chilly, but at least it had yet to snow.

"Don't start. He's off the sauce."

"Just as long as he doesn't try and lead us in a blessing before dinner."

Lori barked laughter. Her laugh was infectious, and Owen joined in. They sat in the living room, on the same old sofa and loveseat they'd sat on as kids. On the television, much bigger than the one they'd had when they both lived at home, Dorothy skipped hand-in-hand with the Tin Man, the Scarecrow, and the Cowardly Lion down the Yellow Brick Road. They watched the muted images in silence for a moment as pleasant memories from their youth came drifting back to Owen.

"Remember when you used to sit upside down in that chair?"

She grinned, tucking her sock feet under her knees. "I don't need to anymore. I live my life that way."

Owen nodded. "You look good. Tanned."

"You look like shit. Tired."

"Now that we've got the pleasantries out of the way... I could really use a drink."

"Oh, feeling adventurous, huh? What'll it be? Coke or ginger ale?"

"Just some water."

Lori made to get up, but Owen held up a hand to stop her. "I'll get it. I should put in an appearance, anyway."

Owen went to the kitchen, leaving Lori behind. Gerald leaned against the kitchen counter, drinking a glass of sparkling amber liquid Owen assumed was infused with alcohol. He tipped the glass toward Owen, swallowing and smacking his lips before saying, "Owen! Your mother and I were just talking about you."

"You know I love it when people talk about me, Gerald."

His mother turned with moist stuffing stuck to her bare hands. The pork roast rested in the large roasting pan, tied and dressed with sprigs of rosemary. "Owen, be a lamb and turn on the sink for me." Gerald reached the sink before he could, and she washed her hands thoroughly. Owen stood beside her, waiting to give her a hug.

"Ginger ale, Owen?" Gerald asked, ice clinking as he raised his perspiring glass.

"Is that all that is?"

A scowl flashed on the old man's face, then softened. "How about you, Margaret? Something to drink?"

"I'm fine, thank you." Her hands dried, she allowed Owen to hug her. She was just skin and bones under the apron, her sweater, and pleated pants. He thought that, if Lori had hugged her with the same enthusiasm she'd showed him, dear old mum might have broken something.

"Can I help you with anything?" Owen asked.

He turned to Gerald, who seemed to be eyeing him queerly. *Probably thinks I'm sucking up*, he thought. He had been surprised to smell nothing but pop in Gerald's drink. Maybe he really was off the sauce, like Lori had said.

"We're fine," Margaret said. "Spend time with your sister. Never know when you might see her again."

Not such an odd thing to say, considering Lori's constant

globetrotting. Owen kissed his mother on the forehead and shuffled back to the living room, where Lori was watching the grease-painted winged monkeys attack the gang. Toto barked as they flew off carrying a screaming Dorothy with them.

"You ever feel like Dorothy?" Lori asked suddenly, looking over.

"I usually feel like Toto."

"The dog or the band?"

Owen chuckled. "That reminds me, where are you off to next? If you're heading to Africa, maybe you could—"

"*Bless the rain*," they said in unison.

"Oh, you've heard that one," he said, grinning.

"Once or twice." She turned back to the TV, fidgeting with the drawstring of her Baja hoodie—avoiding the question, he noticed. Typically she'd go into great detail about her next destination: the culture, the food, the sights, and the indigenous people.

"I'll zip it if you think it'll upset Mom," he said.

She turned to him with her lips pressed flat, then back to the movie. He decided to drop it. If she wanted to tell him, she would tell him. They watched the rest of *The Wizard of Oz* in silence.

"How's the roast?" Gerald asked during dinner.

"Porktastic," Lori said. She'd been off meat for a few years, but had come back with gusto.

"It's a little dry," Owen admitted, making his mother scowl. "But good," he added, pouring on more gravy.

"It's the white meat," Gerald informed him. "White meat is always dry." He patted Margaret's hand, who smiled thinly. Then he lumped mashed potatoes onto a bit of meat from the gristly end, and forked it into his mouth.

They ate in silence a few moments, the only sound the clink of cutlery on dinnerware, and the occasional smack of lips.

"How's that... uhh... What is it you're working on again, Owen?"

Owen finished chewing, sure Gerald was only faking interest and had deliberately waited for him to have food in his mouth, like an overeager server in a restaurant.

"He's doing the new wind farm, up past Streetsville," Lori said for him.

"Right, the turbines." He sipped his ginger ale, probably wishing he'd added scotch to it. "Aren't those things supposed to be dangerous? I heard something about that."

"Don't believe everything you hear, Dad."

"Wind-turbine syndrome," Owen said. "It's only been documented by a handful of scientists going under the assumption that infrasound is damaging to the brain. Chronic sleep loss, headaches, etcetera. I mean, who knows? The ones we're using are sound-dampening, so we're hoping to cut down on these incidents, whether they're real or just perceived."

"I'll tell you what the real headache is," Margaret said. They all awaited her next words, while she scraped up the last of the corn from her plate. "Shop talk at the dinner table."

They finished in silence. When Margaret brought out the pumpkin pie, she spotted Lori fiddling with the necklace Owen had bought her twenty-some-odd years earlier. She dropped the pie plate on the table. It struck heavily, rattling the salt and pepper shakers, the undercooked pie filling sloshing in its crust.

"What on earth is that... *thing*?"

Owen took a closer look, wondering what had troubled her. She'd known about the unicorn pendant since a few days after Christmas that year. Lori hadn't been able to keep it a secret for long. But the faded unicorn dangled from its chain. Between her fingers was a new pendant: this one a shiny crucifix.

"You don't like it?"

"I most certainly do *not*."

Lori wore a smirk, baiting their mother. He remembered the last time they'd played Lori's game, finding the Bible in their mother's closet. It was the last time he'd gone into his mother's room when she wasn't home. Something about that closet had both intrigued and repelled him, but he'd never been quite sure what had made him so ill at ease, considering the contents of the shoebox had been just a water-damaged Bible and a bunch of old pictures of people he didn't know. He'd wanted to forget all about it, and though it had often nagged at him when he'd passed her room on the way up the stairs to his own, or the bathroom, he'd successfully pushed it out of his mind elsewhere.

"Maybe I've had a religious awakening. Anyway, it's just a symbol. What's so bad about it?"

"Just take it off at the dinner table!" Margaret's thighs struck the table, shaking it again, startling everyone seated around it. She composed herself, smoothed the tablecloth, and sat. "I've put up with your silly Rastafarian hair and your incense burning; I should at least be able to eat in my own house without feeling uncomfortable. There. I've said my peace."

"Better listen to your mother," Gerald muttered, and sipped his ginger ale.

"Fine," Lori said, lifting her "Rastafarian hair" to unclasp the chain. She tucked the necklace and both of its pendants into her hoodie pocket.

After dessert, while Gerald and Margaret sat silently, watching an old black-and-white movie on Turner Classics, Owen followed Lori upstairs. "Why were you baiting Mom like that?"

She turned at the top of the steps. "She'll get over it."

"That's not the point. You know she hates that stuff."

"*Does* she?" She lowered her voice, peering over his shoulder at the stairs. "Don't you ever wonder why Mom has a Bible? About who all those people were in those pictures Mom keeps in her shoebox? Why she never talks about anything that happened before I came along?"

He made note of that: how she'd said "keeps," in the present tense, and decided to leave it alone. Accusing her of going into their mother's closet would only exacerbate the rift that had formed between them in her latest absence. "Mom's old life is her own business. If she doesn't want you dredging up her past, you should probably just leave it alone."

She fixed him with a look of concern. "Don't you ever wonder about your dad?"

Of course he wondered. All he'd ever known of him was what his mother had told him over the years, and it hadn't been much: that he was a strong and determined man, a "great mind," that he'd loved them "fiercely," but he'd "wandered off" when Owen was five. He'd wondered why his father had left them, left *him*. He'd wondered what he looked like now. If he was still alive, or dead, or had run away from the law. It was hard to know how not to grow up like his deadbeat father when he knew so little about him. "No," he said. "I don't think about it. It doesn't concern me."

Lori gave him a hard look, her blue eyes glistening so that Owen thought she might be about to cry. "Don't lie to me, Owns." Her voice was unnaturally quiet.

"I don't *care*, Lori. Honestly, I couldn't give a shit if the man was dead."

Her lower lip quivered. She turned from him, storming off to her bedroom and slammed the door. After a moment of indecision, Owen followed.

"What's all that racket up there?" Margaret called from below.

"Nothing, Mom!" He thumped softly on Lori's door. "Lori, I'm sorry, okay? I don't even know what I did, but I'm sorry."

"Forget it," he heard her say, her voice muffled.

He leaned his forehead against the door, wondering why things couldn't be like they'd been when they were kids. Wondering why they had drifted apart. But he knew it had probably been his fault. He'd always been distant and indifferent. Lori had brought the best out of him, but that had been a long time ago, in a different life. They were adults now. They were very different people.

Owen pushed himself up from the door. He turned from her room, about to head back downstairs, when Lori's sniffle brought him back. "Do you remember that ghost you saw when we were kids?" she said, her voice tremulous. "You always called it my ghost, but it was never mine."

He answered weakly, "That was a long time ago, Lori."

"No. No, it really wasn't. He's been following you your whole life, you see, and you don't even know it. You don't even care enough to wonder what that means."

"No," he said. He felt something close to tears. "I don't."

Lori said nothing more. A moment later, she came out with her giant backpack slung over her shoulders, cinched at the waist.

"Where are you going?"

She scowled at him. "I thought you didn't care." She pushed past him, heading for the stairs.

"Don't leave, Lori."

Her footsteps thudded down the steps.

"Lori..." He stayed put, having followed Lori and her crazy whims too many times in the past. "Come on, Lori."

She reached the first floor, and disappeared around the corner into the living room. Owen, still standing at the top of the stairs, heard Gerald protest her leaving.

"I've got somewhere I need to go," she said. "The bus leaves in an hour."

"Where are you going?"

"I'll call you when I get there. Love you, Mom, Dad."

She stepped out through the archway, blowing them kisses from the foyer. Owen hadn't moved from the top of the stairs when she looked up from the open front door with a forlorn expression.

Owen merely shook his head.

Lori's shoulders sagged. She pressed her lips together, resolute. Then she turned and walked out the door, pulling it shut behind her. He let her go.

# PART THREE

HOLY GHOSTS

# CHAPTER 10

## BURNT OFFERINGS

I

OWEN WOKE WITH the sun in his eyes. He'd slept through the night with no two o'clock wakeup call, and he felt well-rested for the first time in months. Rolling over, he expected to find Jo asleep beside him, but the other side of the bed was empty and cold, the sheet flipped back like the dog-eared page of a paperback.

*Must have left while I was sleeping. I guess I should be glad she came inside at all, considering the way I found her.*

She'd led him by the hand to the bedroom, where they'd lain in each other's arms, two desperately lonely souls enjoying the warmth of each other's bodies, the rush of blood in their veins. They'd breathed, without speaking, to the night music drifting in through the window—the lonely cry of the loon, the chorus of frogs, the far-off drone of a motorboat echoing across the lake—and had eventually drifted asleep.

Owen drew his arms behind his head and lay in a warm place on the pillow for a moment, thinking about everything that had happened the past few days. The stories, the mysteries, the revelations, the friends made and lost, friends found again, the sudden, tragic departures. He'd lived more in the last week than he had in the last several years. If he made it out of Chapel Lake alive, he'd be sure to make a lot of changes back home.

*Maybe Jo could come with me*, he thought. Then again, maybe not. She hadn't even been willing to spend the whole night.

Smiling, Owen climbed out of bed and got dressed. The lake had washed away their sweat. He thought he'd be fine without a shower, and he didn't want to step into the bath anyhow. Twisting the sink handle warily, he brushed his teeth, spat into the sink, rinsed out his mouth under the tap.

He smiled at his reflection in the mirror. All the sun he'd gotten on the lake and reading on the deck had given him a healthy look. Lori was still dead, but the smile felt right on his face. He felt born again, not quite in a spiritual way—more that he felt like a new person. A *different* person. Someone whose decisions and actions might surprise even himself.

The smile remained as he peered down into the living room to find Jo in the recliner, but faltered when he saw the book in her lap. It was Lori's journal, her letters to him. To find Jo reading his sister's words felt like a terrible violation, like someone listening in on a private conversation.

Yesterday, Owen would have reacted in anger. Today, he managed to shrug it off. "You're still here," he said.

Jo raised her head from the journal, closing the book quickly and straightening up as if she'd been caught in the act of something. "I guess you hoped I'd be gone, huh?"

"I'd hoped you'd stay in bed. Make up for lost time." He crossed to her, planted a kiss on her forehead. It occurred to him the last person he'd kissed on the forehead was his mother, after Lori's funeral, but he didn't let the memory sour his mood. "I see you found my sister's journal," he said, sitting beside her on the armrest.

Jo tilted her head up to him with a guilty look. "I hope you don't mind..."

"Why would I mind?"

"I don't know." She set the book on the table beside the unplugged lamp. "It's like reading someone else's mail."

"You probably know most of it anyway. The stuff you don't, what she said about me—"

"The stuff about the sandcastle? It's a helluva lot more complimentary than what she says about me later on," she admitted.

"I haven't gotten that far."

"Where did you leave off?"

"Crouch's visit."

"He visited me, too. The other night."

They both looked toward the journal, then to each other. Neither dared pick it up.

"Do you think he might have come to visit her a second time?" he said. "I mean, could he have been here the night she died?"

Jo let out a heavy breath. "I don't know. Didn't they say she was diving? Had all her gear on?" She shrugged. "I mean, I suppose she could have followed him out there. To the church."

Owen muttered in solemn agreement, wondering if that was what Crouch had wanted him to do the other night.

"What I do know is your sister was right," Jo said, pointing at the journal. "This place is haunted, Owen. *All of it*. And it's not just the church, it's that lake—you have no idea what it did to us. To this *town*. It divided us. It tore us apart. The ones who stayed with the church after the Purification, you and your mother, my parents and me—they *shunned* us, Owen. People literally cross the street when they see me coming, *to this day*. 'There goes Crazy Jo Dunsmuir. Church runs away from her, even her own parents crash their car just to get away from her.'"

"I'm sorry to hear that," he said. "Honestly."

She shrugged it off. "People die," she said, putting on a good poker face, but she couldn't keep the sadness from creeping into her voice.

"That seems to be a common theme around here."

She chuckled morosely. "You know, the first time I saw Father Crouch after the flood, I was fifteen. He was at my parents' funeral, watching from afar. I thought for sure what people had said was true, that the Blessed Trinity had run away and left us behind, that you and your mother left with them. But when I saw him standing in the trees beyond the tombstones, that's when I knew the Blessed Trinity hadn't run away. Because *Father Crouch hadn't aged a day*. He was the exact same man who used to bounce me on his knee, ten years before."

Owen couldn't picture the man having ever bounced anyone on his knee. Then again, he couldn't imagine Everett Crouch having ever lived in a single family home with a wife and a young son. Clearly, his father was full of surprises.

"For ten years I wondered what happened to you," Jo said. "I kept thinking you'd come back, and we'd pick up right where we left off. We'd be best friends again, and no one would make fun of me anymore because they'd have to deal with two of us. But when I saw Crouch standing there, white as chalk, as young as the day we left the Trinity, I knew then you were never coming back to save me. Or if you did, it would just make people think I was even crazier." Her eyes grew large as she looked up at him. "*You'd died with him*, Owen. That's what I believed. And that's when I lost all hope."

Owen smoothed the hair on the back of her head. "I'm here now," he said. She gave him a weak smile, took his hand in hers and tucked it into her lap.

"For a long time I believed I was in love with you," she said, and mocked herself in the voices of her bullies: "'In love with a dead kid, what'll Crazy Jo think of next?' But I was just obsessed with the idea of you. You were my White Knight."

Owen nodded thoughtfully. "Now you're mine," he said, and grinned.

"Ha. I guess that's true, isn't it? Don't get any crazy ideas, Owen. Crazier than all the rest of this, I mean."

The two of them laughed. Their laughter died quickly.

"After the funeral," she said, "I guess I traded you in for another obsession. Pete Jebson taught me how to dive. He's always been a good friend to me. My *only* friend. He believed me when I said you all were dead. He told me he sees them, too. Mostly in his dreams, but once..."

"Once, what?"

"He was the one who found my parents," she said.

Owen took a seat across from her on the couch and watched her intently.

"It was right near his house on the county road where it happened. He was putting in a new mailbox—they still delivered door-to-door back then, now they've got everyone in boxes at the post office. Jeb was hammering his mailbox into the dirt when my parents drove by. They were driving really slow with their windows down, he said, singing 'Old-Time Religion,' you know, the one that goes 'Gimme that—'"

"I know it," he said, sparing her from singing it.

She offered a shy smile of gratitude before continuing. "They were driving really slow, like I said, singing that song at the top of their lungs. Jeb recognized their car long before they passed. It was pretty easy to spot, probably the only Lada left in existence in North America around that time. It was only the two of them singing, but someone was in the backseat, and at first he thought it was me."

"It wasn't you."

Jo shook her head. "No, I wasn't there," she said, looking at her hands.

"It was Crouch."

She agreed silently. "Jeb said if he hadn't had the mailbox there to hold him up he would have fallen over out of pure shock. Sitting there in the backseat was a man he hadn't seen in ten years, who hadn't aged a day, smiling out at Jeb while my parents drove by singing spirituals at the top of their lungs. Only he said, 'In a kind of religious fervor,' which sounds like my parents one-hundred percent, even after we'd left the church.

"They thought they'd gotten away, Owen. But Crouch was just biding his time. *Good things come to those who wait*. Isn't that what the Bible says?"

"I think it's from something else. Like how the thing about give a man a fish he'll eat for a day, teach him to fish he'll eat for a lifetime is usually thought to be from the Bible, but it's actually—" She was looking askance at him. "What?"

"You sure took a lot more from Sunday school than I did."

"Sorry. It's been coming back. Go on."

She eyed him to be sure he was through interrupting. Then, "Jeb heard the tires squeal, and then a loud crash. They were barely going twenty, but he knew it was a pretty steep drop down to the marsh, and it gets deep out there on the county road since they put in the dam. He ran out there in his work boots. They were still singing, he told me, 'Still rejoicing even while they were dying,' he said, while he ran toward the car. Then their voices just stopped."

Jo licked her lips. It seemed like she wouldn't go on, but she gathered herself, and continued. "They'd gone about a kilometer up the road while Jeb stood frozen at the end of his driveway, holding himself up by his mailbox. When he got to where their tires peeled-up on the asphalt, the car had already sunk up to the back doors, half buried in wild rice shoots as tall as him. He climbed down to the ditch, just about slipped all the way down in the soft gravel and twisted up his ankle. When he got one of the back doors open, all this brown water came rushing out. Crouch wasn't there in the backseat anymore. My parents still had their seat belts on. He said they were smiling."

*He'd whispered in their ears,* Owen thought. *He'd filled their minds full of his black filth, full of his poison. Maybe he made them think it was their own idea, so they'd go on believing their suicide was righteous until the very end.*

"There's only a handful of us left now," Jo said. "You and me, your mother, Howard Lansall, Mr. Wickman, and Beau Parrish. I don't have proof, Owen, but I believe it in my heart: your father and the Blessed Trinity are down there, under that lake. *In that church.*"

"Howard Lansall said the same," Owen said, and told Jo the story Howard had told him. By the time he was through, she had tears standing in her eyes.

"He knew all this time, he knew everything people said about me, and he never told me a thing," she said. The tears fell. She wiped them away angrily.

"Maybe he was afraid you'd tell someone."

"I *told* everyone when my parents died. Nobody believed me then. Why would they believe me now?"

"Because it's getting worse. My sister, and now Howie. This town has lived in the dark for *thirty years.* Now's your chance to show them the light. *Our* chance."

She smiled, sadly hopeful. "But how...?"

"Maybe if—I don't know, if we could prove they're down there, if we could find their remains, and give them a proper Christian burial..." He chuckled. "It sounds so ridiculous out loud. Like something out of a movie."

"But that lake is *haunted* by the Blessed Trinity—you've seen it yourself, Owen. They're much stronger in that lake, but they don't *need* it to hurt us. You saw them somewhere before you came to Chapel Lake, didn't you? Somewhere near water? A puddle in a birdbath, the rainbow from a sprinkler? He *uses the water,* Owen."

"He tried to drown me the night before I came here," Owen said. "If my neighbor hadn't come by at just the right moment with Lori's postcard, I would've drowned in my own bathtub. Everyone would have thought it was suicide, even my mother." He squinted off at the sun streaming in through the kitchen windows, chickadees chirping in the swaying trees. "Who knows? Maybe they would've been right."

Jo put a hand on his knee, nodding in sympathy.

"We have to risk it," he said. "We have to go down there, even if it kills us. People need to know. 'Earth, do not cover my blood,' those were Crouch's last words. 'May my cry never be laid to rest.'"

"It sounds like a curse," Jo said, bitterly.

Owen looked at her. "*Isn't* it?"

2

ON THE FAR EASTERN end of the cottage road, which stretched and curved its way around the north side of Chapel Lake, past the trailer park and the dump where Howie Lansall had lost his life, Jo had lived alone in her family home for almost twenty years.

After the car crash, Jo's great aunt had taken custody of her, moving some of her things into the old house, but mostly she had left Jo to herself. She'd found her niece's daughter odd and moody. She'd never understood her niece's love for "that man" (Jo's father), nor their mutual admiration of Crouch and his "death cult." These were Grenada Thériault's own words, repeated by Jo while they drove. In the eyes of Grenada Thériault, sole heir to a small logging fortune, Joelle Dunsmuir was a product of her niece's forbidden love. She had thrown the term "cult baby" around often.

"She didn't want anything to do with me," Jo said, "but the courts forced me on her. In the end, while the government thought she was living in both houses, mostly she just used my house as a place to store all the junk she'd bought from the shopping channel. When the children's aid people came around, which wasn't very often, they'd always call first. It gave Grenada enough time to drive over from Dunsmuir and make herself at home. I remember she always used to bake cookies when they came. Those were the only times she ever did anything nice, but it was all for show. She gave me a small allowance, and I bought my own groceries with it, did small repairs on the house when it needed them, if I could afford them. I got a job at the Masterfeeds store to supplement what she gave me, which wasn't much, even back then. And once I turned eighteen, I was legally my own guardian. The house was finally mine. I kicked that old bag to the curb, and tossed all her shit out on the lawn."

"Good for you," Owen said, and meant it.

Jo grinned. "You should've seen her face. She was pretty pissed. But I think she was glad she didn't have to deal with me anymore."

"She sounds like a nice lady."

"*So* nice."

Owen pulled up to a stop sign, let a dusty minivan through the intersection of the cottage and trailer park roads. Jo inspected the van as it drove by, and they continued on their way. After a moment, she flicked on the radio on a howling wolf—a promo for the station, a gruff voice announcing it as "*The Wolf... 101.5 FM.*" They sang along to Guns N' Roses "Sweet Child O' Mine." The next song was "Dirty Water," an '80s hit by Canadian band Rock and Hyde. Owen turned off the radio.

"I like that song," Jo said, but Owen left it off.

In another five minutes they reached her house. The brown lawn stretched back from the road to a small, neat bungalow surrounded by forest. Off to the right stood an old water well, with crumbling stone sides and a rotted wood roof. Out near the gate a FOR SALE sign stood, with Skip's face smiling from it.

"You're moving?"

"If it ever sells. Seems like the right time, don't you think?"

Owen thought about what to say. After so many years haunted by the past, Jo Dunsmuir had finally decided to put it behind her. He wondered how long the house had been on the market, if his or his sister's arrival had sparked her decision. He said nothing, only opened the door and climbed out. He followed her to the house.

"Sorry about the mess," she said. "I haven't had time to clean."

"I'm sure it's fine."

Jo unlocked the door. It creaked open on a dim cavern of newspapers and file folders, stacked chest-high. Shoes were scattered in the corner behind the door, both men's and women's. He supposed they must have belonged to her parents. The house smelled dank, like a basement.

Jo must have seen his nostrils flare, because she said, "I had a flood. The pipes burst one night while I was sleeping. Filled the whole basement."

"Was that recent?"

"It happens a lot. I've fixed those old pipes so many times..." She shrugged. "I wouldn't be surprised if it was Crouch, trying to mess with my head. Can I get you something to drink?" she asked him, wandering into the house.

"As long as it's not from the sink."

Jo's laughter echoed through the empty house. Passing the living room doorway, Owen saw more of the same: papers of all kinds, men and women's clothing in scattered piles, sad, sagging curtains, ugly beige broadloom, all of it layered with dust. On the coffee table, more pages were spread out. Blue leaflets from the Blessed Trinity Mission emblazoned with the words he'd seen on his first day at Chapel Lake: *WILL YOU BE EM-BRACED BY THE ARMS OF THE FATHER?*

He stepped into the kitchen, the only bright, clean space in the house, aside from a few dirty dishes in the sink, and found Jo holding a glass under the running tap. The windows behind her overlooked a miserable backyard. Broken lawn furniture, a sad, leafless tree, a lawn consisting almost entirely of dirt. Beyond this was a forest so thick with pines the sunlight couldn't penetrate it.

*This is how she lives*, he thought. *This is her life. Because of* them. *Because Crouch won't leave her in peace.*

Jo held out the glass to him. He knew the water's cloudiness was a harmless release of oxygen, but after all he knew about Chapel Lake, he couldn't bring himself to take the glass. "Don't you have some orange juice? Some Tang?"

"Fresh out."

"I'll pass."

"Suit yourself." She shrugged, and guzzled it, and set it down empty on the counter. After a satisfied gasp, Jo said: "All that stuff in the living room is what I've collected concerning the church. I've got every legitimate piece of Blessed Trinity ephemera I could get my hands on. Some of the original church documents are photocopies, but the blue ones on the coffee table are originals I got in a new haul. Everything else is cult-related. Jonestown. The Moonies, the Raelians and the Branch Davidians. The Solar Temple. Early Mormonism, pre-LDS. Scientology." She sat down hard at the kitchen table. "It's everything I could find, and not a single bit of it explained what I was going through."

He sat beside her on a mismatched stool with a frayed, pea-green vinyl seat cover. "It'll be over soon," he said, hoping to be reassuring, but sounding doubtful even to his own ears.

"Will it?"

He didn't answer, only fiddled with a torn flap of the ugly tablecloth. "You know, I heard about something on a radio call-in show once. I think it might apply to your situation." He considered it. "Hell, it probably applies to both of us. It's called survivor guilt."

"Oh, Christ..." Jo muttered, rolling her eyes.

"I know, I know. But we're kind of stuck together now, so you're obligated to listen to at least one completely uninteresting thing a day. That's a rule, I think."

She rolled her eyes, sighing dramatically. "Fine. But don't think I won't remember this, Saddler."

"You're a gem."

She winked.

"For survivors of traumatic events," he said, "like a death in the family, or war, natural disasters, or, like us, escaping from a cult—having PTSD symptoms is apparently pretty common. Depression, blaming yourself for what happened, vivid nightmares, withdrawing from social situations," he counted them off on his fingers.

"You sound like an ad for a new medication."

Owen laughed. "You know, now that I think about it, I pretty much experienced every one of those at one point or another long before Lori died." Jo laid a hand on his. "With your parents passing, learning as much as you have about the church... it's no wonder you might think Crouch was haunting you because of something you did." He studied her face. "That you maybe deserved it."

She nodded. After a moment, she looked at him dubiously. "Wait a minute. You learned all that from a radio call-in show?"

"It was pretty good." Owen grinned. "I think they were actually talking about alien abductions, but I'm sure you can extrapolate." When she giggled, he slipped a hand into her hair, smoothing his fingers against her scalp, and she leaned into his touch. "Think you're ready to go through those papers, or do you need a minute?"

"Let's get it over with," she said, getting up from the table.

The Blessed Trinity Mission's literature was filled with paranoid ramblings, peppered with Bible quotes whose meanings Crouch had deliberately warped to suit his agenda—typical evangelical rhetoric. What Owen found most fascinating were communiqués, both typed and handwritten, between Everett Crouch and various businesses, legal officials and politicos, not just in Canada but throughout the world. Several were still tucked in envelopes marked RETURN TO SENDER in a hand pointing toward the offending address. And NO SUCH STREET. And UNABLE TO FORWARD.

One of these was written to Roman Polanski at the Benedict Canyon address Charles Manson and his followers had broken into, killing his young wife and unborn child. In it, Everett Crouch urged the director to turn himself in to the authorities for what Crouch called "the impure corruption of an impressionable young woman." Another was addressed to Fidel Castro, pointing to their shared plight, and requesting assistance with his own, noting that American officials "have dismissed Cuba as a nation in much the same way my own government has dismissed my Ministry as a ragtag band of Bible-thumping zealots."

Letters to the Prime Minister's office had been opened and returned, most of them requesting a renewal of tax exemption status for a religious organization under the Charter of Rights and Freedoms. Letters to the Department of Public Works and Minister J. Judd Buchanan demanded the Peace Falls hydroelectric dam project "immediately cease and desist with any and all further disruptions." Form replies from several governing bodies insisted the dam would be "beneficial for the growth and stability of Canada as a nation," and "we regret to inform you that we are unable to grant your organization status as an official religion... Therefore, your request for tax exemption is denied."

Much of the rest was hate mail received by the church, most

of it handwritten, scrawled with angry immediacy. Some were Crouch's responses to these that had been "returned to sender" in the case of an incorrect address.

"Listen to this," Owen said, sitting cross legged on one of many stains in the carpet in front of the coffee table, holding a letter in his hand. "'My friend,'" he read, "'I am deeply troubled you have chosen to accept the deal (read: serpent's temptation) proffered by the Devil's Pimp. Eat of this tree, if you must, but bear in mind that the Lord God Almighty *banished* Adam and Eve from the Garden of Eden! You might also consider the divine words of Jesus Himself: *It is easier for a camel to pass through the eye of a needle, than for a rich man to enter the Kingdom of Heaven.* Yours in Truth'—and truth is capitalized," Owen added, "'The Reverend Everett Crouch.'"

"That's one of my favorites," Jo said, bent over by a bookshelf packed with file folders and stacks of printouts. "I guess he wasn't a big fan of hyperbole."

Owen chuckled. "No, I guess not." He held up the original envelope it had been stuffed back into so she could see. He had to assume the addressee had returned it directly to the church doors by hand, as the offended party had scrawled across the envelope in red marker, *FUCK YOU AND FUCK JESUS!*

Jo barked out a tired laugh, and Owen joined in. The contagious laughter brought them close to tears. But his reflection in the cracked and smudgy mirror leaning against the wall reminded him of the mirror in his childhood bedroom, startling him back to reality, and the laughter caught in his throat. Jo continued a moment longer, then she too returned to the search.

But for what? Neither of them spoke of what they hoped to find. He supposed they were searching for evidence that Crouch and his Ministry were planning to martyr themselves, of Crouch's motivations, for a way to put their spirits to rest... but after a while, it started to seem like busy work. Bills, receipts, and legal documents passed through their hands. Bureaucratic form letters, hate mail, and Crouch's passive-aggressive replies. None of it seemed to matter. And there was nothing, absolutely *nothing* about a man named Brother Woodrow.

They sat quietly, the only sounds the rustling of papers, the ticking of an old grandfather clock, the chirrup of birds outside. Somebody, somewhere, was mowing their lawn. The smell of fresh-cut grass was stronger than the sound was loud. It was a perfect summer day, not too hot or humid. A cool breeze blew in through the window, helped by a fan Jo had stuck in front of it.

*Woulda been a great day to get out on that lake*, Owen thought.

A short while later, Jo discovered a letter among what was clearly worthless correspondence, this one written in the thick, shaky script of someone who'd had difficulty holding a pen. She showed it to Owen.

*My dearest Maggie. For your tireless efforts in transcribing my often rambling thoughts to paper, a thankless task to be sure, and for bearing us a son, whom—God willing—will one day fill my shoes at the pulpit, I pledge to you my undying love.*

It was signed below with a simple *E*.

"It looks like Crouch might have had Parkinson's," she said, referring to the jittery handwriting.

"Or a bad drinking habit," Owen added, remembering Gerald's terrible penmanship.

He sifted through loose papers in a cardboard box, and found what he'd been looking for. They were notes, written in the same scrawling print as the letter Jo had found to his mother. Crouch rambled on for a time before coming to any sort of point. Finally, Crouch mentioned Woodrow by name:

*Brother Woodrow says I'm too soft on the boy. He says a boy needs discipline from his father, not mercy. If the boy wants mercy, it should come from the mother. That's what Woodrow believes, anyhow. Me, I'm not so sure...*

And later:

*Woodrow says I'm preaching too much "God is love" and not enough "God is wrath." He makes a good point, although inadvertently, about the dual nature of the Bible's depiction of God.*

*These two halves of the Bible don't entirely contradict themselves, but they come close many times. The Old Testament God is a vengeful, jealous God, seemingly disappointed in His own creation. "Vengeance is Mine," and "Thou shalt have no other gods before Me." He ejects us angrily from the Garden of Eden, and wipes us all out with a flood, sparing only two of every animal. In the New Testament, God preaches forgiveness through Jesus Christ and salvation through performing good works. He loves His fellow man, in particular the meek, the poor, and those who have sinned.*

*This dualism mirrors what we often feel in our hearts. I'll tell you what I believe: I believe every man has two selves, in constant battle with one another—the man who is, and <u>the man he's meant to be</u>.*

*If one can reconcile these two halves, he will have solved the mystery of what it is to be truly human.*

"'The man who is, and the man he's meant to be,'" Owen said aloud. He liked the sound of it.

"Huh?" Jo said, leafing through a folder.

"Just something Crouch wrote. Not sure if it's profound or complete bullshit."

"Hmm."

Jo didn't appear to be paying attention, absorbed by something in the folder, so Owen returned to the box. He unfolded a page of the *Chapel Lake Breeze* next. This *Special Second Installment* of the biweekly paper was dated December 12, 1979. On the back was the crossword, the bridge column, and a few comics reprinted from major publications. On the front, p. 2, the last half of an article titled "BLESSED TRINITY (CONT.)" took up most of the page. A small crime section in the right margin, listing a break-in at a dairy farm, and a fistfight at the Red Pony during its opening night. An editorial cartoon filled the rest of the page: the caricature of a mustached man running away from church with a briefcase spilling money. The man had a nametag, CROUCH, his briefcase not-so-cleverly labeled INSURANCE PAYOUT.

Curious, Owen read the article:

*Meanwhile, speculation continues as to where Rev. Crouch and his remaining followers have gone. It would seem they have been swept away on the same winds which blew the Plague of Locusts into the Red Sea. Whatever the case may be, this "plague" on*

*Peace Falls (Chapel Lake, rather—Ed.) has ostensibly run its course. As Everett Crouch was fond of reinterpreting and paraphrasing Biblical verse to his somewhat nefarious requirements, I hope you will permit me my own, this from Dickens'* Little Dorrit: *"The old proverb says to* Let sleeping dogs lie. *In the case of the Mad Preacher and his Blessed Missionaries, it is advisable to* Let missing dogs go. *"*

Later, Owen found an entire folder dedicated to financial documents, signed by Everett Crouch and Peter Jebson, the church accountant, which contradicted the cartoonist's idea of monetary gain. "The church really was flat broke," Owen said, shuffling through past-due notices and official letters of foreclosure.

"They would have lost it, with or without the flood," Jo said.

"But they still fought against it," he added. "They still went down with the ship. That's pretty goddamned determined."

"Don't confuse determination with crazy," she said, leaning into a cardboard box and rooting through it. "There it is," she muttered to herself, and came back with a classroom cassette player, and a tape, which she clunkily inserted into it.

Suddenly a man's voice filled the dusty, cramped living room. Owen recognized it right away: blustering, pompous; a televangelist's voice. It could only be Crouch. He pictured the man pacing before a soft chair, speaking into a small microphone, and wondered if what he saw was memory or imagination.

"—beyond which none of us may travel," the voice intoned, "a dark void much like space—" Jo pushed a button, zipping Crouch's voice along at warp speed. Another clunk as she pressed play. "I stood before it, shaking with despair, *thundering* my fists upon the soil—"

"Listen to this," Jo said, as if he could help it. As if Crouch's voice hadn't already wormed its way into his subconscious, deep and pleasant and unwavering. He sounded a lot like Gregory Peck—a voice tailor-made for orating. A voice you couldn't help but *believe.*

"—in the darkness I cried out to God, 'Take this burden from me, Lord!'" A crinkle of paper. It went on for a moment. Then: "I cried out to God, 'Why have you put this obstacle in our path? Why, when all we do is spread your Good Word?'"

Jo was watching for his reaction.

"What is this?" he asked her.

"Crouch recorded all of his sermons when he rehearsed them. This one is where—" She shrugged. "Just listen."

"—the mighty Mushkoweban, awash in moonlight—" Crouch corrected himself. "A *jewel* in moonlight. And as I knelt there in the dirt, garments filthy with my own impudence, my *hubris*. For it was certainly the sin of Pride which put me on the shore that night, brothers and sisters, I confess this to you right here and now." He cleared his throat. A tiny scratch of pen on paper. "And as I knelt there, I noticed the water wasn't making the splishy-splashy sounds you and I have grown accustomed to, brothers and sisters. The water was *speaking to me*."

"It's his burning bush story," Owen said.

Nodding, Jo said, "*Listen.*"

"—it was speaking my name. 'Crouch!' it said. 'Crouch! Crouch!' And at first I thought, 'I must be mad.' Isn't that what they call me out there in the big bad world? The Mad Preacher? Yes, yes," he calmed his imagined defenders. "I'm no stranger to the epithets. I may be a sinner like the rest of us, but willful ignorance is not my sin of choice. I thought I must be mad. Firstly, to wander out to the river in the dead of night, and then to hear voices in the waterfall calling out my name! I put myself in their shoes for a moment, the men and women who curse me as Noah was cursed in his time, or Lot and his wife, and I thought to myself, 'It's no wonder they call me a lunatic!' And yet where the ungodly trusts not his eyes, and turns away his ears, the holy man instead must *listen*. Don't we all yearn to hear the voice of God, our Creator? So I listened, brothers and sisters. I opened up my heart, and the Lord filled me with the Word.

"I said to Him, *I am here*!"

Owen felt his heartbeat quicken, hearing his sister's words in Crouch's voice.

"And God said unto me—" Crouch paused. "I know that, Woodrow. I'm getting to that part now."

Jo stopped the tape, looking up at Owen expectantly.

"*Woodrow!*" Owen said. "He was there in the room with him. He was telling him what to say!"

"I didn't hear his voice," Jo said. "Did you?"

She rewound the tape, pushed play.

"—filled me with the Word. I said to Him, 'I am here!'" Jo leaned close and cranked the volume as high as it would go. Tape hiss filled the air, as loud as a storm in the trees. Crouch's voice boomed, rattling the photos of Jo and her parents on the bookshelf: "AND GOD SAID UNTO ME—"

For a moment there was nothing. Owen and Jo moved close to the tape player, straining to hear through the hiss, the click and whir of the spools. Suddenly a strange, alien muttering made Jo flinch back from the machine, a sound like unintelligible, muffled words spoken through a loudspeaker.

"I KNOW THAT, WOODROW."

Jo reached out, stretching an arm toward the cassette player as if she were afraid to go near, and stopped the tape.

"What was that?"

"I don't know," she said, her eyes widened in fear. "Maybe he was talking to Woodrow over the phone?"

"Maybe." Crouch could just as easily have been speaking to him from the next room. "Maybe it was God speaking to him," he said jokingly.

Jo flashed him a look, turned the volume down, and set the tape whirring again.

"And God said unto me, 'I have seen the misery of My people in your village, and I am concerned about their suffering.' These, you may recall, are the *very same words* God spoke to Moses through the burning bush. God does not love suffering, people, contrary to what the unbelievers would have you think. He feels the suffering of *a single person* as much as He feels that of *an entire people*. That is the lesson of Job in the land of Uz. It was not a test of Job's faith in *Him*, but a testament to *God's own love for Man*.

"There's no question Job was pious," Crouch said, to his imagined parishioners. "A little holier than thou—we can agree on that, can't we?" He chuckled softly, as he if he were laughing along with his congregation. "*Each morning* Job sacrificed a burnt offering for each one of his children—if we count them up, it was *ten* burnt offerings *every single day*—in the *vainglorious* belief that his *children* might not be as holy as their father, and that they may have *cursed* God's name in the night. This was an affront to God, I tell you—this insinuation!"

He paused a moment, cleared his throat.

"But never mind that. Biblical scholars would have you believe the misery set upon Job was at the behest of the Lord, though if you remember, God said to Satan, 'Behold, all that *he* (he, meaning Job) all that *he* hath is in *thy* power; only upon himself put not forth *thine* hand.' *Thy* and *thine*. Well, it's clear enough to me the Lord is giving instructions to Satan, which means it was *Satan*, not God, who *slaughtered* Job's livestock, who *murdered* his children. It is the *Adversary himself* who afflicted Job with boils from the soles of his feet to the crown of his head!"

That inhuman muttering filled the next pause.

"Yes, I'm aware of that. Would you let me continue?" Another pause. "Yet Job... blames God. He accuses God of having *mercy* for evil men, yet no pity for the *devout*, such as himself. Job's friends *implore* him to confess his sins. God would not punish a righteous man unjustly, they tell him. But Job persists. He argues his own innocence. He pleads his case. He *begs* the Lord—in some, let's face it, rather flowery speech—to *erase his birth from history*. To *cast* him into the *darkness*!

"In the meantime, God seems to have put aside his little deal with Satan, at least until pious Job starts finding fault in Creation itself." He chuckled softly. "And the Lord so loveth Job that He spoke to him through the whirlwind, justifying *His work* to Job, all the while under the pretense of *challenging* Job for his insolence!

"The Lord then proceeds to punish Eliphaz, Bidlad, Zophar and Elihu for *daring* to question Job's critique of His Good Work. He punishes *them* for defending *Him*. He then *doubles* Job's fortunes and bestows upon him new, ever more beautiful daughters to replace those children Satan had murdered. All of this Job receives for *daring* to challenge the Lord's wisdom.

"What I'm saying to you, friends, is that God is forgiving. God is *understanding*. He sees our despair, yours and mine, and like Moses at the burning bush, like Job and the whirlwind, He spoke to *me* through that waterfall—the *very instrument* of our impending ruin. But from it... He offered salvation for our Ministry. 'The firstborn of your sons you shall give to Me,' the Lord said—'"

As if on cue, a baby began to cry in the background. "Lord help us," Crouch cursed under his breath. "Can't I get a moment's *peace*?"

The recording ended suddenly, leaving only the hiss of blank tape. After a moment, Jo pressed the stop button.

"'The firstborn son you shall give to Me,'" Owen repeated. "I'm his firstborn son. His only son, as far as I know. If he was planning to—to *sacrifice* me..." He shook his head, feeling sick to his stomach, to his *soul*, unable to believe his own father, as sick as he was, had meant to murder him to save their church.

*The old man was sicker than you thought, Lori. And he's still trying to finish the job, even now. Does he actually believe God will part the water? Does he still think there's a chance?*

Owen answered himself aloud: "He died believing my death would spare them. They probably believed it right up to the end, that if my mother and I had stayed, if he'd gone through with the sacrifice... God would have spared the church."

"You want to know what I think?" Jo offered. "I think Everett Crouch was an undiagnosed schizophrenic, and instead of medication, Peace Falls gave him a pulpit. It's one of history's most flammable combinations: power and paranoia. They go together like Christian terrorists and abortion clinics."

Owen considered it. "I just don't understand why no one noticed until it was too late."

"Can *you* tell the difference between old-fashioned religious fervor and a schizophrenic's religious preoccupation? Before it becomes dangerous, I mean." She waited for his reply. When none came, she continued, "I mean, think about it for a second. There's a giant angry man in the sky who created *everything*, and lets us do whatever we want. But if we don't fear him, he'll send us to a lake of fire for *allll* eternity. Imagine somebody telling you this, if you'd never heard anything about God before. Do you think you'd look up in the sky and tremble? Or would you dismiss it as the ramblings of a madman?"

"Good point, I guess," Owen said.

"George W. Bush said God *told* him to end Saddam Hussein's tyranny in Iraq," she said. "Pope Benedict said God told him to quit being the Pope and devote his life to prayer. Now are we meant to believe God *literally* spoke to them? Why would God ignore extreme poverty, rape, torture, terrorism, one environmental catastrophe after another... and then give His undivided attention to a couple of right-wing megalomaniacs?"

"You're starting to sound a bit like Job," Owen said.

"Maybe that's because, if God exists, *Job was right.*" There was fire in the dark pits of her eyes. "*That's* why God gave everything back to him—along with some new daughters who were even prettier than the ones he'd had before, but let's not even get into that. Maybe God didn't do all that because He *loved* Job, but because God realized what He'd done to Job was the biggest of all dick moves."

Owen grunted in agreement.

"Anyway, we've gotten way off topic," Jo said. "All I know for sure is that God didn't speak to Crouch through the waterfall that night or any night. *Crouch* spoke to Crouch. *In his own mind.*"

"Or this Brother Woodrow. You heard the voice on the tape."

"I heard *something*. Whether it was a voice or not, I don't know."

"Whatever it was, all this stuff only cements what I said earlier. It's me he wants. Lori knew it all along. He's been following me my whole life. *Haunting* me. I've tried to ignore him, to push him away, but if I just... maybe he'll leave the rest of you alone, if I just let him *take* me."

Jo fell back from her knees, dropping down on her butt with her back against the sofa. "Don't say that, Owen. There are other ways. There *has* to be another way."

"What if there aren't?"

"Can't we at least *try*? What if we can—I don't know, what if we can reunite him with Woodrow?"

"What makes you think that would help?" Owen only realized he'd snapped at Jo when her mouth closed hard. "Sorry," he said. "The problem is, we'd have to find him first. And there's no telling if that would even work. I'm the one he wants, not Woodrow. I have to go back down there. I have to find *them.*"

"Then I'm coming with you," she said, the look in her eyes suggesting devotion—or a death wish.

He nodded. She would follow him whether he wanted her to or not, he knew that. Just as he used to follow Lori around, as if she'd been the older sibling, there would be no stopping Jo.

# CHAPTER 11

## ABADDON UNCOVERED

I

TWO LOVERS STOOD side-by-side on the dock at Fisherman's Wharf, dressed in their diving gear. Jo turned to him. "Are we crazy, Owen?"

"This is the only way," he said.

"No, I mean, are we *crazy*? Maybe all of this is just a bunch of awful coincidences. Maybe that church down there drove the whole town nuts, and we're the only ones stupid enough to believe our own eyes."

"What happened to the girl who practically dragged me into the water last night?" he said.

Her shoulders drooped. "Maybe a part of me hoped they would take us, the way they took my parents," she said. "It'd be a pretty poetic death, as far as deaths go, don't you think?"

"Yeah," he said. "Real Romeo and Juliet."

"*All I know* is death, Owen. At least you had your mother and sister. I had no one. I *have* no one."

Owen draped an arm over her waist. "You've got me now," he told her. "I'm not going anywhere without you."

Her voice was small when she said, "You mean that?"

He nodded. She looked up, met his eyes, and kissed his lips. A bead of saliva stretched from her mouth to his as she pulled away. He wiped it from her lips with his thumb, and she smiled at the easy tenderness of the gesture.

"Are you ready?" he asked her.

"I guess I've been preparing for this dive almost my whole

life, so I should be." She shrugged. "If we don't make it out of this alive, I want you to know..." She started to speak, then hesitated. Finally, it came out in a rush. "I could love you again, if that's what you want."

Owen smiled at the thought of it. He couldn't remember if he'd ever really loved anyone, not even Allison, whom he'd been with the longest—or if she'd even loved him. Their relationship, the two or three years or so it had lasted, had been one of convenience. Lori had introduced them at a party, and they'd fallen into bed together, fallen into step with each other. They'd had many of the same interests, architecture being one of the main ones, but their lives had eventually drifted apart. "I guess, maybe, I could love you, too," he said.

Crazy Jo Dunsmuir threw a good punch at his shoulder. He laughed. "What?"

"Don't be a jerk," she said. "I'm trying to have a moment here."

"You're gonna have to get used to me spoiling the moment," he said, shrugging. "It's kind of my thing."

"Is that a threat?" she said, raising an eyebrow.

"It's a promise," Owen told her.

He dove in. Jo was mere steps behind.

———

2

OTHER DIVERS SWAM languidly through the ruins in rays of sediment-mottled sunshine, floating among schools of crappies and sunfish, plucking rocks and junk from the dirt and tossing them away in mild frustration, searching for treasured keepsakes and knickknacks left behind when Peace Falls had been abandoned. Most of them would leave empty-handed. They might find a rusted Zippo lighter, or an old toothbrush scaled with silt, and imagine who they'd belonged to some thirty years ago —but the real secrets lay elsewhere, in a place none of them had dared go. The church cast a menacing shadow over the old town. According to Jo, few had attempted to gain entry since the Crucified Jesus had crushed a young boy to death in 1981 and the windows had been boarded, the doors chained shut.

Jo and Owen stood in its gloom, craning their necks to see the opening she'd kicked out in the second story window. Her plan had been to kick out all the boards barring entry, to let in the light, to provide the most daring explorers access, hoping they would find what others hadn't—what Jo herself *couldn't*, because Crouch wouldn't let her get close.

"I almost died down there," she'd said the night before, as the two of them lay in Hordyke's small bed under the dim glow of the moon. "There was a cave-in. The stairs collapsed on me, pinned me down halfway to the basement. If the landing below hadn't finally given away on its own, I would have drowned, for sure."

Standing in the shadow of the church, Jo pointed to the opening she'd made, and then turned to him, shrugging up her shoulders with a troubled look. *Still want to risk it?*

He nodded.

Jo swam ahead, kicking up silt. Owen followed. He saw Jo slip in through the window and into the darkness beyond. He paused at the windowsill, unable to see through the murk inside. He drew the LED from his belt, flicked it on, and aimed it into the black maw of the haunted church, expecting to find the Reverend Everett Crouch inside, a welcoming smile on his dead man's face, and seated in a comfortable chair, bidding him to his side. There was nothing. He breathed a sigh of relief into the regulator, and then hauled himself in through the window.

His flippers came down on a heap of sediment that had been swept up against the window by the internal current of the church. He stood in front of a large desk and chair, close enough that he'd almost banged his knees climbing in. He swept the LED over the rest of the room. More eyes rose from the gloom, human eyes, flat and tacked to the walls: tattered posters that had somehow weathered the flood. Combo chair desks were scattered about the floor, others were gathered in a pile by the far wall. The pile shifted suddenly in a small avalanche, as if something had disturbed their rest.

*This must have been our Sunday school. Maybe even our only school, after the Schism. Was it just Jo and me, sitting in the front of the class, listening to—who? My mother, or one of the others Selkie couldn't name, teaching us our ABCs and 1-2-3s? Or Crouch, rapping to us about God?*

*Where is Jo, anyway?* he wondered, shining his light over a mural of smiling, round-faced children with chubby arms and legs. All of them had big blue eyes full of joy and wonder, white, black, Asian and Native. They played hopscotch and Cowboys and Indians; they rode Big Wheel tricycles and hung by their legs from trees. One girl was dressed as an angel with wings and halo, praying over a dolly in a casket, while another stood in mourning, wearing a pillbox hat with a veil. Several others wore animal costumes beneath a sign for a production of *Peter and the Wolf*. The entire mural was hand-painted, but the sign for the play had apparently been meant to look as if it had been painted by the children. The wolf, another boy in a costume, peeked out from behind a bush in the background. He appeared to be licking his lips.

Inscribed above all this was a motto, carved into a wooden panel along the length of the wall. The words *LITTLE CHILDREN* stood out under the LED, but the rest was covered in too much silt to be read from a distance. Owen swam to the beginning and wiped it clean, pulling himself along its edge, reading it letter by letter, until the whole motto was revealed. When he had finished, he swam back to take it all in at once.

*SUFFER THE CHILDREN,*
*AND FORBID THEM NOT*
*TO COME UNTO ME:*
*FOR SUCH IS THE*
*KINGDOM OF HEAVEN*

*All we've done is suffer*, Owen thought, though he knew the word had a different meaning here. *Crouch wouldn't let us do anything else.*

His face prickled with oncoming tears, but he'd cried enough for his lost childhood. This place brought no fresh memories, only pain. It was as unmemorable as the child's—*his* —bedroom in the house behind the church. A single doorway led out of the classroom. The small hill of broken school desks beside it tumbled with a hollow metallic *thunk*. Owen swam out, eager to be gone, hoping he'd never have to come back.

He found Jo swimming near the end of the hall. She turned and waved as his LED caught her. Pitch black everywhere except in their little circles of light, the hall was an underwater topiary, its walls caked with mossy algae, the floors littered with broken boards and loose trash (*Refuse*, Owen corrected himself, causing another twinge of sadness), and baseboards sprouting a brownish, lettuce-like plant along its edge. The ceiling had rotted out entirely in places, revealing bare joists where track lights hung loose, their florescent tubes slick with algae. Boards littered the floor. A patch of spruce-like weeds reached out from a large hole between the exposed slats, swaying in the gentle undercurrent. Long, fibrous strands of dark green algae floated elsewhere. Owen pulled a slimy glob from his hair and cast it aside.

*Brings a new meaning to the term "green building,"* he thought, vaguely amused.

Jo swam toward an even darker stairwell, ignoring the doors on either side. Owen tried one, found the handle rusted solid and impossible to open without a great deal of force behind him. He skipped the other door, which was slightly ajar and blocked from the inside by several large wooden crates, and followed Jo to the stairwell, as her head sank beneath the rise into the yawning darkness.

The stairs lay twenty or so feet below. Jo's flashlight swept across a toothy jangle of steps, broken handrails, and balusters, before she disappeared out of sight below the second floor.

*Must be the cave-in Jo mentioned. Lucky she made it out alive.*

Owen followed, a dreamlike feeling washing over him as the perspective shifted, the objects and surroundings so normal and yet somehow otherworldly. Though he'd evidently been here before, this was no world he was used to: here was a realm of scaly, hard-shelled creatures and deadly microbes, a beautiful, shadowy microcosm of algae and human waste, a hauntingly beautiful aquarium. Before the flood, he imagined it would have been scrubbed and swept and polished. It truly was God's House now, more than when he and his mother had come to worship.

He swam down, down, following Jo's lamplight, and when he reached the jagged remains of the stairs, he performed an easy somersault. What he saw when his feet came to rest on the decayed floorboards left him breathless.

The collapsed stairwell opened on the nave, or sanctuary, a

hall so high his light caught nothing of the cathedral ceiling, only brightening as high as the balconies, cluttered with damaged seating. Black stretched above them, like an endless upward-stretching abyss. He felt its oppressive weight as he followed Jo toward the altar.

The baptismal font had tipped and cracked in two. Pews were toppled like dominoes on either side. Bibles, and footwear of all sizes and styles, at least a dozen shoes in all—some paired, but mostly singles—littered the floor by the altar. The Blessed Trinity had left their shoes behind, unable or unwilling to carry them into the afterlife.

Dull colored light shimmered in through cracks in the boards covering the giant stained glass depiction of Moses and the Israelites standing before the parted Red Sea. Crouch had put the mural in after the Schism, perhaps to inspire his followers to believe they could, with divine intervention, part the flood and spare their place of worship from destruction. And when, at last, the Blessed Trinity understood God would not intervene on their behalf, they'd slipped out of their shoes and cast aside their Holy Books. Their Pied Piper had promised salvation in martyrdom, and they'd swallowed Crouch's lies until all that was left to swallow had been water.

Owen sat in the front pew, where he assumed he and his mother had sat when they'd been part of the church, the Dunsmuirs possibly sitting at their side. He closed his eyes, trying to reach into the past and dredge up memories of Father Crouch preaching damnation at the pulpit, of voices raised in song and prayer, of surreptitiously kicking Jo's saddle shoes to get her attention, and, when she turned, pulling a face to make her giggle.

He listened, trying to conjure up the voice of Crouch—whom he refused to think of as his father, no matter what the evidence said. He'd seen enough televangelists to know the shtick: *Put your hand on your television set, brothers and sisters, and the Lord will relieve you of your pain! Reach, brother, reach into the past and you shall see the light. The past is a bright, shining beacon, leading you home. Your soul is sick, your heart is sore! Here I come, Lord, I'm coming home!*

He saw Crouch pacing the floor behind the pulpit, wringing his hands together obsessively, muttering to himself—

*Speaking to God*, Owen's mother would have told him. *Speaking to God*. Owen tried to imagine what the words had meant to a five-year-old. He tried to imagine what he'd been doing in church while his father paced. Something like a memory slowly percolated into his consciousness. He seemed to remember lining up his army men on the pews, playing war until he heard his father's voice. He'd been sitting on the floor between pews, and his father hadn't seen him. Owen had peered over at the sound of his father's voice, had seen the man pull down on a candelabrum to the right of the pulpit, had heard a sharp click echo throughout the nave.

Crouch had opened a passage in the wall. He'd stepped into it, and the door had clicked shut behind him, flush with the wall. Invisible to anyone but those who knew of its existence. The divers looking for treasure, the police searching for the missing members of the Blessed Trinity, would have swam by without ever seeing it.

Jo floated near the secret door, looking but not seeing it, either. Owen pushed up from the pew and swam for her. He found the rusted remains of the candelabrum, and pulled with all his strength. A portion of the wall swung into the darkness with a cloud of silt. Jo turned to him, her eyes wide. She grabbed him in an excited hug before the two of them peered into the darkness.

Owen stepped in first, LED illuminating the wall directly in front of him, no more than three feet away. A bare bulb hung from the low ceiling, and a rusted chain pulley. It wasn't a room, as he'd expected—it was a *stairwell*.

He threw a look over his shoulder. Jo nodded, urging him forward.

The stairs were undamaged, eerily free of debris and algae, and descended to a riser before a sharp left into pitch dark. Owen swam down into the watery darkness.

Jo's light fell over his shoulder, throwing his long shadow in a snaking pattern down the steps. He settled his flippers down on the first riser, heart beating rapidly.

*He's here, Owns.* His sister's words echoed in his mind. *Crouch is here, I can* feel *it. This is the place.*

He waited for Jo to meet him on the riser, waited until she

was standing right beside him, then he pulled himself around the wall, and shined his light into the dark.

A mere ten steps led down to a steel door of what was likely a fallout shelter. The large crucifix from the altar had been wedged between it and the stairs, barricading the door. Owen didn't know what to make of this; it didn't jibe with what they'd learned. From Jo's expression, neither did she.

Owen got down on his knees and began to pull. Jo crouched beside him, and the two of them strained their muscles until the cross came unstuck with a great groan, reverberating the stairs and shaking silt from the ceiling like flakes of brown-green snow. Together they moved the cross aside. It stood a good eight feet against the wall, even leaning.

He turned to Jo. They shared an anxious look.

*How long has she been trying to find this place?* he wondered. *Years? If she finds what she's looking for, will she let that be the end of it?*

Owen nodded her ahead. Jo descended the last two steps, reached out for the uppermost door handle. He came down behind her, reluctantly, and took the handle nearest the floor. They twisted them together.

The door came open with a groan of rusted metal and swung heavily outward. Its weight and the suddenness of its opening threw them back against the stairs. The regulator rattled between Owen's teeth as his ass struck a stair, sending a judder of pain up his jaw. They sat there a moment, both of them winded, peering into the cold, dark abyss of the cellar.

Jo shined her light inside. The chamber resembled the inside of a cave, walls coated with thick algae the color of sick phlegm, jagged stalactites of the same orange-brown oozing down from the ceiling. It covered the floor, too, mottled and bubbled, repulsive and slimy. The shelves lining the walls were so thickly buried it was impossible to determine the objects beneath.

Jo grabbed him by the shoulder. She pointed at her nose, her mouth, and then shook her head roughly: *Don't breathe this. Don't drink this.*

She took a cautious step inside, her foot in the sock of her wetsuit squishing down into the phlegmy mess. She kneeled a few paces in through the doorway and began tearing at the sludge. She cast the clumps aside, breaking apart into smaller bits that floated between him and Jo like dust. Her fingers reached bare earth without finding anything, and she crawled a few feet to try again, digging furiously.

He knew what she was looking for, and pushed aside his disgust to crouch down beside her, where he reached into the muck himself and tore it up in big hunks that broke apart, sifting through the fingers of his gloves like handfuls of beach sand. It wasn't long before he grabbed onto something solid, and he pulled the thing up to examine it under his LED.

It was a bone, long and naked. He turned, holding it out to Jo—but she'd dug up remains herself, and pulled out a half-buried skull from the sludge, unmistakeably human. In the place he'd found the limb, he found the rotted bones of a hand hanging limp at its end. Brushing away more loose, slimy detritus, he exposed a ribcage, scraps of black fabric hanging from the bones. The ribs were shattered in places, as if something had punctured the chest. A small, leather-bound book lay beside it in the muck, its remaining pages clumped together. Owen wiped scum from the cover, several bits of paper tore and floated away in a cloud of silt. The words HOLY BIBLE did not surprise him.

Owen remembered his dream of the corpse hand that had dragged him under the water, and his whole body wracked with a sudden shudder. The walls, the shelves along them, the floor and the ceiling, all of it congealed with a sloppy mass of organisms formed by the decomposition of human remains. Under the living sludge lay the moldered skeletons of Everett Crouch and his Blessed Trinity.

He almost gagged, but managed to fight it back, struggling to keep his lips tight around the regulator, for fear of getting any loose detritus in his mouth.

*Howie was right: the lake is poisoned, but not by the dump—by the dead.*

Jo stopped digging and crawled to him, snatched the bones from his hand. Behind her mask, her eyes had changed, her brow knitted. It was difficult to decipher the emotion—fear, vindication, sadness, or some combination of the three, he couldn't tell.

Owen had seen enough, had never wanted to flee from

somewhere as badly in his whole life. But he didn't dare go without her—for his own safety as much as Jo's. Crouch was *everywhere* down here. Molecules of him drifted in the water around them; no wonder he could manipulate it, no wonder he could use it to kill. Everett Crouch wasn't just *a part* of the water. He *was* the water.

Jo raised the bone over her head and drove it down onto the bare earth, shattering it to bits.

Owen twisted his look of shock into sympathy—but Jo whirled away from his touch, and flung herself from the shelter, kicking away, raising a cloud of filth around him.

He was alone. Alone with *them*.

*Have to leave. I have to go* now.

The sludge on the cellar floor began to writhe beneath his feet—it was *living*. Shapes formed in the gelatinous soup, gnarled limbs and misshapen heads, twisted faces crying out in voiceless agony.

*The dead are in deep anguish, those beneath the waters and all that live in them... Abaddonuncovered...*

Owen turned with dreamlike sluggishness, swimming for the door. The viscous sludge reached out for him, clawing at his legs, stretching down from the ceiling to snatch at his arms, his shoulders.

He squirmed out of its reach, kicking out into the stairwell, taking shallow, quick breaths of cold, dead air, hyperventilation inevitable now. Jo had slipped away into the dark. Without turning to see the horrid things at his heels, Owen pushed the door closed. The living sludge slammed against it, throwing him back, but he dug his heel in against the bottom stair and pushed with all his strength. It wasn't enough. His muscles strained under the pressure, stiffening painfully.

He threw his shoulder against the door, then reached out for the cross with his free hand and pulled it down. It struck the door with a reverberating clang like the toll of a bell, forcing the evil sludge back into the darkness and slamming the door shut.

Hastily, Owen jerked up the rusted handles, locking the shelter door, and swam up from the tomb, leaving only death in his wake.

3

JO WAITED for him on the dock, the regulator hanging between her legs, face cradled in her hands, shoulders hitching as she wept.

Owen sat down beside her. After a long moment, Jo felt him there, and pressed up against him. He put an arm around her shoulder to draw her close.

"It's all death down there," she said finally, speaking into his chest. "They were *murdered*, Owen. It wasn't suicide. *Somebody locked them in there*." She wiped a forearm under her nose. "We have to let people know. We have to let them *all* know."

"They won't like it."

"*I don't care*." she told him, and the cold look in her eyes made him uneasy.

Owen turned to face the church. Waves crashed against the steeple, the cross a black silhouette against the bright sky as the sun broke free from the clouds. A gull shrieked out on the lake, flying so high it was almost invisible.

He peered into the choppy water at his feet, looking for the dark shape of the church below. Crouch's last words—*Earth, do not cover my blood. May my cry never be laid to rest*—had been somewhat prophetic. However it had happened, the church had survived the flood and so had Everett Crouch. His mortal remains had been buried, but not by earth, and his voice had never been silenced. Until recently, it had only been heard by a few, in the chuckle of the waterfall, in the groan of rusted pipes. In nightmares. In death.

Soon, the doors of that monstrous church would be blown wide open, and the whole world would hear their cries. Soon, Everett Crouch and his Blessed Trinity would be laid to rest.

---

4

THEY DROVE the cottage road to town, Jo sitting silently in the passenger seat, staring blankly out the window the way a trauma victim would. She'd bunched her hands into fists and jammed them between her legs, as if she were cold and struggling to keep herself warm.

As the gate to Hordyke House passed behind them, she turned to him. "The Catholic Church said atheists who are good and just will go to Heaven," she said.

Owen remembered. He used to think of himself as an atheist, a skeptic. He'd never believed in God, at least not as far back as he could remember. He supposed when he was a child he must have believed, and maybe if he'd never left Peace Falls, if the dam had never happened and the flood had never come, if he and his mother had stayed with the church and his father had remained in their lives, he'd be an entirely different man today. He might have followed in his father's footsteps. He might have become a minister—he might have been the Reverend Owen Crouch, minister of the Blessed Trinity Mission, preparing for his next sermon. Of course, it was just as likely he would have rebelled, become the Lost Son. If his father really had been insane, he and his mother might have left whether the flood had swept away their hometown or not.

"The Pope believes in the Big Bang, and evolution," Jo continued. "He said that God isn't some magician who waved a magic wand to create the Earth in seven days." She looked at him finally, her eyes misty. "Who knows what we'll find out about God next?"

Owen considered it. "Do you believe in God?"

Her dark eyes seemed to search for a motive behind the question. "Do *you*?"

Owen considered it. "I guess if I truly believed, the answer would be easy," he said, struggling for the words to express what he'd felt his whole life. "But maybe faith is supposed to be a... a constant struggle between the known and unknown, the rational and the spiritual." He turned to see if she was following along; she'd pooched out her lower lip in deliberation, but otherwise expressed no opinion. "Faith doesn't look for proof," he said, "faith exists in the *absence* of proof. In that way, belief in God is a lot like believing in love, I think." Jo scowled at this, though he couldn't tell if she disagreed or was merely considering it. "Science tells us love is chemical, right? A reaction in our brains. But we can *feel* love swell in our hearts. Losing someone we love feels like a hole in ourselves. Like a... like a vast emptiness. It's like a piece of us is missing."

"I think you're avoiding the question."

"Well, it's complicated," he said. "Okay, more to the point. My sister believed that ghosts and God couldn't exist in the same universe. You've read her journal, you know what I mean. See, the Bible does talk about spirit beings, but they're generally interpreted as angels and demons. There's only one instance of an actual haunting in the Bible, but it's not by a ghost, it's a man possessed by demons, haunting a graveyard."

"So... what? You think Crouch and the others are *demons*? Or angels?"

"I don't know what I believe," he said. "I'd never even considered the *possibility* of ghosts until last week."

"I wish I could say the same," she said, turning back to the trees that whipped by her window, squinting out, her face brightened by intermittent sunlight.

They drove in silence, gravel crunching under the tires. In the rear-view mirror, a big old black '70s monster with a shiny, toothy grill emerged from the cloud of dust kicked up behind them. Owen took the corner, and for a moment, it disappeared behind the trees. Then it was back, hogging the road, swerving wildly.

*Maniac*, Owen thought. "If we take what the Bible says literally," he said, trying to ignore his creeping paranoia, "demons, or a single demon, has been using Crouch and his congregation as puppets, for their own nefarious purposes. That's one interpretation."

"You're using rationality to explain the irrational. Isn't believing in ghosts the same as faith, too?"

"Whether it's demons or ghosts we're dealing with, we're in trouble."

"Right."

Behind them, the elderly engine roared. The big American car lurched forward, catching up, and the driver laid on the horn. Jo twisted to look over the seat.

"Who the hell is this?" Owen asked.

"That's Jeb's car. Pete Jebson." She scowled. "What's he *doing?*"

Owen kept driving to a long, straight stretch and pulled

over into the soft ditch. Jeb's behemoth tore up gravel as it ground to a halt behind them.

The old man wore a look of deep concern as he hauled himself out, visible even before he stood alongside his car. Something was wrong. Smoke or steam rose from the hood. The engine rattled angrily.

Owen and Jo got out of the car. Owen recognized Pete Jebson right away—he was the bearded old man from Lori's funeral, the man who'd told Owen he looked just like his father. He understood now the old man had meant Crouch, although having seen his father, Owen hardly thought they looked alike. The argument Jeb and his mother had must have been about him being at the funeral. She must have been worried the old man would reveal the truth to Owen, and ordered him to leave.

"Jeb?" Jo said, moving toward him. "What's wrong?"

The old man began waving his arms fervently, gesturing for her to steer clear. "You aren't safe!" he shouted. "None of us are! I never should have trusted him! Dink... oh, God, Dink Deakins is dead! Drowned in his canoe! I never should have—"

The hood shot upward with a vicious *BOOM!*

Blackened debris shot out on a gust of blistering steam. Owen and Jo ducked back from the explosion; Pete Jebson wasn't so lucky. A small chunk of metal smashed through the rear window of Owen's car, while Jeb threw his hands up to his face. In a moment, blood began to pour from between his fingers.

Jo cried Jeb's name, hurrying to his side, and Owen took up behind her, eyeballing the steam still rising from the hood with caution, his mind making unconscious connections: *Steam and water, water and Crouch, Crouch and death.*

"Get away from the car!" he shouted to Jo, who threw an irritated look over her shoulder before reaching out to the old man, saying something softly to Jeb, trying to keep him calm. Jeb pushed her hands away, revealing his face. Looking at Jeb's ruined face reminded Owen of Brother Woodrow in his dream, though Jeb had suffered far worse: flaps of skin and white, blood-streaked hair hung loose from glistening muscle and bone, his right eye obliterated, the other rolling wildly in its socket. Jeb's lower lip had been completely torn off, his teeth shattered, sharp little pink and white bits left in his moaning, bloody hole of a mouth that opened and closed as if Jeb were a fish gasping for breath.

Jo stumbled back, a look of horror in her tear-rimmed eyes as she brought a hand to her widened lips. "Jeb—" she said, quietly, as if raising her voice might make his injuries somehow worse, "Jeb, we need to take you to the hospital."

The old man shook his head violently, red flaps of flesh waggling like lures on a fishing vest. "*Ay... away,*" the old man said with his lipless mouth, and he stumbled off half-blind into the woods.

Jo turned to Owen with a distressed look, then followed after the old man. Owen gave the old car a wide berth and chased after her.

Pete Jebson slid down the gravel ditch on his ass. He got to his feet unsteadily, snagged himself in the brambles of a raspberry bush, and tore his shirt breaking free to the other side. Jo avoided the bushes, trudging over a slightly less prickly juniper, and Owen followed in her footsteps. The old man broke for the trees then, swinging his arms out before him, low spruce branches springing forward then back again as he brushed through. He bumped headfirst into a white birch as Owen and Jo caught up to him. His blood streaked its pale flesh, looking like a blazing red trail marker.

Owen took the old man by the shoulder, trying to be both forceful and delicate. Jeb jerked free and lurched onward, dead leaves crunching underfoot. It was a straight shot through the stand of birches to the clear blue sky.

"He's heading for the water," he told Jo.

She nodded, sickly grim. "Crouch is calling him home," she said, watching the old man stagger away.

Owen rushed after him. Jo hurried alongside him, but when Owen glanced at her and saw the look in her eyes, he knew her heart was no longer in it. She merely pushed on with a vacant stare. They finally caught up to Jeb at the cliff's edge, where he stood silhouetted against the clear blue sky and a skeletal line of hydro towers teetering on the smooth, round bedrock. The loose white sack of his obliterated eye swung on its socket like a clock's pendulum as he turned drunkenly toward Jo and Owen, holding out his arms to steady himself. Off to the right was the massive Mushkoweban Falls Hydroelectric Dam, a smooth wall of concrete with eight sluice tunnels pouring water down into the river below. The roaring water spread out like a frothy cloud.

"*I'ng... solly,*" the old man said, an apology uttered without lips, a look of shame and guilt still recognizable on the ruin of his face. He took a lurching step backward before either of them could seize him.

Jo gasped as the old man tumbled over the edge. A moment later, they heard the dull crunch of the old man's bones. Something had broken his fall toward the lake. Owen stepped to the edge and looked down. Jeb had landed on an outcrop a few feet from where they stood, his broken body twisted back around the stump of a tree that had grown at the edge of the cliff. Twenty, thirty feet farther along the edge, and he would have dashed his brains out on the rocky shore below; here, he'd only succeeding in drawing out his pain. He groaned. His tongue came out to lick at his splintered teeth, and came away bloodied.

Owen looked for a way to climb down without killing himself. The bedrock was smooth, and seemed to have no footholds. Far below, waves crashed against jagged rocks, a vertiginous height. Jeb groaned again, his legs jittering like a dead insect's.

"*Look,*" Jo said.

At first Owen couldn't see what she was pointing at. He had to shade his eyes with a hand before he spotted the glistening moisture creeping up the rocks at the base of the cliff. He turned to Jo, catching something in her eyes he couldn't place.

"What the hell is—?" he started, but he understood before he'd finished. Crouch had called Pete Jebson home; and the Blessed Trinity were rolling out the welcome mat.

A puddle of water began spreading on the ground around them. Dead pine needles crept forward as the rising water gathered bark and twigs and bits of moss—along with a snail, the stalks of its eyes writhing confusedly—and moved it toward Jeb with a gentle *ssshhhhhh*. Unholy terror seized Owen, then, as the water suddenly rose from the ground, sloughing off the detritus it had gathered—rose and *took shape*, swirling like a cyclone, lifting Jeb into the air as he moaned in anguish, his limbs jerking outward, his tongue twisting like a blind snake. His remaining eye bulged in dazed fear. Blood spilled from his gaping jaw, and seemed to ooze from his pores as the water spout eddied around him.

Owen thought he recognized the look in Jo's eyes then: she'd seen this thing before.

The water spout splashed onto the ground as if it had been poured from a bucket, pitching the old man's ragged remains back over the edge, this time to the rocks below. With a meaty thud, what was left of Pete Jebson bounded off the rocks and into the surge.

———

5

OWEN AND JO stood at the edge of the cliff, gazing down at the place where Pete Jebson had disappeared into the whitewater, watching for the river to creep upward again, to *shape itself* —but the water that had been solid enough to fling a man to his death moments before merely evaporated on the hot rocks, and nothing further emerged from the churning river.

Jo suddenly stalked away.

"Wait," Owen called, chasing after her. "What *was* that?"

She kept walking, facing the road. "I don't know."

"You've seen it before. Don't lie to me, Jo."

She rounded on him. "Yes, I've seen it before! What difference does it make? Is it gonna bring Jeb back? Howie Lansall? Your *sister*?"

Owen felt the fresh sting of Lori's death as if he'd only just now heard of it. He stood there, hollowed out, mouth agape, as Jo approached him with an accusing finger.

"If Crouch hadn't wanted you back here, *none* of this would have happened! That lake was quiet until *she* came here! Crouch probably had no idea you and your mother had survived the flood until Lori stepped into that lake!"

"What, so you're blaming *me* for this? Like it's my fault I was *born*? Like it's my fault that monster is my father?"

"You never should have come back," she said weakly, shaking her head. She struck him in the chest. "You should have stayed away."

Owen took her by the wrist. She struggled, turning her face

away. He snatched her other hand and pulled her close. "If you really think this wouldn't have happened without me, what do you think Crouch is doing? *He brought me here to end this*. One way or the other, I'm going to make them rest."

She faced him, a look of concern twisting her lips. "What do you mean, 'or the other'?"

"He wants me to drown; I think we've established that much. If busting open that church and burying what's left of them doesn't work..."

Jo looked up at him expectantly, fearfully. Owen thought back to that night in his mother's house, the sound of the faucet drawing him to the bathroom, the plunk of drops into a full tub. He remembered running his own bath, needing desperately to know how it had felt for Lori to drown. His father's poison had already entered his mind by then. Owen remembered the bliss in Crouch's eyes as his father held him under. "We have to end this," he said. "And I think I know how. But first we need to warn the others. Beau Parrish and Mr. Wickman could be in danger."

They pulled into Beau's Self-Serve on the way to Skip's office. The grease-covered kid Owen had seen on his first day in town approached the car. He peered down through the window, first at Owen, then at Jo, squinting when he saw her. Owen wondered if this kid knew her as Crazy Jo, or if the younger generation was unaware of the name.

"He'p you?" he said.

"I hope so. Is Beau around?"

"Beau went off to his kid's place in Haliburton, left me to take care of the shop. Whatcha want with Beau, anyways?"

"Never mind," Jo said, leaning over Owen to look out at the boy. "Thanks for your help."

The kid looked confused. "You don't want no gas or nothin?"

Owen glanced at the gas gauge. "Looks like we're good, thanks."

The kid gave the car the same look Beau had given it, looking at it as if it were an alien spacecraft, then took off his hat and wiped his grease-streaked brow with his forearm.

Pulling out of the station, Jo remarked, "I guess he's safe if he's not Beau's kin."

"*Kin?*" Owen said, and giggled.

She shrugged. "It felt appropriate."

Owen agreed with a nod. "Let's find Skip."

Less than five minutes later, they pulled up in front of the realtor's office. The lot was empty, but it was possible Skip had walked to work on such a nice day. They approached the door together. It was locked, the lights out inside. A CLOSED sign had been placed in the window.

"This doesn't look good," Owen said.

"He's probably just out on a showing. Don't be so paranoid."

Owen shaded his eyes to peer into the darkened office. Nothing looked out of place. He noted, gratefully, the lack of puddles on the floor. "Maybe," he said.

Jo was looking at FOR SALE postings in the window when he stepped away from the door. "Owen, I think I know where to find him."

He came to her side. She pointed at a bungalow advertised as a "starter home," a cozy fixer-upper with "excellent bones."

"Why there?"

"Location, location, location," she said.

Fifteen minutes later, they found Skip's Caddy parked in the long drive at 12 Peace Falls Road, a hatchback behind it. The man himself was shaking the hands of a young, nicely dressed couple with their child in a stroller. Owen and Jo got out of Owen's car and bustled up the drive as the couple tucked their child in its car seat, both father and mother smiling and twiddling their fingers in its face. Owen felt a twinge of sadness, seeing this: the happy family he'd never had.

The bungalow stood on a hill overlooking the lake, an ugly house on a beautiful piece of valuable waterfront property. Skip spotted them. "Owen!" he said, coming toward them and sticking out a hand. While Owen shook it, Skip turned his winning smile on Jo. "Well, well, the old crew's back together, huh? To what do I owe this extreme pleasure?"

"Not what," Owen said, "*who*. Everett Crouch."

Skip's brow furrowed. He peered between them at the young family, who were standing by their car with puzzled looks. "Will you excuse us a moment?" The woman nodded, and Skip ushered Jo and Owen aside. "I guess I should have known seeing the two of you back together was bad news," he muttered. "What's this about Crouch?"

"He's back, Skip," Owen said.

"He never left," Jo corrected.

Skip gazed at the two of them, expressionless. Then he laughed as if it were the funniest thing he'd ever heard. "*Crouch*," he said dubiously, eyes watering.

"He just took another victim back to his church," Jo said. Owen watched Skip's face for a response, disbelief, perhaps; but the man's face remained expressionless, passive. "A waterspout picked Pete Jebson up and dragged him into the river."

"The Hand of God," Skip said ominously, looking off toward the lake. He turned to Owen, perhaps unsure whether he should put his trust in Crazy Jo. "You saw this, too?"

"His radiator exploded in his face," Owen said. "Crouch is using the water. You're not safe; none of us are safe anywhere there's water."

"And what do you expect me to do?" Skip said. "Run away? Barricade myself in my house?" He pulled a sarcastic look of surprise. "Oh, wait. I suppose I can't do that, can I? Running water."

"We just came to tell you to be careful," Jo said, seemingly aggravated. Owen guessed she thought they were wasting their time, that Skip would never believe her.

"Look," Skip said, "let me say goodbye to these lovely people and I'll be right back." He gave Jo a look. "Is that okay?"

Jo shrugged up her shoulders, nodding. Skip walked away. "He won't believe us," she said, once Skip had stepped out of earshot.

"We'll make him believe us. We'll take him out to Jeb's car."

"We should have called the cops."

"And tell them what? We tell the police, and I'm gonna be a suspect. First my sister, then Howie, who I was seen with the day before he died, and now I'm *present* at the scene of Pete Jebson's death? It's cut and dry."

"I'd back up your story."

"You think Constable Selkie would believe you? He still calls you Crazy Jo."

She looked at Owen, his words having obviously stung her.

"I'm sorry, okay?" She shied from his touch. "But just... we have to keep this to ourselves. Just for a little while longer. A day or two, no more. They go digging up those bones down there and bury them, and we'll never figure out what happened to those people in that church."

"Unless someone confesses."

"Whoever did it has lived with their guilt for thirty years. Why would they confess now? Dink and Jeb are already the fall guys. We need to figure out how to end this without involving anyone else. Without getting anyone else hurt." He watched her eyes, waiting for a reaction. "Right?"

She nodded, somewhat sulkily.

A moment later, the family were driving down the driveway, and Skip came back. "I had a feeling this might be on the horizon," he admitted. "Well, not *this*, specifically. I mean, who could predict the Hand of God would rise from the lake to take vengeance on poor old Jeb? But *something* bad."

"What do you mean, 'take vengeance'?" Owen asked.

"'Vengeance is mine, saith the Lord—'"

"I know the verse, Mr. Wickman."

Skip chuckled morosely. "Yes, I imagine you would. I suppose I'm not sure what you mean."

"Why would God take vengeance on Mr. Jebson? For what reason?"

"For betraying the church. For leaving the Trinity in their hour of need. Just like I did."

"It wasn't God's hand, Mr. Wickman," Jo said, with obvious scorn. "It was Crouch."

Skip favored her with a doubtful look. "Everett Crouch is dead, Joelle."

"Somebody oughta tell *him* that."

"Owen—is she serious?"

"I'm afraid so, Mr. Wickman."

"Skip," the man said distractedly, looking ashen. "There's no such thing as ghosts. The Bible says—"

"*Whatever* it is," Jo interrupted, "ghosts, demons, Puff the Magic Dragon—it's *Crouch*. He's bringing us back, one by one. It's wearing his *face*."

"The Devil has many faces," Skip muttered, swallowing a lump in his throat. "You know, I'd always prayed that Crouch and the others had run off to start a *real* mission in some impoverished country. Like Haiti. Or Guatemala. Like our friend Jim Jones," he said, his expression bleak. "Your father really was a good man, Owen, and one heck of a preacher. It's a terrible thing when a good man falls apart. But his whole world had come undone. That's what made it so hard to leave him, in the end. Especially with his illness."

"Illness?" Owen said, remembering what Lori had written in her journal: *Your father didn't leave you and Mom. He went crazy.*

"Disorder?" Skip asked, making a face like he'd stepped in something nasty. "I never know what to call these things anymore. Your father was unwell. Mentally. Manic depression, schizophrenia. I'm not sure which it was. I'm not even sure how many of his wild ideas were his own, and how many belonged to this... Brother Woodrow he kept talking about."

"*Brother Woodrow?*"

"You know him? They spoke to each other regularly, though I never saw the man myself."

So Woodrow was a real man—and maybe, just maybe, he was still hanging around Chapel Lake. Or *under* it. "Thank you so much for your help, Mr. Wickman."

"My pleasure. And thank you for your concern."

"Stay safe," Jo said with a foreboding look.

Again, Skip smiled. "If they do come for me, Joelle, I'll be ready," he said, placid. "I know the Mystery."

Owen flinched. Skip had heard of Brother Woodrow, and now he was using the man's words. "What is that?" he asked. "What's this Mystery?"

"God's word," Skip said, as if it were self-evident, beaming his beatific smile at them. "I'll tell you a secret if you promise not to spread it around. Things like what I'm about to tell you aren't quite good for business."

"Of course," Owen said. He and Jo moved closer to the man, listening intently.

"God told me the Mystery in person," Skip said. That smile swept across his face again. So confident. So at peace. "He whispered it in my ear while I slept."

Owen and Jo shared a look, awaiting Skip's big reveal.

"The Lord said to me, 'Skip, fear not: for *death is not the end.*'"

# CHAPTER 12

## LEVIATHAN

I

OWEN AND JO lay on their backs in her twin bed, looking up at the dayglow stars she'd stuck on the ceiling as a child. Dim light filtered in through the curtains. He watched her dark eyes, seemingly captivated by relics of her lost childhood. He saw the slight lines between her eyebrows, and at the corners of her mouth, evidence she'd spent at least a portion of her life smiling, despite everything she'd been through. Her dusty blonde hair was raggedly chopped, as if she'd done it herself, but it caught in the dim moonlight from the window, giving her an almost angelic look.

He thought he could love this woman. He thought he might have loved her all his life, and hadn't even known it.

She caught him looking, and smiled. Dimples formed at the upturned corners of her lips, reminding him, briefly, of the children they'd been. He flashed suddenly on a memory of chasing her through darkened streets, her golden hair shimmering under the streetlamps as a purple dusk fell, shooting playful looks back over her shoulder that said *Catch me, I want you to catch me*, and laughing when he couldn't reach her. He remembered the faint, sweet smell of lavender in her hair, and the wide, dark brown of her eyes staring at him in naked curiosity.

He smiled back, thinking, *This is the man I was meant to be. This is what Lori was trying to bring out of me all these years. If only she could see me now.*

"When Lori and I were kids," he found himself saying, "she

was always running headlong into another exciting adventure. I was the kid who stayed behind. The one who stood against the wall, while the other kids danced. The one who kept all his clothes on when everyone else jumped into the pool."

"That's not the Owen Saddler *I* remember," Jo said.

"That Owen died when he left Peace Falls, I think. But Lori.... When Lori got old enough to start getting into trouble, she dragged me along with her. I didn't want to go, but there was something about her... you couldn't help but get swept along in her wake."

Jo smiled, and let him speak.

"I was thinking about this the other day, about the time she taught me to swim. I'd always hated the water. I guess now I know why. When we were kids, my stepdad tried to throw me into the lake we used to go to some summers, this really nice place called China Cove. I didn't want to go in, not just because I was afraid, but because of Crouch, because of my father. I'd seen him standing on the water. I didn't know who he was, but looking at him... Just thinking about it now is giving me chills."

He held out his arm for Jo to touch the goose bumps on his forearm, and she ran her hand over them, the hairs tingling.

"I didn't know who he was back then," he said. "I just knew that I had to get away from him. This was maybe seven or eight years after we left Peace Falls. It's like he'd been obliterated from my memory. Anyway, this happened years later, when Lori was... I don't know, nine or ten. We were back at China Cove, and she told me something that stuck with me, even though I might not have heeded the advice. I told her I'd always been afraid of the water, and couldn't swim with her. What she said to me was, 'Forget about the before. All that matters is now.'" He smiled. "For some reason, that did the trick. I didn't worry about why I was scared, or what might happen if I went in, I just jumped in. And after a little bit of struggling, I realized I'd must have been a pretty good swimmer when I was little."

Jo's smile became so joyful she might have been on the verge of tears. "You were," she said, and Owen felt his heart swell up with the same joy. If this feeling was just a chemical reaction, what did it matter? He'd fill himself up with it and ask for more.

She took his hand, her fingers entwining with his, and

kissed it. They lay in silence for a while, comforted by each other's breathing.

"I need to tell you something," Jo said suddenly, sitting up. "It's not as nice as your story, but I want to tell you. I *need* to tell you. What happened to my parents, it should have happened to me, too."

Owen sat up beside her. "What do you mean?"

"I was with them that day," she said.

"You were—? What, in the car? With them?"

She nodded grimly. "I was with them. It just seemed like a normal day. We were on our way into town, and they were singing, just like normal. I mouthed along with the words in the backseat, just like normal."

She took a deep, shuddery breath, and went on: "My parents woke me up early that morning, rushed me to get dressed, said we were going to town to get new clothes. Back then I was always begging them for new clothes. I wore secondhand, mostly, so I was excited. But also suspicious. 'Why are they all of a sudden gonna buy me new clothes?' We didn't have much money, as you can see." She indicated the house with a small gesture.

"It's not a bad sized house," he said. "A house like this would go for half-a-million in Toronto."

"I'm sure Skip would tell you the market's not quite that good here," she said, and shrugged. "We'll see how it does. Regardless, we didn't have much, aside from our not-bad sized house. My parents took odd jobs after the flood, wherever someone who didn't know about Crouch and the Purification would hire them. My mom waitressed for a while, did some temp secretarial work in Peterborough, and my dad painted cottages and did small building projects around the lake. 'Decks and docks,' he liked to say. Cottagers don't seem to know or care much about local gossip. Salvage divers, they like to dabble in the lake's history, but they're generally 'renters and tenters,' as my dad used to say."

"He liked to rhyme, huh?" Owen said.

"He used to make up his own spirituals," Jo said, smiling in reminiscence. "He'd play them on his guitar, and he and my mom would sing harmony. They were actually pretty good. I've got some recordings downstairs. They're not professional, just home-jobs on cassette. If we get bored, I'll play them for you."

"I'd like that," he said, genuinely curious. He'd always had a vague memory of a group of children sitting cross-legged, listening to a man and woman play guitar and sing "Michael, Row the Boat Ashore," and "Whole World in His Hands," and The Byrds' "Turn! Turn! Turn!" He'd always assumed these people had been children's entertainers, but he supposed now they must have been Joan and Edam Dunsmuir.

"I saw the look in Mr. Jebson's eyes as we passed him on the road, and I started to get scared. I mean really, gripping-the-seat terrified. I turned to watch him out the back window. He dropped the sledgehammer he'd been using and ran after us, like there was something wrong with the car only he could see. My parents must have heard him shouting at us, seen him in the rearview mirror, at least, but they just kept on singing and driving. And when I turned back to them, to tell them to stop the car, that Mr. Jebson was running after us to beat the Devil, there was Crouch, buckled into the seat beside me. I remember his seat belt being buckled more clearly than anything, because I wondered why a ghost would need one. And that thought was what really struck it home: Crouch's ghost was sitting beside me, and my parents kept singing 'Swing Low, Sweet Chariot, comin' for to carry me home.'

"That's when I realized we were driving toward the lake. I heard Crouch whispering something, but I couldn't tell what, muttering low and quiet and smiling, like you'd sometimes see him walking down the street, whispering and smiling, and you'd think he was praying.

"I wanted to shout for my dad to stop the car, to pull over so I could get out, but I couldn't talk. My lips moved, but my breath was caught in my lungs, like in dreams, where you're so scared you can't scream. And all of a sudden, Crouch turned to me and sang the next verse in my face at the top of his lungs: '*When Jesus WASHED my sins aWAY!*'"

Her shout cut through the silence of the night, startling him, making his heart beat faster.

"My dad jerked the wheel. It was marsh on one side, trees on the other. Either way he took us would have been bad, but Crouch wanted us in the water, so my dad went right. We went down in the ditch before I really clued in what was happening, and my parents never stopped singing, 'If you get there before I do,' and I saw them hold hands and smile at each other as the front end hit the water, 'tell all my friends I'm coming there too.' They sang until the words were just bubbles on the surface of the water."

"I'm so sorry," Owen said, because he genuinely was, and he understood then why people recited platitudes at funerals—because more precise words would cut them open, would lay their emotions bare. Platitudes allowed them to express sympathy without making themselves vulnerable.

Jo shrugged. "It's all right. It was a long time ago. I'm not gonna dwell on the past anymore. My whole life, I've been living with these ghosts, and I'm tired of it, Owen. I'm tired of living for my parents. I want to live for me," she said, reaching out for his hand. He took it, smiling. "For *us*."

"I want that, too."

She was silent for a moment. Then she said, "Something else always bothered me about that day. Crouch sat beside me and smiled at the back of my parents' heads the whole time they were drowning. The car went in at a steep angle, so my head was still above water when theirs had been under for a while already. I tried to unlatch my seat belt, to get free, but Crouch put his hand on it, holding it in place, and I froze up. I couldn't make myself touch it with his hand there, even if it killed me. All I could do was struggle and wriggle while my parents grew still, and eventually, a sense of calm came over me. *I knew I was going to die*. Mr. Jebson had left us, and I'd drown in the car with my parents dead already and Crouch's ghost muttering prayers.

"Except it wasn't prayers, Owen. He was *talking* to someone. Somebody who wasn't there—and I heard him say, 'Brother Woodrow.'"

"Woodrow?"

She nodded. "So I asked him, I was curious, and I guess my curiosity must have overcome my fear, because all of a sudden I could speak again. I asked him, 'Who's Brother Woodrow?' And suddenly Crouch stopped smiling. He looked at me with *fear* in his eyes, Owen. 'You were talking to him,' I said. 'Who's Brother Woodrow?' Crouch opened his mouth to say something, I don't know if he was going to answer me or what, but right about then I heard Mr. Jebson calling out from up on the road, and Crouch looked out the back window, still terrified, like *he* was the one who'd seen a ghost. Then he unlatched my seat belt."

She looked like she couldn't believe it herself. "He let me go, Owen. I tore open the door; the windows were open already, so it was easy, and I stumbled out up to my hips in the cold, mucky marsh water, and Mr. Jebson met me on his way down the ditch, and I just about jumped into his arms, babbling and crying. He hugged me for what seemed like forever, before we remembered my parents were still in the car. Anyway, that's all I remember. The rest is just a blur, the sort of crime scene stuff I might have mixed up with memories from a thousand TV shows."

"That's awful," Owen said. "That's gotta be the worst thing that could happen to a kid, and you survived it. You've lived with that for twenty years."

"But it's odd, isn't it? Crouch could have drowned me, and instead he spared my life, all because I mentioned Woodrow. Woodrow was the man who had all kinds of parenting advice for Crouch, don't forget. I wonder if he's the one who put the idea in Crouch's head that you had to die to save the ministry."

"That seems likely," Owen said. "Woodrow was the Old Testament fire and brimstone guy. Crouch was 'God is Love.'"

"Right. Whatever the reason, it seemed to me like Crouch came to his senses just then. Like hearing Woodrow's name snapped him out of a trance. And he spared my life. He *saved* me. Crouch saved my life, and all this time I've been trying to figure out why." She ran her fingers through his bangs, absently. "When I saw you that day at the lake, that's when I put it all together. He saved me to help *you*, Owen. To put an end to this, once and for all. He's still under Brother Woodrow's spell, I think, *whoever* Woodrow is. And the two of them together are a dangerous combination."

She smiled triumphantly. The smile faltered as something occurred to her. "I need to pee," she said. "Will you be okay for a minute?"

"Go ahead," Owen said. "I'm thirsty. After all that, all I can think of is a tall, cool glass of water."

"You're a tall, cool glass of water," Jo said, smirking as she made a show of looking him up and down.

Owen laughed heartily before stepping out of bed. She followed him. Owen planted a kiss on her lips. "You need anything?"

"I'm good, thanks." She smacked him on the butt as he moved down the hall ahead of her. "Don't flash the neighbors!"

"Aw. Party pooper."

He padded down the small, carpeted stairs and into the kitchen of the backsplit house. Jo and her family hadn't used their share of the money to haul their house up the hill. He'd noticed on their way in that the house was as old as the foundation, mid-'60s, most likely.

At the sink, he peered out the window at the sad lawn and the trees, making sure there were no neighbors to flash. Then he turned on the cold water, let it run for a moment, and dipped the glass Jo had drank from under the tap.

The faucet rumbled, loose parts in the plumbing. He turned off the water, and brought the glass to his lips.

"*OWEN!*"

A loud crash startled him. Cursing under his breath, he ran barefoot to the hall.

"*Help! Owen!*"

Owen's blood raced as he bounded up the steps, still carrying his water glass, and what he saw through the open bathroom door nearly made him stumble back down the steps. The far wall and bathroom window were warped and rippled as if he were looking through old glass. Just as it had done at the dam, the water had risen up, this time from the tub, this time holding Jo several feet above the floor in colossal, translucent fingers. A second shape like a human head formed a grin as it studied Jo's bloodless face, her eyes widened in terror, her mouth an agonized rictus. The hand made of water closed around her, crushing her alive. The face, *Crouch's* face, watched as she died.

"*... help...*"

Owen threw the glass. It splashed through Crouch at the throat, shattering against the far wall. Crouch whipped his massive, rippling head round to observe the interloper, and as his giant's face formed a scowl, a second hand emerged from the tub, as big as the first, which was still tightening its hold on Jo's midsection, cracking her ribs with a wet crunch. Jo's eyes met

Owen's for the last time, and a look of peace washed over her. In the next moment, Crouch's other hand swatted angrily at the door.

The door struck him on the forehead, knocking him backward, and still it slammed shut. Fireworks exploded across his vision as he stumbled back toward the stairs. He grabbed the stair rail, stopping short of tumbling down backwards. Blood from the gash in his forehead fell on the carpet in a rapid stream of fat, heavy drips while he steadied himself. Dizzy, he staggered back to the bathroom door, shouting Jo's name. He jerked the handle, pounded his fists—*thundering my fists upon the soil*—against it, all to no avail. "*Jo!* Oh, please, don't let him kill her, *please!*" He threw himself against the door, once, twice, so hard his teeth rattled. He tasted blood from his tongue. Blood dripped down into his eyes. His vision went momentarily pink, and he blinked it away. On the third strike, the door cracked open, and he stumbled forward, slipping on the wet tiles.

Jo lay sprawled over the toilet. Blood streamed from her nose, her ears, her mouth. The bones in her chest and arms were so badly broken she had the look of a marionette with its strings cut.

Owen slipped again and staggered to her, a gurgle in the drain capturing his attention just long enough to see the water that had been a monstrous version of his father disappearing down the drain. The Reverend Everett Crouch had killed Jo Dunsmuir, the same girl he'd bounced on his knee when she'd been a child, and now that his work was done, he returned home, back to the lake.

Owen hurled curses at him, kicked at the tub, and fell down on his knees beside Jo. He saw right away she wasn't breathing, or if she was, it was so shallow her chest didn't move at all.

"Please don't be dead, Jo, *please.*"

He pressed his fingers against her throat, felt no blood move beneath her wet skin. He took her wrist and felt the same. He brought her to the floor and breathed into her mouth, as she'd done for him only recently, breathing him back to life. He pounded on her chest, and breathed again. He hadn't trained for this, was only following what they did on TV. On television, just when it seemed like she'd never wake up, Jo would turn her head and vomit up water. She'd gasp for air and look into his eyes, disoriented and relieved, and smile her dimpled smile.

He breathed and pumped. *Breathed. Pumped.*

"Please, Jo, please, *please...*" Weeping. Shuddering.

The tub made one last gurgle—a long, groaning death rattle —then fell silent.

Jo made no sound at all.

He drew her into his lap and held her. She felt brittle and jagged in his arms, not at all like she'd felt that night in the lake. He wept, loud and messily. He thundered his fist against the tub and kicked the wall until it cracked, and hurled accusations at the giant angry man in the sky. After a long while, the small room began to darken, seemingly in tandem with the light draining out of his life. He stood and hoisted Jo into his arms.

Owen brought her to the biggest bedroom—which had once been her parents, but which she must have taken for herself, since the covers were ruffled and the room looked lived in. He placed her on the bed, drew her arms across her chest, then changed his mind, not liking the gruesome image it made, and laid them at her sides. He brushed damp hair back from her face and kissed her forehead.

"It's over, now, Jo," he whispered in her ear. "Wherever you are, I hope there's no more pain."

Downstairs in the living room, he found a box of cassette tapes with hand-printed labels, the spirituals she'd mentioned before. He found one labeled *The Dunsmuirs HOUSE OF MY DREAMS: DEMO* and liked the sound of it, and he thought Jo might have liked it, too. The master bedroom had a stereo on the vanity. Owen inserted the tape, already wound to the beginning. He pushed play, and sat on the edge of the bed in his damp clothes, looking down at what remained of Crazy Jo Dunsmuir, his first and only real love.

A tune strummed out on an acoustic guitar, both heartbreakingly sweet and hauntingly sad. Edam Dunsmuir's gravelly vibrato joined it, belting out the lyrics with a slight country twang. During the chorus, Jo's mother sang along in a pleasing falsetto.

> *If you stay with me tonight,*
> *I'll swear we'll build a Heaven on Earth*

> *How we'll live there,*
> *I don't know*
> *Take me down to the water*
> *Where the green grass grow*
> *Take me down to the house*
> *Of my dreams*

He let the tape play out, then wound it back and played it again. At first, the lyrics seemed a fitting tribute to the Dunsmuir family, though the second time through he decided Jo might not have felt the same, considering how her parents had died, he *she'd* died, and shut it off. He came back to her side, leaned down, and kissed her cold, blue lips. He brushed her hair away from her ear, as blonde and fine as it had been when she was a girl.

"You remember what Mr. Wickman said? Death isn't the end, Jo. Death isn't the end," he said again, sitting down beside her, trying his damnedest to make himself believe it.

# CHAPTER 13

## LAID TO REST

I

OWEN MADE HIS way down to the living room, where he'd left his cell phone. He sat on the sofa in his wet clothes, dialing the long-distance number. After four rings, his mother picked up from two-hundred kilometers away.

"Saddler residence," she said.

For a long moment Owen said nothing, didn't know how to begin. It had all come apart: all the progress he'd made, shattered in an instant of carelessness and stupidity.

"Mom," he said finally, "it's me."

"Owen." She sounded neither thrilled nor disappointed to hear his voice. "Where are you calling from? You sound odd."

"Mom, Jo is dead."

"Jo. Am I supposed to know this person?"

"Joelle Dunsmuir," Owen said, annoyed by her brusqueness.

"Joelle—" She clued in. "*Little Jo*? Where on earth did you...?"

Silence, filled by the hiss of dead air. "Mom."

"You're *there* now, aren't you? You went up to that awful place—"

"Mom, I have a right to know—"

"You have *no idea* what I went through to get you away from that damned place, and you had the nerve to go *back*? Just when were you planning to tell me, hmm? After what happened to—" She made herself finish it, "to your sister. How *could* you, Owen? *How could you?*"

He held the phone away, her scream ringing in his ear. It was the most emotion he'd gotten out of his mother in years, since the days he used to argue and fight with everyone; he hadn't sought out anger, but it was better than the flat tone she'd taken before. Now that Jo had died he'd been stumbling around on autopilot, like a man in a dream. Night had slipped its cold hands over the world without him noticing, the windows now entirely black. Anyone could be out there in the dark, with the cicadas and the frogs chirping out spirituals of their own. Their somber music helped him focus his thoughts.

"Lori came up here for me, Mom. Because of my depression."

"Pish posh."

"She was looking for my father," he said, becoming angry. "For Crouch."

A long pause, the hiss of distance between them: metaphorical and physical. "And I suppose she found him," his mother said after a time.

"In a way. He's dead. He's been dead for years, Mom. Since the day we left."

"What do you mean? Your father's not dead."

"Mom, I was down there in that church—"

"*You went down there?*"

"Twice. The people we left behind drowned down there. They meant to kill themselves, but I think they changed their mind at the last moment. Somebody murdered them."

Margaret Saddler clucked her tongue.

"*Mom.*"

"You can't possibly know all that. How could you know all that?" she said, as if asking herself.

"What do you think I've been doing up here, taking a vacation? I've been researching. I've been diving. I found a journal Lori wrote to me, Mom, and I met Jo Dunsmuir and we..." He swallowed his sadness. "...and now she's, she's *dead*, Mom. Because of Crouch. Because of the lies you told me."

The distant hiss. "You *blame* me. Well, I'm sorry, Owen. I'm sorry that had to happen to your little friend. She was a fine girl. Your father—" She seemed to choke on her own words, sorrow cracking the veneer. "Your father loved her very much. He loved both of you. But he was sick. He'd been sick for quite a while. I saw the signs—I should have, I transcribed all his sermons—but I chose to ignore them."

She cupped the receiver to politely blow her nose. "You don't remember how he was," she said when she came back. "His *fury*. He never struck either of us, not with his fists. He wielded God's Word like a weapon, bullying us into submission with Eternal Damnation and Hellfire, abusing and demoralizing us with scripture. Not just the two of us, Owen, but the whole church. The whole *town*. He was sick, your father. Sick."

"He should've been on medication."

"I suggested it, when the worst of it began. He spat at my feet. On the *kitchen floor* he did this, Owen. 'Many are the afflictions of the righteous,' he said, 'but the Lord delivers him from them all!' And I told him, 'Shepherd the flock that is among you, not domineering over those in your charge, but being an example to the flock.' We went on and on like that. Everett would say 'Those who are well do not need a physician. Do you not know the body is a temple of the Holy Spirit?' I reminded him God's ways are not our ways, and if we were expected to follow everything the Old Testament told us to the letter, we'd all be out toiling in the fields and stoning hippies to death for smelling like patchouli."

Odd as it was to hear his mother quote scripture, even odder was the tone in which she spoke about her relationship with his father. She was angry, impassioned—but affection trickled through the bitterness. It hadn't all been bad times in the Crouch house, after all. They'd been a family. There'd been *love*.

"He used to like that we could debate religion," she said. "But that night I think I must have pushed him over the edge. It was Woodrow's influence, I don't fully blame Everett."

"Brother Woodrow?"

"That's what Everett called him," she said. "We'd been arguing for hours before you wandered into the kitchen in your pajamas. It was the first time I saw venom in your father's eyes, every bit of it aimed at you. Three years old at the time, you were. It was the first time he truly frightened me. He'd always been a passionate man, I'd known that from the moment I met him. It's what fueled his sermons. It put butts in the seats. But *rage*? Toward his own *flesh and blood*?"

"So it's true," Owen said. "He really was going to murder me."

"Oh, no. No, no, I don't think he'd ever have gone that far. When you were very little, Everett baptised you," she explained. "You nearly died. We would only ever do full-body immersions. When Philip baptized the Ethiopian, he took him down *into* the water. He didn't just sprinkle water from the font on the man's forehead. So that's what we did in the Blessed Trinity. It was the same ceremony for adults as it was for the children.

"By the time we started this, you were barely a year old. You didn't like the water, not one bit. Not the bath, and especially not the river. And you struggled. You screamed bloody murder. Everett used... a little more force than he'd meant to, I think—I *hope* that's what it was, because the alternative scares the life out of me."

Owen pictured Crouch pushing him under the water, the great holy glory in his eyes. The scene came back to him in a flash, Crouch pushing him down, smiling darkly, the pocket watch hung from a chain in his pocket, the men and women whose faces he recognized: Dink Deakins, and Edam and Joan Dunsmuir, who'd rejoined their brethren and sistren in death, and the little blonde girl who was Jo, he knew that now, the same child Woodrow had been baptizing in the lake, held in her parents' loving arms. She'd been with them all along, had spent her entire life living under the shadow of that terrible church, living just like the dead, and now she was back in the tender bosom of her loving family.

"Secondary drowning, the doctors said," his mother was saying. "They were able to save you, by some miracle. The dam was proposed near about the same time; I suppose Everett must have made a connection between the two. Thinking perhaps it wasn't God's Will that saved you, but Man's intervention, and maybe you were *meant* to have drowned that day. That maybe God was testing him, like He'd tested Job and Abraham. That if he'd sacrificed you, if he'd *drowned* you, in the same water that would soon come to destroy his church, that God would spare it. Of course it was insane. Muddy thinking."

"Jo thinks—" He corrected himself with a morose glance up

the stairs toward her bedroom, where her remains cooled and stiffened on the bedspread. "Jo *thought* the same thing. She thought he was schizophrenic."

"She always was smart as a whip, that Jo. In any case, I don't think he could have gone through with it. I don't think so. But I wasn't about to give him the chance to change his mind."

"Why didn't the others see it? Couldn't you have rallied them against him?"

"By that point, he'd built up their passion to a fever pitch. He'd passed on his delusions to the rest of us, like he was passing on a cold. We *yearned* for confrontation. I know that now. Having to defend your beliefs only makes them stronger. We weren't chaining ourselves to trees to stop some men in bulldozers, like your sister might've done. We were standing in front of a *tidal wave*, praying for a trickle." She chuckled softly, laughing at her own blindness. "It wasn't even all that difficult to convince them to do it, either. And once you've been convinced of such insanity, it's often harder to turn back than to see the madness through to the end. Turning back doesn't just mean you were *wrong*, it means you were *duped*. You have to admit you've been a fool, and that's difficult for most people to do."

"Where was Brother Woodrow during all this?"

"Oh, he was there with Everett. He was always there, whispering in his ear. Like Rasputin."

"So he died with Crouch."

"If it's true your father died down there, Woodrow died with him, I've no doubt of that." She fell silent. The mechanical hiss filled it.

"So why did we leave that day? Why didn't you stay, if you thought there'd be a miracle?"

"Because *I never believed*," she said.

"You didn't?"

"I transcribed every one of Everett's tapes myself. If nothing else, it gave me a front row seat to his machinations. I saw what he was doing somewhere along the line, the only thing I didn't know was whether he'd been doing it *purposefully* or not. Was it the man, or the sickness? Your father used to say, 'Every man has two selves—"

"'—the man who is, and the man he's meant to be,'" Owen finished for her.

"Precisely. Perhaps if I'd understood he'd meant it *literally*, I could have done more for him. For *them*. I suppose that's my cross to bear. I loved those people, and I loved *him*, in spite of it. He was your father, my husband. In sickness and in health, I'd made those vows. There were moments of tenderness, when I'd find it difficult to remember the bad times. I still love him dearly, as crazy as it sounds."

"Love *is* crazy," he said, thinking of Jo, of the easy way they'd fallen into step with each other. "Did he—" He found himself swallowing back tears at the thought. "Mom, do you think he ever loved me?"

"Owen," she said, her tone reproachful. "*Of course* he loved you. He was your *father*."

"So was Gerald."

"And he loved you too, in his way. He always said you reminded him of himself when he was young. So stubborn and impulsive."

"*Gerald* said that?"

"Mm-hmm."

It wasn't exactly a compliment, but maybe he hadn't given Gerald the chance he'd needed to be a father figure. Maybe he'd shut Gerald out because of the way Crouch had abandoned them, which in the end had turned out to be untrue. "You know, I think that's the first time I've heard you say something nice about him," Owen remarked.

"Gerald was sick too, in his way," she said wearily. "I hadn't the strength to see him through it. I'd already tried to save one husband. You know now how that turned out. I certainly wasn't ready to try it again."

"I don't blame you."

"I spent years waiting for the man Everett meant himself to be to step into the light. But the other man had taken him over, and he was ugly, Owen. The Devil wears many faces. Often it's a face you know too well. Still, I'm not sure I would have had the courage to go if not for Howard. He was the angel on my shoulder. He was our lawyer—"

"I know."

"Did he tell you I used to work for him? I was his legal secretary before I met Everett."

"He never said that, no."

"He didn't like me going to that church, and he sure didn't like me getting close to Everett. He tried to argue me out of making a 'life-altering decision,' as he called it, but I was just as stubborn as your father. As you are. I suppose when he saw he couldn't beat me, he joined me. He joined *us*. He was there for all the picnics and the sermons and the squabbling, but he never believed in Everett, not like the rest of them. He helped us as far as he could with the legal troubles, after what people in town started referring to as the Schism—what your father called the Purification—but I could tell his heart wasn't in it.

"He hadn't gone to a sermon in over a year when he came back one Sunday and sat himself down in the back row. Your father was reciting his speech about you, the one in which God told him to sacrifice his firstborn son to save the church, and Howard stood up and called him a liar. The whole church, there wasn't much left of us by then, but we all turned around to gawk. He was drunk as a skunk and swaying on his feet. He called your father a fraud, a wolf in sheep's clothing, and told the rest of us we were following Everett straight to Hell."

"Wow."

"He'd stood idly by, he said, but he couldn't do it any longer, and anyone who wanted to leave could come with him right then and never look back. 'Like Lot from Sodom,' he said, and that got Everett going, I think. Your father said, 'Nor thieves, nor the greedy, nor drunkards, nor revilers, nor swindlers will inherit the kingdom of God.' And Howard made a raspberry, thumbing his nose at all of us, I think, and stumbled outside."

"Nobody followed him?"

"Not right then. But I could tell the Dunsmuirs were considering it, because when he said the thing about Sodom, they hugged Little Joelle up tight, and the next Sunday Joan was too sick to attend, and the Sunday after that they had to visit their dying aunt in the town named after Edam's family.

"After the incident in the church, Howard got drunker and drunker, stewing in booze and his own embarrassment. He resigned, he never said another word to me until the night before the valley was to be flooded, when he crept up to the back door. Your father was going back and forth with Woodrow in his office upstairs. It was cold that night, it'd been a crisp fall day and the trees were just about bare, but I wouldn't let Howard inside, and I'm not sure he would have come in if I'd asked him.

"He was drunk, slurring his words, but they struck me as clearly as if they'd been spoken by God Himself. 'Don't do it for me,' he said, 'don't do it for either of us. Do it for the boy. That church is nothing but death, Maggie,' he said. 'The boy is *life*.' And he was right, Owen. All the arguments we've had over the years, all the screaming and pushing back at each other, *you gave me life*. Without you and your sister to care for, I might as well have locked myself in that church with the rest of them."

A flood of emotion overcame him. Tears welled in his eyes, and he let them fall.

"I love you, too, Mom," he said. He heard his mother's sob on the other end, and she blew her nose loudly, not bothering to muffle it. After some sniffling on both ends of the line, Owen said, "Howard told me to tell you he still does, whatever that means."

Margaret sniffled again, cleared her throat. "Howard used to say he wished you were his son, instead of Everett's."

"He did?"

"He loved you like his own. You don't remember?"

No matter how much he learned, he still remembered so little of what had come before. "No," he said. He remembered what Howard had said in the hospital about his relationship with her being strictly platonic, at the behest of his mom. "Did he love you, do you think?"

"Howard?" She sounded taken aback. "Oh, goodness, no! I mean, I don't *think* so. He certainly never indicated anything to me...." A brief pause. "I suppose he *could* have. Why do you ask? Did he say something to you?"

"Never mind, Mom," he said. "I love you. Don't come up here, okay? I'll be back soon."

She promised she wouldn't.

<hr>

2

Owen headed out to the car in the dark. He'd cleaned up his blood, pouring bleach onto the stains and daubing them with paper towels, wiping his blood from the bathroom door and the tiles by the toilet, feeling guilty and ashamed, as if he were cleaning up evidence of a crime. In a way, he supposed he should feel guilty. If not for him, Jo would still be alive. If not for him, a lot of good people would still be among the living.

"Not my fault," he assured himself, and thought, *Original sin. Blame the child for the crimes of his parents.*

He was sitting in the driver's seat with the engine started, a trash bag of bloodied rags thrown into the back, before he noticed the slip of paper on the passenger seat. It was heavy paper ripped from a book, recycled and textured like cloth—the same paper from Lori's journal. He unfolded it.

*Take her home, Owen.*
*Take her to the lake.*

Scrawled in Lori's hand. He stared at the words on the page until they blurred. "She *knew*," he said. Then he shook his head, blinked hard, and read the note again. "No. It's not possible."

But he held the evidence in his hand. Somehow Lori had written about Jo's death, and Jo had torn it out of the journal and left it on the seat for him to find, almost as if the two of them had known she would die here today.

*Coincidence*, he thought. *If she'd made it, she would have folded this up and tucked it away for tomorrow, or the next day.*

Owen peered back at the darkened house.

He'd left Jo on her bed, not knowing what to do about her. He'd considered calling the police, but even without his blood, evidence of him having been there was all over that house; he'd touched just about everything—especially Jo. He thought about burying her in the yard, but since she'd been ready to sell, she obviously hadn't wanted to spend the rest of her life there, let alone eternity. He'd struggled over the decision for a long time before electing to leave her there, just for the night. Until he'd laid Crouch and the Blessed Trinity to rest once and for all.

Now, the choice was clear: he had to bring her to the lake.

*And hand her over to Crouch? You've gotta be crazy.*

*What other choice is there?*

His shadow stretched out long and gauzy before him under the fat, bright moon, leading the way to the house, which seemed to sigh as he opened the front door. He'd turned off all the lights on his way out. Lit by the moon, long shadows drew across the living room. The refrigerator ticked and rattled in the kitchen. He felt along the wall for the switch, and flicked it on, expecting Crouch and the Blessed Trinity to be standing in his way, but the house was empty.

He padded up the steps to the back room. Jo still lay exactly where he'd left her. Some part of him had expected to find her sitting in front of the vanity by the window, peering at him in the mirror, to be sitting on the edge of the bed, patting the bedspread with a sly grin. He wasn't sure if in these fantasies he'd thought of her as dead or still living; in either case, the thought was morbid.

Not that what he was about to do wasn't equally gruesome, though he supposed undertakers did it several times each day. He slipped his hands under her arms and hoisted her up, so that, to an outsider, it might look as if they'd been dancing and she'd passed out drunk or exhausted in his arms. She was dry now, and still smelled clean, her hair slightly fruity under his nose. Decay hadn't yet begun, and he was grateful for that. If it had, he didn't think he could manage what needed to be done. He wondered idly how long it would take, and supposed she'd be in the lake long before the worst of it began.

Getting her down the stairs took a bit of work, but he managed it without hitting her head on anything, or tripping over her dangling legs. He remembered once having to carry Allison up to bed after she'd had too much to drink; the feeling was remarkably similar, enough that he could easily imagine Jo was just sleeping.

"'Do not weep,'" Owen grunted, while the toes of Jo's bare feet dragged along the hall floor toward the front door, "'for she is not dead but sleeping.'"

The minister had recited this phrase from The Gospel of Luke at Lori's funeral. Owen thought he understood it now. It wouldn't bring her back to him, it didn't diminish the pain of his loss, but he recognized the need for a sense that this life was not the end, that there was more to us than flesh and blood and breath. He felt Jo with him, not the dead woman in his arms but the fiery spirit she'd been. He felt her as a presence very close by, not in his mind but in his heart. *He felt her with him.*

Owen hoisted Jo's lifeless remains onto a knee, to open the front door, and flicked off the living room lights. Out on the porch, with Jo resting in the patio swing, he took one last look at the darkened house, feeling suddenly and desperately alone. Her spirit, her soul, whatever it was he'd felt inside had left him. Just the cool night breeze now, and the trees, and a lonely, unhappy man with a dead woman sitting awkwardly on a patio swing.

Jo's spirit had moved on.

3

HE LAID her remains out on the dock, and the boards gently rocked her to a current from out in the main bay. He thought of their first night together, how she'd been swimming nude and beckoned him in. *Hard to believe that was just two nights ago*, he thought, and he slipped down into the water up to his hips, a perfect depth for Immersion. From there, he drew Jo into his arms. Her lower half splashed heavily off the dock, her cold arms slumped over his shoulders.

Owen waded her out into deeper water, out beyond the low pine boughs to where Brother Woodrow and the Blessed Trinity had performed her baptism. He had to get her out of the bay and into the lake or she'd float up on shore in front of Fisherman's Wharf. She might still, but an attempt had to be made. Jo's legs wanted to float, stretching out in front of them while he trudged along the mucky bottom. It unnerved him, felt unnatural. He was in up to his shoulders before he let her go.

Jo floated a moment, skin so pale under the moon, stark white against the black water surrounding her. Then, ever so slowly, she began to descend. Owen stepped back to watch her slip away into the darkness, into her watery grave. Home, at last.

# CHAPTER 14

## HIS FATHER'S HOUSE HAS MANY ROOMS

I

STANDING UP TO his knees in the water, Owen looked out over the bay for a long time. Somewhere out there the church beckoned. He wondered if it would ever be over, or if it would just go on until every one of them had been sucked kicking and screaming into the water.

*This damned lake*, he thought. *It's taken all the wrong people, all the innocents. If I could go back and change it ... if I could tell my mother to turn the car around... if she'd just let him take me... But then Lori never would have been born... Better that she'd lived and died, than never lived at all... I'm the one who should have never been born... I'm the one who's never had a reason to live.*

"Take me," he said aloud. "Come on, Crouch, *take me*. It's me you want, so let's finish this right now. Take me." He splashed a fist weakly into the water. "Fucking take *me*!"

The shout returned to him in an echo from across the bay. It felt stupid, senseless, standing in water up to his waist, shouting curses at a man who'd been dead almost as long as his son had been alive. If Crouch was out there tonight, the man had turned a deaf ear toward him. Owen supposed he should have been used to being ignored by his father by now, anyway.

Owen trudged out of the lake reluctantly, still eager to confront Crouch. He considered taking the boat out to the church, but even though the moon would light his way, it was much too dark to do any good under the water. Lori's journal, open on the

241

coffee table, drew his attention, but he couldn't bring himself to read more tonight. It was too late for anything but sleep, and he was just tired enough that he thought he could manage to get some.

He dragged himself pathetically upstairs, lay down, and drew the sheet up to his chin. Within minutes, he was out.

Something awoke him from a deep, dark and dreamless sleep. The bedroom was dead dark. A voice—he was sure that was what he'd heard, whether it was someone else's voice or his own, he couldn't be sure. As always, the clock said 2:06.

He rolled over beneath the sheet and smacked his lips, blinking out into the dim moonlight in the hall before realizing someone was standing in the doorway, blocking his view.

"*Jo...*" he breathed. *She came back...*

She stood over him, smiling her dimpled smile, her baptismal robe—the same Lori had worn in his dream—still wet, clinging to her curves. When he met her dark eyes, they were rimmed with gold that sparkled in the glimmer of the moon.

"You found the note," she said. Her voice was different—seemed only half there, as if her words were swimming up from a great darkness, from some dark, unknowable void.

He nodded, unable to speak. All he could manage was a cracked breath.

"It was sweet, what you did," she told him in her ethereal voice. "Playing my parents' song. Taking me to the lake. What you said about death."

Her words sent a shiver of pleasure up his spine. "You heard me?"

She ignored the query. "Owen, the truth is so much worse than we thought," she said, urgency in her ghostly voice. "Howard told you nothing but lies."

Owen sat up in bed, letting the sheet gather in his lap. "No more stories, Jo. Please. My head's all muddled up with them. I just want to *remember*."

"Everett can *help* you remember," she said with a patient smile. "It's what he's wanted from the beginning. For you to open your eyes. For you to see the *truth*."

"How do you know all this?"

"Because you brought me home," she said. "I'm with them now. We're all together. Your sister's there, too."

*"Lori..."*

"And Howie. I know it's difficult for you to believe, but your father only ever wanted to help you. It's *Woodrow* who wanted you dead. Because he knew you'd take Everett away from him. He knew you'd be your father's savior."

Everything pointed to Woodrow: Crouch's letters, his mother comparing the man to Rasputin, Jo's story about the day her parents died. On his first day here, the backwoods pastor had drawn Owen into the water, he'd almost gotten him under, but he'd sensed the truth despite the bearded man's lies and twinkling-eyed smile. If he truly was the dark mastermind behind the curtain, pulling Crouch's strings, Owen needn't fear Crouch, so long as Woodrow wasn't around. If, as his mother seemed to think, Woodrow had drowned with Crouch, how could he know when Crouch was in charge and Woodrow wasn't? They'd already switched places once. What would stop them from doing it again?

*Lori*, he thought. *Howie and Jo. If they're down there with him, maybe they can talk sense into him.*

It was a big *if*, but worth considering.

"What does he want?" Owen said.

"He wants you to come with me. To the lake."

"You *trust* him?"

"I trust *them*. It's Brother Woodrow you can't trust. He's down there, too. But he's sleeping. When Crouch is awake, Woodrow sleeps. That's how it's always been."

*Angels and demons*, Owen thought; *good spirits and evil. And if the Bible is right, it's not Jo's ghost talking to me, pushing me toward the lake, but a* spirit being. *The question is, who's sitting at the head of the table: God or the Devil?*

"I'll protect you," Jo said. She held out a hand to him, palm up.

"My head hurts," he said. The coils squeaked as he rose from the bed and took the hand she offered. It was surprisingly warm, delicate and light. "I'm tired of all of this, Jo. I just want it to be over."

"I know." Even her breath was warm in his ear. "You're so close to the end now. Can you feel it?"

He could. "Let's just go," he said. The carpet was wet at his feet. This didn't surprise him, either. "Let's get it over with. Before I lose my nerve."

"That's the spirit," she said, and smirked at the unintended pun. She drew him to the hall, down the stairs, through the living room, and around the chimney to the open back door. Passing through the darkened house, he was reminded of the dream he'd had of Crouch, when the Blessed Trinity had risen, dead and bloated, from their tomb below, and Woodrow had shown him the Mystery.

"You're going to need this," Jo said, pointing to his wetsuit on the patio railing.

"Where are we going?"

"*You know where.*"

Obediently, Owen tugged the suit on, the legs still damp and cool. He zipped up, drew on the weight belt and life vest, and hoisted the tank over his right shoulder and the mouthpiece over his left. Jo had already taken the stairs, and she stood on the path below, waiting. He came to her side. Her robe trailed behind her down the path to the lake, slightly too long, effulgent under the moon. Owen followed a short distance behind. Whatever she was now, ghost or angel (*Or demon*, a small, paranoid voice whispered in his mind), the way she'd touched him, the way the pine needles dragged along in the wake of her robe, she seemed *real*.

*It's the water. Look what it did for Crouch. He'd found the Fountain of Youth, all he had to do was die. Drown yourself in Chapel Lake and you, too, can live forever!*

Owen didn't find the thought amusing, or very helpful.

Jo looked back over her shoulder at the dock. He noticed, as she moved toward the boat, that at least one thing proved she wasn't entirely *there*: the dock never moved under her feet. Not once did her presence disrupt the water.

He crossed the ramp, the dock bounding up and down with each step, creaking on its hinges and causing ripples to radiate from the dock. Jo had climbed into the boat, and now she looked up at him expectantly from the front seat. He stepped in, sat in the driver's seat, then turned to her.

"Well?" she said.

"I have something to say, but I don't want to upset you."

"You want to know if you can trust me," she said.

He nodded. "How can I be sure?"

She seemed to think about this for a moment, then shrugged. "You'll just have to take it on faith, I guess. Faith doesn't look for proof."

It didn't matter. Owen had already decided he would follow her just about anywhere.

He started the boat.

<hr>

2

OUT IN THE MAIN BAY, there wasn't a single boat in sight. The stars and moon were obscured by a scud of thick, dark clouds. The lake was a sheet of black. The boat engine seemed incredibly loud as it cut through the silence. Owen held a flashlight under his arm as he drove, making Jo's robe shine as bright as a comet against the dark. Every so often, she turned with a tender smile, pointing the way with hand signals.

Finally, she shouted over the roar of the engine, "Here!"

"I see it!" Owen cried back, finally locating the steeple rising from the gloom ahead, darker than the night itself. He cut the motor and looked off toward the bright dots of light on the shore, white in the windows, the orange of bonfires, and wondered if anyone had heard her voice, or just his reply.

Owen paddled the rest of the way to the dock, silent for the most part, the oar cutting through water as flat as glass, occasionally scraping against the side. He secured the boat to the dock and stood.

"This is where we part ways," Jo said.

"You're not coming with me?"

She shook her head with another patient smile. "This is *your* Mystery, Owen. I've already met mine."

"What—?" In that moment, he wasn't sure what he'd meant to ask, but she interrupted him before he could finish.

"Some other time, maybe."

"I'll see you again?"

"Of course you will." She took his hand, turned it palm-up, and kissed it gently. Her lips were warm, soft, wet—not the cold, stiff flesh of the dead. "You said it yourself, Owen: death is not the end."

He hadn't believed it before, had spoken it as if to convince himself of its truth in a time of shattering grief. But while she held his hand against her smooth, tender palm, almost as light as air, it was difficult not to accept the truth. Jo was dead, yet here she sat. Whether or not blood flowed through her veins, she was as real as the cool night air kissing his cheeks and rustling his hair, as the scent of pines and wood smoke and fresh water it carried, as the tin boat rocking under his feet. And the love he felt radiating from her—*toward* her—that was real, too.

"What?" she asked with a playful smirk, as if reading something in his eyes.

"I was just thinking," he said. "I guess maybe I love you."

Jo laughed. It carried in the silence. Out in the dark, a loon called back. "I guess maybe I love you, too," she said.

"Take it on faith."

She smiled. "Take it on faith," she agreed.

He kissed her forehead. Even though it reminded him of doing the same on her deathbed, it felt pleasant this time, to smell her clean skin and the lavender in her hair one last time.

"I guess I should go," he said.

"Good luck."

He climbed out onto the dock and sat down on the edge to don the rest of his equipment, until he finally plunged his flippers into the still water. She twiddled her fingers at him, and he returned the gesture. Then he slipped into the black waters of Chapel Lake for the last time.

3

THE LAKE WAS SO dark he couldn't see a thing until he was a few feet from the church, and by then it was too late to stop himself from bumping into the ledge below the bell tower window.

From there, he swam with his hands out before him, feeling like a blind man as he descended in the dark. Silver-eyed fish loomed toward him out of the murk. He came upon a boarded window and realized somewhere along the way he'd gotten turned upside down; rather than pulling himself *down* the wall, he'd been dragging himself *up*. He righted himself and continued. Finally, his flippers struck the ground, raising a cloud of silt that looked unnaturally green under his LED. Somehow he'd lost the church in the gloom and found himself facing a great wall of murky darkness, what he assumed were the remains of Peace Falls. Out there in the dark were the homes of those the others had left behind. Jo's childhood home stood there, too, in the black abyss of the past. Owen turned from it, swimming toward what he soon found was the church after all. From there, he had little trouble working his way around the side.

He found the first of the Blessed Trinity among the tombstones. Edam and Joan Dunsmuir stood before a stone marked DUNSMUIR, as dead as the forebears whose plot they stood on, but their flesh looked as though they still lived. They held hands, their baptismal robes bathed in the ethereal green light of his LED, and the two of them smiled as they recognized him. With their free hands, they directed him toward his childhood home.

On the path up the small rise to the Crouch house, he saw two of the others, whom he recognized from the photograph he'd shared with Constable Selkie: the chubby woman in the sundress, and the skinny woman with the sour countenance and pantsuit. Both women now wore the same white garments as the others. They sat in a porch swing, swaying gently back and forth, wearing the smiles of children, their feet resting on stones. But as he drew nearer, Owen realized with a sudden shock that their footrests were not rocks at all: Dink Deakins and Pete Jebson had been buried up to their necks beneath the women's bare feet. The men wore identical silent screams.

Owen swam quickly by, heading for the house, not looking back at the strange, ghastly scene. Fear gripped him, but it was much too late to turn back. He had a terrible feeling that, if he tried, he'd only become lost in the darkness, swimming in circles without ever finding the surface.

Howie Lansall sat on the porch steps, whittling something, by the look, and he threw Owen a smiling wave as he approached the house. Owen waved back, unable to return the smile through the regulator, but smiling with his eyes, glad to see Howie had been spared the same fate as Dink and Jeb, though it was likely no picnic seeing the two men slowly tortured.

Owen pointed to the chunk of black wood in Howie's palm, the rusty old blade carving it. Howie held it out for him to see, a quite realistic frog. Howie nodded toward it, gesturing for Owen to take it from him. Since he couldn't figure out how to politely decline without words, Owen took the wooden frog, nodded gratefully, and tucked it into his fanny pack. He patted Howie on the shoulder. Howie smiled, showing teeth. The sight unnerved Owen, somehow. He supposed a part of him still expected to see bubbles emerge from Howie's mouth.

Owen left Howie behind and swam up toward the second floor window, where he pulled himself along the porch roof and climbed into his childhood bedroom. The mirror where he'd seen Crouch now reflected his own anxious gaze. Without Crouch to distract him, Owen noticed words etched around the mirror's edges, and he wiped them clean with a glove.

## THAT ALL MEN MAY KNOW HIS WORK

*This is* my *work*, he thought. *Dealing with Crouch. Laying the Blessed Trinity to rest. Howie, Jo, and my sister. The rest of them. This is no place to spend an eternity.*

Owen opened the bedroom door, imagining the creak of its hinges in the deep silence of this watery tomb. He hesitated only a moment before swimming out into the hall. Nothing here jogged his memory: the walls with their exposed boards, black with rot; the carpet, so sodden and littered with mucky plaster it was impossible to recognize what color it had once been. He came to some photo frames hung from jutting nails. Wiping one clean, he saw a blond boy with a cherubic smile he only vaguely recognized.

*That's me*, he thought with a shiver of pleasure. Aside from the photo Howard had given him, he'd never seen another picture of himself before the age of five. In it, he stood in front of the church in a child's black suit.

The door to his old bedroom faced a set of stairs leading down into a deeper gloom. At the far end of the hall was an open door, the room behind it hidden in darkness. Owen swam toward it, wanting more than ever to remember, desperate to discover the Mystery that awaited him and him alone.

Owen shined his light into the room, which had apparently been an office, looted of everything but the furniture: a desk, a rolling desk chair, a bookshelf, and a straight-backed chair so old, the fabric had been torn away to stuffing and coils.

Crouch sat in the chair, a ruined throne for a ruined king in his empire of death, bathed suddenly in Owen's ghostly green light. His pallid face was unsmiling, hands clasped in his lap.

Owen hesitated in the doorway. Alone in the presence of his father, he couldn't go on. Jo had said he could trust him, that it was Woodrow who wanted him dead—but hadn't Crouch tried to drown him twice already? And wasn't it just as likely that Woodrow held Jo in his sway, too? The scene on the front lawn looked like some sadistic game Woodrow might have dreamed up, a way for his sheep to pass eternity—what had Dink Deakins and Pete Jebson done to deserve such a fate? Was it because they'd been exiles? Because they'd abandoned the others in their hour of need? And what fate did Woodrow have in mind for Owen, Crouch's prodigal son?

Crouch smiled up at his son from his throne.

A hand fell on Owen's shoulder. He wheeled around, expecting to find Woodrow standing beside him, smiling his twinkling-eyed smile. The LED threw menacing shadows along the walls until it came to rest on their visitor.

*Lori...*

She smiled at him, gave his shoulder a tender squeeze. If not for the regulator, he would have cried out her name. He gave her a questioning look, felt fresh tears sting his eyes. She held out her arms and he fell into them, embracing her. Her soft white robe billowed around the both of them like the wings of an angel. Hugging her was not like it had been with Jo; he felt none of the physical warmth radiating from her, but a heat began to spread from inside his chest, as if being with her again was filling up the hole she'd left in his heart with unimaginable joy.

After a long time—not long enough—Lori broke the embrace, and held out a hand toward the chair, toward his father. She urged him forward with a smiling nod. He turned to face the room, to face the past.

Crouch stood beside the ruined chair now, one hand at rest on the seatback, the other directing Owen to sit. Owen approached, trying to decipher the expression on his father's face, a face he now recognized was very similar to his own: the flat bridge of their noses; the ridged, high forehead; the hairline receding in the same way. Looking at his father was like looking into a warped mirror at himself. They even looked to be about the same age, aside from some gray above his father's ears; the resemblance wasn't a man and his twin, but a man and his brother. The biggest difference between them was the white scar that severed Owen's eyebrow, and since he didn't remember the incident, Owen often forgot it was there.

He turned to Lori, but the doorway was empty. She had slipped away without him noticing. His father nodded toward the chair.

Owen sat. He waited. Nothing happened for maybe ten seconds, and he looked up expectantly at Crouch.

Black rivulets poured from his father's eyes, from his nose, mouth, ears, and fingertips. The tendrils gathered in front of him like a cloud of black soot, and in a moment of revelation Owen understood what he was seeing—*this was Crouch's Mystery*. What he'd seen, what he'd smelled, what he'd heard and touched, this black cloud was not filth or poison, but *memories*. It was the story of the Blessed Trinity Mission's final days. He wasn't certain how he knew, but the feeling was unshakable.

His father had never meant to hurt him. He'd only ever wanted to show Owen what had become of the Blessed Trinity and its people.

The cloud flowed toward him. The urge to rid himself of his diving equipment overpowered reason. He peeled back his hood, and took off his gloves. The tendrils reached out toward him, wispy black tentacles. He shrank away, hesitating for a moment, like a child reaching out to pet a spider. Regaining his courage, he tore the mask off his face, relieved to take the pressure off the throbbing wound on his forehead, and let it settle on the floor beside him. Before removing the regulator from his mouth, he looked up at his father for approval.

The dead man nodded weakly, seemingly drained, as if unburdening himself of his memories had taken all his strength.

Owen pulled out the mouthpiece last, and let it fall to his lap. He held his breath a moment, then inhaled.

Crouch's memories flooded into him, darting toward his fingers, filling his ears with the roar of rushing water, filling his eyes with darkness, clotting out his breath.

———

4

There was a void.

From out of the void came light, pinpricks at first, then steadily growing until he could see the space around himself. His father sat in the chair, though in this memory—if that was what it was—sunlight spilled in through the windows. There was no water. Photos of his family hung on the walls, the same photos that had always hung there, since there'd been a family to have photos of—the boy, the wife, the husband. In many of them he was smiling. In others, a darkness had already begun growing within his father, his eyes clouded, and his smile grim.

Crouch blinked, and sat up groggily. A runner of drool had crusted from his lips to his chin, and he wiped it away with slight disgust. Somehow, the way he sometimes knew things in dreams, Owen knew this was a childhood shame his father had long hoped to have left behind. Crouch's mother had tried to make him stop, but some habits stick no matter how hard you try to rid yourself of them.

*Every man has two selves, in constant battle with one another.* Crouch's thoughts came to him like the voiceover in a film. *The man who is, and the man he's meant to be. I suppose I'm just meant to be a drooler.*

Crouch glanced at his watch lying on the table. "Blast!" he cried, and peered out the window at the afternoon sun. "One o'clock? *Lord, Lord, Lord,*" he said anxiously, rising from the chair, which squeaked as he lifted his weight.

*Late. Got to get to the church on time, or Woodrow will be upset.* He put on the watch and hurried out, not wanting to think about Woodrow, passing by the shelf full of books and out into the hall.

The hall was bright, the carpet patterned with First Nations glyphs in pine green and burnt red. Photos lined the flocked wallpaper that never failed to remind Everett of his mother's house in Peterborough, where she had lived with her two dogs until all three of them had passed. Now she lived in the House of God, and her dogs, Blackie and Bozo, were buried in a backyard belonging to someone new.

The house was silent. No clatter of toys—*Blasted things*, he thought—from downstairs, nor the sound of Margaret's piano.

"Owen?" Everett called out. "Maggie?"

No cheerful voices returned his call. He felt like the lonely loon, howling out into the dark on Mushkoweban Lake. Thinking of this reminded him of the dam, and Satan's Pimps, and the Good Work he and the others would do today once he got them all to the church on time.

"Owen?" He peered into the boy's room, shook his head at the silly *Battlestar Galactica* bedspread Margaret had bought him in the city, at the opened toy box vomiting plastic spaceships and dolls. The boy was always filling his head with nonsense, when he should be filling it with the wisdom of the ages. *The time has come to do away with childish things*, he thought, and the thought felt poisonous.

*I ought to give the boy some slack*, he thought, but this thought felt wrong, too.

Crouch walked across the braided rug and peered into the mirror, the only thing in the room that retained something of his influence over the boy. The phrase from Job, THAT ALL MEN MAY KNOW HIS WORK, had been arranged in a square around the empty place in the glass where Everett's face peered back at him. Hair graying at the temples a little. His moustache needed tweezing, but it could wait until after the Miracle, he supposed. His gaze left his eyes for only a moment, but when they returned, they were not his own eyes looking back at him, and this was not his face in the mirror...

He jumped back, startled and dismayed.

It was *Woodrow*.

"*You*," he said, pointing at the bearded man in the mirror, and who pointed back at him with as much accusation. "Haven't you taken enough from me? Why can't you leave us alone! Aren't I doing everything God asked of us?" Woodrow's lips curled up in a sneer. "Why don't you *speak*?"

"'Why is light given to those in misery,'" Woodrow responded in his faux-Southern twang, "'and life to the bitter of soul, to those who long for death that does not come, who search for it more than for hidden treasure, who are filled with gladness and rejoice when they reach the grave?'"

"What is your obsession with Job?" Everett snapped.

"A wife is bound to her husband so long as he lives," the voice of Woodrow said back, "First Corinthians 7:39."

"Don't quote scripture to me. You think I don't know that?"

Sometimes the voices had spoken to him from the radiators, and often from the faucets, the showerhead, and drains. Woodrow's voice, however, had always emanated from within Everett's own mind—and there was always a curious familiarity to it, though he was certain he'd never heard it before the day he met the man himself. When Everett returned his gaze to the mirror, the bearded pastor had vanished. All he saw looking back at him were his own desperate brown eyes. He wiped sweat from his forehead and turned to the hall.

*Where are they?* he wondered, growing more concerned as he came downstairs and found the living room just as empty.

"Maggie?" Desperation cracked his voice. He rushed into the kitchen: empty. The backyard: empty. Shouting their names now—"MAGGIE! OWEN!"—certain that they had abandoned him, forsaken him.

In the instant he touched the front door handle, a horn sounded—*BWAAAAAAAA!*—louder than any human instrument, a deep bass rumble that rattled Crouch from head to toe. The man pulled back his hand as the door handle rattled, and the sticky, fleshy wall jostled, and the floor shook beneath him.

*The flood*, Crouch thought. *The sirens must have woken me.*

The sound died away. Crouch reached out again, and twisted the handle.

The door blew inward, tearing off its hinges and flinging into a dazzling oblivion, a blinding light shining out from the open doorway. When his vision cleared, a screen slid open, revealing the lattice of a confessional booth, hung with a crucifix and rosary, and beyond it, the silhouette of a man—a priest. The boy sitting there, about nine or ten years old, made the sign of the cross.

"Bless me father, for I have sinned," he said.

"How long has it been since your last confession?"

"A week," the boy said. "But last time I lied."

Silence greeted him.

"Father...?"

"I'm here," the priest said. "Why did you lie, son?"

"Because I didn't want to say..."

"Say, what? You can tell me. God sees all. He is all-knowing, but through Jesus Christ all sins are forgiven." He paused, letting the gravity of this hang in the musty confessional. "Even lying."

"Even *murder*?"

The priest cleared his throat. "Murder?"

"I killed him." Tears filled his eyes. "I—I k-killed my daddy."

"Surely you didn't *kill* your father. Did somebody tell you that? They may have been exaggerating, embellishing the truth. As it says in James, 'No human being can tame the tongue. It is a restless evil, full of deadly poison.'"

"It wasn't that," young Everett said. "I seen it happen. I did it, I seen him die."

"Son, these are serious things you're saying. You mustn't speak lightly—"

"I don't wanna go to Hell!" the boy cried, his small hands clasped desperately together over the Holy Bible on the kneeler, wringing them in an all too familiar way. "Mama says all murderers go to Hell, but I don't wanna burn for all eternalty! I don't *wanna!*" Everett wept then, his whole body shaking.

"Every sin is forgiven through our Lord Jesus Christ," the priest said patiently. "Even murder."

"But Mama says—"

"Your mother is not a priest, is she?"

Everett sniffled. "Girls can't be priests."

"Is she a nun?"

He sputtered. "Nuns ain't s'posed to get married."

"That's right. Neither am I. You might say we've entered into a sort of spiritual marriage with God."

"Huh?"

"Never mind," the priest said. "Go back to the day it happened. Tell me why you think you've harmed your father."

The scene shifted to a man sprawled at the foot of the stairs, a man Owen was entirely unsurprised to discover looked exactly like Brother Woodrow—and it was only then that Owen saw the family resemblance: the flat bridge of his nose, the high forehead, the flat pink lips. Owen's recollection of Woodrow's beard had drawn his attention away from these features. Owen stood behind young Everett at the top of the stairs, looking down at his grandfather. The toys scattered at their feet, toys Everett's father had stepped on and had sent him hurtling down the stairs, breaking his bones, the man flailing his arms all the way down, cracking his head on the floor below, where he now lay in a growing pool of blood.

*WHAT ARE YOU DOING IN THERE?* Woodrow's voice boomed, seeming to arise from everywhere at once, just as the horn had before it, rattling the crucifix against the lattice and shaking the tiny confessional.

"Son, I want you to know that whatever you did or think you've done, God forgives you..." the priest was assuring him, but his voice was very far away.

*THIS IS NO PLACE FOR A LIAR LIKE YOU!*

The screen slammed shut. Everett scrambled back against the corner, shuddering in unholy terror. When it opened a moment later, a giant green-gray eye peered through, swimming with whorls of blue, every fleck and flaw visible as the pupil dilated to peer into the dim booth at Everett.

*FEE-FI-FO-FUM! I SMELL THE LIES OF A LITTLE CRUMB-BUM!*

Everett shrank back against the far wall.

"Are you all right in there?" The priest. Speaking from another world. Another cosmos.

*ME MY, HO HUM, NEVER TELL ANOTHER ONE!* Woodrow sang, his giant's eye squinting through the lattice at the boy, his breath rattling the thin walls. Everett moaned, a runner of drool spilling from the corner of his lips.

"Son...? *Son...?*"

The wood groaned and creaked. The giant eye twinkled in a dark smile. A tremendous, earth-shattering crack pierced the air, and the roof of the confessional tore off, Woodrow's massive, neatly manicured fingers tearing it away like the top of a toy box. Woodrow himself towered above the opening, peering down at the boy from the cathedral ceiling, the hairs in his nose the width of tree branches, each of his straight, yellow teeth as big as the boy's head.

*I SEEEEEE YOUUU...*

Everett's shaking grew more pronounced. Suddenly, he fell back against the seat, and his eyes fluttered back as he seized madly, violently. His head struck the wall just as the door flung open.

"*My God!*" the priest said. "*Somebody call an ambulance!*"

The priest rushed to the boy's side.

*GOD MAY FORGIVE YOU, BUT I DON'T FORGIVE, BOY, AND I'LL NEVER FORGET! YOU'RE MINE! YOU'LL ALWAYS BE MINE! ...AND YOU'LL DIE BEFORE I LET YOU TELL!*

"What is it, Brother Woodrow?" an altar boy asked the priest, stepping up behind them.

*BROTHER WOODROW!* Owen's mind cried out, as further twists and shudders ran through the boy's fragile body.

"Everett Crouch is having a seizure," the priest said, his voice far-off now, and as the man peeled back Everett's eyelids, Crouch shook this memory from his head, finding himself behind the church in the harsh sunlight, on a day brisk enough to see his breath but not cold enough to require a jacket. Already the streets were flooding, the sidewalks turning to rivers, the holes where family homes had once been—good, God-fearing people, most of them—filling with brown water, with branches and leaves and splintered two-by-fours and sodden children's toys that looked like ugly little imps. That drunkard Selkie, who'd lost his job as a detective because of his love for the Devil's drink, sat in a rowboat in the middle of King Street.

"In those days before the flood," Crouch muttered to himself, "they were eating and drinking right up to the day Noah went into the Ark, and they did not understand until the flood came and destroyed them all." He rubbed his hands against the chill as he made his way to the church.

In the street, Howard's old pickup truck stood idling outside his office. Looking out through his father's eyes, Owen saw a young, blond boy he knew instinctively was himself at age five —and at such a young age, the family resemblance was nearly perfect. The boy heaved a duffel bag into the back, while Margaret stepped out of the office.

She glanced up the street, and locked eyes with Everett Crouch. He shouted her name, approaching them at a fast pace. Young Owen smiled—until he saw the look on his father's face. Howard was nowhere in sight.

"What is this?" Everett demanded. "Where do you think you're going?"

Margaret stepped between Owen and his father, hiding him behind her. "We're leaving, Everett. This is madness, what you've got planned. I'll be no part of it."

"You'll be no—? It's what God wants, Maggie! He spoke to me—"

"Nobody *spoke* to you! Those voices, that damned monster Woodrow—they're all in your head! You're a sick man, Rett. You need help. You need to let those poor, deluded people go home."

"We'll all be going home, if you take him away from us. Going home to be with the Lord."

"Owen, get in the truck," his mother said.

Everett pointed. "Don't you get in that truck, boy!"

Owen hesitated, torn between his parents. Finally, the decision was made for him. Everett strode toward them, and pushed Margaret out of the way. She yelped as she stumbled to her knees, surprised by the blow, and dropped her purse on the sidewalk, its contents spilling out.

Everett snatched Owen by the arm and dragged him away from the car. The boy yelled back, "Mom!" Margaret got to her feet and chased after them, hobbling on the broken heel of her left shoe. She stopped to remove both shoes, then splashed through the brown, shin-deep water in her stockings.

Owen stumbled along behind Everett, reaching back to his mother while his father dragged him along toward the church. "Dad! Dad, please, let me go!"

"No one is going anywhere," Everett said distractedly. "You're coming with me. God has a plan for the two of us."

Margaret had fallen behind, and was looking up the hill at them in despair. She turned from them, and Owen cried out for her once more. But rather than look back, she headed toward the office, while Everett continued onward determinedly. They soon reached the big church doors, and Everett threw them open to discover the nave empty. He dragged Owen inside, and slammed the door shut.

"Don't you think you're being a tad firm with the boy?" A lanky old man with sunken cheeks and leathery skin had emerged from the basement stairwell, his voice startling Crouch and the boy. In everyday life, Rusty "Red" Adams chewed straw and wore red suspenders to hold up his paint-stained slacks, but today he wore the same wispy white robe as the rest of the congregation.

"'Whoever spares the rod hates his son,'" Crouch said absently, and looked down at Owen, who wept silently, standing a few steps away from his father. "Owen's been a terrible boy, and now he must make amends."

"Fair enough," the old man said.

Crouch looked around, still holding Owen by the arm. "Where are the others?"

"Downstairs, as God commanded."

Crouch nodded. "Good, good." His eyes were on the baptismal font. He looked away to question the old man. "And why aren't you with them?"

Red looked disgruntled. "Forgot to leave my shoes," he said, and crossed to the altar. He sat with a pained groan, and removed them one by one, casting them alongside those that the rest of the flock had left behind.

Crouch peered anxiously toward the big church doors. "Must you do that now?"

"I do as the Lord asks." Red gave him a questioning look. "Unless, of course, He's changed His mind again."

"No, no, do as you must," Crouch said with a sigh, his eye on the door. Finally, the old man grunted as he pushed himself up barefoot from the altar. His gnarled feet swished against the wood floor as he headed back toward the basement.

"See you down there," he said.

"We'll be down shortly," Crouch said hurriedly. He looked at Owen. "Stay there," he said. He went to the door himself and closed it gently. Then he came back to Owen and led him to the baptismal font. "Don't cry. Hush now, Owen. Everything will be all right. You'll be with your mother again, soon enough. We have to cleanse you, Owen, before you step into the presence of the Lord." He held his arms out. "Come up into Daddy's arms," he said. Owen shuffled over warily, and allowed himself to be picked up.

Crouch groaned from Owen's weight. "You're getting big," he said, hoisting the boy onto his shoulder. Against his will, the boy found himself smiling through his tears.

"Dad...?"

"Yes, son." He hugged Owen to his chest.

"Mom says you're sick. But you don't look sick."

"No man is sick, who is full of God's love." He held Owen back from himself, regarding him. "It's too late. I know it's too late," he said.

Owen reached out and brushed the tear from his father's eye. "What's too late?"

Without another word, Crouch spun Owen around and thrust the boy's face into the holy water. Owen kicked his legs, his small fists thrashing in the water. "Let not your hearts be troubled," Crouch said over the splashing, turning his head from the sight. "Believe in God; believe also in me. In my Father's house are many rooms. If it were not so, would I have told you that I go to prepare a place for you? And if I go and prepare a place for you, I will come again and will take you to myself—"

The heavy doors crashed open. Howard Lansall stood in the doorway, Owen's mother standing behind him. She cried out in terror when she saw what Crouch was doing.

Startled, his grip slackened, and Owen rose from the font choking and gasping for air, his hair dripping holy water.

"Let the boy go!" Howard said.

"It's for his own good. Can't you see that?"

"You're mad, Crouch. The Mad Preacher. Kill yourselves if you must, but the boy needs his mother."

"No," Crouch said. He thrust Owen's face toward the font again. Owen screamed, and Howard stepped in through the vestibule.

"Put him down!"

"God demands it!" Crouch shouted back. "He was meant to drown, don't you see? I'm only doing what God asks!"

"You're doing what Woodrow asks," Margaret said, stepping up beside Howard. "You can't seem to tell the two apart anymore."

"No..."

"Woodrow speaks, and you listen. Woodrow says jump, you say 'How high?'"

Crouch shook his head.

"What do you think God would have to say about that? 'Worship no one before Me, for I am the Lord thy God.'"

Crouch's shoulders fell. He let go of Owen, who ran bawling to his mother and hugged her fiercely.

"Come with us," Margaret said to Crouch. "It's not too late."

"It *is* too late," he said, hanging his head. "Go. Go now. The flood will be at the doors any moment."

Howard made to leave, but Margaret hung back. "He's made up his mind, Madge. We have to leave."

Margaret nodded. She lifted Owen into her arms, and turned to leave. Looking over her shoulder, Owen watched his father slump down onto the altar. The man never once looked up.

When the doors had closed behind his wife and son, Crouch stood and descended the stairs toward the basement shelter, comforted to know his congregation would follow him to Abaddon, if it came down to it. They were survivors. Together they would build a new Eden on the ruins of Peace Falls, once the Lord had washed away the sins of the past.

Crouch stopped by the door and listened to his followers speaking in hushed voices inside the shelter. Their words were unclear. The tone seemed to signify worry. He pulled the big door open and stepped inside.

The others were slipping out of their shoes. Already they wore their baptismal robes. There were close to ten of them left in all, but Crouch was afraid it wouldn't be enough. Without the children, the Lord would surely turn His gaze from them. Their prayers, however loud, however fervent, would go unheard.

The others came over, barefoot in their robes of purest white. "Where's Margaret? Where's Owen?" Several of them spoke at once, overlapping as the voices sometimes did in his head. He couldn't tell them the Backstabbing Brit had run off with them. He couldn't say that Howard had been working on Margaret since the Purification. The snake Lansall had been whispering in her ear like a Devil on her shoulder.

"They've left us," he said.

Shocked eyes met his words. Gasps of fear.

"Worry not," he assured them. "We don't need them. God spoke to me again, my brothers and sisters, but not from the water. This time, he addressed me through the *fire*."

A sudden image flashed in Owen's mind: a pillar of fire standing in the middle of Everett's office. A deep monotone mumbling arose from it, the same sound Owen had heard on the tape of his father's sermon, the sound Crouch had addressed as Woodrow.

When Crouch spoke again to the remaining members of the Blessed Trinity it was in a rush: "God said we're to stay in the basement and pray until the flood passes. He said He will spare us and our church, because we are true believers. We are *Seekers of the Mystery*. The water will *pass over us*, as the Lord passed over the first-born Hebrew sons in Egypt. But only if we *pray*."

The congregation turned to each other, mumbling their concern, nodding aggressively to one another, psyching themselves up for the confrontation. Finally, Émile Tremblay—a man with slicked dark hair and a large mole on his cheek, and faded tattoos visible under his sleeves—spoke up in his heavy Quebecois accent. "If dis is what God wants, who are we to argue?"

The others nodded in agreement. Jesus hung from his cross behind them, unable to intervene.

"God will intervene," Glenda decided, nodding along with the rest. "We're His faithful."

"We must kneel," Crouch said, moving to each of his flock one by one and laying his right hand on their foreheads. As he came around to them, they each knelt and closed their eyes. "Kneel and pray."

A sound of trickling water startled him, and he turned to look at the door, where a black puddle had begun to gather, drawing closer. Crouch's brow furrowed, the sight troubling him.

Velma Kampf, opened one eye, her hands clasped tight in prayer. "I thought you said this room vas vaterproof," the German immigrant said.

The others opened their eyes to see what she had.

"It is," Crouch said, flustered. "God is merely—uh—testing our faith." He was stammering, the same as Brother Woodrow.

"That looks like a puddle to me," Red said, his mouth conspicuously empty of all but insinuation.

"The shelter is waterproof," Crouch assured them. The congregation turned to look with scowls of concern. Crouch wiped a runner of drool from his lips, absently, with the back of his hand. Then he suddenly jabbed an accusing finger at his faithful. "You're *unbelievers*! *All* of you!"

The congregation murmured amongst each other, becoming agitated and distrustful. Émile Tremblay rose cautiously onto one knee. "Everett!" Tremblay approached Crouch, hands held out in supplication. Crouch turned his dazed eyes toward the man. "You say God will protect us, but you don't tell us nothing. If God speaks to you now, why you don't tell us what he say?"

Everett's eyes came alight abruptly. He nodded stupidly, a child finding an easy out in his lies. "Yes," he said, and addressed the congregation. "Yes, Émile is right. God *is* talking to me."

"Everett, tell us God's word," Red Adams said.

"Tell us!" the others chimed in.

Crouch gathered his thoughts. Water trickled under the door in the silence. Some of the members of his flock gave it troubled glances, waiting for their leader to speak. Overhead, footsteps crossed from the front of the church to the back.

Owen knew it was too late; the killers were on their way.

Crouch flashed his followers a God-loves-us-all smile, and his arms rose with the corners of his lips until his hands faced the crowd, palm-out. "God has sent his righteous to spare our lives!" he cried. He went to each of them, taking their hands, ushering them into a rough circle.

From above, a thunderous crash startled the entire ministry. They all looked up with terror-stricken eyes as plaster dust fell around them.

Owen pictured the men upstairs dragging the massive crucifix across the floor. *They aren't coming to save you, Everett*, he thought, but it was like warning actors in a film. *They mean to kill you.*

Crouch squinted up at the ceiling, eyes following the footsteps, the loud screeching of the crucifix being dragged across the wood floor. "They mean to kill me," he muttered, as if he'd heard Owen's warning. "They hate me, because of what I did. Because of what I did to my father."

"Father Crouch, no," Glenda said, smiling through a haze of tears. "We *love* you."

The others nodded. Still holding hands. Still faithful.

"No," Everett said, anxious now. "They'll never forgive me. *They'll never forgive me!*" He jabbed a finger toward the ceiling, where the footsteps, the dragging, grew louder. "These people are not our friends. They've come to destroy us."

"They're coming to *save* us," Émile said uncertainly. "God tell you this, you say so yourself."

Everett broke the circle, grasping Glenda's plump-fingers in his own, looking her dead in the eyes. "We have to go," Everett told her, told everyone. "We have to leave, *right now.*"

Glenda seemed to see the dread in his eyes and dragged old man Adams along by the hand. "Come on," she urged the others. Reluctantly, they followed Everett to the door. He twisted the handle. Outside, the footsteps and the dragging continued. Each drag was followed by a loud thump that shook the walls: they had reached the stairs.

Everett and Glenda yanked on the door together. It came open with a groan, letting a gush of water in, ankle-deep and cold.

Howard Lansall stood in the doorway, blocking their intended exodus. Behind him, Dink Deakins and Pete Jebson lugged the crucifix over their shoulders. Howard held the pocket watch, its loop of chain tucked into the breast pocket of his gray vest. He'd apparently been studying the time when the door opened, and he looked up with a cold grin, snatching the lid closed.

"Time's up, Crouch," he said.

"Oh, thank God," Everett said. "Howard, I've made a terrible mistake."

"You're bloody well right, you have," Howard said, and with the grin still on his face, he slugged Everett in the stomach. The wind escaped Everett's diaphragm with a whistling gasp. The others moved in to protect their patriarch, but Howard tucked the watch into his pocket, and neat as a magic trick, he produced a snub-nosed revolver with steady hands.

The congregation stepped back in fright. Everett, doubled-over and catching his breath, looked up to see the gun.

The other two men finished lugging the crucifix down onto the concrete floor of the stairwell.

"Let us out of here!" Velma shouted.

"You're not going anywhere," said Jeb, peeling off his hat to wipe sweat from his forehead, the T of the cross draped over his shoulder.

"It's over, Crouch," Howard said. "Madge and the boy have gone up the hill. They're with me, now." Everett shook his head meekly, veins standing out on his forehead. Howard nodded. "You *lost*."

"Let us go, Lansall!" Émile Tremblay shouted. The others shouted similar sentiments.

"You can't..." Everett took a breath. "...do this."

"It's already done," Howard said with a bored sigh. "'What's done is done and gone,' isn't that what the Voice says? Well, Crouch, 'I will tell you what's to come, even before the events are brand-new.'" He grinned, pleased with himself. His words had the feel of a prepared speech, an oration worthy of Everett himself. "You and your pathetic flunkies are going to drown in this pit. And the rest of us will go on with our lives on the hill above your grave, as if the lot of you never existed."

Everett rose to his full height, his face still red from the blow. "You won't take these peoples' lives. You'll have to shoot me dead," he said, and stepped forward until the barrel pressed into his chest.

Howard's eyes widened in surprise. He drew the pistol back, seeming to reconsider, with a glance back at his cronies for affirmation. Jeb shook his head, a look on his face as if he'd just woken from a nightmare, having come to his senses. Dink Deakins's scowl deepened.

In a flash, Howard thrust the pistol between Crouch's ribs and pulled the trigger. Everyone, even the men on the stairs, tried to cover their ears. The Blessed Trinity howled and moaned in agony.

Everett's eyes opened in stunned amazement. He looked down at himself, at the blood spilling freely down the front of his white work shirt, at the black tendrils of smoke rising from the barrel of the gun. He reached out to grasp Howard's vest, but his fingers only managed to snag the chain of Howard's pocket watch. The watch slipped from Howard's pocket. Howard reached for it as Everett dropped, the chain snapping. Everett's fingers loosened as his knees splashed down in the rising flood water. The watch fell face down on the floor with a crunch of glass, and Everett toppled sideways, sprawling out beside it in the growing pool.

Howard bent to scoop up his watch, but the Blessed Trinity hurried to their patriarch, circling him, protecting him from further harm.

"Come on, Howard!" Dink said from the doorway, eagerness to flee obvious in his face.

While the Blessed Trinity threw accusing stares at their captors, their Shepherd's eyes fluttered open and regarded them. He groaned. He panted. His lips formed a weak smile.

"Give me the watch, and I'll go," Howard told the weeping parishioners.

"You don't 'ave enough bullet to kill us all," Émile said. "Go now! *Leave* us!"

"You'll be judged accordingly," old man Adams shouted up at Howard and his cronies through gritted teeth. "The Lake of Fire awaits you!"

"I'm sure Hell will greet me warmly," Howard chuckled, stepping back from the door and drawing it shut with a loud clang. Shouting, Émile and Glenda rose to their feet and threw themselves against the door, thundering their fists upon the dense metal. The outside handles were pulled.

They were locked in.

"Everett," Glenda said. "Everett, we won't let Howard get away with this."

Crouch shook his head weakly. His eyes had filled with tears. Black water had soaked through his shirt. His blood oozed out in a dispersing pool before him. Blood poured out when he opened his mouth to speak. He wheezed in a breath.

"He's trying to say something!" old man Adams said to the two at the door. They both stopped their hammering and returned to Everett's side.

Outside the door, metal screeched—a sound Owen realized was the three men wedging it shut with the crucifix.

"*For...*" Crouch groaned. His chest hitched. "*For...*"

"For what?" Velma said. Tears stood in their eyes, the congregation looking to each other with dashed hopes.

"*Give...*" Crouch said finally, and the breath on which he'd said it continued until there was nothing left in his lungs but blood. His arm slipped out from under him, and he fell back into black water deep enough to cover half his face.

Everett's flock gave each other confused looks. "Give?" Émile Tremblay said.

"Give *what*?" Glenda said.

"*For*give," Red Adams said, sitting down hard in the rising water, looking down at what was left of the man who'd been his pastor, his spiritual guide.

"Forgive?" they wondered aloud.

As the water rose around them, the Blessed Trinity pondered their leader's last word, and told stories of the past to buoy their spirits as the end came. Everett stayed with them throughout, hovering above them in spirit. He tried to soothe them with spiritual guidance and scripture, but his words, in death, could not find their ears. In the end, all he could do was pray for them. They would be martyrs; but to what end? Everything they'd been fighting for seemed so silly now. So trivial. The business of ants.

Soon, the Blessed Trinity abandoned the Mystery of their leader's words for their own survival, clawing their way up the shelves as the water rose above their heads, then treading water, their tears lost to the flood, their cries muffled by the last four walls they would ever see. Everett's body did not rise with the water, while the limbs of the others thrashed above his head, and finally, when their muscles seized and their lungs filled with water, the six of them slowly descended to the earth, one by one, the expressions on their faces not bliss, but suffering.

# CHAPTER 15

## CONFESSION IS GOOD FOR THE SOUL

I

OWEN SNAPPED AWAKE, gagging and spitting up water.

He rolled over onto his side and blinked at the terrain. He'd washed up on a muddy shore beneath a jagged hill of bedrock that shone bone white under the moon hanging on the horizon. The cool air reeked of fish. His hood and regulator hung loose. The tank had come free of one shoulder, and he shook it weakly off the other. It clanged heavily into the dirt.

He sat up, feeling like he'd just awakened from a terrible nightmare. But he knew everything Crouch had shown him had been real, the unvarnished truth.

Woodrow was Everett's other half, his dark side. Everett had been young when his father died, about the same age Owen had been when he and his mother had left Peace Falls. A tender age; a *formative* age. He'd lived with the guilt of the accident festering inside him, until it had formed a sort of schism in his mind. A part of him, the part that even now maintained his innocence, believed he should be forgiven. Brother Woodrow— not the *real* Woodrow, of course, but a shadow who'd appropriated his name, a manifestation, a *boogeyman* who'd taken on the shape and the bushy red beard of Everett's father—would never let the boy forget that his Old Testament God required an eye for an eye. Woodrow would never forgive, and so, in essence, Everett could not forgive himself.

It hurt Owen to think what his father might have been,

what *their family* might have been, if not for that traumatic accident.

*Every man has two selves*, he thought, *the man who is, and the man he's meant to be.*

Everett Crouch had the charisma, the intelligence, the passion required to be a great leader. But Woodrow would never let him be more than a snake in the grass, a conniving, selfish, evil man who'd plotted to murder his own son, who'd led eight innocents to their deaths.

*May your cries be laid to rest.*

Owen turned to gather up his tank and found the wooden frog in the muck, near the gutted carcass of a trout. Owen stared at it for a long time, thinking he was hallucinating. Finally, he picked it up, felt its weight, and turned it over in the moonlight. There were smooth ridges where Howie's knife had carved, and splinters elsewhere. He put it back in his fanny pack, which he supposed he must have left open, and zipped it closed.

Pushing himself up from the dirt, he looked out at the dark lake, trying to orient himself. The lights of the marina were just about straight ahead. The moon had settled above a black line of trees to his immediate left, in a cloudy haze. Between the marina and where he'd awakened was the church, which meant he'd washed up on a northern shore, on the same side of the lake as the trailer park and the dump. It would take hours to walk around the lake back to Hordyke Bay; dark, silent hours during which bears roamed the woods.

Owen threw the tank over his shoulder and crab-walked awkwardly up the smooth bedrock to the trees.

"Well, it's a little better than night diving," he said, able to make out individual trees in the moonlight. If it got too dark or too dense, he had his LED. If he heard the enormous crash of a bear in the trees, he'd snatch up a twig and strike it against the oxygen tank, hoping to frighten it with the clang.

Owen set off on his journey. Within minutes, he'd found a dirt road. From then on, it was clear sailing.

2

THE SUN HAD JUST BEGUN to rise by the time he reached Hordyke House. The roads had been bare, but as he passed the dump he'd seen a handful of eager fisherman out on the lake. He tore the heavy tank off his aching shoulders as soon as he got through the gate, and dropped it on the patio, where he peeled out of the wetsuit.

Hunger had struck him halfway back, and he filled the painful pit in his stomach with two full bowls of cereal, too tired to cook. He practically crawled up the stairs, flopped down on the bed, and was asleep in moments.

When he woke, the hot afternoon sun was blasting through the gauzy curtains. He rolled over, yawning. The alarm clock still showed 2:06, and his wristwatch had stopped at 3:16, apparently having cracked under the pressure of the water while he'd sat in his father's chair, reliving the Blessed Trinity's final hour. It had stopped on that famous verse from John, probably the most quoted line in the Bible: *For God so loved the world that he gave his one and only Son, that whoever believes in Him shall not perish but have eternal life.*

"Huh," Owen said, amused by the coincidence. He supposed there were probably a dozen verses that corresponded to 2:06, or 2:6, but he couldn't recite them from memory, and he wasn't about to look them up. He was still tired, but there was work to be done—*That all men may know His work*—and he wanted to get back on the lake before dusk.

Howard still needed to answer for his sins, and on his walk back to the house in the wee hours of the morning, Owen had made a rough plan for getting the old man out on the lake.

He got up, ran a cool shower in the tub to rinse off the smell of fish and the rest of his fatigue. He put on fresh clothes, the last clean pair of jeans and underwear in his suitcase, and the socks he'd worn on his first day, which he'd aired out on the windowsill. In a moment of inspiration, he snatched up the least flowery sun hat he could find in the wardrobe, along with a pair of lime green women's slacks and a cream blouse that could easily fit his mother. He made the bed neatly, folded the clothes as his mother would have on the bedspread, and hurried downstairs with the hat.

Looking out the front windows on his way down the stairs, he saw a car he didn't recognize parked in the driveway. A vaguely familiar men's cologne stung his nostrils, and it wasn't his own. His immediate thought was: *Mike Selkie*. But the voice that greeted him was not the Constable's.

"Have a little lie-down, did you?"

He recognized the accent before he saw Howard in the recliner, sifting through Lori's journal. *Speak of the Devil*, he thought. The old man was dressed in the same clothes he'd worn to the hospital, down to the wacky '70s cravat. He'd slung the tweed professor's jacket over the edge of the coffee table.

"I really wish you wouldn't touch that," Owen said.

"Oh?" Howard riffled its pages, the yellow hospital bracelet rattling softly on his wrist. "Something in here you wouldn't want me to see?"

"What are you doing out of the hospital, Howard?"

Howard grinned. "My son-in-law called. Some busybody or another spotted you out on the lake again last night. Michael wondered if I might know what you'd been up to."

Owen shrugged. "Just a little night diving," he said. "I was actually just running out a sun hat for my mom. Wouldn't want her to get heat stroke, you know."

"*Madge*—?" Howard swallowed his enthusiasm. "Your mother is here?"

Nodding, Owen said, "She came up for a visit last night. I'm sure she'd be happy to know you're here."

Now that Owen knew the truth, Howard's presence here made him edgy. That Howard had been sitting there for God knew how long, waiting for him to wake from his nap, disturbed him in some primal way. That he'd been reading Lori's journal bothered him even more—he had no idea what she might have written about Howard, if she'd already pieced together what had happened or not. He wished he'd spent more time reading it, though it would have meant spending less time with Jo in her final days. It was obvious Howard hadn't just popped by for a casual visit. The Devil's business had brought him here, and Owen wouldn't be the least bit surprised to find that Howard might be concealing the same gun he'd used to murder Everett Crouch.

*At least with Howard here*, he thought, *I won't have to drive an hour to Peterborough and back. At least there's that.*

"Mom's just out sunning on the dock." He gestured with

the hat toward the kitchen. In reality, Margaret Saddler never would have suntanned, but it had been almost thirty years since Howard had seen her, and Owen figured he'd be safe with the lie. "Said she might go for a swim," he added, casting out his bait.

"A *swim*?" Howard blinked rapidly. He wore the look of a man choking at a polite dinner party, trying not to make a scene. The ruse had worked better than Owen could have imagined. Howard had taken the bait, and Owen had gained the upper hand. He intended to use it to his advantage.

"Sure. The water's perfect, Howard. I was thinking of taking a dip myself, if you want to join us."

The old man shook his head fearfully.

"Oh, that's right. You don't swim."

The shake became an equally mindless nod.

"Well, how 'bout coming down to the dock to say hi?"

Howard considered it for a moment. "I suppose there's no harm in that," he said finally, though the fear hadn't left his eyes. He stood, groaning with effort. "Let's go see your mother, then."

They headed to the kitchen, Howard a little ways behind, moving warily. Owen caught him peeking out the window before he followed Owen to the door, but with just a glance he wouldn't have been able to see the dock through the trees. The barometer's needle had settled on *Change*. Owen wasn't surprised.

He held the door open. "After you."

Howard eyed him, and then stepped out onto the patio. The wetsuit was still dripping into a puddle on the deck boards. He gave this a brief look. "Just some night diving, hmm?" Howard said.

"I wanted to see how easy it would be for someone to drown out there in the dark."

Howard cocked his head, curious. "And...?"

"Lori wouldn't have known which way was up. Even with a strong light and the moon, you can't see five feet in front of you."

The old man nodded. "Chapel Lake is dangerous in the best of conditions," he said.

"I'm sure Howie didn't suffer," Owen said.

"No," Howard agreed, caught off-guard by the still-fresh wound. "I'm sure he didn't." As an afterthought, he added, "I'd like to believe your sister didn't, either."

"Thank you. But I know that's not true."

The old man threw him an indecipherable look, and though it hadn't been Owen's intention—he'd only meant she must have suffered, lost in a dark void, circling endlessly until she'd run out of air—he seemed to have touched on something in Howard, and he wasn't sure what to make of it. "Oh?" the old man said, his bristly Adam's apple working unpleasantly.

"I don't need it sugarcoated," Owen said "She drowned. It's not a pleasant way to die. At least Howie was unconscious before he hit the water."

Howard nodded mechanically, and blinked away a tear. "I don't see your mother down there," he said, making a show of peering under the trees.

"She's probably in the lake, then."

"I'd rather not go down there..."

"We could sit and wait, if you'd prefer. She might be a while."

Howard narrowed his eyes out at the lake. "Right, let's go see, shall we?" He led the way. "Madge?" he called. "Madge, dear, guess who's come to dinner!" Howard stopped several steps from the water and looked out. "I don't see her."

Owen faked concern. "Mom?" He dropped Mrs. Hordyke's hat on the stone path. "*Mom!*" Owen hurried down to the dock. The hinges creaked and the floats bounced as he ran out, shading his eyes and looking around frantically. "Howard, I don't—"

"Madge, where the Devil are you?" the old man called out, staying put a few feet from the water.

"The boat's gone," Owen said, returning to the shore, glad to have washed up on the shore with the boat still back at the church.

"What would she be doing in the boat?" Howard asked.

"I don't even think she knows how to drive it," Owen said, and shot a fake nervous look out at the opening of the bay. Howard followed his gaze. "You don't think—?" Owen began.

"Dear, God, I should hope not!"

"Maybe we oughta go check. If she's out there at the church—"

"Madge..." Howard said under his breath, fingering his cravat.

Owen headed up the hill, toward the overturned canoe under its canvas tarp. He looked back, hoping the anxiety in his eyes looked real. "You coming?"

"Coming?" Howard looked at the lake. "In *that*?"

"I'll need help steering the canoe," Owen said. "Do you wanna help find her, or not?"

Howard nodded. He stepped gingerly up the hill to Owen's side. "It's just that I've never been in a canoe before."

"Neither have I," Owen admitted, and Howard snapped a look at him, more frightened now than before. "I'm sure we'll get the hang of it. Just don't stand up and rock the boat."

Howard's nod was slow and deliberate. "All right. Give it the old Dunkirk spirit," he said, then uttered a high, nervous chuckle.

Owen removed the tarpaulin, shaking off dead pine needles. The canoe was wooden—cedar, at a guess—and varnished to a high shine. He bent to take the end closest to the lake, and looked up to see Howard watching him curiously. "Ready?"

Howard nodded and scurried to the high end. Owen counted to three, and both men lifted simultaneously, Howard exhaling noisily. The paddles fell from inside, landing on a pair of sodden yellow life cushions. A bailing can, really a rusted old juice tin, lay beside them.

Slowly they trudged the canoe toward the lake, Owen lifting it behind his back. Howard's rhythm was a few steps off, and the pointy end—whether it was the bow or stern, Owen had no idea—kept bumping Owen in the tailbone. All the way down, he thought Howard could easily ram him into the lake and push him under, and put the situation with the Blessed Trinity behind him for good. But Howard never made a move. Owen guessed he was genuinely concerned for Margaret, no matter what he'd originally planned to do to her only son at Fisherman's Wharf.

Owen turned to the old man at the water's edge. "We're gonna flip it now, okay? On my count."

Howard agreed with a nod. Owen counted, and they turned the canoe right side up. The inside was mottled with black water stains, the varnish worn from use. "You keep pushing, and I'll go around the side," Owen directed. Howard did as he was told, while Owen stepped out onto the rock wall, carrying what turned out to be the bow out into the water. Once it was fully in the lake, he told Howard to let go. The old man did so eagerly, worried he'd be pulled into the lake along with the canoe.

"Perhaps you'd better get your wetsuit?" Howard said.

"Why would I—?" Then Owen understood. "You don't think...?"

Howard had looked like a man asleep at the wheel, but now his eyes came alight. "Of course not. Though it doesn't hurt to put on our belt and braces." Owen gave him a clueless look. "It's an expression," Howard said. "It means to be cautious."

"You're right," Owen said. He held out the frayed rope to him. "Can you hold the boat in?"

Howard looked uneasily at the rock wall—so close to the water, and shallow as it was—then the rope. He stepped up onto the wall like a man climbing onto a tightrope. His nice shiny shoes, Owen noted, were about to get wet. Howard treaded delicately toward Owen and held out his hand. Owen's skin crawled at the thought of holding hands with his father's killer, but he took it and helped him pass. Once the old man had situated himself, balancing precariously despite the wall being several feet wide, Owen handed him the rope.

"I'll just be a minute," he said, then headed up the path. It occurred to him as he reached the dark patch where the canoe had been that it was odd for Howard to suggest he put on the wetsuit. Even being overly cautious, what did Howard expect to happen out there? *I don't need a wetsuit to help him if he falls out of the boat*, he thought. *What's he got in mind?*

He reached the patio, slipped out of his shoes, and began tugging the damp wetsuit onto his legs. It was difficult to pull on. He jerked hard on the right leg, the material stretching. It would have been easier dressing a mannequin, or someone else.

It hit him like a flood, as if he were seeing it with his own eyes, like some hazy reenactment on television. Mike Selkie had told Howard that Lori was snooping into the disappearance of the Blessed Trinity. Howard suspected she might have learned something dangerous, and had confronted her here. And once he'd learned who she was (her resemblance to their mother, despite the difference in their hair color, was close enough to guess), he knew he couldn't simply pay her off to forget all about it. In true Saddler fashion, Lori wouldn't have let it go; she'd have had it in her jaws like a dog with a bone. Howard had likely snapped. He'd probably broken her chain in the struggle, had forced her to the sink or the tub upstairs and held her head underwater until she'd stopped struggling. Then he'd found the crucifix and threw it in the trash, and wiped away his fingerprints. He'd dressed her in her scuba gear, drove her out to the church, and, just as Owen had done with Jo, he'd slipped Lori's lifeless remains into the lake, where she'd be found the next morning, face down in the reeds.

Owen swallowed his grief, tasting nothing but bitter rage. "*You killed her.* You killed Lori, you old fuck," he said under his breath. He threw a look over his shoulder, suddenly afraid he'd said it loud enough for Howard to hear. But the old man was peering down dreamily into the water.

"All right down there?" Owen called, as cheerily as he could manage.

Howard looked up from his ruminating. "Fine and dandy!"

"'Fine and dandy,'" Owen mimicked, zipping up the suit. "We'll just see how fine and dandy you are out on that lake, Howard, my boy."

Owen returned to the water, carrying the tank and flippers under his arms. He placed them in the canoe, then gave Howard a thin smile. The old man returned it with a sickly one of his own. "All right for another minute? I have to get the paddles and the life jackets. Must put on the belt and braces, eh, old chap?" he added, smiling jovially, while inside he seethed.

Howard agreed, and Owen went back up the hill. He carried the remaining equipment down awkwardly, leaving the bailing can in the dirt. He laid the paddles in the bottom of the canoe, and put a cushion on each wicker seat. "Ready?"

"I suppose I'll have to be," Howard said with a trepidatious look at the canoe, a look that said he didn't trust that it wouldn't slip out from underneath him. Then he turned to Owen. "Tally ho," he said unenthusiastically, and stepped into the canoe. It wobbled, and he threw his arms out wide. Owen held the side, stabilizing it. "Easy, peasy," the old man said, and sat in the front, but facing toward the rear.

"I think you're facing the wrong way."

Howard scowled, then swung his legs around in the other direction one by one, wary of the gentle rocking. "Better?"

"Perfect," Owen said, grinning slyly. Putting Howard in the front kept the man in his sight, facing away from him, making it difficult for the old man to get the drop on him, as Selkie might have said. Owen stepped in carefully. Howard grasped the sides as the canoe wobbled again and began to float away from shore, sending out ripples.

"You okay?"

Howard nodded but didn't turn or speak. Owen wondered if terror gripped him the way it had Lori when he'd suddenly become violent. He grabbed a paddle and prodded the old man on the shoulder with it. Howard startled. The boat rocked, and he gripped the sides again, white-knuckled. He tried to look over his shoulder, but without daring to turn his body, he couldn't manage.

"What are you trying to do to me, boy? My heart can't take another rattle like that."

"Sorry," Owen said. "Just handing you a paddle."

"Well, Christ, give me a sodding warning next time, would you?" He snatched the paddle and looked at it as if he had no idea what to do with it, then laid it over his lap.

Owen grinned sadistically at the back of Howard's head, dipping his own paddle into the water. He'd seen people paddle canoes on TV, and he had a vague recollection of sitting in the front seat of one, paddling as well as a child of four or five could manage, likely on the river on either side of what had once been the Mushkoweban Falls, possibly with his father steering. He paddled on the left side, then the right, watching the bow swing in the opposite direction each time. Eager to see if he could paddle the thing on his own, he tried various improvised strokes, and found he could steer and push the canoe forward without Howard's assistance. It would be helpful when it was just him in the boat on the return journey.

He steered the canoe out into the bay.

The day was eerily calm, the sky a pure azure blue aside from a heavy slash of steel gray above the trees at the horizon. It was difficult to tell what way the clouds were moving. Out in the main bay, Howard finally began to lackadaisically dip his paddle in the water. A few boats zipped by in the distance, closer to shore, but overall it seemed as though the world was holding its breath. Owen supposed he could be projecting his own anger and anxiety on the lake itself, a sense that it was waiting, waiting for something incredible to happen.

"Deep out here," Owen remarked.

Howard blinked into the dark water. In the same moment, the skeleton of a rooftop loomed out from the depths, and he startled. "Not deep enough," he said, holding the paddle a few feet above the surface as if he thought something might reach up and grab it.

"No," Owen agreed. "Not deep enough at all."

Howard turned to give a queer look over his shoulder, but since he wouldn't dare shift on his seat, his eyes couldn't meet Owen's. "Would these cushions keep a grown man afloat, do you think?"

"Hard to say," Owen said, carving his paddle through the water, steering them toward the church. "I don't think they're legal, if that helps you make an informed decision."

Howard nodded solemnly.

"Boat's still there."

The old man laid his paddle on his lap and shaded his eyes with a hand. Drips from the blade struck the surface of the water, ripples making a triangular pattern as the canoe zipped by, dappled by the sun. "My eyesight's not what it used to be," Howard admitted, and dropped the hand uselessly to his lap. He looked out over the side. "Parish Hardware would have been right here. Funny, that."

Owen didn't care for the old man's reminiscing, but he needed to appear civil, at least for a little while longer. "What's funny?" he asked.

"To know the place you'd spent so many years of your life has become a fish's lavatory."

Below them, a bare telephone pole stretched toward the sun like some bizarre underwater plant. "Is that funny, or sad?" Owen said.

Howard tried to look over his shoulder again. Eventually, he settled on, "It's as broad as it is long, my boy."

"Pardon?"

"It's funny *and* sad." He dipped his paddle again, halfheartedly. "I won't say Peace Falls was a thriving metropolis, but it was a wonderful community, once. Not quite St. Mary Mead, but neither was it Peyton Place. We had our troubles—like any town, I suppose. Before Crouch, that is. He and that Woodrow character turned Peace Falls into an unforgiving place, where a man wasn't sure he could trust his own neighbor."

Howard peered up at the sky, not so blue now, as the clouds that had been perched on the horizon had drawn over it like a curtain. "Looks like the weather might shift," Howard muttered. "Perhaps we should turn back? Call in the maritime police?"

Owen ignored the request. "He wasn't always like that, was he, Howard?"

"Who? Crouch?" He appeared to think. "I suppose he was a good man, once. A *kind* man. It was his peculiar relationship with Woodrow that poisoned him. Changed him. Made a kind, generous man into a tyrant. A *maniac*."

"He didn't stand a chance against Woodrow."

"No, I suppose he didn't," Howard said on a sigh. "You said you met him?"

"In the water. He was baptizing a little blonde girl with his congregation. They called themselves the Blessed Trinity."

"Whomever you may have met wasn't the *real* Brother Woodrow."

"No?"

The old man shook his head. "There *was* no Woodrow. He was simply a figment of Crouch's lunacy. An imaginary friend, though no friend you'd ever want to have. Your mother and I were the only ones who knew. We kept it a secret. We gave Woodrow an imaginary life, told people they'd just missed him walking out the door, I suppose as much to spare Crouch embarrassment as it was to keep the others from knowing the truth. At some point, Woodrow's imaginary life became as real to Crouch as his own. Perhaps more."

"You could have had him committed."

"We *should* have," Howard agreed. The church steeple had come into view near the dock, where the ugly purple and green boat rocked languidly. "But it would have killed him. To lose that church. To lose his life's work."

"So you waited. You waited until it was too late," Owen said, feeling his heart quicken as he prepared his attack.

"Alas."

"Now was it because you loved him, or because you couldn't stand that my mom loved Everett instead of you?"

Howard jerked his head around, too fast. The canoe shook, and this time, with his hands still gripping the paddle, he couldn't reach for the sides. He pitched forward, the paddle scraping along the sides in front of him before it plunged into the water. Owen kept the canoe moving. He watched the paddle float past, bobbing on the tiny waves in their wake.

"Owen, what on earth are you doing?"

"I'm bringing you home, Howard. You're going to rejoin the congregation."

Howard was gripping the sides for dear life, his knees thrust up against the hull. "For God's sake, *why*?"

"You shot my father. You locked the Blessed Trinity in the church and left them to drown."

"You think by simply siring a child it makes you their father?" The old man's voice was high-pitched and anxious. "I was more of a father to you than Crouch ever was."

Owen shook the boat. It rocked from side to side, and Howard yelped. "Please!" he cried. "You're wrong about Crouch! I *never* wanted him dead. It was *him*! Woodrow told him to go down with the ship, and the others lashed themselves to him as if he were a life preserver. They drowned for *his beliefs*, Owen—are you so blind you can't see it? *Please*, stop!"

"Only you can stop this, Howard," Owen said coldly. "*Confess*."

The water around them churned. The placid lake grew violent the closer they came to the old church, as if the chop were rising from the town below, while above, the clouds had stretched out ominously above their heads.

Howard's head swung anxiously, registering the storm that had gathered around them. "I've nothing to confess! I swear it!"

Owen prodded the old man between the shoulders, rocking the boat until water began to splash over the sides. Howard shrank from it, crying out.

"Confess, Howard!"

"There's nothing! *Please!*"

Owen shook the canoe once more. Water splashed in, and in

the same instant, Howard toppled out. He was so frightened he didn't even throw up his arms, simply somersaulted and plunged headfirst into the water. It took a moment for Owen to register what had happened. A part of him regretted it—but the rest of him cried out for vengeance. The rest of him wanted to see the water churn red with Howard's blood.

The old man's head rose above the raging waves, wet gray hair matted on his scalp and in his eyes. He sputtered water from his lips and threw his arms in the air. *"Help!"* He twisted toward the marina, shouting breathlessly to be heard above the chop. "HELP!" The sky had darkened and the water was almost black, as dark as it had been during the final day of the Blessed Trinity. Howard splashed his arms and kicked his feet uselessly. "Please, Owen!"

"Say it, Howard!" Owen shouted to be heard over the storm. "Say you killed them!"

"All right! I did him in!" Howard cried breathlessly. "All of them! He would have killed *you* if not for me! Don't you see? I did what I did to save *you*! The atrocities he'd planned to commit in the name of a God who doesn't exist—*I did what had to be done!*"

"You keep telling yourself that, Howard. I hope it comforts you in your final moments."

"Please! I've told the truth, now please *help me!*"

The current had carried them to within shouting distance from the church, but there was no one out diving this morning to hear them. The Blessed Trinity rose from the water surrounding the steeple of their church, standing hip-deep as the waves churned around them: those who had died in the church, and those who had died *because* of it—Howie and Jo and her parents among them, Dink Deakins and Pete Jebson, too—each pallid face etched with profound sadness as Howard drowned.

And from the water, the figure of Crouch rose, the same monstrous, liquescent doppelganger that had taken Jo. His giant's features regarded Howard's thrashing with curiosity. Howard must have sensed it behind him, because he turned suddenly, violently, and used the last of his breath to scream.

*"Dear God, please, Owen! For the love of God, help me!"*

"It's not up to me anymore," Owen shouted above the

crashing waves. "It's up to him." He said this, uncertain whether he'd meant Crouch, Woodrow, or God.

The water rose up, and the giant Crouch snatched out and grabbed Howard in his colossal fist. The old man trembled, teeth chattering, drenched in the fierce wind, as Crouch brought him close. The scowl deepened. A snarl formed on his aqueous face.

Owen held the sides of the canoe as it rose and fell, eagerly anticipating the clench of Crouch's fist. It wasn't until the canoe pitched further toward the church that he saw Lori standing on the rickety dock, alongside the holy ghosts of the Blessed Trinity.

The old man screamed, his voice breaking. He wouldn't have the air to voice his cries much longer.

Lori held Owen's gaze a moment. It was difficult to tell, the way the dock rocked her up and down, side to side, but in that frozen moment, he could swear he saw her shaking her head. And the thought struck him like a bullet in the chest: *This isn't right*.

He turned from Lori. "Everett!" he shouted, his voice a whisper over the din. He swung the paddle, desperate to get Crouch's attention. *"Everett Crouch!"*

The creature's ferocious eyes snapped from his prey to Owen. The giant's torso sped toward him, the fist holding Howard remaining behind as the massive head came close to inspect the interloper.

*"YOU!"* it boomed, in Woodrow's Southern evangelical twang: *You-uh*.

Terror gripped Owen, but he wouldn't allow himself to flinch. His insides flooded with adrenaline. "You're not real, Woodrow!"

*"YOU HAVE NO BUSINESS HERE, BOY!"*

"It's *you* who's got no business!" Owen shouted, holding out the paddle in self-defense. "Get thee hence, Demon! Everett knows who you really are! You're a big white rabbit! A boogeyman! You aren't real! You can hurt me, but you can't hurt Everett anymore!"

Crouch's face reared away, a look of surprise in his features. Rage flashed again in his glassy eyes and he returned, licking his lips.

*"YOU'RE A LIAR! YOU STINK OF LIES, JUST LIKE THE BOY!"*

The colossal features shifted: rage, fear, anger, recognition, fury. The face rippled, widening; it shimmered and shook. And then it tore itself in two. Now the two men stood facing each other, up to their ankles in the churning froth: Brother Woodrow and Everett Crouch, separated at last. Behind them, the huge fist of their vengeance still held Howard, kicking and whimpering, a good ten feet above the storm.

"NO MORE!" Everett snarled. Thunder and lightning came in unison. A fork of brilliant white struck the church steeple and tore it to splinters. Both men ignored it, seeing only each other in their fury. Nail-studded planks rose up from the depths, floating around the congregation, who watched in anxious anticipation as the battle for control of their patriarch unfolded. The church was coming apart all around them, and none of them seemed to notice or care.

*"You need me,"* Woodrow seethed, almost pathetically, nothing like the giant he'd been, while he moved so close to Everett his bushy red beard brushed against the other man's chin. *"You're* nothing *without me!"*

Everett seemed to weigh this. Then he shook his head. *"You're* nothing," he shouted. "A figment of my imagination, just like Owen said! My son..." He turned to bestow upon Owen a look of profound regret.

Woodrow's sneer rose, showing teeth, fists clenched at his sides. In the same moment, Everett reared back his head and snapped it forward, striking Woodrow's skull with a tremendous crack as loud as thunder. Shock and agony registered on Woodrow's face for less than a second. In the next, his body broke apart in a shower of wet gobs and splashed into the water below like red rain.

The lake calmed almost immediately.

Everett was smiling when he returned his gaze to Owen. The Blessed Trinity waded toward their Shepherd, trudging through the fragments of their ruined church. The giant's fist brought Howard, who lay limp in its grip, unconscious or already dead, back to the canoe, and laid him gently on the hull.

"Forgive," Everett said to Owen.

*"Forgive,"* the others said in chorus.

Owen turned to Howard, finding himself relieved to see the old man take a shallow breath, and then another. He wasn't surprised to feel tears on his cheeks. He nodded. Jo, who stood on the dock with his sister, holding her hand, turned to her and smiled. Then the two women turned their smiles upon Owen.

"I love you," Owen said, his lower lip quivering, recognizing now what his life had always been missing: these people were *his tribe*. He'd grown up with them. He'd shared their joys, their triumphs, their hardships. He might not have experienced it in the same way, having been just a child, but then, nobody experienced anything the same as someone else; it was this fundamental difference that made us unique. "I love you all," he said.

"We love you," the congregation responded.

"*I* love you," Everett said. "You go on home now. Go home, and be with your mother. She needs you."

Lori nodded. It was enough for him to get moving.

3

OWEN TIED the canoe to the back of the boat and towed it home. Howard had come back to consciousness somewhere along the way, and sat up, looking around himself in bleary-eyed relief.

Back on the dock at Fisherman's Wharf, Owen pulled the canoe up so Howard could climb out. The old man was still wet and jittery from fear. He thanked Owen humbly and stepped up onto the dock. He wouldn't meet Owen's eyes as he slipped past him and headed for shore, but then he stopped at the foot of the ramp and turned, eyes downcast. "Will you drive me to the police station?" he said. "I think it's high time I confessed."

Owen nodded. "I think that's a good idea."

4

HOWARD REMAINED silent all the way to town. As they pulled in to Beau's gas station, he turned. "That scar on your forehead," he said, pointing a finger at his own eyebrow. Owen noticed the old man's hand no longer shook, as if unburdening himself of his secret had stopped his tremors. "You remember where it came from, don't you?"

Owen looked at him. The old man was smiling wistfully out the windshield. Owen turned back to the road, feeling the resentment curl in his chest. *It's a hard thing, to forgive,* he thought. *Sometimes it's harder than anything in the world.* "No," he said.

"We were on our way up the hill, you and your mother and I," Howard said. "I must confess, I felt a little like Lot, fleeing Sodom with another man's wife and child. Only *you* couldn't stop yourself from looking back, ever hopeful your father would be along soon. I told you to let it alone, to turn around and face the front, face the *future,* or you'd turn into a pillar of salt. But you wouldn't listen, and what did you get? You banged your head on the window frame, just like I'd said you would." He chuckled and shook his head, smiling at the memory.

Owen reached up and touched the scar on his eyebrow.

"And here you sit," Howard said, "not a child anymore, but a grown man. Still as cheeky as that boy who'd refused to listen."

Owen scowled, wishing he could turn the old man's volume down. In the garage, Beau stood up from a lawnmower and wiped his greasy hands on a rag.

"And do you know what? You were right, Owen. I was wrong. *Always* keep looking back. Bury the past, and the past will surely bury you." A small smile crossed his lips. "I know that now. I've done a lot of drinking to keep myself from truly understanding that. The past doesn't die."

"'The past is a bright and shining beacon, lighting the way home,'" Owen said, quoting words that had suddenly sprung to mind, words his sister had written to him. *About* him.

"Who wrote that?" Howard wondered. "Fitzgerald?"

Owen grinned. He felt Beau's presence in the window before he saw the man's shadow there. Beau knocked on the glass. His knuckles left a black smudge. Owen rolled it down.

"Fill 'er up, sport?"

"That'd be great, Beau," Owen said, pronouncing it Bew, like the man had told him.

Beau grabbed the nozzle and pushed it into the tank. He stood for a moment squinting out at the clouds, still retreating from the afternoon sun, while the gas pump ticked away. "Don't suspect we'll see another storm like that for some time," Beau remarked.

"No," Owen agreed. "I don't think you will."

Beau considered Owen's reply, and bounced on the soles of his boots. "Some fella or another said the ol' church finally bit the biscuit. Wouldn't that-a been a sight?"

Owen turned to Howard. The old man shrugged. "I'm sure it's been a long time coming," Owen said to Beau.

"You got that right," Beau said, and spat in the dust at his feet.

5

CONSTABLE SELKIE ld Howard back to the interrogation room, shooting Owen a look over his shoulder that said he thought the old man had finally lost the last of his tiddlywinks. Owen wished the two of them good luck, and returned to his car.

He sat behind the wheel for a long moment before starting the engine. There were miles to put behind him yet, but he thought he might go back to the house, and take one last dip in the lake.

He threw the car in reverse, and drove the cottage road back to Hordyke House. Once his things were packed into the car, he headed down the old stone path. At the water's edge, he rolled up his pant legs and stepped down onto the cement dock, into the cool, refreshing water. Minnows circled his bare legs.

This was paradise. An Eden among the trees—and like Eden, Owen knew he would never return.

# Epilogue

## Meeting Again

B ACK TO THE city, and back to the grind. Avery was glad
for his return, and the two of them greeted protestors at
the job site every day. Even the man with the spooky eyes and
his STOP GREEN FASCISM sign was still around, though
when Owen said hello on his first day back at the future site of
the Jackson's Creek Wind Farm, the man he'd attacked didn't
seem to recognize him.

Owen began visiting his mother once a week. On his return
visit, he'd sat her down on the sofa and read Lori's journal to
her. Margaret Saddler had turned off the TV. She wept at first,
then smiled, and found herself laughing uproariously, often
through her tears. He laughed with her. He joined in her tears.
They hugged, with Lori's journal between them on their knees.
The remaining Saddlers let themselves grieve. At times, it felt as
if Lori might be standing over them, watching them, laughing
with them. But the room was always empty when Owen turned
to look.

After his mother had gone to her room and shut off the
light, Owen sat on Lori's bed and rummaged through her box
of things. He rifled through her wallet, the one she'd made at
some summer camp out of duct tape and plastic thread. He
found black & white photos of people she'd seen around
Chapel Lake: Beau, and Skip, and Pete Jebson, and Jo Dunsmuir. He'd laughed at some of their expressions, and he'd held
Jo's photo, with her thin, grim smile, for a long time, looking
into her dark, cheerless eyes. Less than a week later, Owen
learned that Jo's body had been found very near where they'd

found Lori, washed up on the shore among fragments of the old church. In the meantime, OPP divers made the discovery of dozens of human bones in the same area, and forensics determined they'd been dead as long as thirty years. Howard Lansall II, who had confessed to the murder of the eight remaining Blessed Trinity members and their pastor, Everett Crouch, and to the recent murder of Lori Saddler, would stand trial for his crimes in September. He was expected to plead guilty.

Owen drove up and attended Jo's funeral the following Saturday. Dozens of people showed up at the cemetery, surprising the hell out of him. Now that the church was gone, the town seemed to have forgiven the small part Crazy Jo Dunsmuir played in keeping it alive in their memories. Many of them wept, and a few of them, especially Skip Wickman, wore smiles. He'd seen the Mystery. Death was not the end, just the beginning of some new journey, another bend in the long road home. The minister, who'd driven out from Locust, assured them so in his choice of verse. Owen waited until the gatherers had dispersed, and placed Howie's wooden frog on Jo's headstone.

A week later, Owen found himself in another cemetery: St. John's Norway, very near the neighborhood where he and Lori had grown up. He worked his way through the tombstones, past garish mausoleums and stone angels and monuments flat against the earth. Lori's stone, dulled a little since the last time he'd seen it, still glimmered under the hot sun. He stood before it, remembering her funeral, his bitterness, and the pocket full of smooth dirt he'd fingered, pretending it was ash. He'd come a long way since then. With Lori's help, and Jo's, and the people of the Blessed Trinity, he'd finally become the man he was meant to be.

He felt a presence behind him, and turned, expecting to find the two of them there, Lori and Jo, perhaps holding hands in the grove of bright-green cedar. It was neither. Gerald Kinsman reared back behind a tree. He seemed to realize he'd been caught, then, and came out from hiding.

"Why are you hiding back there?" Owen said.

Gerald's face reddened. He wringed his hands. "I didn't want to disturb you," he admitted.

"Hanging back there like a ghost is disturbing. Why don't you come join me?"

A hopeful look crossed the old man's face. Uncertainty followed it. "You're sure I won't be interrupting?"

"You've got just as much right to be here as I do," Owen said. "You're her father."

Gerald smiled, a goofy sort of smile that was kind of loveable, in Owen's opinion, and he hurried over to Owen's side. He smelled of aftershave and fresh cut grass. Owen remembered his mother had said Gerald was doing yard maintenance now, hard work that kept him in the sun and kept his mind off the booze. They stood in a reverent silence a moment, while the trees blew and the birds chirped and the sun beat hot on their scalps.

"She really loved you, you know," Gerald said.

"She loved you, too. She told me that once."

Gerald nodded, looking down at the stone. "We were trying to reconnect."

"She told me that, too." He let the silence hang a moment, wondering how to start the conversation. Finally, he said, "I never gave you much of a chance in the past. I'm sorry for that."

Gerald shrugged it off. "I gave you plenty of opportunity to dislike me. I just hope you can forgive me, too."

Owen nodded. "I think I can," he said.

The two of them turned their gaze to Lori's grave, just a six foot plot of drying grass and a fancy stone in the earth. A smile crept across Gerald's lips as they stood there. Owen watched him for a long moment, the old man's ginger comb-over ruffling in the strong wind.

He faced his sister's grave. Then he looked up, beyond the uneven rows of stones and the whispering oaks. Owen Saddler, forty years old, looked up at the wide blue sky, and smiled.

# Afterword

I BEGAN WRITING *Salvage* during a time of deep depression, and finished it during a prolonged period of (mostly) happiness. Often, I found it difficult plunging back into the well of darkness without bringing a little of it back up with me.

No one person's depression defines another's. This book was never meant to be an entirely accurate representation of mental disorders or mental illness. It is a work of fiction, and any inaccuracies were for the benefit (I hope) of the story.

The initial seed for the idea was the video for Radiohead's "Pyramid Song," which I saw way back in 2002. In it, a person dives into a body of water with an entire city below the surface and eventually swims into a house by the end and sits down in a comfortable-looking chair. That image stuck with me for a long time, but it wouldn't become the complete concept of the story you've just read until a little while later. (You may notice I took that final scene verbatim for Owen's confrontation with Crouch.) One thing I still remember from little over twenty or so years ago, on the night I came up with the haunted underwater church concept I had a lucid dream in which I could fly. I was floating about a hundred feet above a lake and thought to myself, *I bet if I can fly I might be able to breath underwater.* So I flew down to test that theory, and—it being a dream—discovered that I could. I dove straight to the bottom and began pulling up handfuls of gold doubloons from the silt. I woke up that morning and knew what I'd written down the day before was "solid gold," metaphorically speaking.

I've always been fascinated by ghost towns in general, so the idea of a ghost town submerged underwater really struck a chord. I'd seen *O Brother, Where Art Thou?* a couple of years before, so the concept of flooding towns to build reservoirs was still fresh in my mind. I had no idea back then it would take me more than ten years to finally get around to writing and publishing it.

When I *did* finally sit down to start writing it, an odd coincidence occurred within that same week. I'd just written a scene in which Owen dreams his mother's house has flooded. His entire childhood—what he remembers of it—floats out of the dark water around him. Eventually, he gets pulled under, and wakes.

A pipe burst in the house I was renting the same night I wrote this scene, and the basement flooded. I'd experienced this once before, when I was renting a basement apartment, which was a far worse situation, leading to me having to spend two weeks in a hotel. This time there was less damage, as most of the stuff we had down in the basement was about two or three inches off the floor. But it was another sign, or I believed at the time, that I was on the right track.

As I mentioned in the afterword for *Gristle & Bone*, I plotted this novel while in the hospital after surgery, but it became a very different beast than what I'd written. For the better, I think. For one thing, the editor from Booktrope, William Campbell, suggested I write interlude segments to build up the relationship between Owen and his sister prior to her death. I felt that was a smart choice and quickly added them. For another, in the outline Owen planned to blow up the dam, effectively dredging the lake and (theoretically) purging the ghosts. I felt like that would have been a big, bombastic—so to speak—climax, but I decided once I'd written the rest that a more toned-down ending would better suit the story. I'm relatively certain I made the right choice, though blowing up the dam would have been cool, for sure.

*Salvage* became my debut novel in 2015 (though my true debut was the fiction collection released the year before, *Gristle & Bone*), first published by the now-defunct Booktrope, and while I don't think it's necessarily my best work to date, I still believe it's quite a good little ghost mystery. I poured a lot of my own journey into Owen's, so I suppose it's also my most personal work, as well. I hope you've enjoyed this story, and possibly gotten a little more out of it than just light entertainment

# About the Author

Author of the cult smash-hit *Woom* and *Ghostland* and more than 15 other books that aren't the cult smash-hit *Woom* or *Ghostland*. His debut collection was blurbed positively by the legendary Jack Ketchum. His novel, *Pedo Island Bloodbath*, was nominated for a 2024 Splatterpunk Award for Best Novel.

For 7 FREE dark fiction short stories/novellas including the prequel to GHOSTLAND, "The Moving House," signed copies of Woom, bookplates and merch, please visit www.dun canralston.com.

For more delicious dark fiction, please visit
www.duncanralston.com and
www.shadowworkpublishing.com.

www.ingramcontent.com/pod-product-compliance
Lightning Source LLC
Chambersburg PA
CBHW031555310726
48973CB00003B/836